SAS:
FORTRESS

ANDY
AUTHOR OF *BRAVO TWO ZERO*
McNAB
SAS:
FORTRESS

WELBECK

Published in 2021 by Welbeck Fiction Limited, part of Welbeck
Publishing Group 20 Mortimer Street London W1T 3JW

First published in Great Britain in 2014 by Bantam Press,
an imprint of Penguin Random House

Copyright © Andy McNab 2015

The moral right of the author has been asserted.

ISBN: 978–1–78739–716–3

Printed in Canada

10 9 8 7 6 5 4 3 2 1

1

Walthamstow, East London
28 June

The target's hands hovered each side of his head, shaking so much that they looked like they were about to fall off. Callum's forefinger curled round the trigger of his Heckler & Koch MP5SF, his right eye studying the target's wide-eyed grimace down the night sight. The man, IC6—Middle Eastern, early thirties, six one, well built—stood framed in the Transit's open passenger door, lit by the glare of the halogens from one of their 5 Series ARVs.

"Name?"

All that came back was the high-pitched whinnying sound of the man, who was either a terrified van passenger or a wannabe suicide bomber.

"Name, *now!*"

"Still no DSO," shouted Vic from the car, his headset mic flipped down, cell pressed to his ear. But it didn't matter at that stage. Even if they hadn't lost radio contact, SCO19's designated senior officer back in the control room at Scotland Yard couldn't see what they were seeing. Soon they would have cameras on helmets, but not yet. Right now they were on their own, the choice theirs: to kill or not to kill. Callum was the lead; it was his call, his neck if they fucked up.

"No wheelman."

Cook, who'd taken off after the driver had done a runner, had given up the chase, his words pushed out between gasps of breath.

Even though it was past two a.m., the hottest day of the year was showing no sign of cooling. A short, sharp shock of rain had merely covered the street with a sticky slick of gloss that was now steaming the place up. Vic was dripping with it and even Callum who, a few lives back, had seen service in hell-hot Sierra Leone and, even further back, had had a few sweltering holidays with his gran in Jamaica, was feeling it.

His brain scrolled through standard procedure.

Target should drop like liquid. Aim for the head to avoid triggering explosive devices attached to chest or waist: tick. *Confrontation to be made in secluded location to avoid risk to personnel or public:* tick. *Prepare to fire multiple shots at the brain stem to minimize the risk of detonation.* Brain stem? Who wrote this shit? This wasn't keyhole surgery.

The man's mouth moved. "Suleiman."

At last, a name.

"Suleiman what?"

"Suleiman, *sir*?"

You had to laugh.

"The rest of your *name*."

"Nazul. Suleiman Nazul."

Callum could hear Vic's fingers dancing over the laptop, then an agonizing pause.

"Negative on that. No form coming up."

The sweat pouring down Suleiman's face was being blotted up by the T-shirt under his padded gilet. Who wears a fucking padded gilet on a night like this? What's in it? Duck down or Semtex? One of his wobbling hands strayed close to his streaming head.

2

"Hands back up! *Up!*"

There had been no warning, no build-up, no plan. Fresh intelligence from a trusted source, the control room had said. Scramble. The Transit, white, 02 plate; contents on board reported to include syringes, latex gloves, clamps, drills, aerosols and a generous quantity of hydrogen peroxide. Someone fitting out a hair-dressing salon? Right. And a .380 starter pistol converted to fire live rounds. The passenger, believed to be a British jihadi recently returned from Syria, *nom de guerre*: Abu Salayman de Britaini; given name unknown. *Was this him?*

Callum nodded at Wren beside him. Wren moved towards the rear of the van, tried the door, opened it a bit, then wider, then both doors.

"Negative."

Wrong van?

Wrong man?

Callum adjusted his stance and lifted his head an inch above the sight so he was looking at the man eye to eye. He was fresh from his annual requalifying at Gravesend, stuffed to the gills with the latest guidance, essential if he was to keep his firearms ticket.

"Okay, Suleiman, here's what's going to happen. When I say so, you're going to keep your hands as high as you can while you get down on your knees, then, keeping your arms stretched, lower them to the ground and lie face down. You got that?"

He nodded eagerly. Maybe he thought his life wasn't over after all.

"Okay: one, two, *three* . . ."

On *three*, two things happened. Callum heard the crack of a round passing him at supersonic speed, followed by the thump of a weapon's report. Suleiman spun round as if someone had cut his strings and dropped—like liquid—to the ground in a cloud of pink mist.

"—the fuck?"

Callum wheeled round, leaped behind the car for cover and scanned the building behind them. Less than half a second between the crack and the thump meant a firing point less than a hundred and fifty yards from the target. An oblong slab of flats, unlit, deserted, awaiting demolition.

In seconds, Vic was at Suleiman's side with the emergency equipment, rolled him over and cradled his head, the half that was still intact. He looked up at Callum.

Nothing to be done.

2

Camp Bastion, Helmand Province, Afghanistan

"I've decided."

Dave Whitehead peeled off his equipment and let it drop onto his cot—M4, vest stashed with extra rounds, Sig 9mm, Kevlar helmet, Gen 3 NVs, sat phone, sweat-sodden MTP, vest, socks, and boots: it came off in layers until all that remained was the basic soldier in a pair of boxers featuring Stewie the homicidal baby from *Family Guy*.

"Decided what?"

Tom Buckingham was only half listening as he steered his laptop round their quarters in search of the ever elusive Wi-Fi signal. The whole row of trailers had been plagued by glitches all week. He glanced at the time: 23.00. Six thirty in Hereford. Ten minutes to his Skype with Delphine. He needed to be ready, and alone.

"Came to me in a flash while we were out there today."

The screen burst into life. The BBC News Home page: *Outrage at killing sparks nationwide riots. Nine dead, hundreds injured.* Tom lowered the laptop onto the shelf under the window, checked the signal strength, clicked Skype onto standby and tried to absorb the news from home.

"Hey, listen up."

Something about Dave's tone told him he'd better pay attention. He turned away from the screen.

"I'm serious. When this ends, it's time to get out."

It was the start of their second sweltering month at Bastion, tasked with babysitting an Afghan National Army mission to lift a Taliban chief as he broke cover and crossed from the Tribal Areas into Helmand for a *shura*, a tribal meeting. They wanted him alive, so no taking him out with a drone. But the *shura* kept getting postponed. So they waited, rehearsed and waited some more. Today should have been The Day. But when they'd hit the safe-house the guy was supposed to be in, it was deserted.

Tom, already down to his vest, glanced in the mirror. Dave, behind, signaled to him to pay attention.

"You know, forget it while I'm ahead."

He had confided in him about leaving a few days ago, starting a new life, getting on the troops-to-teachers program. Tom had thought it was a wind-up. He gestured at the laptop, his mind elsewhere. "Can this wait? I'm kind of on standby here."

Dave, ignoring him, popped a can of Monster and poured it down his throat. "After all, I'm great with kids, aren't I?"

Only last week, on an exercise with the ANA, Dave had covered himself in glory by pulling an eight-year-old boy out of the rubble that had been his home and delivering him into the arms of his frantic parents. When they'd gone back to see the family, Dave had taken a basketball he'd liberated from the same US Marines that now made up the vast majority of troops in Helmand, fixed up a makeshift hoop for the kid and shown him the ropes. Within minutes he was surrounded by ten more eager players.

"Yeah, it's a great idea. Now can you fuck off for a bit while I talk to Mademoiselle?"

Dave threw his head back, drained the dregs of his drink, tossed the can into the trash or garbage with deadly accuracy and lay back, wiping droplets of liquid from his blond stubble. Flung together by the SAS, they were planets apart. Tom, all blue chip and silver spoon, had seen pictures of Dave as a kid, a skinny, scruffy urchin with spindly legs, scabs on his elbows and big flappy ears. Removed from his drug-addicted mother at four, he had weathered every indignity the care system could heap on him, as he was bounced through a succession of homes and foster placements, his spirit undimmed, until the Army had thrown him a lifeline. There, he had blossomed, single-mindedly transforming himself into the fine fighting machine that now lay spread-eagled on the cot and scratching his balls.

"I mean, look at you, playing soldier while your ball and chain waits in vain. When you gonna get your act together?"

Dave had a theory he loved to expound on about doing *one thing at a time* and had given Tom a hard time for saddling himself with a fiancée.

"Tell you what," said Tom. "Just fuck off to the gym."

"I've decided. Don't try to talk me out of it."

"There's a new USAF one. They've got a whole rig of great equipment in there, chest press, pec fly, gyroscopic dumbbells. An hour of those and you'll sleep like a baby. With a nice clear head when you wake up."

"My head is clear."

"Sure, sure, I know. Their AC runs off its own genny. You'll look cool and *be* cool. Now split."

"You sound like an ad for deodorant."

"I'll catch you up, okay?"

Dave reared up and was on his way out of the door.

"Where's your weapon?"

He patted his holster.

"I'm going to the gym, man—not patrol. Hey . . ."

Tom paused, his fingers on the keyboard.

Dave grinned. "You're a lucky bastard, you know that?"

The door swung shut and he was alone.

Tom glared at the laptop, not relishing the upcoming communication. Skype seemed to be the worst of both worlds. He used to like to write letters. At prep school, every Sunday after chapel, they'd been made to. He'd listed the week's academic achievements—that bit didn't take long—then his various triumphs on the field. *Dear Mom, I got two trys in rugby and got sent to the Head for fiyting Robbo only it was just play. Nothing broken so you don't need to tell Dad. The ginger cake is all gone. Please send a bigger one this time if poss. Love from Tom.* He'd carried on after he'd enlisted, deaf to the hoots of derision from his mates. But it was easier than phoning—no grief coming back at him.

He clicked on BBC News again, scrolled through pictures of a street of shops in flames, a mounted policeman, face bloodied, helmet gone. Even the ANA had heard about it, the interpreter raising an eyebrow at him at breakfast, as if to say, *Welcome to our world.*

Delphine would have something to say about all this.

He stared at his reflection in the window. A hundred meters away, he saw a small glow of light. It flickered once, then twice more—a lighter, perhaps. Maybe a cigarette would help. After a long abstinence he'd lapsed, then promised Delphine he'd stop.

That had lasted about three days. A pair of Ospreys thundered overhead, landing lights off to deter enemy fire, yet plain to see from all the light thrown up by the base. It was huge: as big as Reading, its air traffic busier than Gatwick's. Brits, Americans, Danes and the fledgling Afghan National Army were all here. The ANA were in charge now, the end in sight for the Coalition, though it didn't feel much like it.

The aircon stuttered to a stop and, in a matter of moments, the room heated up to an uncomfortable level. Great. Fucking perfect.

The laptop came to life. Delphine was there.

"Hey, babe." Seeing her lifted his spirits instantly.

"*Bonsoir, mon chéri.*"

She blew him a kiss. He blew one back. Why did this make him think of prison visits?

"You've caught the sun again."

"Hard not to—it's up to forty-five."

Neither of them had got the hang of this.

"How's your day going?"

"Oh, you know. Same old."

Her colloquial English was coming on. But it was clear something was wrong. She looked tired and drawn and, although she'd probably touched her face up for the chat, he could see her eyes were red from crying.

"Are you okay?"

"Tom, it's not good here. I don't like it, what's happening—all this trouble, I don't feel safe."

"It's just people letting off steam, taking advantage."

Instantly he felt the shallow gloss of his words. "There'll be nothing like that where you are, trust me."

Her shoulders rose and she let out a dismissive sigh. "You say that, but people right here in the bar, they're saying terrible things about what should happen to the protesters. It's all so ugly."

Delphine was right. It *was* ugly, but the chances of her coming to any harm at the Green Dragon in Hereford were less than zero. The guys back at the Lines would see to that. He'd told a couple of them to look out for her.

"Trust me, it'll all die down. Stuff like this happens all over— this could be Paris or Lyon or Marseille." Now he could hear the impatience in his tone. Civil strife, ethnic tensions, tribal conflicts, you name it, he'd seen it—in Benghazi, Beirut, Kinshasa, Kirkuk. *In Western Europe we don't know we're born*, he felt like saying, but that was the last thing she needed to hear.

"Why do they keep extending you? Tell them you want to come home."

Now it was hitting them what different worlds they occupied, what it meant to be an army fiancée—let alone a wife, if they ever got that far. Had he misled her? She knew some of the wives back in Hereford and must have heard the gripes. This was his first long job away since they had got together. It had all happened so fast: just forty-eight hours' notice. This was how it was going to be: she had to realize that.

"It doesn't work like that, babe. They give the orders. I do what I'm told."

Her face disappeared from the screen for a moment. When it reappeared she was dabbing her eyes with a tissue. "I keep thinking how different it could have been."

He didn't need to ask what she meant. First there had been the Eurostar incident. She had been so brave, standing up to

10

the hijackers, helping him defeat them. His respect for her then was total. But it had taken its toll on her—with flashbacks, nightmares and an understandable fear of tunnels. And then losing the baby, *their* baby. Their different responses to grief had opened a void between them. He knew all about loss. He could have written a book about it. But none of it was working for her.

"Look, we've got the whole of our lives ahead of us. We can try again."

It sounded weak and clichéd, but what else could he say? How could he comfort her, reassure her from a desert fortress more than three thousand miles away? The pregnancy had been a complete accident, parenthood something he hadn't even considered. But he'd supported her all the way, even fancied himself as potential good dad material—when he was around. But it wasn't to be.

He had dealt with more than his fair share of death: seen mates killed, shredded, vaporized, smashed to pieces so small there was nothing to bury. But watching your own child die as it was being born, and its distraught mother turn her face away from you in grief? There was no training for that.

"Look . . ." he began. The screen flickered, but he soldiered on. "Why don't you go home for a bit, get away from all this? Find some . . ." He'd been going to say "perspective" but that would have sounded as if he thought she was being irrational. "Get some decent rest. Clean French air. Your mom's cooking. *Cassoulet* and *tarte Tatin*. Mmm, *fantastique*."

This time she couldn't help smiling. He had only stayed with them once and had overeaten spectacularly. Her father's expression had implied concern that a man with so little self-control should be allowed anywhere near live ammunition.

"The pub can arrange cover, I'm sure, and—"

"They have. Moira has found someone."

"So it's already sorted?" He tried to keep the dismay out of his voice. "Good! That's—good. You need to get away."

Then the line was gone. Her sad, perfect face was sliced and diced into pixels, then discrete blocks of color that froze and slid away, like a surreal, digitized version of Jenga.

"Fuck it."

He grabbed his pistol and followed Dave out into the baking night.

3

Perimeter of Camp Bastion

They flattened themselves against the dirt, head to toe like a line of ants, moving forward in the darkness, out of the mud-walled village towards the poppy field. There were twelve and the Leader, levering themselves forward on their elbows, four of them not yet out of their teens. Isamuddin's face was still completely smooth, without even the beginnings of a mustache. All were full of hope for the better life awaiting them.

Every day for two months they had trained under cover, behind walls and under improvised awnings, building their strength, assembling the devices, memorizing the layout of the infidel base, the size of a city, from a map scratched onto the wall of the room that had been their living quarters. As he pulled himself forward, Isamuddin risked a glance behind him at his brother. But Aynaddin wasn't looking. His eyes were tight shut, tiny points of light betraying the presence of his tears. Only his lips moved in silent recitation. Isa tried to send him a thought message: *Do not worry, little brother. You and I will soon be in glory.* But all Ayna heard was the verses he repeated over and over to jam all his other thoughts—of doubt and paralyzing fear.

Isa looked up into the starless night, a vast cavern that guarded their ultimate destination. His heart thumped at the thought of what awaited them after they had done their duty. The poppy was their last cover. Once through that they would be out in the open, with only a quarter of a mile of dirt before the perimeter. The orange glow of the floodlights was already visible beyond the foliage. He heard a sharp hiss a few feet ahead from the Leader, invisible in the darkness, who seemed to have eyes that glowed in the dark. Isa dropped his head so his nose scraped the dirt as he had been told, and kept on moving towards the poppy, where they would switch to a crouching run, guarded by the tall stalks, quickening their pace towards the target.

The base had been there barely four years. It had taken shape with astounding speed, an instant fortress city of concrete, metal and wire on a previously barren plain. So many thousands lived behind its walls that the sewage run-off had given life to the desert, and fields of poppy had sprung up. Before, the invaders had destroyed the crop, eradicating the extra source of income. But all that had done was antagonize the population.

They look strong with all their machines and missiles but, as you will see, they are weak, the Leader had explained. *They have grown too sure of themselves, and because of that they are lazy. And on their useless diet of junk they have become fat and slow, while we have speed and patience, which is why we will prevail.* The Leader had many such explanations for why victory was assured. The last reason, he had said, was *They do not give their lives as you have chosen to. For this reason we will prevail.*

Isa didn't remember choosing. He remembered the Leader appearing one night on a gray mare and telling his father that the boys of the village had been chosen to serve the Almighty, and that he should celebrate his good fortune. When his father had stood there, dumbstruck, the Leader had swung the AK47 into his face and knocked him to the ground. Before he could rise, the Leader had pushed the barrel of the gun into his mouth. Only Mother's dramatic display of gratitude had stopped him pulling the trigger.

Inches in front of his face Isa could just make out the heels of Khanay, his cousin, the hard calloused shells of skin built up over years of going barefoot, the loose legs of the oversized Afghan National Army uniform flapping around his ankles. And on his back, the dark mound of his pack stuffed with the devices they had prepared. Khanay had got the message. *This is the greatest day of our lives!* he had exclaimed, his eyes wild. *Until this night we have been peasants of no value. Tomorrow we shall be princes, honored by our family forever.*

The stolen uniforms were strange. Isa had never worn new clothes before. The stiff fabric between his legs chafed. They had forgone the boots, which had felt like metal cases round their feet, once they knew that the ANA themselves often went without, preferring sandals or bare feet. Four hours earlier they had stood in front of a video camera while the Leader recited his speech to the world in English. *I give this message to the infidel crusaders . . . We will burn you and your weapons . . .*

Only Ayna understood. He was the educated one. He could read and count. They all marveled at his capacity to remember things—the names of every village ancestor going back eight generations, and his unrivalled mastery of the Koran. He had even learned some English. He knew the names of all the invaders' aeroplanes: Osprey, the half-plane, half-helicopter, Huey, with two rotors, Apache, and the AV-8 jump jets that it was said could even fly backwards. There was so much in his head—and so much more he could know. Isa thought perhaps that was what made him cry: he didn't know if he could take his earthly knowledge with him to Heaven.

They brushed past the first poppy stalks but stayed flat to the earth. Before they had left the room, they had taken a last look at the map, the route across the huge base to their destination—the aircraft hangars. Was it yards or miles? They had no idea of the scale. Only today had the Leader let them into his secret. *Don't worry, my brothers, friends will be waiting. You will be transported.*

A miracle? Isa asked.

And the Leader laughed. *In a way, yes.*

They lifted themselves to take their first look. Stretching from one horizon to the other, the perimeter fence looked like the border to another land. Above them in the starless sky a pair of jets thundered past, their black cut-out shapes almost invisible in the darkness, except for the twin circles of fire, low enough to shake the ground beneath their feet. In the brief orange glow of the engines Isa again saw the glint of tears on Ayna's face. He reached out and gave his arm a squeeze—but then the Leader spoke.

"Here we wait for the signal."

4

They were in the open now, moving swiftly in the dark, their packs heavy with weapons and ammunition bouncing on their backs, pounding the rough dirt underfoot. They ran heads down towards the towering walls, giant mesh barriers filled with sand and topped with razor wire. Up ahead the Leader looked round every few seconds, as if any of them would dare to turn back. Isa glanced at Ayna and saw that his previously tearful face had hardened into a mask of concentration, as if he had finally found something to focus on, perhaps knowing that there was no alternative fate, nothing to do but resign himself to what was ahead.

They were now within range of the giant arc lights that swept the area round the gate, the light bouncing off the sweat on their faces. Any other day, the guards in the towers would have seen them. Loudspeakers would have ordered them to halt and identify themselves. But this wasn't any day.

A brother will prepare our welcome, the Leader had told them. *The gates will open: no guards will fire*. They must wait for a signal to approach. Three flashes five seconds apart, and the same a minute later. They were all commanded to watch so no one would miss it. On the third they were to move forward, like a detachment of real ANA soldiers returning from a perimeter patrol. Never mind that they were on foot and it was night. The ANA were famous among the other nationalities for doing strange things.

Beyond the wire, the lights of the airfield shone with a ghostly glow. Even at night they appeared to shimmer, the heat of the day still rising. Below they could make out the sharp outlines of the Ospreys, the Huey gunships, Cobras and Harrier jump jets, loaded with rockets and bombs. These machines—unassailable, so the enemy believed—were their targets.

Ayna saw it first. Three flashes a few meters to the left of the gate. He tugged Isa's tunic and Isa squeezed the forearm of the Leader.

Who is he, the man on the other side? Ayna had asked. How is he our brother if he is with the enemy?

We have many brothers everywhere, came the Leader's reply. *They are biding their time, waiting to act. As well as courage, they have great patience, which is why we will win and the glory will be ours*.

Now they advanced again, in twos, as they had been instructed, like tired soldiers after a long day. But none of them was tired. Their hearts were beating fiercely. What they all knew was that this was their last march, and that the end would be soon—and spectacular.

5

Tom set a course for the gym near the perimeter of the flight line. He jogged down a street lined with rows of trailers occasionally interrupted by the odd ISO container. The pervasive whiff of aviation fuel hung in the air along with a thin clouding of dust. He'd known bases of all kinds around the world, but none on this scale. This was a vast fortress capable of handling an entire invasion force. Its sheer size alone should have been enough to get the message across to the enemy about who was boss round here. And despite all the talk about a phased withdrawal, construction was still going on, the runways being extended, rumor had it, so B-52s could be based there in the event of war with Iran.

Yet Tom felt its very enormity, along with its arsenal of weaponry, created a false sense of security. Last week they had deployed to a forward patrol base, under canvas; no air-conditioned gym, just a pot to piss in and furniture improvised from wooden pallets and the wire frames of the Hescos. At least you knew what was at stake out in the field. He preferred it to this prefabricated metal city in the desert, a giant, very costly waste of money that the bean counters in Whitehall and Washington longed to be rid of. But despite the politicians' proclamations of "mission accomplished" and the start of a phased handover to the Afghan National Army, to Tom it didn't look like this long war was anywhere near done.

A moonless sky hung over the camp, the moisture in the air reflecting the dull orange glow that came from the floodlights. At the end of the street of trailers a wide open space bordered on the USAF maintenance compound. To the left, about fifty meters away, was the South Gate, and straight ahead the gym, about another three minutes if he upped his pace. A small detachment of troops crossed the end of the street and turned towards the airfield. Just from their size Tom could tell they were ANA. Generations of deprivation and the habitual lack of decent nutrition had kept their average height several inches below that of the other nationalities. Once they had cleared he saw another figure in front of the gym, bareheaded, carrying a flashlight but no obvious weapon. The figure lit a cigarette, then lifted his head to blow a long plume of smoke up into the night.

Qazi.

That morning Tom had witnessed him being fêted by the US camp commander, Major General Carthage, in front of a gathering that included a number of press—quite a large number.

"You are looking at the future, gentlemen." Carthage, towering over Qazi, patted him on the shoulder in a way that made Tom squirm, as if he was his pet. Qazi stood expressionless, with a faraway look in his eyes that revealed nothing.

"Second Lieutenant Amhamid Qazi, like many in the ANA, enlisted out of patriotism and devotion to his country. As a member of the first Commando Battalion of the 3rd Brigade Quick Reaction Force he sure has shown us what he's made of and just what the ANA is capable of doing."

Tom had felt himself cringe even more as he watched Carthage pour treacly praise over the Afghan.

20

". . . and then his weapon became inoperable. What did he do? Did he stop? The hell he did. He charged right on, leading his men up the ridge, heedless of the enemy fire all around . . ."

After Carthage had come to the end of his sermon, Qazi had addressed the group in perfect English. "My companion soldiers were very brave and energetic, and they are very eager to bring peace and stability to the area, to Afghanistan and to the region as a whole."

Carthage had started to clap. He was keen to get on with his day, but Qazi wasn't done. Carthage lowered his hands and kept smiling.

"In fact, sir, Afghanistan's forces will soon be in a position to defend every province and not allow any foreign invaders to use our country ever again."

Carthage's lipless smile twitched at the edges, working hard to pretend he hadn't caught the thinly veiled slight.

Now Qazi appeared to be alone, finishing his cigarette under the ghostly orange of the floodlights. He turned and levelled his gaze as Tom approached.

"As-salamu" alaykum."

"Peace be with you too," replied Qazi in English.

"Saw you in front of the cameras today."

"I do what I can." He shrugged as if he didn't want to be reminded and took another long pull on the roll-up pinched between his fingers as he wiped his other hand on his thigh. "The major general was very generous." He snorted. "I saw on CNN that the war's getting closer to home for you now."

"Sad, but true. The only way this ends is if we stand together."

Qazi looked blank.

"Shona be shona."

21

Qazi grinned, recognizing the ISAF motto in Dari. "'Shoulder to shoulder.' Of course." He turned back to the end of his cigarette.

Tom had learned a fair bit about the ANA on his tours. They were a mixed bunch, from various tribal backgrounds, and not by any means always loyal to the government. Some pragmatic families had hedged their bets by sending one son to the ANA and another to fight with the Taliban. But the biggest attraction was the $240 a month, not bad in a country where pay averaged $614 a year.

Like soldiers the world over, they complained about everything— it was part of the job description—but they had now actually begun to look more like soldiers. They didn't always use body armor and helmets but they had them, along with boots. They told Tom they didn't like the American-issued M16s and, when he asked why, explained they weren't strong enough: the Russian AKs they were used to didn't break when they used them to hit people.

Tom nodded as he went past the Afghan, up the steps into the gym. Inside, the equipment was all new, smelling strongly of fresh paint and rubber. A recent shipment from the US, it was all set to do battle with the hearts—and, more importantly, stomachs—of the American troops. But he was the only one there. Sure enough, thought Tom, at this time of day they'd be more likely working on their endless appetites. There was no sign of Dave either. Maybe he was in the can. He looked at the brand new weights, then selected a couple of dumbbells, nothing too heavy. He weighed them in each hand as he carried them over to the bench, set them down while he adjusted the height, and sat. Then, with his spine flat against the pad, he reached down and lifted the weights. Gripping them not too hard, his elbows aligned with his hips, he brought them up, breathing out as he lifted. Held them there, then lowered them, breathing in as they came down. Sweat beads immediately popped out on his forehead; he was out of shape. If nothing else, it would dissipate the tension after the talk with Delphine and tire him out enough for a decent sleep. He repeated the move ten times, then ten more. Even though it hurt he embarked on another ten. Just as he raised his hands, the distant "crump" of a muffled explosion broke the silence somewhere to the west.

He put down the weights and stood up, just as a second, far bigger, bang rocked the gym, blasting out the windows. He dived out of the way of the flying splinters, snatched up his weapon and, still crouching, ran to the door. A huge column of fiery smoke funneled into the night sky. Pieces of debris rained down. And as he stepped back into the doorway he caught sight of a mound between the two trailers opposite, illuminated by the blaze.

He sped across the roadway and into the gap, dropping to his knees as he came up to the huddled shape. He shone his flashlight into the face.

Dave.

His bright blue eyes stared past him as if with a faint look of surprise that they were meeting like this. Blood oozed from a deep gash across his throat, still warm, the front of his T-shirt sodden. Tom thrust his fingers into the wound, feeling for a pulse. Nothing. While he was lifting weights just a few meters away, Dave must have bled out. Tom embraced his friend, then laid him down again. There was nothing he could do. He removed his wallet for safekeeping and drew down his pistol. There was no doubt the smoke was from an aircraft on the tarmac that had been hit. His

23

first thought was a mortar attack from outside the fence. But now he could hear small-arms fire, followed by a prolonged burst from a machine gun. This wasn't from outside. And tracer bouncing skywards confirmed it. This was a ground assault—an attack from *inside*.

6

Tom approached the USAF command tent from the rear. Inside, it was filled with a choking cloud of dust from a freshly exploded grenade. There were two dead, their body armor only half on, and a bloody trail where a third had crawled a few meters before succumbing to his injuries. There was nothing he could do for them. And there was firing outside. He ducked out, flattened himself against the Hesco wall and got his first sight of the insurgents. Two hundred meters away, a dozen or more were advancing on the next aircraft. They looked like ANA; one was carrying an RPG launcher, another lugging a heavy machine gun.

Tom darted forward, staying parallel but out of their line of sight, heading towards a maintenance hangar. A bullet zinged over his head, which could only have come from the hangar.

"I'm a Brit!" he yelled, into the darkness.

Inside, a bunch of night crew, mechanics and supply clerks were holed up behind tool cabinets, the muzzles of their rifles trained on the doors. What the fuck were they doing, crammed together like sitting ducks? The walls of the hangar were no more than thin aluminium sheeting. If their attackers felt like it, they could just dump a few rounds on them and they'd be gone.

A dazed-looking mechanic lifted his head from behind a pile of tyres. "What the fuck's going on?"

These guys packed wrenches and wielded power drills, but as US Marines they were also trained in basic infantry tactics. There wasn't much time to think. The camp's size was also its weakness: the base operations center was at least two miles away. The staff there could well be oblivious. By the time a response team was on site the insurgents would have done their worst. The other question troubling Tom—where had they come from? Was this really an insider attack, or just designed to look like one?

Out on the flight line Tom saw one of them shoulder his RPG launcher and take aim. A second later another Harrier exploded in a massive balloon of flame. Loaded with over ten thousand pounds of fuel, the first plane was now no more than a flaming carcass, the three hundred explosive rounds in its armory going off like a giant demented firework. Debris showered the hangar's thin roof. He crouched and addressed the mechanics.

"No point staying here—they find you, they'll fry you. You guys give me cover. I'll get near enough to take some out."

He snatched up one of their weapons and a couple of mags. No one argued.

From the door he scanned the flight line and made a plan. Once in motion he had no way of communicating with these men so he had to keep it simple. The insurgents clearly aimed to take out as many of the aircraft as they could. What was more, they seemed to know where they were going. A sickening thought came to him. Beyond the flight line, surrounded by earth embankments, were the fuel farms, massive rubber bladders holding millions of gallons of aviation fuel.

Covering fire would get him to the blast barriers, ten-foot-high concrete walls, which were supposed to stop incoming mortars or anything else the enemy might want to hurl at the aircraft. It might also deflect the insurgents, who would then return fire, or perhaps cause them to split up. Even in the few seconds he had eyes on them it was clear that they were committed and fearless but had evidently decided—or been told—to stick together in one clump. That at least made them vulnerable.

He sprinted up to the first blast barrier. Automatic-weapons fire ripped over his head as he dashed to the second. Another RPG streaked out of the darkness and slammed into one of the bladders, briefly turning night into day.

He flattened himself against the barrier, trying to get sight of the ANA uniformed men. He picked off the furthest of the five he could see first. Seeing their brother fall, the rest hesitated—just long enough for Tom to hit each of them. The nearest, also one of the smallest, had just set down a heavy belt-fed machinegun. Tom aimed and took him down before he could fire. But a second even smaller man, perhaps a boy, sprang forward out of the gloom and embraced his fallen comrade. Seconds later the boy had grabbed the ancient weapon and swung it in Tom's direction. Bullets spewed out of it, peppering the wall behind him. The shooter could barely control it, but seemed intent on emptying the belt regardless. Tom raised himself to get an angle, and found the insurgent in his optic. It was clear now that he was no more than a boy. Remembering he had only a handful of rounds, Tom took a breath to steady his aim and fired a single into the figure, who slumped lifelessly against the concrete.

Now the airfield was alive with troops, pouring fire down on the remaining insurgents. Slow to react, the full force of the ISAF had now been brought to bear. It was as good as over.

Tom ran up to the two boys spread-eagled on the flight line. One was dead, the other wounded but conscious, on his back, his right arm trapped under him. He couldn't have been more than thirteen, the new ANA uniform stiff and several sizes too large, the old sneakers dangling off his feet split at the sides, the soles completely worn through. He had taken a bullet in the shoulder. On its way it had burst the breast pocket of his tunic, exploding a bag of nuts and raisins that were now scattered over his chest. He was saying something over and over. *Isa, Isa.*

Tom dropped to his haunches and addressed him in Dari. "Which way did you come?" The boy didn't move. His eyes were full of tears. Tom repeated the question in Pashto. "Which way?"

The boy tilted his head and glanced towards the East Gate.

"Through the wire or through the gate?"

The boy coughed.

"You need medicine. I can get you medicine. Just answer the question."

The boy jerked to the left and brought out his right hand. The muzzle of an ancient Chinese QSZ 92 9mm pistol was pointing straight at Tom. You had to admire the kid's persistence.

Tom jumped back and kicked out. The pistol flew out of the boy's hand, just as the sound exploded behind him. For a fraction of a second Tom thought the pistol had discharged as it clattered onto the tarmac, the air next to his cheek displaced by the bullet's journey. But the boy's head jolted back, a three-inch crater where his left ear had been. The fatal bullet had come from behind Tom. He swung round. Three meters away, Qazi's weapon was still aimed at the boy. He raised his eyebrows at Tom. "That was close."

"Why'd you do that? The kid was down."

Qazi ignored the question. He came forward and took out a knife, then bent down and cut the straps of the dead insurgent's backpack and pulled it from under him. But Tom's gaze was concentrated on the dark stain on his right thigh, where he had seen him wiping his palm when they met by the gym.

Tom glanced at the knife, then back at the stain. And saw Dave's lifeless face, the empty blue eyes, the long, seeping gash across his throat.

And then he knew.

Qazi pocketed the knife. Lifted the backpack and started to walk away.

"Stop."

Qazi turned slowly, a withering look on his face. Tom flung himself at the Afghan and they both slammed onto the ground and rolled. Tom heard the clink of the knife, saw it, lunged for it, grabbed it.

An American officer and two others rushed towards them, seized Tom and pulled him off, twisting the weapon out of his grip.

"What the fuck is this?"

Tom shoved the American away and threw himself again at Qazi, taking him down in a rugby tackle as Qazi kicked back at him. As they struggled, Tom gripped the seam of the Afghan's fatigues until the Americans leaped on him and wrenched him free.

Qazi stood motionless, his eyes boring into Tom's. But all Tom could see was Dave's face, his eyes gazing upwards and past him, the life in them gone. Qazi reached down slowly, picked up the knife and put it back in its sheath.

7

A hard hot morning sun had just appeared over the blast barriers and was already training its unforgiving glare on Tom. He could feel the sweat trickling itchily downwards under the body armor that all personnel had been ordered to wear after the raid. On the surface it looked like just another day at the base. But underneath everyone was on edge. There had been no sleep. An acrid smog of burned rubber and fuel still hung in the air.

His body aching from head to toe, he found some shade under the awning stretched out over the front of the brigade commander's trailer. A few feet away a Yank was balancing on his haunches, dark aviators and a whitewall haircut, sand-colored cargoes, black nylon web belt and dark blue polo shirt under his armor. Had to be CIA.

"You before me, sir?"

The spook said nothing, just looked at him.

Eventually the door opened and an orderly beckoned to Tom. As he went forward the Yank eased himself to his feet and followed. Tom frowned at him.

"Don't mind me, soldier. Just making sure that what needs doing gets done."

The one-star British Task Force commander, Brigadier Kershaw, was bent over a mass of papers on his desk. Beside him a fan stirred the syrupy air. He waved Tom to a chair without glancing up.

The spook took a seat at the back of the room. Eventually Kershaw raised his eyes. He looked like a man shouldering more than his fair share of the world's woes.

"First of all, your quick action against the insurgents last night—consider it noted."

"It was all hands to the pumps, sir. I just did what I could."

Kershaw frowned into the cup of black tea by his elbow: they were out of milk again. "However we have a problem. I don't need to remind you, we're under the operational command of the ANA now. ISAF's role is purely to assist."

Tom didn't like where this was going. He took a deep breath and let it out as slowly as he could. A restraining voice somewhere in his burning head told him to hear out the one-star.

"Let me remind you of just where we stand—and where you stand. Our political masters are looking for a smooth exit out of here, which leaves us in effect trying to put the genie back in the bottle. Incidents like this set us all back. Suddenly the bridges we've been building stone by stone between ISAF and the ANA go to Hell. This sort of thing saps Afghan morale and ISAF confidence. Assaulting an ANA officer—that has political implications, plays into the hands of all the sceptics back home. It's not helpful and that is why you're in front of me."

Kershaw's gaze flicked to the Yank seated behind.

"The last thing ISAF, Whitehall, and the White House want right now is yet another scrap with Kabul. So I'm afraid they're taking rather a hard line on it."

The Task Force commander's frustration with what he was having to say was plain. His expression softened.

"This is very delicate, Buckingham."

32

But Tom was fighting a losing battle with his own anger. "Unlike Sergeant Dave Whitehead's murder, sir. Nothing delicate about that."

Kershaw reddened. "Sergeant Whitehead's death is deeply regretted. Your comments on the matter have already been noted."

"Noted, sir?"

The brigadier slammed both hands on the desk, sending papers flying in all directions. "Don't be an arse, Tom. Can't you see I'm giving you an exit? Qazi is an ANA hero. He's also a cousin of the ANA five-star in Kabul. Their fathers fought together with the Muj. When we get the hell out of here it's the likes of him who'll have to pick up the pieces. The fact is that, as you know, Sergeant Whitehead was killed by insurgents."

Tom could feel his own face burning as well. For a moment neither of them spoke. The only sound in the room was the fan and the Yank's foot tapping his chair.

"Who let them in? Who got them past the sentries?"

Kershaw waved the question away. "All this will be examined."

"What are the media saying?"

"They don't have the story—and it's staying that way."

Tom felt a jolt of outrage course through his body. He fixed the one-star with a venomous glare.

"Wind your neck in, Sergeant. As I said, I'm giving you an exit here. Do not fuck that up. You're booked on the next transport to Brize."

"The fuck—?" Tom couldn't help himself.

Kershaw's face was purple now. Again, his eyes flicked across to the American and back to Tom. "Carry on like this and you'll need a new career."

Tom got to his feet. The American opened the door and held it. Outside, a convoy of salvage vehicles was taking away the charred carcasses from the night's inferno.

Tom looked at the American, his expression masked by the dark glasses. "After you. Sir."

Deaf to his sarcasm, the Yank shook his head. "You Brits! Always so polite."

As the American disappeared into the brightness, Kershaw coughed. "This isn't my way of doing things. It came down from Kabul. Welcome to the snake pit."

Tom reached into his pocket and took out a small plastic bag. He turned and placed it on Kershaw's desk.

"What's this?"

"A memento, sir."

Inside was a scrap of bloodstained fabric.

"A piece of Qazi's ACU. You might want to get someone to check whose blood that is."

8

Pimlico, London

The solitary police van started to rock. It was surrounded and prone, like an animal separated from its herd, with half a dozen uniforms trapped inside. Several of the mob wore white robes. With each shove the van tipped further until it teetered tantalizingly in the balance, then crashed onto its side. A huge roar went up from the mob in the street and the spectators on the balconies of a nearby block of flats. The back doors of the van sprang open as some of the occupants tried to make their escape. Flames erupted from underneath.

Sarah Garvey aimed the remote and froze the picture. "Jesus Christ."

She slumped back on the sofa. Her eyes were sore and gritty from three days of semi-sleepless nights. She reached for the glass on the coffee-table and downed the remains of the Evian.

Roger Spate leaned against the fireplace. "I do advise you to keep going, Home Secretary."

"I think I've got the gist."

"We can stop, of course, if it's upsetting." There was a small twitch of mock pity around Spate's mouth.

They were in the front room of her Georgian town house with the blinds down, the muffled chat of the press pack camped on her doorstep filtering through the reinforced windows.

"It does get better, trust me," he added.

Trusting her press officer was an indulgence she had so far not allowed herself. *Screw you, Roger*, she thought, knowing that her glare would say it for her. She pressed play.

He pointed at the screen, excited. "Stand by for the money shot."

Spoken like a true hack.

Just as the mob fell on the escaping cops, a huge white truck lurched round the corner.

"Remember the water cannon you okayed? *Voilà*—just off the boat from Belfast, courtesy of the PSNI."

The jet of water from the turret above its cab simultaneously doused the fire and scattered the mob, like bowling pins, leaving the cops drenched but safe.

"Thank Christ for that."

Spate coughed quietly into his fist.

Typical of him to look so pleased with himself, as if he had personally saved the day.

"What one could almost call a very welcome good-news story. The media haven't exactly been cooperative when it comes to showing us getting a grip. And the ones in the white robes. We're just getting confirmation that three of them are returnee jihadis, back from Syria."

She could only marvel at his gift for remaining smug at the direst of moments. She jabbed at the screen. "Good news for whom? When did we last see water cannon trained on mainland British subjects?"

Spate gazed at her, clearly surprised at being wrong-footed. He said nothing while she pressed on.

"The ring-leaders *may* be jihadi returnees. Yes, it shows the police getting stuck in, but what's the fallout? What kind of message does it send to the rest of the Muslim community? You think this is going to make people think twice about taking to the streets? Think again."

Spate sagged a little as if he could sense a speech coming. Garvey was in full flow. The only option was to keep mom and listen.

"See that orange glow in the background? That's the Leafhaven Mall left to burn out of control. The BBC's claiming that the fire brigade are so stretched they've decided to let it burn and concentrate on the surrounding dwellings. There are major blazes in five other cities. This isn't going away, Roger. People are starting to wonder if anyone's in charge."

Spate lifted a finger. "Are you suggesting we fly the PM back from Camp David?"

We? Who the fuck does he think he is?

In any case, she knew damn well that neither wild horses nor even parts of the country in flames would make the PM abandon his love-in with the President.

The news package cut to a line of people wrapped in blankets being ushered into a school hall, which had been commandeered as a temporary shelter. Spate was pointing again. "Well, Home Secretary, if I may, this does look like someone's in charge— caring for the victims."

Garvey looked at him, amazed by his capacity to detect the thinnest silver lining in even the darkest cloud. That was a talent, she supposed, of sorts.

"Those people." She jabbed a finger at the group of residents being ushered towards the hall. "Who d'you think they're going to be voting for in the next election?"

37

Her phone buzzed: the prime minister. She snatched it up, at the same time shooing Spate out of the room.

"Sarah! So sorry I've been incommunicado. POTUS has been keeping us under lock and key."

"Bit hard to hear you—there's a loud buzzing."

"Cicadas: the trees are alive with them. It's practically tropical here."

The photo call with the President—*on a golf course, for fuck's sake*—had been a disaster, an absolute gift for *Private Eye* and *Mock the Week*.

"You've seen the latest, Prime Minister?" She had just forwarded him a briefing, a stark rundown of the latest casualties: twenty dead and at least six hundred injured. All police leave canceled indefinitely; army medics drafted into overflowing A and E departments.

"Yes, yes. Very troubling."

She knew he hadn't read it, and he knew she knew.

"Look, Sarah, we really appreciate all you're doing." *We? As if the President himself were patting her on the head.* "We're cracking on here . . ." *Cracking on eating twelve-course fucking banquets and downing the President's personal bourbon.* "And they're talking openly about us speeding up our exit from Afghanistan. But for that fracas in Helmand . . . "

"Sorry to butt in, Geoff." She couldn't give a flying fuck about Afghanistan. "May I speak bluntly?"

"You always do, Sarah. That's why I put you in the job." He gave one of his falsetto laughs, which she recognized as a sign he wasn't amused.

"The war on everyone's minds is right here on their doorstep, not three thousand miles away in Helmand. It's not going away."

"Yes, yes, I appreciate that—but, Sarah, this is a win-win. We get our boys home *and* we're not fighting Islam any more. Should send the right messages to both sides. We—that's the President and I—see this as a real opportunity to press the reset button on our relationship with the Muslim world, and he's prepared to put some real economic muscle behind it. And, by the way, just to give you a little bit more . . . support, I've asked the office to go hard on finding some young Muslim voices—you know, who we can put up to show we're *inclusive*."

Seriously? "I think we've rather passed that point." His feeble Tiggerish enthusiasm made her want to beat him to death with his own golf clubs.

"Come on, Sarah, positive thinking. Crises can bring out the best in us. Let's use this opportunity to shake the Party up a bit. With all this kerfuffle at home, it's a good moment to start widening the gene pool."

Kerfuffle?

She felt the chill of despair setting in.

"Look, just do whatever you can to keep a lid on things. You've got my total confidence. And—you never know—it could be your finest hour. Anyway, must dash. The President wants us to get going again."

The line went dead just as Spate slid back into the room. "The car's ready, Home Secretary."

A second, and her mental diary had gone blank.

"For COBRA."

She let out a low groan and reached for her bag. "I'm not getting into a car to travel three hundred meters down Whitehall."

"Under the current circumstances, Home Secretary . . ."

"There's a press scrum on my doorstep. I'm bloody well not going to be photographed climbing into a bulletproof Range Rover to go half a block. People need to see that someone's got some fucking balls around here."

"Absolutely, Home Secretary."

Was that the hint of a smirk she detected? It had better bloody not be. The PM had already put her in a foul mood and, if necessary, she was prepared to get the nutcrackers out. In fact, she was looking forward to it.

9

COBRA Briefing Room, Whitehall

The COBRA room smelt as if the same air had been inhaled and expelled by successive bureaucrats, through a filter of tobacco, alcohol, pizza, and curry. Buried as it was in a blast-proof windowless basement under Whitehall, to keep the inhabitants breathing it relied on an ancient air-conditioning system that should have been donated to the Science Museum long ago.

As Garvey entered, she paused and looked over the sea of male faces. For a moment she was propelled back to her schooldays, the solitary female in her Latin class. *Nothing changes.* "Sorry I'm late. The PM kept me on the phone."

The room went quiet. Their petty smugness at having started without her was trumped by the fact that she'd had a private call with the prime minister, as she'd known it would. Curiosity compelled them to listen.

"He wants to bring in some fresh Muslim voices—'press the reset button' on relations with the Islamic community." She looked up. "Fine, so long as it's not wired to blow up in our faces."

Round the table, uncomfortable titters broke out. Her off-the-cuff remarks had often got her into trouble but she didn't care; they were part of her arsenal in the guerrilla warfare of politics. She allowed herself a rare smile of satisfaction that she could

41

control the atmosphere in a room full of male self-importance. As she took her seat she scanned the attendees. Conspicuous by their absence were any cabinet members: with the PM away, the imperative to show up was gone. And, in turn, department heads had sent their deputies or their deputies' deputies. This was supposed to be *the* decision-making forum for domestic crisis management. Fat chance.

The only exceptions were John Halford, the Metropolitan Police commissioner, who was in deep conversation with the deputy head of the Civil Contingencies Secretariat, and Delamere, the army chief of general staff. The owner of the only unfamiliar face was seated slightly apart, his tie askew. She glared at him until he eventually looked up.

"Woolf, ma'am, MI5."

"Don't 'ma'am' me, Woolf. I'm not the bloody Queen—yet."

Another titter went round the room until the sound of a pen tapping a cup brought them to order.

Alec Clements, the Foreign Office mandarin recently seconded to the Cabinet Office, seemed to have appointed himself chair in the prime minister's absence. He leaned back and spread his hands. "Shall we make a start?"

To her annoyance, he had also bagged the head of the table. This constant manoeuvring and jockeying for position was both pathetic and tiresome, but it went with the territory. She cleared her throat and from her seat, directly opposite Halford, raised her voice just enough to make sure she had everyone's attention. She had already made up her mind what she wanted out of this.

"Thank you, Alec. Let's keep this brief, shall we? We all need to get back to our posts."

Having seized the initiative, she fixed her gaze on the commissioner, who was doing a lot of silent nodding with the army chief.

"John, shall we start with your update on the Suleiman shooting?"

Halford looked at her, unblinking. He was in uniform, his cap occupying the space on the table in front of him. Perhaps he thought it made him look more powerful. Instead the effect was the opposite. The starchiness of his tunic and the way that the collar rode rather high round his short neck gave him the air of a schoolboy whose mother had got him a too-large blazer to "grow into". Hired by her predecessor, he had never once said anything she agreed with.

Clements's eyes darted towards her and away again as he attempted to regain control of the room. "Ah, we were rather expecting to focus on civil security, Home Secretary. There are a number of pressing decisions regarding co-ordination, deployment and resources."

Garvey, knowing exactly where this was leading, waved his words away. "We're not putting troops on the streets, Alec. You can forget it."

"We're just talking about a visible presence. To send the message that—"

"The only message *that*'s going to send is that we think we're at war."

Delamere, the army chief, pursed his lips. "Just for the record, if matters deteriorate, there'll have to be a rethink about the PM's plans to cut troop numbers."

She brought him to a halt. "You can go on the offensive with the Treasury later about that. What I want to hear from the commissioner is where we're at with how all this started."

Clements wasn't ready to give up yet. "We, that is the commissioner and I, feel strongly that there should be national co-ordination to the policing—"

"Yes, good idea, sort it." She smiled. "There—that wasn't so hard."

She turned back to Halford. "So, John, who fired the shot that started all this?"

He moistened his lips with a small serpent-like tongue. "Sarah, I really think that at this stage it's too early to—"

She cut him off with the sweep of a hand that had the makings of a karate chop to his Adam's apple. "If we don't bottom out how this started we're never going to get a proper grip on it. As far as the public's concerned, an unarmed British Muslim, a popular community worker with no criminal record or terrorist connections, who was trying to build bridges with the wider community, has been shot by the police."

"Which, as I'm sure you are aware, is complete and utter—"

"But, nevertheless, a popular view, which we have yet convincingly to counter. Meanwhile the entire Muslim community comes onto the streets and here we are."

Halford straightened up, as if to launch into a long speech. "I've put the head of Homicide and Serious Crime Command in direct control. He's confident that we're going to find our man in the drug world."

"Well, *that* narrows it down."

A murmur of amusement rippled round the table. Her and the commissioner's loathing for each other was no secret in the corridors of Whitehall. She glanced at Clements, sitting back, arms folded to enjoy the joust.

Halford plowed on: "Suleiman's vocal opposition to drug- and gang-related crime inevitably made him some enemies. But because of the volatile atmosphere on the streets we're having to move forward with a significant degree of caution to ensure our interventions do not exacerbate the situation by further raising tension in the community."

"So—after five days—no actual suspects." Garvey glanced at Woolf, but the MI5 man was frowning intently at his clasped hands, as if he had forgotten how to work them.

Halford pressed on: "We have a number of persons of interest among the criminal fraternity who had reason to be upset with this individual."

"Sufficiently upset to commission a professional hit?"

They all stared at her.

Garvey sighed. "From my limited and inferior third-hand knowledge, drug shootings are almost always close range and even then frequently botched, resulting in multiple discharges to get the job done. This was a single shot to the head—or, more precisely, the left temple—a direct hit. The shooter was obviously a trained marksman, perhaps a sniper or—"

"For Christ's sake, Sarah, this was not a hard stop and this was not one of my men."

All eyes were on Halford now. He coughed slightly, needlessly adjusted his collar, and attempted to continue in a calmer tone: "The pursuit team came upon the victim's car when it was already stationary."

The room fell eerily silent. Garvey's eyes burned. Halford had tried to shut off her questions by addressing her as if she were a child. Bad idea. She kept her tone measured. "Yet it was your officers, was it not, who ordered him out of the car, with their weapons drawn?"

"We had reason to believe the driver had a weapon in the vehicle."

"And Suleiman complied—presumably because your men were pointing their MP5s at him."

"Home Secretary, I'm not prepared to be questioned like this."

"No, Commissioner, you clearly aren't."

Halford was now bright red and speechless with rage. Clements's barely contained glee at the spectacle erupted into a loud snort, which he half concealed behind his hand.

Garvey was well into her stride now, the atmosphere in the room electric. "Where are the bullets?"

"They've been sent for examination."

"So you did find them."

"They were removed from the body."

"So they hadn't exited. How come?"

Halford's voice was low and cold. "I don't follow."

She leaned forward. "Well, unless I'm mistaken, all police rounds are designed to embed themselves in the target with the minimum possible likelihood of their exiting and injuring someone else."

There was an awed silence. Halford fiddled with his cap, lying in front of him on the desk. "Are you suggesting that we're covering something up?"

"Perish the thought, Commissioner. I'm just putting it out there that perhaps the shooter *intended* to make the hit look like it was one of your chaps."

There was another ripple of surprise from round the table. Garvey knew that, not for the first time, she was out on a limb. She had to be sure of her facts. "Since the shooting took place less than four minutes after the victim's car came to a stop, it's unlikely that the assailant was tailing him and was most probably lying in wait. So, this was in all likelihood a carefully planned assassination by a professional who had scouted the location and chosen his position in advance, knowing the target would come to a halt right where his weapon was aimed. This killing ground was carefully chosen."

Clements's triumph was complete, but he made sure his expression remained grave.

Halford's eyes bulged. "And exactly how did you deduce that?"

As soon as he spoke it was clear he wished he hadn't. The home secretary was not known for her great intellect but she more than made up for it with her grasp of detail.

"Do you know what kind of car Suleiman was travelling in?"

"I don't think that's—"

"Correct. It wasn't a car, it was a van—and since it was parked facing away from the direction of the shots, the gunman needed Suleiman *out* of the vehicle to get a clean shot. So you might ask yourself if the shooter also *expected* your lot to be there to get his man into the open for him."

"Home Secretary, I really think that airing untested theories in this forum is unwise."

"Why?" She looked round the room. "Since you're not telling us anything, what's going to leak? All I'm asking is, you look closely at the possibility that this was no drug shooting but a carefully planned assassination in which the Metropolitan Police appear to have been—no doubt unwittingly—complicit. What if the shooter *wanted* your men there to make it look like they did it? Where did your team get the information that Suleiman and his driver were supposedly armed? Surely it's the *source* of that intelligence which might lead you to whoever lured both Suleiman and your men to the site, where they were made to look like complete pricks."

She stared at Halford, who looked as though his balls had shrunk to the size of acorns. Sweat was spreading around his high-riding collar. He made one last attempt to regain some kind of authority. "Home Secretary, I completely fail to see what value there is in pursuing this unwarranted line of interrogation. The whole point of COBRA—"

"Is to get to the heart of things. I know, John, and you shouldn't take it so personally. We can all see you're in a tight spot."

That was the *coup de grâce*—the final twist of the knife. Having floored him she now turned to Woolf. "I'm sure MI5 would be the first to agree that this one's going to take a lot of digging to resolve. Woolf, don't you agree?"

He looked startled to have the spotlight suddenly trained on him. "Er—absolutely, ma—Home Secretary."

"Can you bring us up to speed on their thinking?"

He fiddled with his tie as if to check it was still there holding his head in place, discovered it was loose, made an attempt to tighten it, failed and gave up. "All our intelligence seems to confirm that Suleiman was clean, which *may* have put him at odds with the drug lords." He stole a glance at Halford, who was staring at his cap. "But if there turns out to be no drug-crime-related motive, then we could be looking at extremist elements wanting to open divisions between Muslims and the, er—well, the rest."

Garvey was ready to pounce. "Which elements? You're supposed to be the people with their fingers on the extremist pulse."

She watched Woolf scan the room. All eyes were on him. Evidently he hadn't anticipated being put on the spot like this. She knew just what was going through his head; Mandler would have told him to sit tight and take notes, but say as little as possible. But now she had put him on the spot. He would have to try to *sound* as though he was answering the question, while not actually doing so at all. "We're preparing a dossier for you, which we'll be sharing with all of the security services by the end of play today."

"Oh, marvelous."

They give nothing away, that lot. Garvey gave him an empty smile. She needed him to know that he wasn't in the clear yet.

Clements was trying to get her attention. "Since we are without an FCO presence today . . ." He cleared his throat.

Trust him to try to ride more than one horse, she thought.

He took off his annoying little half-glasses and twirled them. "There is the matter of Britons who've been fighting in Syria rotating back to the UK. We have to factor in that some of these folk have seen some pretty serious action and acquired, in some cases, some equally serious training. I just thought I should add that to the pot as our people are pretty stretched keeping tabs on them all, particularly in view of their increasing use of, and for once this phrase is appropriate, *noms de guerre*."

Garvey looked at him. Pretentious twat.

He paused and glanced at Woolf. "I'm sure MI5's doing a fine job of monitoring all the would-be jihadis in our midst, but if you're looking for someone with the skills to carry out an assassination such as this, our eager returnees from Syria might be a good place to start."

She turned to Woolf. "Well?"

49

Woolf bit his bottom lip while he crafted the appropriate answer. "The cabinet secretary is quite right that the returnees are a source of concern. And we will, of course, continue to rule nothing out."

She pursed her lips. Typical bloody opaque MI5 answer. Something was going on in his head that he wasn't broadcasting to the room. She could sense it. She spread her hands flat on the table. "Well, I suggest we get back to work. No use fiddling while Britain burns."

As the meeting broke up she remained seated. She caught Woolf's eye and, with a tiny movement of her forefinger, gestured for him to sit back down.

10

Woolf sat motionless, mentally checking his body language, trying to look composed, not defensive. Inside he was in turmoil.

"Either you know something and aren't saying or you genuinely haven't a clue."

Garvey's eyes bored into his. She could practically see the cogs in his brain frantically spinning. Clearly, he hadn't bargained for this. The DG had probably only sent him along because he happened to be standing outside his office trying to get his attention. *Just be there—say nothing to the room.* Those would have been Mandler's instructions.

"Come on, man. We're both on the same side here. Spit it out."

Halford had been easy: his hubris and defensiveness made him vulnerable. But Woolf looked like a more complex creature, harder to read: junior, dishevelled, very bright, yet seemingly unambitious. She suspected that was just a cover. She had noted the care he had taken not to rile Halford, while subtly distancing himself from the commissioner's hare-brained theories about gangsters. He was an operator, all right.

Woolf passed a hand over his chin; he had forgotten to shave. "It's early days, and a lot of it is conjecture."

"Well, it can't be any worse than Halford's effort. Keep going."

He checked his tie again. "I'm going out on a limb here."

"Do I hear the sound of distant chainsaws?"

51

"Even the Service is divided."

Ah, she thought. Does this mean he's actually got something worth hearing?

He looked at her properly for the first time since they had been alone. "The Muslim extremist cells—those we know of—they're still our main focus, but—well, they don't want this."

She reached over to a jug and poured herself some water. She didn't offer him any. "What do you mean?"

"Anything that brings the police out in big numbers, any step-up in surveillance, makes their lives harder."

"What about Clements's point—the returnees from Syria? One of them could have the capability."

"But it still comes back to motive. *Why* would they?" He clamped his hands together in front of him. "Since Seven/Seven, MI5 has been all about the Islamist threat. We've put so much effort into recruiting from the Muslim community, turning informers, the surveillance of would-be jihadis, there's not been much left over for anything else. We've become obsessed with them. There's a few of us who think we need to look elsewhere."

Garvey guessed what was coming and launched a preemptive strike. "If this is about resources, forget it. We're all running on empty, so don't even think of asking."

Woolf shook his head. "Elsewhere—by which I mean other disgruntled groups who are pissed off with the status quo and have a reason to make trouble and embarrass the government."

"Such as who? You're not making sense."

He reddened, but had no option other than to continue. "Your party's in danger of losing the next election, but the opposition aren't exactly electable, given their leadership. There's a gap in the market, if you will."

"The far right's become a disorganized joke."

"Exactly. But I'm not talking about a political party, more a groundswell of collective discontent. Which other groups out on the streets have reason to be disgruntled?"

She couldn't see where this was going, but he didn't seem to need prompting. She sat back and let him talk.

"Former members of Her Majesty's Armed Forces. In the last three years we've put another four thousand of them out of a job, one that most of them loved, that they thought was theirs for life. They view the withdrawal from Afghanistan very much as a retreat—they think we've thrown in the towel."

"Well, the government is committed to spending cuts. There's no going back on that."

"They don't see it that way. They feel their lives are being cut from under them. And they see we're not winning the war on terror. And one thing they've all got in common—they're trained to fight. Plus you've taken out a layer of police, who also didn't expect to be looking for work. It's a smaller number, but one that could be significant."

She hadn't heard this one before, though now he mentioned it, her inbox was full of complaints from ex-service constituents with one grievance or another.

Woolf took a breath. "The shooting: Halford's in a hole because he *knows* it was a professional hit. And what he hasn't told you is that they've confirmed the bullets *were* from a police firearm. But not one that was being carried by any of his team that night."

She raised an eyebrow. "Someone with access to specialist police equipment. Are you ready to point the finger at anyone?"

"We think we may have found the shooter."

"Do the police know?"

"Not yet, and we want to keep it that way for now. We don't think he's acting alone, so if we bring him in it'll tip off the group who's running him."

"So if it's not resources you're after, what is it?"

Woolf sat back, bit his bottom lip. "Time."

"It's virtual civil war out there. And you want time?"

"To bring in a recruit, someone credible we can put in with them. He's got to be completely kosher, an ex-serviceman who's been fucked over."

"Ask the MoD. They probably know hundreds."

He leaned closer and knitted his fingers together. "We don't want them in on this."

She started to laugh. "You really are going out on a limb if you think the MoD are involved."

He showed no sign of sharing her mirth, which alarmed her.

"Is your DG across this?"

Once more, she imagined Mandler's instructions to him. *Here's some rope: try not to hang us with it, there's a good chap.* She could see he was struggling to find the right words. "We've been looking for the right man."

"And have you found him yet?"

"I think we have."

11

The hold of the Starlifter was almost empty, a giant aluminium airborne metal cave. Before it had finished the climb out of Afghanistan, Tom, too wired to sit or sleep, unstrapped himself and paced the length of the plane's vast hold while the events of the last twenty-four hours replayed themselves over and over again. Oblivious of the thunder from the engines and the temperature at this altitude, he was numb.

But one thing he couldn't shut out, couldn't stop replaying, was Dave's death. Wherever he looked, his face gazed back at him, the inert glassy stare in the semi-darkness where he had found him, his features frozen for ever in the moment he must have known his charmed life was about to come to an end. Had those eyes seen his assailant? The devastating slash to his throat suggested he had been killed from behind. The fact that Qazi had appeared not to be bloodspattered supported that, with just the tell-tale stain on the thigh of his fatigues where he'd wiped his bloodied hand.

So here he was on his way home. What would that mean at the other end? An inquiry, a court-martial, a quiet word? Tom realized he didn't care. Something had snapped. The unimaginable had happened. The Army, which he had loved, which had been his second family, had turned on him.

Even the prospect of being reunited with Delphine didn't lift his mood. He was in limbo, his world pulled from under him.

Yet he'd been in dark places before. Collecting body parts of men he'd been playing poker with the previous night. Coming upon an entire house of dead—a village wedding feast, the guests lying sprawled, mixed up with the dead livestock. He needed to reach into wherever he kept the resources to deal with bad stuff—if he still had any. In the meantime, however, he needed a distraction.

On a stretcher surrounded by aeromedics was Rifleman Cliff Blakey. Tom thought he might prefer to be left alone, but Blakey tipped his head, indicating for him to come nearer. The whites of his eyes were completely red from conjunctival haemorrhages, which gave him a vampiric appearance, but other than that he looked all right.

"Never die a virgin."

Tom surveyed the apparently intact frame beneath the sheet. "Why?"

"Cos in Heaven they'll make you fuck a suicide bomber."

Blakey managed a wheezy giggle at his own joke. Tom laughed. Blakey had an audience.

"What you call a gay suicide bomber? A poof." More laughing that descended into a cough.

One of the aeromedics gave him a weary look.

"Hundreds more where that came from. Was gonna be a stand-up comic—but now . . . Geddit?"

Tom grinned. "Still got your right hand, then. That'll be a relief."

Blakey liked that. But as the medics finished changing his drip they rolled him onto his side, and Tom saw that his body—though visually unmarked—was, from the chest down, a lifeless

56

sack. "Fuckers didn't finish the job did they, eh? Just shattered me spine. Fuckin' useless twats."

The blast of the IED had pulverized several vertebrae and severed his spinal cord.

Blakey winced, a jolt of pain in the part where he could still feel.

"Sorry, Cliff, be done in a jiffy."

Blakey was doing his level best to put a positive spin on his situation but Tom wondered how long he would keep it up. He lifted his head to free his hand and pointed at a laptop balanced on top of his pack. Tom picked it up, opened it and put it on Blakey's chest as he indicated. Then he tilted the screen towards Tom and stroked the track pad. The image sprang to life: a flaming car being pushed down a half-destroyed street towards retreating mounted police.

Blakey's expression changed and his eyes filled with tears. "That's my fucking estate. How'm I gonna protect my mom from that? And they're letting even more in! It's totally fucked up."

Tom tried to think of some consoling words, discarding them as they came to him. It was one thing to be facing a life in a wheelchair, another when the home you were coming back to had become a war zone. "It can't go on like this. It'll run out of steam."

That was the line he had taken with Delphine, to no avail. With Blakey it also fell wide of the mark. He snorted, his face reddening with rage. "And where's the cops? I'm like this from fighting these bastards—and now they're fucking taking over at home. They don't deal with them, someone else is gonna have to."

12

Tom's plan, as soon as he touched down at Brize, was to hire a car and get to Hereford to see Delphine. But she wasn't picking up. Perhaps she didn't want to talk on the phone. Soon she'd see him face to face; that would start to mend things. The Lines could wait. For the first time in his military life he had no desire to touch base. It shocked him. He also wanted to go and see Dave's girlfriend. He would have to work out what to say to her but he owed her a visit at the very least.

But he was knackered after the flight and grimy with the Afghan dust. He'd go home first, clean up. As he walked away from the Starlifter into the gloom of the English evening he wasn't expecting any kind of reception. Least of all to see his CO.

Ashton was leaning on the bonnet of a Range Rover, arms folded. Despite the too-young hoodie and trackies, he exuded authority, having risen quickly from squadron commander to the Regiment's CO. They were a tribe and he was the leader, all knowing, all seeing, whose word was law. But for all Tom's love of the Regiment, there had always been a flicker of tension between the two men. As if Ashton threatened him in a way none of the others did, or something about Tom's background rubbed him up the wrong way. There had been an unspoken understanding between them that they would ignore it and get on with the job.

But now was different. Ashton put out his hand. Tom took it, gave it one curt shake. "Thought we should check in before you head home."

"I've given a full account in Bastion. If you want me to go over it all again—"

Ashton cut him off. "I've read it. A few things have come up since."

Tom held out a slim hope that the fragment of Qazi's fatigues had tested positive for Dave's blood.

"The ANA's conducting their own investigation. Seems they're still suspicious about the nature of Dave's death."

"I bet they are."

"But not in the way you'd expect. They're focused on the fact that you were the last one to see him alive."

"So?"

"They found your prints on his face and neck, and one of your hairs on his MTP."

Tom felt his chest tighten as Ashton's words sank in. "Of course they did. I'm the one who found him."

There was an uncomfortable pause.

"What—so I'm a suspect?"

"They want to know if you'd argued, had some kind of disagreement over something."

"Like he beat me at cards so I cut his throat? What planet are they on?"

Ashton held up a hand. "It doesn't help that we shipped you home in double-quick time before they had a chance to talk to you."

"For fuck's sake." Tom smashed a fist on the bonnet of the Range Rover.

"Steady. Just suck it up. There's also the fact that you pointed the finger at one of theirs. Right now, this is the last thing the Regiment needs."

"So the ANA are claiming I ran amok, killed one of our own for no reason, helped defend the base against an attack and then tried to have a go at Qazi—again for no reason."

Ashton didn't reply. His look said it all.

"This is so fucked up."

"The MoD agree with you on that one for sure."

"I should fucking hope they do."

"Not in the way you think. This couldn't have come at a worse time. The DSF is in the midst of trying to win the argument for us to be part of the lot that stays behind to help the Afghans try to keep a lid on things, stave off the cuts that are most likely coming our way. Trouble is, the Yanks have the same agenda. They see all this kicking off and are whispering in Kabul's ear, saying they should give the job exclusively to them." Ashton shrugged.

"You're going to be RTU'd. You go back to the Rifles as a WO2."

Tom felt as if the ground under his boots had just turned to mush. "You taking the piss?"

Ashton shook his head. "It's just come down from Whitehall. If I had my way it'd all be different—but you know how it is. You have a month's leave—it'll give you time to get the idea bedded in."

"Or just forget it altogether." Tom thought he detected a flicker of satisfaction in Ashton's face as if a dark part of him was enjoying this. He couldn't help but admire the CO's toughness, his

60

focus, how he never flinched or cracked, and the care with which he tended the comradery that held them all together, but now they were alone, the void between them was all too plain.

Ashton eased himself off the Range Rover. "Give you a lift?"

"I'll make my own way."

"Suit yourself. Oh, one more thing. Steer clear of Dave's girl. She's understandably . . . very upset."

13

Watching this exchange from his car-pool Mondeo, parked on the other side of the apron, James Woolf bit into his cheeseburger without lowering his binoculars and smiled. Even though a fine rain blurred his view, he could tell by the body language how badly the encounter was going. As the two men parted, Ashton in his Range Rover back to the Lines, Buckingham towards the Europcar booth in the terminal, Woolf dropped the remains of the burger into the bag in his lap, screwed it up, threw it into the passenger footwell and speed-dialed Stephen Mandler.

"Woolf, what a surprise."

There was a familiar weariness in the boss's voice that he had learned to ignore.

"I just wondered if you'd had a chance to read my last briefing."

There was a muffled exchange while Mandler shooed someone out of his office. "I've got it here. Give me a minute."

A soft clicking came down the phone: Mandler's tongue tapping the roof of his mouth, which he often did when scanning Woolf's latest missives. There followed a long sigh. "You really are rather a cunt, aren't you, James?"

Woolf said nothing.

"If I were Buckingham, I think I'd want to punch you very hard in the face. The man's whole life is the SAS. His part in Eurostar was exemplary. Wouldn't it have been more decent to just take him aside and make him an offer?"

Mandler had taken Woolf to task before for his over-elaborate schemes, but Woolf had already rehearsed his answer. "That would have meant involving his CO—too much of a risk. There can't be any suspicion. This way the whole world thinks it's all for real, including Buckingham."

There was a long silence at the other end of the phone. Woolf knew what was going on. Mandler was more than just his boss: he was his mentor and his protector, but there were limits to how far the old man would go to protect his protégé. Everyone who managed Woolf thought him a handful. Expelled from more than one school, sent down from Oxford and sacked from the BBC, he intimidated some with his intellect, while for others it was his brutal intolerance of inferiors that had dogged his career. Only MI5, his last-chance saloon, had managed to accommodate him, and then only with Mandler's patronage. And there, as in every job before, his seemingly wilful determination to take the opposite view, which the DG could only describe as pathological, got right up the nose of the staff. That, and his lack of grace, had on more than one occasion brought aggrieved colleagues to Mandler's door. "You're playing with fire, Woolf, you know that."

Woolf didn't respond.

"Let me spell it out. You are accusing British ex-servicemen of terrorism—on British soil—and you're proposing to place an SAS sergeant with an exemplary record among them to help you join up the dots."

Getting it wrong wouldn't just be Woolf's undoing: it would be Mandler's head as well.

"I think we're going to have to take some soundings before I let you off the leash. All right?"

14

Newland Hall, Malvern Hills, Worcestershire

Mary Buckingham brushed a few crumbs off the ancient oak table as she put his coffee in front of him, black, no sugar. Tom had appeared at the door without any warning. She hadn't even known he was back in the country. Usually she got a call to say that he was on his way. She touched his shoulder, felt the tension in it, then sat down and tried not to make it too obvious that she was watching him intently.

"Thanks, Mom." He smiled at her, then let his gaze drift back to a vacant space on the kitchen wall.

She was torn. Every homecoming was a cause for celebration, a huge wave of relief that brought the knowledge he was safe and in one piece. But she had learned to keep her joy to herself, just as she hid her tears whenever he left. She used to think that it would get easier, that the heart-aching wrench of seeing her son, so recently a child to her, going off to dangerous places—he could never say where—would diminish over time. In fact, it was the opposite, as if a malign calculator in the back of her mind was totting up the probability that the longer he stayed in the Regiment the more likely it was that the worst would happen. She had accepted that she couldn't know where he was going or what he was doing, knew that it was probably better that way. But she still tensed when the news came on, or if Hugh paused when answering the phone, even held her breath. So the relief when he reappeared usually made her almost light-headed with joy.

But not today. Something was wrong.

"How was the flight?"

There were a million other questions she lacked the courage to ask.

"Fine. Flew back with a young lad from Brum."

"Oh, yes? Was that nice?"

Tom said nothing.

She couldn't remember a time when he had been so distant. When Delphine had lost the baby, he had been full of sorrow, but he'd handled it, talked about it. He wasn't one to push things down. But something had sucked the energy out of him.

Of course he had grown out of overt displays of emotion at a young age. Seared into her memory was the first time they'd left him at school, aged just seven, trussed up in his stiff new uniform. In the car on the way and again when they'd arrived, he had given her strict orders: *Just a quick hug, okay, Mom, and NO TEARS.* And the same had applied to school holidays. After a few days he would let his guard down—but then, as if he was preparing her for what was to come, he would terrify the life out of her by climbing the tallest trees and crossing the lake when it froze. Once he'd come back drenched and half frozen, almost hysterical with delight after the ice had cracked. Nothing had fazed him even then. He simply had no sense of fear.

But now that he was sitting at the table with the untouched coffee in front of him, that was what she was seeing in his face: fear.

He scanned the familiar kitchen landscape, the timeless Welsh dresser with the blue and white "Old Luxembourg" Villeroy & Boch dinner service, passed on by his grandmother and, miraculously, still complete, though one of the soup bowls displayed multiple joins from its surgery when, aged four, he used it as a soldier's helmet. He looked at the clock, a rectangular Dutch antique with a twisted barley-sugar pole on either side of its face, and a soft chime that measured out life at home in reassuring quarter-hours, the parquet floor, pleasantly worn but good for another century, and the black retriever resting its chin on his thigh: Horace, one of a long line of more or less identical animals that had graced the Buckingham kitchen since he'd been in a high chair. Thank God some things never changed. Except that everything just had.

He looked at her. "I'm done—it's over." There was something cold in his gaze that Mary didn't recognize. She was bewildered—she had no idea what he was talking about. "The Regiment—I'm out."

As she took this in, two opposing emotions went into battle inside her. This was the day she had secretly prayed for, that one day he would just outgrow it and there would be life beyond all the anxiety. She had hoped at one point that Delphine would bring it about, but the relationship hadn't changed anything.

So she was happy—for herself. She knew the Army was his whole world. He'd always made it clear that was where he was headed, that nothing else would do—so if he was quitting, something completely unprecedented must have happened. Unless *it* was quitting *him*—in which case he would be devastated.

"Well, that's . . ." now she had started she had to finish ". . . it's—I'm sure you know when the right time—"

His face darkened. He brought the mug down hard, sending some of the coffee splashing over the table. The dog yelped, equally confused. "There's *nothing* right about it."

Now she was scared. On the few occasions she had ever seen him angry he had been truly alarming—when a neighbor had run over a previous Horace, and when he had surprised some burglars to whom he gave such a beating that the police nearly charged him with GBH. Only Hugh's measured intervention, and the fact that he and the policeman were both on the board of the soccer club, had saved him.

She opened her mouth to speak, still not sure what she was going to say. But he put up his hand. "Let's talk about something else—anything."

She went into conversation autopilot: the neighbors' flood; the campaign to save the row of poplars that lined the main road, beyond the pheasant woods; the youth club his father had championed, but the locals were opposed to. None of it required him to do anything other than listen—if he was hearing any of it. She couldn't tell. "But all we seem to be talking about at the moment is what's happening in the cities. Your father says he can't remember a time like it. Even the miners' strike wasn't anything like this, he says. He thinks they might declare a state of emergency."

"Where is he, anyway?"

"Up in town, staying at the club."

If only Hugh was here, he and Tom could have gone off to the pub and Tom could have unloaded. But she was alone and that made the atmosphere more intense. Maybe she could get him to come back on some pretext.

"I'm going to get cleaned up, then go and see Delphine."

She put a hand on his. He flinched slightly but she left it there. He frowned at her.

"Haven't you spoken to her?"

"Her phone was off so—no. Why?"

His voice trailed away: he could see his mother had something to say.

"Darling, she's gone home—to France. She came by to tell us. She said she thought she needed a bit of time at home. All the trouble here—and everything else."

They both knew what "everything else" meant.

"She didn't want to just disappear without saying goodbye."

"To you! I need to see her."

"Darling, I think you should let her be—for now. Just let her know you're safe. I'm sure she'll be glad to hear that."

He got up, his jaw set. Was he even listening?

"She's had so much to deal with. Losing the baby—it's something a woman doesn't really get over. I'm not saying it doesn't affect men too. But it can be devastating."

He stared at her vacantly. No Regiment and now no Delphine. His whole life had just ground to a shuddering stop.

15

Doncaster

Sam was soaked through. His linen jacket and even the T-shirt under it had fused themselves into a sodden outer skin. His backpack was a limp wet lump drooping from its straps. He hadn't bargained on a walk from the station. At the taxi stand he had given the address and the cabbie's face had contorted with dismay.

"You 'avin' a laugh?"

The second had just taken off.

"Forget it," said the third.

He'd tried waiting for a 42, the bus he used to take to school, but a passer-by told him he was wasting his time. "All suspended cos of the riots. Four buses were torched. Where have you been—Mars?"

He didn't have to walk far to see it: the bright orange glow to the east, and emanating from it, the almost continuous shriek of sirens, though the streets near the station were eerily empty.

Twenty-five rain-soaked minutes later, he reached the foot of Trap Hill. A cordon stretched along the east side of Farley Street. The side door of a police van slid open and a PC in riot gear poked his head out. "Oi, you. Get over here." After four days of semi-continuous battle pleasantries were unlikely to be forthcoming.

Inside the van were several more cops—all in various stages of sleep.

Sam set his face to reasonable, accompanied by a small enquiring smile. "How can I help, Officer?"

The cop glanced at one of his mates, who leaned out to look at him, then exchanged glances with his colleagues in the time-honored fashion, as if to say, *We've got a right one here.*

"You lost or summat?"

"No, I'm not, actually."

"You're not from round here."

Sam pointed to Jimmy's Kebabs, halfway up Trap Hill, still intact, albeit with a plywood front window. "See the kebab shop? That's where I grew up."

They stared at him. He knew what they were thinking. His hair was black, but his skin was pale and he'd always made a point of staying out of the sun. The linen suit—albeit drenched—along with the designer backpack, was what he considered to be the uniform of an ambitious young academic. No one round here looked like this.

"What's your name?"

"Kovacevic, *Dr.* Kovacevic."

Sam was a convenient Anglicization. His mother had protested but eventually given way and, apart from her, no one called him Sahim.

The cop raised his eyebrows. "Hospital's that way." He jabbed a thumb in the direction of the orange glow. He snorted. "They're a bit short right now."

"Not a medical doctor, I'm afraid."

"What, then?"

"Criminology."

They burst out laughing.

"Well, you've come to the right place."

They continued to laugh, sharing the news with the others in the van.

"Here, your mam won't be at home, son. The street's been evacuated."

All he'd had from her was a text from an unknown number. *Help—they've taken me refuge. Help. Mamina.* By the time he'd tried to call back a recording said the number was disconnected.

A cop got out and lifted the police tape for him to go through. "Try the Krypt. They've put some of them up in there."

Sam frowned.

"The church hall, as was."

"Oh, okay. Thanks for your help."

Again, the cops looked at each other. Probably the first thanks they'd had in quite a few days, he thought, as he plodded up the empty street towards his old home.

It was six weeks since he had spoken to his mother, a year since he'd seen her, and that was only when she'd got herself admitted to hospital after his brother had taken off. *I think it's her heart—it's broken*, explained a weary houseman, a fellow Muslim, who said he had tried his best to find a medical explanation for her condition. "Best treatment? Get your brother back. He's all she talks about."

All his life, it seemed, he had been at the mercy of her pleas: help Karza with his homework, fetch him back from friends, help him find a job, get him from the police station. And all the while Sam had got top marks, never got drunk or mixed with the wrong people, and had got into a good university, with no acknowledgement from her. Always it was Karza. *What does she still see in him—after all I've done?* The unfairness was infuriating.

He had been in Oxford when the riots kicked off, giving a lecture on gang culture: how was that for timing? *When the community is undermined by the exodus of wealth and skills caused by lack of opportunity, setting off a downward spiral, and the traditional authorities—family, male role models—retreat from their stabilizing role or are absent, gangs fill the vacuum. The young seek protection; ancient concepts of revenge and the preservation of honor become paramount again.*

He had been applying for a lecturing post. He'd thought it was his for the taking. He had already made a name for himself with appearances on TV. His lines about self-help and responsibility made good sound-bites, and he had just the right tone to appeal to every kind of audience.

But this lot had looked bored and none of the faculty had even turned up. The applause was tepid, just a few desultory questions. For the first time in a long while, he had felt the cloak of inferiority wrap itself around him. Once attached, it was hard to shake off. When the board had finally convened to interview him he could tell that they were just going through the motions, and when the professor had started texting during one of Sam's answers, he had stopped mid-sentence, picked up his bag and walked out. On the bus to the station, still fuming, it had occurred to him that now he knew what it felt like, the incoherent rage some of the thugs he'd studied talked about.

The former church hall stank like the refugee camp they had stayed in when they'd first arrived in England, of sweat, boiled vegetables, and unflushed bathrooms. Inside was a sea of camp beds, mostly mothers with small children. He approached a huddle

72

of women in scarves, in the midst of which, holding forth, in a tacky fake-fur coat and ankle boots, was his mother.

"Hello, Mom."

They stopped talking and gazed up at him. He smiled back. He knew what they were thinking. Here comes Sammy, the *doctorate*. Too bad his mother couldn't share in the admiration.

"Ah, good," she said, as if he had just come back from the shops.

Eighteen years ago, just a few months after they had settled in Doncaster, his father had stepped out for a pint of milk and never come back. Recently Sam had done some digging and found out that he had gone back to Bosnia and started another family.

She got up, took his hands and kissed him purposefully on both cheeks. He noticed that, despite the privations of the last few days, her makeup was still being liberally applied. Wherever she was, she always had a mirror.

"So wonderful of you to spare the time to come all this way."

He looked at the crowd. *Not exactly starved of attention.* Was this new-found appreciation of him mainly for their benefit? "So, what happened?"

She smacked her forehead as if dispatching a mosquito. "Ugh! They came down the street, smashing everything. Oh, it was terrible, terrible! Jimmy's away so I was all on my own."

"Did they hurt you?"

"Oh, no. I'd put the shutters down. But they stood there and banged and banged. And the dreadful things they shouted. It was just like Bosnia."

"Well, I don't think there've been any massacres." It was an ill-chosen remark but he couldn't help himself. She was adept at exaggeration.

73

"After they'd gone the police came, asking if I was okay. I told them how traumatized I was alone so they said I'd better come here. Can you take me to the airport?"

Fuck—had she gone senile?

"You don't want to go *home*?"

"No, silly boy! Jimmy's booked me a flight to Málaga tomorrow. He says we should stay there where it's safe."

"In *Spain*?"

She shrugged, as if it was what any sensible person would do. "He has a sea-view flat."

"Oh, fine then."

He could feel the familiar simmering irritation. She had dragged him back from Oxford to book her a minicab.

Suddenly her face crumpled.

"What is it, Mom?"

She turned her eyes up to him, wide, full of love and longing. "It's Karza."

"Right." His heart sank.

"They still don't know where he is. Jimmy's been onto the Foreigners' Office again—"

"*Foreign* Office, Mom."

"Yes, that's right, and they wash their hands of him."

She didn't need to say any more. A year ago, his brother and two of his equally useless and misguided mates had boarded a flight to Istanbul, made their way to the border, crossed over to Syria and enlisted with the rebels. Knowing Karza, Sam expected he'd be back in three weeks. But after a month they'd got a photo of him holding an AK47, a pair of bandoliers crossed over his shoulders. And for the first time in as long as

Sam could remember, Karza was grinning. He had found his calling.

"Have you asked Bala?"

She threw up her hands and clasped her forehead. He had heard that Bala, one of Karza's fellow fuckwits, had come back four months earlier with a serious leg wound. "He stays in his room twenty-four seven. Says nothing to his mama, not even please and thank you for his foods. So I go there myself. I ask, I beg, 'Where is Karza?' He tells me to—I can't say the dreadful words. Sammy, please, can't you do something?" His mother tilted her head to one side and looked him up and down, as if his drenched linen suit was a uniform that conferred on him some official status.

"Now you are a *doctorate*, can't you at least do that one thing?"

From as early as he could remember he and his brother had gone separate ways. While Karza had stuck resolutely with the other Muslim kids, Sam had made a point of courting English friends, copying their habits and manners, like a method actor studying for a role he intended to play for the rest of his life. He had adored Britain from the moment they arrived. He couldn't believe his luck to have been exiled from what he saw as a backward place, a cauldron of prejudice and religious dogma. He loved school, and his teachers loved him: he gobbled up knowledge as if it was ice cream. He had had no time for Karza and his friends, who seemed bent on denying themselves any hope of advancement.

And yet their mother doted on his brother.

"Mom, he'll be lucky if he's allowed back without a struggle. He can't expect to go off to Syria and just come home when he's had enough."

"But he has passport. He's British citizen."

Before he could reply, she shut her eyes and shook her head as she always did when she wanted to warn him that she would be deaf to whatever he said. Then, just as he was cursing himself for having made the journey, she reached up to him. He sighed, lowered himself into her embrace and just for a moment let himself go—felt the soft warmth that he had so loved as a boy.

"Mamina's baby," she whispered. "I am so proud of you."

He knew this was a lie. *Why do you do this with criminals? Where is the job?* she had blurted out once when he showed her a conference program that featured his name. He still looked forward to when he could tell her he was officially a lecturer, though that goal seemed to have receded beyond his reach—again. Bursaries and fellowships were way beyond her understanding, yet all the time his brother had been at home on his arse in front of *Medal of Honor*, it was "poor Karza".

She waved at the group of friends who had respectfully withdrawn so they could have this moment together. "They all saw you on the television."

They, not you, he wanted to say. But he didn't. He smiled and took the compliment anyway. He couldn't help it: he had always been a sucker for her praise—however guarded. A part of him that he didn't want to own up to was aware that it was almost worth coming all the way up here for.

But he knew the moment would be short-lived.

"Since Karza left, you don't know how hard it's been."

He loosened the embrace and stepped back. "Well, you've got Jimmy now."

76

He had noticed her charming their Cypriot landlord even before his father had left, praising him for letting them live in the cramped, badly ventilated flat above his shop. *Such a kind man, so good to my boys.* It was true: Jimmy gave them Cokes from his fridge, change for the slot machine, and free kebabs. Then she had appeared in new earrings, shoes, a winter coat. He soon realized what she was doing to secure these favors, as he turned up the TV to drown the squeals and gasps that floated up from Jimmy's room behind the shop when she was "helping downstairs".

But even as a teenager, he was relieved that someone else had come along to take the heat off him and carry the burden of bankrolling her and Karza. One major upside of Karza taking off: he wasn't leeching off them any more. But no matter where he was, dead or alive, he still exerted a powerful force over her.

"But no Karza . . ." She was still talking about him, her face clouded with sorrow.

Jesus, families, thought Sam. *They really do fuck you up.*

She looked at him with those sad Labrador eyes. "Jimmy is the kindest man but there can be no joy, only pain, while Karza is . . ." She couldn't finish the sentence.

He put his arm round her.

She nestled her head against his neck. "Will you do something—anything—to bring him back? Will you?" She lifted her head away and fixed him with one of her trademark stares, gradually taking a deep breath that, depending on his response, would erupt in a wail of pure sorrow or an exclamation of love and joy.

He heard the words leave his mouth as if with a will of their own. "All right, I promise."

Her face lit up. She pulled him to her again, squeezing him tight. Then, just as quickly, her mood changed. "Sahim, please go now to the flat and get my passport." She rummaged in her bag and produced a huge ring of keys. "It's in my nightstand—top drawer."

16

Sam slept fitfully in an antiseptic hotel near the station. He had nodded off watching Sky News and it was still playing when he woke up. *Another night of violence . . .*

His phone was buzzing: Helen.

"Hey, sweetheart. So glad you called back." He had left several messages the night before.

"Where are you?"

"I had to go up north." He knew that would do. She never asked what he was up to.

"Oh." She sounded put out.

"Baby, I'm so sorry. Are you missing me? I thought you had a big shoot today." He seemed to remember her talking about a chocolate commercial.

"Um—well, I just wanted to talk."

"Did you have a bad day?"

"No—I'm just a bit freaked out about everything that's going on."

She had never mentioned the riots before.

"Look, I'll be back tonight. Promise. Okay? And I can put your mind at rest about everything."

The thought of being back in her arms, smothering his face in her blonde curls, filled him with excitement. God, he fancied her.

"Okay." Her voice was muted. Oh, well. "Bye. Love you."

Bala's estate was a two-mile walk. In the daylight the center of town seemed to have returned to business as usual. The exercise sharpened him and he soon forgot about Helen's ominous tone. Further away from the center, the damage was apparent. The estate was a ghost town of abandoned houses. Sidewalks were strewn with litter from overturned bins, glass from smashed windows and windshield. A burned-out corner shop still smoldered. His mother had been right. Not since Bosnia had he seen anything like this. He didn't expect to find someone home but at least he could say he'd made the effort. He'd ask anyone he did see around the estate, then get the hell out.

But they hadn't fled. Bala's father was up a ladder, nailing plywood over a smashed upstairs window. All the others had been boarded up.

"Hi, Mr. Pazic."

Mr. Pazic looked down at him, said nothing, and carried on hammering. Sam guessed they blamed Karza for pressuring Bala to go with him to Syria.

The front door wasn't locked. He pushed it open. From the front room came the sound of a TV talk show turned up loud.

"Anyone home? It's Sam."

In the semi-darkness, he could just make out a small child gazing at him from a doorway before she was pulled back. A woman's face appeared. He almost didn't recognize her: Bala's sister, Jana. She kept her eyes lowered. Another ghost from his past—but one he wasn't unhappy to see. "Jana. Hello. Is Bala home? I need to talk to him."

She looked at him for what seemed a long time, a mixture of emotions passing over her face, like fast-moving clouds. Somewhere under the pasty olive skin and tired, sunken eyes was the idealistic teenager he had once kissed in the bus shelter. The headscarf made her seem much older, as did the expression of sullen resignation. He nodded at the child clinging to her skirt. "Yours?"

She said nothing, but indicated the room where the TV sound was coming from. He knocked, but the volume was too high. She stepped forward and hammered on the door. "Bala! Someone here for you."

There was no answer. She shrugged. "Just go in."

"Why's he got it up so loud?"

She stared at him for a few seconds. "He says it drowns it out— the stuff in his head. That and the skunk."

The room was thick with the sweet, heavy smoke. Sam looked back at her and smiled, but she gazed past him blankly and pulled the child into the kitchen.

The TV volume shot up as the door swung open.

"And I'm tellin' 'im, she shows 'er face round our 'ouse, I'll not be answerable for my actions, bladdered or not. Same goes for any of them kids what he's had with her."

On the TV a huge woman in a strapless top was jabbing the air with a heavily ringed finger. Two other women, similar but younger, were holding on to her as if she was liable to launch herself at the skinny, bearded, ponytailed man she was pointing at, seated in a separate chair the other side of Jerry Springer.

Sam focused on the solitary armchair pulled up close to the screen. He wouldn't have recognized Bala. The beard was new, as was the shaved head. A stick lay tucked against the chair. He had put on at least forty pounds. He wore a khaki vest and shorts. The stump of his left leg was wrapped in gauze.

"Hey, bro."

Bala lifted his eyes and frowned.

"It's Sam, Karza's brother."

"I'm not blind."

"Well, it's been a while."

Sam lifted his hands and let them drop to his sides. He couldn't think what to say next. The sight of the stump made him feel queasy. What if something like that happened to Karza? Or worse?

"So—ah, a lot's happened since I was last round here."

He remembered sitting alone in this room with Jana, waiting for Karza and Bala to come in so he could take his brother home. He had liked her, all right, but he'd known that at the first sign of anything serious between them, her parents would have seen it as permanent and he had other plans.

Bala let out a long, smoky sigh and turned back to the screen.

"I need your help."

At least that made Bala smile. "That's a first."

"Mom's worried about Karza. She wants me to find him."

Bala snorted. "Good luck with that."

"She hasn't heard from him in five months. She doesn't even know if he's still alive."

He raised his shoulders, let them drop, then looked back at the screen.

"Anything you can tell me to make a start, like where you last saw him?"

"When they drove off and left me for dead, you mean? About fifty K east of Aleppo. That help you?"

Sam had always assumed that Bala was the more reckless of the two. Their mother had always said he was a bad influence. But listening to him now, and thinking of Karza posing absurdly with his ammunition belts, it occurred to Sam that maybe he had got it wrong and it was the other way round. Their mother would have been in denial, of course, as she so often was where Karza was concerned, and having Bala to blame would have perfectly suited her picture of his brother as the innocent, misguided dupe of more dominant personalities.

"Can you just give me something? Who bought your tickets or who got you across the border? Someone I can ask."

"We drove."

"To Syria? From here?"

"Taking medical supplies for a charity."

"Which one?"

He shrugged.

"Which group were you with?"

"Jaish Muhajireen wa Ansar. That's the Army of Emigrants and Helpers—since you don't speak the language."

God, he was a pain. Sam bet he didn't speak more than two words of Arabic either, but he was fluent in self-righteousness.

"We were in an assault on a Scud base near Aleppo, then an army barracks at the airport." He shook his head. "Karza got lucky—he always does. They let him use the RPG and he scored a direct hit on a bus full of government conscripts. Went right to his head."

Sam struggled to get *his* head round the idea of his little brother as a killer. Even after they'd received the photograph and he had seen Karza's expression, he had dismissed it as showing off.

Bala sucked on the spliff until it glowed back to life. He reached forward and scratched his ankle, where something was bulging inside his sock.

"What's that?"

"You should know. Aren't criminals your special subject?"

Bala pushed his sock down. An electronic tag. "Cos I'm such a danger to society. I'm on a TPIM. You'll know what that is."

Sam did: Terrorism and Prevention Investigation Measures had replaced Control Orders but did much the same, a blunt instrument to keep tabs on would-be terrorists.

"Just cos of going to Syria, never mind I didn't fire a single shot."

The smoke was starting to get to him, irritating his eyes. Bala coughed heavily into the hand that held the spliff, then waved it at Sam. "You don't get it, do you? They've declared war on us. How're we gonna fight back?"

Sam said nothing. He let him rant on.

"Even you, with your degree, you're still a target. We're all targets. Better make up your mind which side you're on."

Sam decided not to engage with this. He'd come about Karza. "The Army of Helpers—do they have anyone based in the UK?"

Bala gave him a withering look.

"Okay then, whoever organized the van you drove there. Just somewhere I can start. Come on, man. Mom's bloody desperate."

Bala reached for a Biro and tore off a corner of the local paper, scribbled something and passed it to him. On it was the name "Leanne" and an address on the other side of Doncaster. "They worked out of there."

"Leanne?"

"It was her house. She was the co-ordinator. Your brother had a bit of a thing for her. Maybe she'll know something."

"Any phone number or surname?"

But Bala was done. He turned back to Jerry Springer. The large beanbag of a woman had dissolved into sobs and was being comforted by her similarly-shaped supporters.

Sam exited the room and turned towards the front door, but Jana was there, the child still clutching her long skirt. Like him, she had gravitated away from the other Muslims at school. Once, Sam and she had even talked about taking off for London together, escaping the stranglehold of family life. He tried to think of something to say. "Last time I saw you, you were in hot pants."

It sounded clumsy and out of place.

She looked at him blankly. "Then you've not seen me in a long time."

He gestured at her clothes. "How come?"

She ignored the question. "You going to help him or what?"

"Bala?"

"You saw that thing on his leg."

"It's up to the authorities. The TPIM expires after two years. He needs to stay out of trouble, though."

"Yeah, like he's going to blow up a bus or something."

He tensed, prepared himself for another speech. *You don't like this? Try Egypt, or Libya*, he felt like saying. If only they understood how lucky they were to be here. In a hundred other countries Bala would have been locked up and forgotten—or tortured.

"And that lot who've attacked us all along, before this kicked off. They gonna be tagged? How long do we have to go on getting battered, shit through our letter-box, bricks in our windows before *you* do something about it?"

"Look, Jana . . ."

She pursed her lips.

". . . I'm just trying to find my brother."

"Fuck your brother. He got Bala into this."

Victimhood: he could have written a whole dissertation on it. It was like a plague that had crippled the community, breeding a toxic combination of self-pity and thwarted entitlement. Thank God he hadn't got involved with her. Instead he had got away. But something about the way the light had gone from her eyes touched him. "You've changed."

She glared at him, then gestured at the boarded-up windows round the front door. "It's not me that's changed. It's out there that's changed."

17

Doncaster

The house was Victorian, one of a terrace that seemed to go on for ever, winding up the hill. There was no sign of rioting in this part of town and, for that matter, no sign of any Muslim presence. A removal van was parked outside, its engine idling, the driver reading a paper propped on the steering wheel. "War Zone Britain" was the headline.

Sam pressed the intercom. Above it there was a small security camera. He looked into it, trying to appear pleasant and unthreatening.

"Yes?" asked a metallic voice, through the speaker.

"I'm here to see Leanne."

Silence. He was about to press again when the door inched open. An elderly Asian man in a suit jacket that was too large for him peered out.

"Is she here—Leanne?"

The old man continued to stare at him. "Wait."

He shut the door.

It was raining hard. Sam started to feel foolish, his already battered morale ebbing away. Then the door opened again and a woman in her mid-twenties, pale but with large dark brown eyes, stood in front of him. Her face was attractive but unanimated, like an empty canvas waiting for someone to add the character.

"Leanne?"

She didn't answer, just waited for him to say something else.

"I'm here about my brother—in Syria."

She frowned. He guessed what she was thinking: that he didn't look the part.

"We're from Bosnia originally."

He couldn't remember the last time he had owned up to this. He'd never raised it with Helen and she hadn't asked. It sounded weird and out of context.

She opened the door wider and gestured for him to enter. For a second she reminded him of Helen. He felt a sharp pain as his conversation with her came back to him.

"Are you Leanne?"

She had a maroon scarf draped over her head, and wore a long dark green smock with loose pants. He followed her down a hall stacked with boxes into the kitchen where there were more boxes and black sacks. She stood in their midst.

"Leanne's not with us any more."

Her speech was oddly formal. He also detected the trace of an American accent.

"I'm Sahim." He felt the occasion merited his real name.

"Nasima."

"Are you with the same organization?"

"Just the medical supplies."

Her tone was cool. Even though she had invited him in he felt he had already outstayed his welcome.

"Look, I'm not—I'm just trying to trace my brother. He went to Syria—with this organization's—seemingly with the help of this Leanne. A friend went with him—Bala Pazic—but he came back. He was injured. He was the one who told me to come here."

She peered at him, frowning. "I've seen you on TV."

For the first time in a grim twenty-four hours he felt a small glow of pleasure. "Oh. Thanks. It was just—a few appearances."

She made no comment as she moved towards the cooker and opened a cupboard. "Tea?"

All her movements were as economical as her speech, as if she was conserving her energy. She retained the same fixed half-smile she had greeted him with at the door.

"Yes, thank you."

Something about her accent told him she wasn't British by birth, but her manner suggested she was very much assimilated, just like him. He felt comforted by that.

He heard floorboards creaking above.

"Do you know where in Syria your brother is?"

It all rushed out of him, like air from a balloon: how Karza and Bala had suddenly volunteered, the picture his brother had sent back. As he talked, he realized what little information he had. She listened with the same blank expression. The kettle boiled, and she dropped a teabag into a mug with the Red Crescent emblem on the side. Maybe they really were organizing medical supplies. He couldn't tell if she was paying any attention.

"Milk and sugar?"

"Both, please."

She put the mug down. "What motivated him? Was he very committed?"

This wasn't the moment to be honest.

"I think they felt they could make a difference—though I don't think he knew what he was getting into."

The truth was far more banal. Sam likened it to the lure of gang culture. He imagined Karza's childish glee at being given a gun for the first time and a sense of importance. His lack of imagination would have stood him in good stead. That much Sam had learned from his studies. Some of the most effective gang members were the least imaginative. No risk of seeing the other side of the argument or the consequences of their deeds.

Feeling better, the tea lubricating his scratchy throat, he gave her a version of his visit to his mother, her emotional plea to him to find Karza, and the encounter with Bala, his stump and the tag. There didn't seem any point in holding back.

"He got back. He's lucky." Her voice had a harder edge.

"So what happened to Leanne?"

"She's gone."

"To Syria?"

Her face clouded. "She's in custody. There was some confusion about the priorities of the charity. It was supposed to be about taking medical supplies to the victims of conflict. But because they started sending people over, it's having to be wound up." She waved at the bags and boxes.

Sam felt the chances of finding his brother diminishing by the minute. "Bala thought she might know where he is."

"Do you want to go and find him?" There was more than a trace of irritation in her voice.

"Well, not exactly." He didn't want to sound like a coward, but nothing would induce him to go anywhere near the place. He hadn't even any desire to go back to Bosnia. "You know, work commitments," he added weakly, because she looked like someone who would appreciate what he meant—then flushed; it sounded like a cop-out.

But she didn't react. He had no idea what she was thinking.

She focused on him again. "What are your work commitments, exactly?"

He gave her a quick rundown, leaving out the Oxford debacle. He hoped she was impressed and wouldn't notice that he didn't actually have a job. But he carried on regardless, as if her blank stillness and lack of response was a vacuum he had to fill. "But Karza's not had the same luck as me. I think going to Syria could have been the making of him."

"So you love him very much," she said, without looking up.

"Well, it's just us and Mom. They're all I've got. And he is the apple of her eye."

"It must be terrible for her, not knowing if he's alive or dead— or something in between."

Her gaze was cold, as if she couldn't conceal her contempt for these naïve recruits, blundering into a war zone hopelessly unprepared. "People coming from the West, if they fall into the hands of government forces they tend to get singled out for—special punishment. And some of the rebel groups are also hostile to them."

He closed his eyes for a moment, at the thought of having to tell his mother that her darling younger son was being tortured. "Is there anything you can do?"

She handed him a pad. "Write down your brother's name, parents, date of birth, last known address, email, and any phone numbers. Yours too."

"Can I ask why?"

"Not all our callers come with the best of intentions."

He reddened. "Of course, and I understand, but rest assured you've no reason to be suspicious of me."

She left the room. He heard her go up the stairs, then more footsteps above. He sipped the tea. He had no experience of charities or organizations that sent people to war zones. All his focus was on domestic criminal behavior, understanding what turned people into thieves and drug-dealers. He hadn't a clue what had inspired his brother or Bala to go to Syria, other than some foolish search for excitement inspired by too much computer gaming and the belief, common to young men, that they were invincible. The last time they had met, Karza had talked with great reverence about his own internal jihad, the challenge to live according to his new-found faith. He hadn't said anything about fighting the actual war. Prior to that, the two of them had never had a serious conversation about anything, except Karza's lack of work or money. Now he thought about it, he should have seen it for what it was: a turning point.

Eventually Nasima reappeared, holding a printout. She looked troubled. "It's not very good news. I'm sorry."

Immediately he imagined breaking news of Karza's death to their mother and somehow being blamed for it. "The militia he was with have been absorbed by ISIS."

"What's that?"

"The Islamic State of Iraq in Syria. They're affiliated with Al Qaeda." She seemed slightly disappointed at his ignorance. "They captured them in the Salahedin district of Aleppo. It's not clear whether they're being held against their will or if they've joined them. There are some confirmed deaths but your brother's name's not among them, so that's one good thing. He could have been injured and they're treating him—or he might have escaped."

"Are there any hospitals?"

"All medical facilities in the rebel-held areas are regarded by the government as legitimate targets. If he's in need of attention he's probably either in a safe-house or out in the hills somewhere."

"Can you get him out?"

"You mean send him a ticket for easyJet?"

The gibe seemed to come out of nowhere.

He blushed. "I didn't mean to imply that I thought it was easy."

To his huge relief, she smiled slightly. "I'm sorry. It's just that we get a lot of relatives asking the same question when our focus should be on helping the Syrian casualties."

"Of course. What would it take? Is it a question of money? Not that I have much."

"We are a charity, Sahim."

The room filled with the sound of sirens. Several police vehicles sped past the front door. She sighed. "Not a good situation." She seemed to expect a response.

"Well, no."

"You don't seem very bothered."

He didn't have a ready answer. The struggles of the Muslim community bored him. He had devoted his life to getting away from all that. Ranting imams, extremists rejecting modern society, women covering themselves and hiding away: it was a tragedy. Look at Jana: all the spark ground out of her. She summed up everything he hated about his culture. But so much of what they were struggling with they had brought on themselves. Even Bala's tag. He'd had it coming to him.

But if he said this to Nasima, it might end his chances of finding Karza. So he settled for one of his stock sound bites. "This country's been good to me. I've a lot to be grateful for. I know it's not a popular view."

She tipped her head while she digested this. In fact, it wasn't a stock response: it was what he really believed. But now he was wondering if he had said the right thing. He was beginning to get the feeling he was being auditioned. Was this the right line to be taking if he was going to get them to help him find Karza?

She stood up. "We'll try to find out more about your brother. I'll contact you if we get anywhere."

"Or I could call you?"

She smiled bleakly. "All our calls and emails are monitored. Leave it with me." She moved towards the door. "I've got your address. I know where to find you."

18

Malvern Hills, Worcestershire

The track was rutted and puddled, speckling Tom's legs with mud as he pounded along. He ran fast, filling his lungs with damp English air to clear out the last of the sticky Helmand dust. He came to the brow of the hill and paused to take in the view. A gray mist hung in the trees like smoke. Even in this light, with the rain falling around him, it was serene. There was no sound other than that of a pair of blackbirds in conversation and, further away, the drill of a woodpecker. Just where the track dipped down and disappeared into the trees a Mondeo was parked, no lights on, but a wisp of exhaust indicated it was occupied. The car looked as if it had been driven a long distance down a rainy highway, its color almost completely obscured by a thick coat of road grime out of which the wipers had cut clean semi-circles.

Everyone in the village and its environs knew each other, and Tom dreaded a conversation with some well-meaning neighbor eager to hear about what he was doing for his country and so on. He kept going, but something about the car bugged him. He had seen it before. As he pounded on, he replayed his movements since his return but couldn't place it. By the time he stopped to take a second look it was gone.

For the first twenty-four hours he had done nothing but sleep—turbulent semi-consciousness crowded with shattering dreams: Dave's limp, blood-drenched frame, his frozen, wide-eyed expression; Qazi's contemptuous sneer. The poor Afghan kid, already wounded, helpless as he died. He knew better than to try to resist these replays. They were part of a process that had to be gone through. Emotional cold turkey, he'd once heard an army shrink call it. He woke drenched with sweat, gasping for breath, as if some unseen hand had got him by the neck, mistaking the sweat for Dave's blood. He had taken the precaution of locking himself in his bedroom. One of his mates had once broken his daughter's nose when she came in to wake him.

He also dreamed of Delphine, the early carefree days, but then her face dissolved into frozen blocks of pixels.

During the day he virtually barricaded himself into the TV room, flipping between the BBC and Sky's rolling news as they ran a continuous commentary on the riots. Not only had his own world been pulled from under him, the country itself was in turmoil. No wonder Delphine had wanted out. He thought of Blakey, coming home from fighting the Taliban to this.

He turned off the track and dived into the woods, following a trail he had blazed as a boy. These were the happy hunting grounds of his childhood, where long school holidays passed in a flash as he and his mates became SOE operatives dropped by Lysanders into the French forests to blow up Nazi trains. At the edge of the woods he paused to take in the view, the field falling away to their Georgian pile, shaded by century-old lime trees, against the backdrop of the Precambrian hills, 680 million years old. Most of their land was leased to a local farmer now, since he had shown no interest in farming. Was this what was waiting for him? Was he staring at his future? What the hell was he going to do next?

When he turned on his phone there were four missed calls, three from a withheld number, no messages. He hadn't the energy to be curious right now.

The fourth was his father. Tom dialed and waited.

"Hello, old boy! Welcome home and all that."

Breezy and positive was Hugh Buckingham's default mode. Tom guessed his mother had been on to him, full of worry, but Hugh would know better than to ask questions or offer sympathy. "Soaking up some of your mother's TLC, I trust."

"Yeah!"

"Well, when you've had enough of that, come up to town and have lunch. I need your perspective."

"On what?"

"On what the hell's going on." Hugh knew he wouldn't survive more than a few days down there without getting cabin fever.

"Yeah, okay."

His father tried not to overplay his joy. "Come to the club and we'll take it from there. And . . ." He paused, sounding uncharacteristically hesitant. "Did that chap Rolt get hold of you?"

Rolt? Tom couldn't place the name.

"You know, the Invicta chap—patron saint of ex-soldiers. You were at school with him."

They'd been in the same house—hardly best buds. "What does he want?"

"Just asked you to call. He's quite a big deal now."

Tom had no inclination to talk to anyone, and especially not if they were connected with the forces. "Okay, Dad. Will do. See you."

19

Westford Airfield, Oxfordshire

Gusts of wind blowing across the airfield rattled the ancient hangar, which creaked in protest. Hastily painted white during some brief conscription for a UN project, it was revealing its much hardier original khaki, showing through here and there, the last remnant of its Battle of Britain glory days. From outside, the only suggestion of activity, apart from a few parked cars, was a cell scanner, its ten-meter dish pointing skywards to send and receive all encrypted communications. Inside, the resident pair of Cessnas had been shunted to one side to make room for Woolf's makeshift operations base. Half a dozen work stations had been erected, along with a couple of large flat-screen monitors and the long table, at the head of which stood Woolf. He hated presentations but Mandler had insisted. "Think of it as a peer review," he'd suggested unhelpfully. But Woolf knew there would be no arguing. MI5's section heads would have to be brought into the tent sooner or later.

"Ladies and gentlemen, my apologies for dragging you away from your desks to this godforsaken back-water." Mandler gazed down at the group. "What you're about to hear is known only to myself, Woolf and . . ." he glanced at his notes while he tried to remember the names of Woolf's team ". . . these two bright young things who have been watching his back."

Cindy and Rafiq smiled in unison. Mandler smiled back, reflecting silently that Cindy, with her pierced lip, and Rafiq, with his iPod lead permanently trailing out of his pants pocket, were both less than half his age.

"The Joint Intelligence Committee has yet to be informed, same for SIS, GCHQ, and DIS. Why we are keeping this so close to our chests should become apparent. So . . ." he paused to frown at Woolf ". . . only the home secretary has been given a sneak peek inside the kimono in case we need to bring her on-side."

He rubbed his hands together. "You all know James. He doesn't just think outside the box. He tends to squash the box flat, toss it in the trash or garbage and leave us to pick up the pieces."

There was a ripple of amusement.

"Any questions, don't hold back."

He motioned to Woolf to begin. The group stared at him stone-faced, except Cindy and Rafiq, who maintained their frozen smiles.

Woolf stepped in front of the screen. "Ladies and gentlemen, meet the new face of British terrorism."

He tapped a key to bring up the next shot, a soldier in dress uniform: gingery hair, freckles, intense gaze. "Retired Corporal Mick Vestey. Household Cavalry sniper, commended for killing two Taliban from more than a mile away. Here he is in his prime: Kandahar, 2007."

The image changed to a shot of Vestey beside a Scimitar armored reconnaissance vehicle, posing with his crew, tanned and oozing confidence.

"Three days after this was taken the armored vehicle he was travelling in hit an IED. He was blown clean out of it, suffered just cuts and bruises. The rest died underneath it, despite his frantic efforts to reach them. Two months later he was out of the Army, dishonorably discharged after attacking his CO with a knife."

Woolf clicked onto the next picture. "Here he is that Christmas."

Vestey was already looking the worse for wear: florid face, sunken cheeks, and an air of defeat.

"And by the following summer . . ."

He was almost unrecognizable in a police mug shot, eyes glazed and emaciated, in a filthy hoodie.

Woolf turned back to the group as the next photo appeared. "But here's our same Mr. Vestey just a few months ago."

He was transformed, a slightly older version of the man he had been in Helmand, showing none of the scars of his trip to the dark side, in a sports jacket, white shirt, and blue tie.

"Quite a comeback, wouldn't you say? Clean as a whistle, gainfully self-employed in VIP security, guarding the rich and famous."

A man at the back raised a forefinger. "Membership of shooting clubs?"

Woolf grinned. "Aha. Since you ask . . ." He hit the pad and up came a still of the gated entrance to what looked like a very well-defended hotel. To the side of the gate was a large sign in gold lettering—"Invicta".

"This organization should need no introduction. Since the post 9/11 wars it has become Britain's foremost charity for ex-service personnel."

Woolf flicked through a sequence, which showed an impressive campus of buildings surrounded by mature trees and rolling lawns, a lecture theater, an Olympic-sized pool, an extensive gym, and a golf course. "This is their HQ in Hampshire. Among the state-of-the-art facilities there does indeed happen to be a shooting range."

The screen changed to another shot of Vestey, this time in Iraq, posing with his L115a3 sniper rifle.

"Now, let me take you back to the early hours of June the twenty-eighth this year."

A series of images from the Suleiman shooting flicked past, with blurred images of the police SCO19s, their faces hidden by their baseball caps. Then a full-face photo of Suleiman.

"The target: a blameless community worker, widely respected for his campaign against drug-dealers and gangs. A devout Muslim but also an avid promoter of integration. Absolutely nothing to connect him with crime or terrorism. But whose killing *apparently* by the Metropolitan Police, despite their strenuous denials, brings the entire British Muslim community out on the streets in protest."

Woolf paused to glance at Rafiq, who nodded his agreement. "And the rest, as they say, is history." He scrolled through a sequence showing the worst of the riots, looting even in "respectable" areas, and more than one police van on fire. "The most widespread civil unrest in my lifetime, certainly. And no sign of its abating.

"The Met insist they were acting on flashed intelligence about a purported cell bomb factory in the back of a Transit van, also carrying a passenger suggested to be a returnee from Syria. Their source, not one of ours, you'll be glad to know."

Woolf looked round the table. The assembly stared back at him.

Ferris, group director for the north-east, chipped in: "We get about a hundred and fifty false leads like that a day. Does there have to be a conspiracy here?"

Woolf nodded eagerly. He was in his stride now. "Quite so. But here's the thing." He punched up another slide: a middle-aged man in a police uniform. "SCO19 control room officer: John Philip Vestey." The next shot showed both men.

"Mick's brother. He was on duty the night of the shooting— though unable to communicate with his team on the ground due to an alleged radio fault. Make of that what you will."

Woolf stood back to let this revelation sink in. Now the room came alive.

"Are you watching him? Mick."

Woolf smiled ruefully. "You know how many bodies surveillance takes." He pointed at Cindy and Rafiq. "This is the sum total of my team."

"Listening to his calls?"

Cindy shook her head. "He doesn't use a phone."

"Ever?"

"Turns it on every couple of days for just a few minutes. The rest of the time it's off and he leaves it at home."

"Somewhat incriminating."

Jedburgh, ex-Special Branch and a notorious sceptic, launched in: "So you've got a classic loner, who's conquered his demons and trained himself to channel his rage. What's holding him back? Chances are that having started he'll probably keep shooting. I suggest you pull your finger out and bring him in before he does any more damage."

Mandler agreed. "Good point. Keep them coming."

Molly Downham, the only other woman in the group, never spoke up unless she had something pertinent to say. "James, can you share with us exactly why you've been playing your cards even closer to your chest than usual?"

102

Woolf nodded. "That brings me neatly on to part two. We've covered the *who*, but now comes the *why*. Why kill a perfectly decent liberal-minded community worker who's been commended for his work with disaffected youth?" He leaned forward and hit the space bar again. "Recognize him?"

The next sequence was a video of a man in his early thirties standing at a podium, receiving an award from the Mayor of London in front of an audience, who were giving him a standing ovation. "Vernon Rolt, founder of Invicta."

"So his facility is being used as a secret training ground for white British jihadis. That's pretty far-fetched, isn't it?"

Woolf glanced at the other two. "Yes. It's crazy and everyone who's heard it agrees."

It was Molly's turn again. "Are you actually pointing the finger at *Vernon Rolt*?"

Woolf raised his eyebrows inscrutably. "I wouldn't want to go that far . . . just yet."

"But that's why you're keeping this in the family."

Woolf nodded again.

Jedburgh cleared his throat. "Sorry, James, but I'm not buying it. Right now we've got an inundation of returnees from Syria. A lot of them have seen and done unimaginable things, been thrown together with the most out-there extremists. They're trained, they're battle-hardened and we can't keep track of them because they're using different names, keeping away from their families and so on. We just don't have the resources or the intelligence."

This Woolf knew to be true, to his frustration. And Jedburgh wasn't done.

"The sight of one of their own being all lovey-dovey and multi-culti with Christians, athiests, and whatnot, they're going to see that guy as the enemy even more than the Anglos. It's a nice idea, but I think you're going to find you're barking up the wrong tree. Radicalization is the issue, nothing else."

The meeting fell silent. Woolf glanced at Rafiq, then Cindy. Both were studying their hands intently.

Mandler got up and brought the meeting to a close with a speech about how grateful he was to them for sparing the time, and waited while the others filed out to their cars.

"Interesting." He gave Woolf a mischievous look.

"Really?"

"You have to consider all sides of the problem. And the trouble is, what you've got here is conjecture. I think we might park this for now. Perhaps I can find something else on which you can train your enormous brain."

It sounded like a compliment, yet also a putdown.

And with that he folded up his glasses and left.

20

Westminster, Central London

"Can you open your bag, please?"

There was a heavy police presence outside Party Headquarters, checking people before they went through the door. Barriers had been set up to funnel visitors to a table where their belongings were being examined. Sam unzipped his bag. The policewoman glanced in and ran a gray plastic wand over his laptop. "ID?"

"I have an appointment, with—"

"ID, please," she repeated, as if he hadn't heard her.

He felt inside his coat and brought the driver's license out of his wallet. She peered at the details, then examined a clipboard held by her colleague. "Mr. Koverchovich?"

She said it loudly, mispronouncing it. A couple of other uniforms looked up and scanned his face.

"*Dr*. Kovace*vic*. I'm here for a job interview."

The policewoman's mouth twitched with amusement. "Good luck, sir," she said, without a trace of goodwill as she handed back his bag. With a curt flick of her head, she signaled to him to go through.

Sam gave his name at the desk, then sank into a large leather and chrome chair. He tried to collect his thoughts for the interview but the impact of Helen's note blotted out everything else. He had found it on the kitchen table when he got back.

Dear Sam,

I'm going to Mummy's. She thinks it would be better if I stayed with her for now, because of the riots and everything that's going on. Please don't take this the wrong way. You can go on using the apartment till you find somewhere else.

Hx

If the letter was a bombshell, the call that followed it was worse. The first three times he'd tried it went to voicemail, but she picked up after the fourth.

"What is this? Are you dumping me?"

"I'm sorry, Sam."

"What's your mother been saying?"

"Just that it's a bad time for us to be together."

"What the fuck does that mean?" He was practically shouting down the phone.

"I've got to go. Sorry."

She hung up. He dialed again, then decided against it. He threw the phone at the wall. Tears of anger blurred his vision. It took him several minutes to grasp what Helen had meant. Nothing like this had happened before.

When he retrieved the phone he saw there was a voicemail. Even though it was late he had called the number and got straight through to a woman called Pippa, who sounded very important but *terribly keen to meet ASAP*.

A tall woman in her early thirties, in a smart suit with a silky blouse underneath, glided towards him. Her smile and her hair looked immovable.

He got to his feet. She put out a hand. "Hello! I'm Pippa. So, is it Sam or Sahim?"

Sam shook her hand, which felt limp and cool, and smiled. Usually he would have said "Sam" emphatically. But the choice suggested opening himself to more possibilities. "Either's fine."

She tilted her head, sizing him up. "I rather like Sahim. Let's go for that, shall we?"

She gestured for him to follow. Her carriage and manner reminded him of Helen, but he dismissed the thought.

She showed him into a boardroom with a long table and waved at a chair. A carafe of water had been placed in front of it.

"We're just waiting for Derek—he's our marketing wizard. But he's always late so let's see if we can cover a few things first." She gave him a conspiratorial smile as she seated herself opposite him and opened a slim file. "We're so glad you decided to give us a chance."

He laughed, faintly sheepish. "Well, I'm always open to offers." Oh, God, he thought, does that sound desperate? The truth was he had never allied himself with a political party, not because of any determination to remain independent but because politics didn't interest him. They were talking about an actual job, though, and since he didn't have one, he had nothing to lose.

"We thought you must be rather in demand."

"I was up at Oxford for an interview. They've not got back to me yet."

This wasn't a lie, more a creative interpretation of the truth.

She smiled again. "I'm sorry to hear that. Their loss, I'm sure. I'd be lying if I said we weren't pleased. Young Muslims willing to work for the Party are a bit thin on the ground right now."

"Well, I'm not exactly practicing."

She laughed. "Well, I call myself C of E but I can't remember the last time I went to church. You fit the bill, all right."

Her enthusiasm put him at ease. "Well, you haven't interviewed me yet. You may think differently afterwards."

They both laughed politely. She flipped open a file and studied it. "So, just to be absolutely clear, you were born in the former Yugoslavia, is that right?"

"Bosnia. Yes. But I've been here since I was five."

She frowned. "You came as a refugee? Gosh, that must have been horrid for you."

"Actually, no. I count myself very lucky to be here."

She sighed. "If only more people felt that way."

The door flew open and a middle-aged man with a florid face and wispy blond hair burst in, a BlackBerry pressed to one ear. Under his arm was a sheaf of papers that looked as if they were about to cascade from their precarious perch.

"Tell him to do it or he's fucking out of here *today*. I don't care. Well, fuck you too."

The papers slid to the floor.

"Fucking arseholes."

Only then did he become aware of the two of them, watching. "Sorry, all." He grinned at Sam and thrust out a meaty hand. "Derek Farmer. So glad you could come. Boy, do we need someone like you round here." His brow furrowed briefly as he peered at Sam. "So you are Muslim, right? Or, er . . ."

108

He frowned at Sam's linen suit from H&M. Pippa studied her nails.

"I am, but I'm under cover."

They all laughed—a little too long. But for the first time in a while Sam felt as if he was capable of making an impact. "But to answer you properly, yes, I am a Muslim. Born and bred."

"But not about to . . ." Farmer made a gesture as if something was about to explode from his chest.

Sam was mystified. He glanced at Pippa who was looking the other way.

"Oh, y'know. Kaboom!"

Sam laughed again because there was nothing else he could think of doing. So did Farmer, who looked at his watch, then picked up his BlackBerry and gestured with it. "So, here's the deal. The Party's in the shit. Most of your lot think we're the enemy. And, frankly, we deserve everything you're hurling at us—well, maybe not the gas bombs. But the fact is we look like a bunch of fucking dinosaurs. Well, not Pippa, of course, who just looks fucking sexy."

"Fuck off, Derek."

"Oh? Thought it was worth a shot. Anyway, *apart* from Pippa, the Party's a load of WASPs, who look as though the only *hoi-polloi* they know are the beaters on their grouse shoots. As for 'Generation Now', all we've got is a few chinless wonders whose grasp of Estuary English is about as good as their Mandarin, and a posse of Afros we bribed to join up with free iPads."

He looked at Sam expectantly. "We need some Islamic cred. Someone who can speak to the street, reach out to the Muslim community, love them up a bit and make them feel more like we're the party that has their interests at heart. Got it?"

Sam found himself nodding. All his time in academia he'd been surrounded by political correctness. Farmer's refusal even to pay lip service to it was almost refreshing. "Yeah, I think I can help you out there."

Farmer waved him on, like a traffic cop. "Go on, then. Do your stuff." He leaned back in his chair and put his hands behind his head, revealing large sweat stains round his armpits.

Sam looked at Pippa, who was smiling. He leaned forward. "Eh, okay, well. There's a lot of people, not unlike me, really, who just want to get on with their lives. They've either fled tyranny or their parents struggled to get here so they can make something of themselves. None of us in this country have anything to gain by fighting with each other. We all want peace and quiet and prosperity."

Farmer clapped. "Love it. *More!*"

Sam felt like a performing seal but he didn't care: he had their attention and that made a welcome change. "Peace and prosperity only thrive where there's the rule of law. As a criminologist, I know all about what happens when there's no security. This party is right to support the police. Their job is very difficult and, yes, mistakes get made, but what's the alternative?"

Farmer turned to Pippa. "I think our friend here has just talked himself into a job." He returned to Sam. "Got any skeletons?"

"Sorry?"

"Sex, drugs, rock and roll, anything the tabloids could stick you for?"

Was Karza a skeleton? If so, he wasn't about to let on.

"Married? Girlfriend—or boyfriend?"

"None of the above—currently."

110

"Well, if you do snag one, make sure it's a she and, if possible, one of your lot. Some of our backwoodsmen cut up rough when they see their English roses being plucked by brown fingers. Sorry."

Pippa gave Sam an apologetic look while Farmer plowed on. "How'd you like to be on TV tonight?"

"Sure."

"He actually has some media experience," said Pippa.

"Fuck me—then he's perfect. Channel 4 News are doing a hatchet job on us. We could put you up—surprise the shit out of them." Farmer seemed thrilled at the prospect.

Emboldened by their attention, Sam felt a surge of confidence. "I'll need a briefing."

"Good man. Play your cards right, we might even parachute you into a safe seat." Farmer scooped up his papers and winked at Pippa. "Do the necessaries, Princess." He offered Sam a warm, sweaty hand. "See you in Makeup. The anchor is gonna love you."

111

21

Pall Mall

The smell of Hugh Buckingham's club was a rich mixture of floor polish, port and old leather.

"Excuse me, sir, if you would be so good . . ." The ancient porter tottered into Tom's path and raised a gnarled claw to his neck.

"Oh—of course." Tom reached into his pocket and drew out the tie his mother had reminded him to bring. The porter sighed quietly, and glanced apologetically at the portrait of Wellington. But the First Duke's attention was still focused on Waterloo.

"Mr. Buckingham's waiting for you in the library, sir." The old man gestured jerkily, as if his arm was controlled by wires from above.

"Thanks."

As Tom went towards the huge double doors, he remembered his first lunch there with his father, just as he was signing up. It had been a difficult one. Put up to it by Mary, Tom's mother, Hugh had been tasked to make one last-ditch attempt to deter him. Neither of them understood Tom's military ambitions and were convinced it was all down to his wilfully rebellious spirit. His father's pleas had fallen on deaf ears.

"My dear boy!"

Several of the other readers jumped as Hugh Buckingham pierced the silence. He threw down his *Telegraph* and leaped out of his chair with an energy that belied his sixty-eight years. He was tanned and bright-eyed, with strong arms that clasped Tom in a brief but impressively firm hug.

"Hey, Dad." It was months since he had seen his father. He had lost even more weight, having late in life discovered the joys of serious exercise. "Just looking at you makes me feel exhausted."

Hugh clasped his waist.

"Thirty-four and counting—inches not years, of course. And keeping the Alzheimer's at bay." He grabbed Tom's arm and spun him round, as if he was a clockwork toy. "Come on, I'm famished." He marched him towards the dining room, where a table for two was waiting by the window. "Bloody good to see you."

Behind the bonhomie, Tom detected his father's anxious glances. Over the years, Hugh had seen him return from tours thin and bearded, bruised and battered, but always exhilarated by the job that was his life. But Tom knew he could count on Hugh to keep his observations to himself. Tom would discuss what had happened in his own time, if he chose to; there wasn't going to be any third degree.

"They've got rack of lamb on today—seem to remember it's one of your favorites."

"Why are you staying up in town?"

"Board meetings. *Very* bored." Hugh chuckled. "The old firm's in the throes of a takeover." The city company he had served for three decades had persuaded him to come back as a non-executive director.

The wine waiter glided towards them. "Something to start, gentlemen?"

"How about kicking off with a couple of glasses of your house champagne?"

"We're not celebrating anything, are we?"

"Well, we won't let that get in the way of a glass!"

Behind his excitement at seeing Tom, Hugh seemed sheepish.

"You're so transparent, Dad. You would've made a terrible spy."

A waitress passed them in the sort of black and white uniform no one wore any more.

"So what's it to be?"

"Yeah, I'll go with the lamb."

Hugh waved the menu to flag down the waitress, like a ground-crew member directing a jumbo jet. Tom recalled being embarrassed by the expansiveness of his movements when he was a boy. Now his enthusiasm felt life-affirming and rather welcome.

"Two lambs." Hugh winked at Tom. "And leave some space for a Swiss roll—bet you don't get that in Afghanistan."

As the waitress retreated, she gave Tom an appreciative look, which Hugh noticed. He leaned across. "Always good to see my DNA getting the attention it deserves." Tom gave his father a withering look.

The champagne arrived. They raised their glasses and drank.

"Ah, that's better." Hugh's fitness regime had done nothing to dull his appreciation of alcohol.

"Bit of a mess you've come back to. What's your take on it all?"

"I'm still catching up."

Hugh furrowed his brow so it resembled rough terrain. "Some would say—indeed, are saying—that it's the inevitable consequence of open borders." He gestured at the other diners, all older than himself. "That's the prevailing view of many of us wrinklies. And these people coming and going from Syria, that's another bee in their bonnet. Frankly, I think that aspect's been blown out of proportion."

Tom knew he could count on his father not to swim with the tide. In fact, he made a habit of taking the contrary view, something that had brought a good many dinner parties to a premature halt, requiring Mary's anxious apologies to smooth things over. It occurred to Tom, perhaps for the first time, that it was one way in which they were alike.

"What do they think in here, the powers that be?"

Hugh looked round. "Well, Chatham House rules, of course, so one can't pass anything on. But there were very strong words on the subject in here last night. A guy who's quite high up in the civil service hinted that the government's terrified. They daren't do anything drastic for fear of alienating parts of the electorate. And public confidence in the cabinet is ebbing away, never mind in Parliament itself. So the MoD and the police have been meeting privately to lay out emergency measures—even talking about putting your lot on the streets, if things don't die down. The PM's buggered off to the States, you know, and that woman Garvey's been left holding the fort."

Tom winced inwardly at the reference to "your lot" but let it go. His father was getting into his stride and at least it deflected the conversation away from him. "Well, she is the home secretary, Dad."

"Of course, of course."

Hugh leaned across the table and dropped his voice. "You know what I think? There are some people who actually *want* things to get worse, precisely so they can take drastic action."

"Such as?"

"Oh, you know, dumping some of this human rights legislation that keeps coming at us from Brussels, all the politically correct stuff that ties the hands of the police and the judiciary."

"You agree with that?"

"Trouble with today is, the collective memory of the last war—I mean the Second World War, when our fore-bears had to muck in and all pull together, when there was a real threat of invasion— has pretty well died out. The truth is, us baby boomers have had it too easy. So we're panicking."

The lamb arrived: two huge plates of roasted meat and a bowl of vegetables. Gradually, Tom felt himself perking up.

"And let's have some of the house claret to keep this company."

As they tucked in, the waitress returned with a bottle and two fresh glasses.

"That's the one—just pour it."

Hugh fell silent as they attacked their food. Tom was well aware of how little he was giving away, but Hugh would have to lump it as he topped up the claret, no doubt hoping it would oil the wheels.

"Did you um, get back to Rolt?" The question broke the silence. Tom stared at his father warily. "Vernon Rolt. You were at school with him."

"Yeah, you said. Look, I'm not talking to anyone right now." He drained his glass.

His father refilled it. "He's very keen to get hold of you."

"So you gave him my number."

Hugh could tell straight away that this had been a mistake. Tom's face had turned to stone.

"Look, I'm sorry, old boy. I know it's private and all that but I just thought, what with you being back and . . . He's a pretty big deal, these days, as I'm sure you know. Quite a hero—and they seem to be in pretty short supply right now. And he was a mate of yours."

"Hardly. I seem to recall I once decked him in a boxing match. What sort of a 'big deal' is he?"

"You don't know? Well, it's quite an interesting story. He dropped out of university, drifted around America, fell in with the dotcom crowd in California and made himself a fortune. Then he got homesick for Blighty, came back and plowed a load of his savings into starting up Invicta."

"Why? Is there some military angle to his family?"

"Apparently he encountered a homeless guy outside his pad in Mayfair who turned out to be a decorated hero of Iraq Two, and that's where it all started. More than two thousand ex-service chaps have been through his program."

"Impressive."

"He stays out of the limelight and shuns attempts to credit him for what he's done. But among those who know, he's much admired. And there are plenty of people in high places who have the wit to realize his programs saved a lot of these guys' lives and cleared up a lot of sick that the MoD's left behind."

"What did he say he wanted?"

"He was very charming, said he'd heard you were back . . ."

Tom could feel his face heating up. He smelt a rat. As he was going through the army recruitment process, his father had engineered a number of occasions when acquaintances of his with Interesting Jobs in the City had been invited to join them for dinner. It was painfully obvious that he had cajoled them into coming in the vain hope that Tom could be diverted from the army. And having set his heart on that course, Tom had refused to go to Sandhurst and become an officer.

"Hope this isn't another of your career-management initiatives."

Hugh took a gulp of wine. "I learned that lesson a long time ago. I'm sure it's quite innocent. He's making a name for himself through his work with these—"

"Yeah, these people whose lives are in freefall. You aren't suggesting I'm one of them, are you?" Tom realized his voice had risen several decibels. A couple of old buffers at the next table were staring at them.

"What do you mean?" Hugh was stung. "Steady on, old boy. I'm not implying you're on the scrapheap, if that's what you mean. The chap called me out of the blue. I'm sure his intentions are entirely noble."

The room felt stifling. Tom pushed his chair back. His father gazed at him in horror. "I'm going for a leak."

Tom marched out, pushing his way through the doors and nearly knocking over an elderly member. Outside it was starting to rain. He took a deep lungful of gray London air and cursed himself for being so sharp with his father, who only had the best intentions, who had put up with his waywardness, and the uncertainty, all these years, and who loved him.

What the fuck was he going to do anyway? He hadn't given it a second's thought. But before he could descend into any kind of self-pity he found himself thinking of Blakey. He took out his phone and searched the number for Selly Oak.

The nurse on the ward sounded relieved to hear from him. "No one's been to see him at all. Are you a relative?"

"No, just a mate. How is he?"

She didn't answer.

"He is going to make it, isn't he?"

"Yes, it's just—well, he's going to need a lot of help."

"Can I talk to him?"

"He's with the surgeon. Could you come in later?"

"I'm in London, but I'll phone back."

He ended the call and noticed the missed calls from two days before. Maybe Rolt could do something for Blakey.

When he got back to the table his father behaved as if nothing had happened. He was good like that.

"Two Swiss rolls on their way." Hugh grinned at him guiltily, just as he used to when Tom was small, as if the desserts were some kind of transgression. At least some things didn't change.

22

Pimlico

Sarah Garvey reached for her phone, which was buzzing like a trapped fly on her nightstand. She glanced at the time—2:25 a.m.

"Sorry to disturb you, Home Secretary."

It was Halford, the Metropolitan Police commissioner.

"No problem, John," she lied. "I'd only just got to bed."

After giving him such a hard time in COBRA she had made a mental note to be more positive.

"We're just getting reports of a fire at an ex-servicemen's hostel in Redditch, probably the result of an explosion."

"Fatalities?"

"Too early to say. But, looking at the footage, I'd say almost certainly. The front of the building's been blown out. Several passers-by taken to A and E. Should have a clearer picture in an hour."

There was an energy to his tone that had been absent at their meeting. She guessed why. This was off his patch and was sure to take the heat off the shooting.

"Hold back as long as you can on the details. Let's be very careful what we feed to the media. Nothing, repeat *nothing*, suggesting a bombing until it's confirmed by forensics. And even then let's discuss what we say first."

"Well, I'd advise you to prepare for the worst. An eye-witness reported seeing a disturbance in the doorway as if someone was being stopped from going in."

"Okay, thanks for that." She put on the light and found the TV remote.

BBC News was already there, with a reporter standing at the end of a cordoned-off street. Behind her rose a thick funnel of smoke from the flames, which firefighters were battling.

". . . and although the police have yet to confirm that this was a bomb, fire-fighters have just ruled out a gas explosion—"

Her report came to an abrupt halt as she ducked to avoid a flying bottle, which smashed to the ground a few feet behind her. The camera panned round to reveal a group of T-shirted and tattooed men, shouting and gesticulating angrily from behind a police tape.

Right, Garvey thought. We might as well be at war.

23

Fulham, London

Sam's eyes fluttered open. The clock said four twenty. He propped himself up on one elbow. Someone was ringing the doorbell. It was probably one of the other tenants who had lost their keys. He decided to ignore it.

He turned over and glanced at the empty half of the bed. Helen's half—of her bed, in fact—and although she had referred to it as "the apartment", it, too, was hers. He wondered if she had seen him on TV, and what she would make of his new position. Maybe it would induce her to come back. But he was using his real name now. Probably her mother would be even less in favor of her going out with him now he was called Sahim.

The bell went again. He let it ring. He had no inclination to be helpful to her neighbors. He would be out of here just as soon as he had found a room to rent. Besides, he was exhausted. After the Channel 4 News appearance Pippa had whisked him off to the Shard for an informal meet and greet with the home secretary, Sarah Garvey, some Whitehall big-wigs, their special advisers and some senior police. Garvey had been pretty distracted and barely acknowledged him. Nevertheless the heady thrill of rubbing shoulders with Establishment high-ups had boosted his confidence no end, especially when one of her officials patted him on the shoulder and told him he had a gift for a good sound bite. He had been assured this would mean a lot more attention from the media.

The bell sounded yet again. "Fuck off," he said, but this time he struggled to his feet, pulled on a pair of shorts and padded to the door.

"Yeah?"

"Kovacevic?"

A male voice. No one he recognized.

"Who is this?"

"Sahim Kovacevic?"

He put the chain on the door and opened it a fraction. A motorbike messenger, holding a slim envelope. "Yeah, that's me. What do you want?"

"Just take this."

The man thrust the letter through the gap.

"Do I need to sign anything?"

"No."

He went back up to the flat and opened it.

News of your brother. Meet me at your mother's apartment, 22.00. Nasima

24

Tom moved briskly through St. James's Park in the hope that his head would have cleared by the time he reached his destination. Luckily Invicta's headquarters were only a short walk from his father's club, where he had stayed the night after an evening of rather too much drinking. He had read about the explosion in one of their hostels over breakfast but when he'd called Rolt's office they had insisted that the meeting was still on.

The street had been blocked at either end by police Transits with mesh grilles over the windows. Armed police stood at either side of the front doors. One stepped forward as Tom approached.

"Can I help?" he said, in a tone that suggested help was the last thing on offer.

"I've got an appointment with Vernon Rolt."

"Your name, please, sir?"

"Buckingham."

The officer stepped back and knocked on the door. A cop inside opened it. The first repeated Tom's name.

The cop inside consulted a clipboard and nodded. The first officer's expression changed. "Sorry, sir. It's all due to the bombing."

"That's confirmed now?"

"'Fraid so."

Tom went into the reception area. The place was strewn with the silver boxes of a TV crew. The receptionist was taking a call so he went straight past and followed the cables up the stairs.

A powerful light shone out of one of the doorways. In the corridor a young woman was standing beside a TV technician watching a monitor. She looked up as Tom approached and was about to shoo him away when she appeared to recognize him. "Are you Mr. Rolt's eleven o'clock?"

Tom gave her hand a firm, business-like shake. "Tom Buckingham."

"I'm Phoebe. He's overrunning, got the BBC in there. Would you like to wait in the boardroom?"

"This about the hostel?"

She nodded gravely.

"I'll linger here and listen, if that's okay."

He leaned against the wall outside Rolt's office, where a couple of technicians were perched on the silver boxes. Phoebe stood beside him. He could see the two men in profile, Rolt and the BBC man interviewing him, but a monitor in front of one of the technicians showed the live feed. Tom expected Rolt to be smoldering with rage after the bombing. But if he was angry, he had it well under control. He sat upright but relaxed, his hands folded in his lap, a model of British restraint.

"What our government and the opposition haven't faced up to is the true mood of the public. A lot of people aren't saying what they're feeling out loud but it's plain to see. They've just had enough."

The reporter said, "Enough of what exactly?"

Rolt lifted his hands and let them drop again as if the answer was obvious. "Fear. They've had enough of being afraid."

"So, are you saying that the government should be considering more drastic measures?"

"We know they're scared of upsetting one small minority of the electorate for fear it will tip the balance in an election. But they've got to stop trying to be all things to all people. Hundreds of our men and women have died, thousands have sustained life-changing injuries in the War on Terror. And what have we got to show for their sacrifice? The people Invicta helps are asking, 'What about the war *here*?'"

"Are you saying there's *going* to be a war here?"

Rolt wagged a finger at the interviewer. "Don't put words into my mouth. I'm just repeating what they tell me."

Tom observed how Rolt controlled the interview, fending off the reporter but at the same time delivering his message in his own words. The reporter's eyes were gleaming as if he knew that what Rolt was saying would make headlines all over the media, and he'd have got it first.

"And what would you like to say to the people who bombed your hostel?"

"I'd say to them, 'You have just forfeited your welcome in this country. You and your beliefs are not welcome here.' And I would challenge the government to follow through with that. I'd say to them, 'It ends here. Inclusion has failed. It's time to weed out the terrorists and remove them from the community.'"

"To where?"

"To wherever they can't harm us."

"That sounds like a call to arms."

"Let's say more of an *en garde*."

126

"Against the Muslim community?"

"God, no. Don't misunderstand me. Look, I can find you any number of law-abiding British Muslims who would be the first to say, 'Do something about the extremists before it's too late.' The government's tried the warm fluffy approach—that's failed. They've tried control orders—failed. If what these terrorists want is a caliphate, if they want Sharia law, there are places they can go and find that—but not here. The Huguenots, the Jews and all the other persecuted groups who have settled here came to these shores in search of tolerance and freedom. That tolerance and freedom is now under threat and we need to recognize that."

The reporter frowned. "What you're proposing doesn't sound like tolerance to me."

Rolt smiled regretfully. "How can you honestly tolerate people whose stated aim is to kill and maim?"

The reporter looked uncomfortable.

Rolt continued, "We have turned a blind eye to extremist ideologies. We have let them import terror into our green and pleasant land. For their own good as much as ours, they would be happier elsewhere."

"So, let me get this clear. You're advocating we repatriate people we regard as a threat to society?"

"I'm advocating freedom from fear." Rolt leaned forward. "Go to the people staying in our hostels. Talk to the men and women from our armed services who are struggling to find their way back into the country that sent them off to war. Add up the expenditure on policing the potential terrorists, the incarceration of the convicted terrorists, the surveillance of suspects. Then add up what it would take to give those ex-servicemen and women a decent job and a decent home. To give them some dignity, something in return for risking their lives to uphold our freedoms. What's the point of their risking their lives if they come home to find the place awash with folk who want to take their freedom away?"

"That's pretty strong stuff."

"Not really. Ask yourself why none of our politicians is saying this. They're so scared of alienating these 'communities' that they've lost their nerve. Give the electorate some credit. Draw a line between the good, productive, useful members of our society—and those who aren't. Get the good ones to help you weed out the others."

The last time Tom had seen Rolt in fighting form was in the boxing ring. He was a scholarship boy with none of the advantages of his peers, who had tried hard at everything but never came top. Tom had respected him for his dogged determination and refusal to be put down by snobbery. But he had beaten him squarely in three rounds. Rolt had had the drive but not the super-quick reactions to deliver his punches with sufficient surprise or to dodge Tom's relentless battering.

"But, Mr. Rolt, isn't this just your anger talking—because your hostel was bombed?"

"You ask if I'm angry. I'm bloody furious. Furious that this has been allowed to happen. Our politicians have yet to come up with an answer so I'm offering them one."

"One last thing, you've sunk your personal fortune into your hostels and apprenticeships. What happens when the money runs out?"

A flicker of hesitation. He hadn't seen that one coming. "I'll do what any decent businessman does and convince others that my projects are worth investing in."

Phoebe leaned over to Tom and whispered, "Sorry about this. I hope we haven't messed up your day."

"No. It's very useful. He's very measured under the circumstances."

Phoebe's eyes lingered on him. She was in her mid-twenties, he guessed, a blonde English rose, just the sort his mother would like. He thought of Delphine and how far away she seemed now.

Rolt was on his feet. He shook the hand of the interviewer and turned. The cold, focused gaze melted when he saw Tom. He strode towards him, hand outstretched. "I didn't think you'd come."

"Why not?"

Rolt's hand wrapped itself round Tom's. "An old schoolmate calling out of the blue—who needs that?"

They both laughed.

"And with all that's going on."

"I was very sorry to hear about your people." They shared a moment's silence before Tom continued, nodding at the TV crew packing up, "I see you've not lost your taste for a fight."

Rolt gave Tom a knowing smile. "Nor you, I hear."

There was a note of compassion in Rolt's tone. But Tom ignored it. He had other reasons for being there.

Phoebe came and stood by Rolt's elbow. "Perhaps you'd like to get away from this lot. Why don't you go through to the office and I'll fetch some tea?"

Rolt showed Tom the way down the hall. The office was impressive, with floor-to-ceiling windows that looked out onto

St. James's Park. It must be costing him a fortune. And that livid skyscape of red and orange over the fireplace. Was it an original?

"Don't tell me that Turner's real?"

"Isn't it a beaut? They used to think it was pigment degradation. Now it's believed the colors are accurate—refraction by volcanic ash in the atmosphere.

"There were three eruptions in his lifetime, Tambora in 1815, Babuyan Claro in the Philippines in 1831 and Cosigüina in 1835. Not that Turner knew."

"So you were paying attention in class all along."

"I think it got in by osmosis. No actual effort on my part."

Tom turned back to the painting.

"Tambora spat an estimated twelve cubic miles of magma into the atmosphere. There was so much ash in the atmosphere they called 1816 'The Year without Summer'."

Rolt beckoned him to turn round. Hanging opposite was a huge faded tapestry, with the faint images of figures visible in the weave. "It predates Bayeux. I found it at an auction in Texas. God knows how it fetched up there." Rolt pointed at the standard bearing the word "Invicta", held high by solid yeomen, the cliffs of Dover beneath them.

Tom had also remembered something from school. "Undefeated—*Roma Invicta*. The Romans had it stamped on their coins to boost morale when the empire was on the wane."

Rolt smiled. "Correct. And much later, when William defeated Harold at Hastings and set his course for Winchester, these men of Kent, a few with swords but most armed with no more than wooden staves, marched against him. William saw their determination and knew they would fight to the death, so he offered them a deal: safe passage for his army and in return the men of Kent would keep their ancient rights and liberties. Hence 'Invicta' became the motto of the county."

Tom nodded approvingly. "Good name."

Phoebe appeared, carrying a tray laden with a silver teapot and small chocolate cakes, and set it on a low table in front of the fireplace.

"It was Phoebe here who tracked you down."

Tom saw her blush faintly as she lowered the tray. She gave Rolt a mock-disapproving look, which he didn't notice. Tom gazed at her, expecting some kind of explanation, but none came. Instead she lifted the teapot. "Shall I pour?"

Rolt waved her away. "No, that's all right, Phoebe, thanks. Close the door behind you, will you?" He waved at a pair of wing-backed chairs either side of the fireplace. Tom took a seat as he watched her leave.

"Well, it's very good of you to come. I'm sorry about bothering your father."

"Oh, he quite likes to be bothered. He doesn't have enough to do, these days."

Rolt sighed as he poured the tea. "Like so many of his generation. So much wisdom and common sense—such a shame it's not listened to."

"I hope he didn't bang on."

Rolt looked faintly shocked. "No, not at all. We exchanged views on what's been happening here . . ."

"You aren't pulling any punches with the media."

Rolt snorted. "Well, the time's come. Someone's got to say it. And I'm in the enviable position of not having some party line to

131

toe. I can say what I think and they can go screw themselves. How do you like it?"

"Black, no sugar, please."

Tom watched Rolt closely. His movements were studied, precise, not extravagant. He showed none of the arrogance of success. He had been an unmemorable teenager who had grown into a charismatic figure, outwardly charming, but the steel was visible beneath the surface.

He passed him a cup. "I wasn't at all sure you'd get back to me. I'm something of a pariah in certain circles."

Tom seized the opportunity. "Actually, there's something you might be able to help me with." He told him about Rifleman Blakey.

Rolt's eyes gleamed. "He's just what we're all about. Trouble is, we're overflowing."

"What are the chances of squeezing in another one? I might be able to tap my old man to help with funds."

Rolt's face darkened. "The kind of money we need right now to go to the next level is . . . well, let's say significant." He lapsed into silence, frowning into his tea. Eventually he went on. "I'll come clean about the reason I called. Almost all my people, my staff, we've picked up and put back on the rails. They're good, hundred percent loyal, but I need to widen my net. We're looking for—well, to be frank—people like you. Intelligent, capable, self-directed, presentable, from the right sort of background and with a blue-chip military record."

"Well, I'm not sure about the last part." He also wondered what he meant by the "right sort of background".

Rolt ignored this and pressed on. "Able to represent me, represent Invicta, at any kind of event. But I have to go out and recruit.

132

I can't wait for that sort of person to wander in here. So we keep an eye out for who's on the move."

Phoebe knocked and opened the door. The flash of anger from Rolt came without any warning. "I said we weren't to be disturbed."

She held her ground.

"Sorry. The editor of *The Times* is asking if you'd do a piece for tomorrow. They're offering you a whole page."

"Okay, okay." Rolt got up. "Sorry to cut it short. How about you come and have a look at our campus? Get a sense of what we're about. And then let's talk again about your mate."

25

The driver was waiting in Reception, dark suit, REME tie. Even without the tie Tom would have clocked him as ex-Army at fifty yards: the bearing and the battered face were giveaways.

"This way, sir."

The hint of contempt in the "sir" marked him out as a probable ex-RSM.

"Actually it was 'sergeant' till last week. What's your name?"

"Jackman, sir."

A gleaming dark green Bentley was parked outside. "Nice wheels. Good to see your boss is flying the flag."

Tom reached for the front door but Jackman opened the rear.

"I think you'll find the back more comfortable, sir."

Tom slid into the hushed compartment and closed the door. Extra thick windows indicated it had been bullet-proofed. Jackman climbed in and brought the car to life. Tom felt his frame press back in the seat as the twin turbo-charged V8 powered forward.

"Really, it's a Volkswagen underneath. Pains me to say it, but the Krauts have done a bloody good job."

"My great-grandad raced a Bentley in the twenties."

Jackman sighed. "Bet he's turning in his grave knowing that nasty little Führer-cell was what saved it from oblivion."

They swept up Park Lane, the needle touching fifty.

"Watch out—I got pulled over up here on my bike."

"Nah, not us. The cops know whose this is. Mr. Rolt's immune. Makes my job a lot pleasanter, I can tell you."

Tom still had a titanic hangover and wasn't in the mood for conversation, but he decided he might as well milk Jackman for all he could get. "Been with him long?"

"Few years."

"And before?"

"Well, it was the REME till 2008, then a bit of a blank after that." Tom glanced at him, curious.

Jackman's gaze was fixed on the road. "Put it this way: if Mr. Rolt hadn't tripped over me on the sidewalk, I'd most probably be six feet under by now." He shot a glance at Tom. His heavily etched face told its own story.

"So you're more than an employee, would you say?"

Jackman nodded. Just the other side of Victoria, one of the lanes was cordoned off where a Lebanese restaurant on the Edgware Road was still smoldering. Builders in hi-viz overalls were erecting scaffolding. The whole building looked unstable. Jackman shook his head. "I never thought I'd see the day."

Tom murmured assent.

"Mind you, given the situation, it was going to happen, sooner or later, wasn't it?"

Tom nodded, though he wasn't ready to put any of his cards on the table. Right now there were a lot of things he wasn't as sure of as he used to be. His life had been so full of certainties—the job, serving his country. Now it was in bits. "So you went through the Invicta program?"

"One of the first. I was in Basra, and I was in Bosnia, but Basingstoke!" Tom frowned. "Invicta's base is just outside."

Jackman shuddered at the memory. "When you've been chucking back a dozen Special Brew before noon, it's a long climb back up. And coming off the cigs, same time."

"Bloody hell."

"That just about sums it up. Ask me then if I thought I could do it. No way, José."

"But you did."

"With Invicta, once you set foot in there, it's out of your hands. Solitary confinement the first week. No bed. You want a pillow, you got to take your jumpsuit off and roll it up. Only you don't do that cos it stinks of shit and piss.

"Second week, you start running. Each day they double the distance. Fall over, there's no one to get you back up. Just some bastard like I used to be—excuse the language, sir—shouting right in your ear to go back to the start.

"Third week you get a change of equipment and a shower— cold. But you're so glad of it because by that time you look and stink like a hunger striker."

"Bit brutal, isn't it?"

"It's what works."

"Do they have many drop-outs?"

"Zero tolerance. One hundred percent success. And once you're back on your feet, they never lose sight of you—unlike the bloody Army. Invicta's for life. Me, I'm happy with my lot." He patted the soft leather of the dash. "But there's blokes he's put through college, found them jobs."

"What does Invicta demand in return for all this?"

Jackman shrugged. "Just loyalty. But that's worth more than riches."

26

Surrey

The Invicta campus, a decommissioned RAF airfield, looked like a cross between a military base and a country estate. Either side of the gate a line of poplars marked the perimeter and masked the high wire fence behind it. The entrance was discreetly fortified. A metal ramp set into the asphalt would rise to block unwanted traffic. The barriers were quite slim but there was a second, much heavier gate fifty yards in. The grass was perfectly tended, the brickwork freshly repointed.

Even though the guards would have known the car a mile off, Jackman still brought it to a stop and rolled down the window. The one on duty was not some rotund failed bouncer but a trim, well-turned-out man of Jackman's age. "Wotcher, Jacko. Someone famous?"

He peered into the car at Tom, who gave his name.

"Could you step out, please, sir?"

Jackman nodded at Tom. "Best do as they say. No special treatment here."

Tom got out of the car. As he straightened up, the hangover he had almost forgotten about met him again, like a low concrete ceiling.

"Bad night, sir?" The guard patted him down.

"Terrible. You?"

The guard looked at him blankly.

"Zero tolerance," Jackman explained, as they drove on. "One drink and you're back in the slammer."

The administrator of the Invicta campus was a former marine Tom recognized from Iraq. Philips was his name and, though he was professionally civil, he made no reference to the encounter in their previous lives. When Tom casually referred to it, Philips told him it was Invicta policy to ignore past connections. "We keep ourselves facing forward. We're all about today and tomorrow, not yesterday."

But Philips could see he wasn't buying this piece of spin. "Look. Most folk who come through here, one way or another something's done them in. Maybe it was during service or maybe before. But whatever it was, it's driving their behavior. This place is about getting shot of all that. The day a man starts here, he draws a line under everything up to that moment. That's the past. This is now. That's the deal."

"What about families?"

"If they have a problem there, we teach them how to deal with that. If there's something we can do for the relatives we'll do it, but only if it benefits the associate."

"Associate?"

"That's what we're all called. Nice and neutral, no ranks or hierarchy. Helps with the sense of kinship."

As they passed between buildings Tom saw a group of men in full MTPs emerge from a clump of trees and climb into the back of a Land Rover. Even from this distance he could see that they were bent with fatigue.

138

Philips smiled. "They're Phase Fives. Survival skills, self-preservation. They've got to stay out on their own and keep out of each other's way for five days and nights. Bit of fun, really, but it builds that sense of independence and helps them believe in their ability to survive on their own. After all, they don't know what they're going to have to put up with in the future."

The next building they entered was busy with staff in white coats. "Medical area. We pick up where the NHS leaves off." He held open a door to a spacious carpeted ward. There were eight beds and each seemed to have at least one nurse nearby.

"No shortage of staff here, then."

"You noticed. That's a big part of it. Most of these blokes just need attention. A lot of it's basically physio. We leave the invasive stuff to the hospitals, but recovery can be a long old process, two years, sometimes more. We see them through it."

Not for the first time that day Tom's thoughts drifted back to Blakey. "How do you get accepted here?"

Philips shrugged. "Word-of-mouth, recommendations. All pretty informal and low key."

"Is there a long queue?"

"Yeah, that's our problem. We need to grow. The boss is onto it, but it can't come soon enough."

Back outside, they passed through a screen of trees and headed towards a long, low building that resembled a cattle shed. There were no windows, just a small gap between the walls and the roof. From it came a noise Tom couldn't decipher at first. As they got closer it became clearer. It was human. Shouts, screams, whimpers.

"For a lot of us, it started here. Detox—there's no easy way."

He gave Tom a look that confirmed he was a graduate of this part of the program. "We make no apology for the conditions. We keep an eye on them medically, in case they try to do something terminal. Otherwise they're on their own to crack on and get through it. Believe me, when you get out, life never felt so sweet."

"Don't you have Health and Safety or some regulator on your backs?"

Philips smirked. "We don't exactly broadcast our methods."

"You're showing me. I'm a complete stranger."

"Mr. Rolt's instructions were that you should see it all."

Over a roast-beef sandwich and a Coke, Philips opened up.

"Enlisting was all about getting out of where I came from, a fairly typical scenario." He sketched out a family life from hell: Dad in prison most of the time and when he wasn't, drinking himself comatose or beating up his wife and any of the kids who were in reach. His violence was indiscriminate—everybody got equally fucked up.

"The Army was my family, so when I left it was like stepping into a void. Now I've got that family back—and on twice the pay, plus a master's in sociology. Here I've got five-star accommodation, all the amenities and a job for life. More than I could have dreamed of."

"What happens if it doesn't work out—if you screw up?"

"Just doesn't happen. We owe our lives to Invicta, so we just don't allow failure."

It's a bit too good to be true, thought Tom, but there was something about the look on Philips's face that wasn't just PR.

"Bottom line: Invicta delivers. And what with everything that's going on out there right now, the country going to hell, you value what you've got all the more. Frankly, the man's a saint—he should be running the country."

It wasn't the first time Tom had heard that said about Invicta's founder. Rolt professed to have no political ambition, but after witnessing his BBC interview Tom found that becoming harder to believe.

27

They walked on past a golf course and a soccer field. From behind a row of poplars, Tom thought he heard shots.

"Yeah, we've got a range too."

"Can I see it?"

"The range warden's a bit funny about visitors."

His wariness made Tom all the more curious. "I'd hate to miss it."

"Let me make a call."

Philips moved away while he dabbed a number onto his iPhone and spoke.

There were single shots and a short burst of machine gun fire.

Philips pocketed the phone. "He said give him five minutes to clear the range."

He gave Tom an anxious glance.

"Something wrong?"

Philips put his head on one side. "Blokes here, they've been through a lot."

"Yes, I got that."

Philips nodded towards the range. "The warden, how can I put this? Doesn't like to be upstaged, if you get my drift. Used to be a sniper."

Tom smiled. "Don't worry. I wouldn't dream of it."

They walked down a path beside a high fence. Philips punched a code into a keypad and an electric gate glided open.

Tom nodded approvingly. "Extra layer of security—very wise."

They mounted a short flight of steps and entered the club house. The interior consisted of a long, windowless pine-panelled room, lit by a row of low shaded lights. On the right was a gallery of photographs and certificates. The left-hand wall was one long weapons rack.

"Wow, this is some collection." As well as numerous HK and Colt assault rifles, he also spied an Israeli Defense Force Tavor Bullpup semiautomatic carbine, a massive 50-calibre Barrett M107 sniper rifle, and several versions of AK.

A door opened at the other end of the room.

"Here comes our warden."

A man wearing a flat wool cap and green gilet moved slowly towards them.

"Sorry to disturb you, Mick. This is Tom Buckingham, sent by the boss."

"Tom Buckingham: Mick Vestey."

Tom grinned and gave his hand a firm shake. Vestey's face remained impassive.

"Quite a set-up you've got here." Tom gestured at the racks. "Enough to see you through a decent-sized war." A lot of the weapons would be illegal unless held under a section-seven license. But in the privacy of this vast facility, maybe a blind eye was being turned.

Seeing no response from Vestey, Philips chipped in: "It's one of our most popular amenities. The fact is that men in the field get very used to weapon handling. Once they're out, they get with-drawal. And then there's some who just need to get some rounds down the range to relax. We're pretty liberal with the ammo."

For Tom, guns were simply tools of the trade, but he had known plenty of others for whom weapons meant far more—and in some cases too much. This was a gun nut's paradise. "Can we see the range?"

Vestey shrugged. "Six-hundred-meter gallery, electric and twenty-five-meter indoor. We got it all."

Tom kept up his kid-in-a-toyshop look, more eager than wary. "Any chance of a cabby?"

Vestey gestured at the weapons. "Take your pick."

Tom pondered for a second, then pointed at the HK MP5.

Vestey frowned. "You sure?"

"Never tried one. Could be my only chance."

Vestey bent forward and lifted it out of the rack. "Suit yourself. We'll pick up the rounds through here."

Tom followed, listening to Vestey, who sounded as if he had flicked a switch. "The lanes are flood-lit and air-conditioned, with individual shooting benches and a target pulley system. Shoot all year round in perfect conditions. No mud, no rain, no distractions, so you can set up the perfect zero."

They paused while he disappeared into the ammo store.

"Very proud of his domain he is," whispered Philips.

Vestey reappeared with a thirty-round mag for the MP5.

"Twenty-five meters?"

Vestey nodded. "Go all the way, if you like."

He handed Tom a pair of ear defenders and protective eye glasses.

144

The range was eerily deserted, with no sound but the aircon humming from the ceiling vents.

"What happened to everyone else?"

"We clear them out on the hour. You can have too much of a good thing."

Vestey marched them past the indoor range. Tom glanced through a door at the stalls. The American-made silhouetted figure targets appeared to be wearing shemags. "Bit politically incorrect?"

Vestey snorted. "Just a little touch of nostalgia for the lads. We used to go big on OBL targets but now he's history there's less demand."

Philips looked uneasy so Tom let the remark go.

"Standing or prone. Take your pick."

"I'll stand, thanks."

Vestey loaded the weapon and made it ready before handing it to Tom, his forefinger pointing at the safety catch for him to see. "There's a round in the chamber and the safety catch is on."

It felt warm as if it had been recently used.

Tom took up his position, raised the weapon and looked down the sights. He thumbed down the safety, let his aim drift slightly wide and fired.

The first round missed the target altogether.

"Shit."

"Take your time," said Vestey, with a hint of weariness.

Tom aimed again, slightly closer this time. The bullet hit about three inches left of center target. Again, he aimed slightly wide. This time it went four inches left of center. His next three shots did no better.

Tom passed the weapon back to him. "Go on, then. Show me how it's done."

Philips gave Tom another of his anxious looks. But Vestey just shrugged. "Okay."

He held the gun like a pro, like it was part of him, brought it up, aimed and fired. The first was an inch off, the second another inch.

"Good skills," murmured Philips, as if a compliment was required to fill the silence.

Vestey remained in his position, fired five more times. None of them came as close.

"Okay, give me one more chance." Vestey handed the weapon back to Tom. This time he got center mass.

"That's better." The next one hit right home as well. He lowered the weapon and offered it back to Vestey. "Want to match me?"

Vestey's eyes didn't meet his. "Time I was getting back. Got another group in a minute." He turned and headed back the way they had come.

Outside, Philips lit a cigarette. "Sorry he wasn't more forth-coming."

"I hope I didn't wind him up."

"You've got to remember, for the people here, a lot of water's flowed under the bridge. We have to accommodate all sorts."

Tom spied Jackman coming towards them.

"Sorry to butt in, gents, but the boss asks if we could swing by Redditch. That's if you can spare the time."

"Is he at the hostel?"

"He's meeting the police there in an hour."

28

Redditch

Rolt was standing with a group of cops, some in uniform, others in hooded white overalls. Firemen were removing their equipment. A group of noisy onlookers was being kept well away behind a tape. Some carried placards: *Fuck off home and blow up your own people.*

Rolt broke away and came towards Tom. "Care to have a look?"

Tom shook his head, disgusted by the carnage. "Expect the cops don't want too many tramping around their crime scene."

"Yeah, but you've seen the effects of more bombs than any of them."

"It's confirmed, then?"

He nodded, then shivered. "It's only when you see it that the true horror hits you, doesn't it?"

Rolt looked gray and drawn. Whatever anger he was feeling, he was doing his best to keep it at bay. "They've taken away some remains. They said they're hopeful of getting an ID."

Inside, the building was a mass of rubble, everything dripping wet from the fire hoses. Three floors had collapsed in on themselves. They stepped aside as two men in hard hats with lamps attached came through with a body-bag on a stretcher.

"How many casualties?"

147

"Five dead. Fourteen critical, three unaccounted for. A few hours later, the canteen would have been full and the toll would have been triple that."

Tom stood on a plastic sheet that covered the foyer floor. "How many explosions?"

"Just the one, far as we know. The fractured gas pipes did the rest."

"Any ideas on how the guy got so far into the building?"

"One witness claims they heard shots before the blast. The police think he may have shot his way in."

"Any weapon recovered?" Tom surveyed the wreckage with a wearily practiced eye. The bomber would have to have been a giant to carry the weight of bang to make a hole that big. This wasn't some random attack.

"Sorry I dragged you up here."

"Not a problem. And since I'm here, I could look in on that guy Blakey I told you about."

"Let me come with you. I'm only getting in the way here."

29

Selly Oak Hospital, Birmingham

Blakey lay flat on his back, surrounded by a spaghetti of drips and drains. He was staring straight upwards, his eyes glazed. He turned his head as they approached and a smile spread over his face. "They said you'd called."

His voice was small and slurred. He tried to lift his head, gave up. Tom stood right over him so he didn't need to move.

"You're my first visitor."

"What about your mom?"

"She's gone to my sister's in Leamington. They smashed her windows. She'll come when she's got her nerve back. I'll still be here. I'm not going anywhere." He closed his eyes again.

Tom took his hand. It felt limp and lifeless. "How are you doing?"

"How does it look?"

Tom wished he hadn't asked. He introduced Rolt.

Before they had got past the pleasantries a nurse and two orderlies appeared.

"Hello, Cliff. We're taking you down to pre-op. Going to have another look at that spine of yours."

"Whatever."

149

The nurse gave Blakey a wan smile and turned to Tom. "Sorry to break up the party, guys."

Rolt reached forward and gripped Blakey's shoulder.

"We'll get your mom and sister out to see you. That's a promise. Then we'll see what else we can do for them and you."

30

In the car back to London, Tom rode in the rear with Rolt, who spent a long time poring over his laptop, the screen a mass of figures. As he scrolled through them, he sighed frequently but said nothing. Jackman pulled onto the M40, put the Bentley in the fast lane and let the needle wind its way up past a hundred.

"Thanks for offering to help Blakey."

"As I said, it's what we're all about. He's got enough on his plate without having to worry about his mother being too scared to come and visit him." Rolt focused on his figures again.

"You've got quite a set-up, haven't you?"

Rolt smiled. "So you got on okay there?"

"Very interesting."

"Impressed?" He looked as though he really wanted to know.

"The guys I spoke to—they seem to think you saved their necks."

"Well, there *is* a bit of a gap in the market. HMG seems to have forgotten about them."

"I still don't know where you think I fit into all this."

The traffic abruptly backed up and they slowed to under fifty. The inside lane was coned off: armed police had surrounded a minibus. The occupants were lined up facing the vehicle as they were patted down and cuffed.

"See what's happening? People are frightened. This mess we're in—it's scaring them. It's affecting everything: the economy, the markets—tourism." Rolt closed his laptop. "Do you mind if I confide in you?"

"Shoot. I'm all ears."

"What you saw today, I've put everything into it. Become a bit of an obsession. But it's costly and it doesn't exactly pay its way. I've tried the government. They plead cuts and more pressing priorities. No one wants to remember the heroes of a war they're trying to forget before it's even over. And now with this bombing . . ."

There was real anger in his voice. He closed his eyes, pinched the bridge of his nose, then felt in his pocket. He pulled out a silver cigarette case, slid one out and lit it. "But I have got some interest from abroad. Potential investors."

"Where?"

"America—Texas, to be precise. There are people there who want to do something similar. I've proposed a partnership: their cash, Invicta's knowhow and reputation." He sighed. "God knows we've jumped through enough hoops for them. I've lost count of the number of times I've been over there. They've heard my pitch, but to them I'm just another businessman touting for money." He turned to Tom. "You know what'll clinch it? They need to hear it from someone who's been there and done it."

"Who—me?"

"Precisely. Someone with a blue-chip military background, who *isn't* a fully paid-up Invicta graduate. Who can give an objective assessment with a bit of intelligent perspective."

"In which case perhaps you'd better share your agenda—your full agenda."

Rolt looked surprised.

"Up to now you've let Invicta's success speak for itself. You're conspicuously absent from the PR messages it puts out. It's almost as if you've shied away from any applause for what you've achieved. But in that TV interview you put down a marker."

Rolt shrugged as if it had been no more than an unintentional aside.

"And what you've said will send shock waves through Whitehall."

He smiled. "That won't hurt. They could do with a jolt."

"But if you follow your argument to the logical conclusion, what you're talking about is a pretty extreme crackdown on potential terrorists that we don't currently have legislation for. Critics will accuse you of advocating something like—well, ethnic cleansing."

He waved Tom's words away. "Look at you. You've risked your life all over the world in the War on Terror. I don't know the details of why you're suddenly back in Britain, that's your business and I'll respect your desire to keep it to yourself, if you choose to do so, but I'll hazard a guess that you've risked your life—oh, maybe twenty, thirty times for this country, and what have you got in return for it? What has your friend Blakey got to look forward to when he comes out? Freedom from fear—is that such a big thing to ask?"

"What do you want me to do?"

"Okay, cards on the table. My people are loyal—in fact, they'd probably drive over their own grandmothers if I asked them to. But almost all of them, one way or another, we've helped put back on the rails—they're, well, to an extent a bit dependent. Men like you, in their prime, with a record like yours, are different. Be my ambassador, go to the US and get them to commit. With your track record, you'll be the one to convince them. Think of it as just another mission, but with food, drink and hotels instead of warfare."

He raised his hands almost apologetically. "I'm not asking you to sign up to anything. Just go and tell them your story."

Tom knew this wasn't a decision to be made on the spot.

"Let me sleep on it, okay?"

31

Doncaster

An eerie calm seemed to have settled over the town. He passed a gas station. The pumps were covered up, the shop part gutted. There was no sign of the police this time. On the forecourt a pair of foxes battled it out over the contents of a discarded KFC box. He was irritated at having to leave London. Only one day into his new job and he had had to ask to be excused from a seminar they'd wanted him to attend at the LSE. But Pippa was full of understanding, as if he could do no wrong.

"Of course, Sam! Family must come first. It's a Party motto," she'd told him.

Not that he had let on what the family matter was: if they found out about Karza, it would be a disaster. He still didn't quite know what to make of his important new role. He was glad of the money as well as the attention. It felt good to have a position and be listened to, though it was new to him to be trading on his background.

He rounded the corner at the bottom of his mother's street. Part of him dreaded what Nasima would have to say, but he was looking forward to seeing her again. There was something intriguing about her—and she was the complete opposite of Helen. The brutally perfunctory way she had ditched him, the implication that he was the wrong race and religion, had stung him hard.

He heard the steps about ten meters behind. At first it felt like a good sound, that he wasn't alone on these deserted streets. The cops had the place on lockdown so surely there was no need for alarm.

But an unmistakable *clack clack* said the steps were boots with metal tips. A sound that, as a kid, he had read as a warning: trouble.

"Hey, it's Kovacevic the *Arse*hole."

His first thought was to ignore it. But that word, one he had hoped never to be called again, meant he had been recognized. And he knew from the voice who it was. The steps quickened; he felt a hand on his arm, breathed the smell of alcohol and weed. The street was deserted, with no sign of the police van that had been at the bottom of the hill. Right. He stopped and turned.

There was a look of furious indignation on Dink's face. He was still small, but he had filled out, a mixture of workouts, steroids and making up for all the calories he'd missed out on as a kid. His pink, shaven head seemed to rise out of his tattooed shoulders like a plug amid the flesh and muscle, his features crowded into the middle of his face, as if they'd been grafted on from a much smaller head. His disconcertingly full, feminine lips parted and Sam saw the straight white teeth of a man with money to burn on dentistry, and the ability to manage a drug habit, a sure sign that he had got where he wanted to be.

"What's in the bag, *Arsehole*?"

Although he was three years younger—in the same year as Karza—age had never inhibited Dink from taking on his elders. He had two others with him, half a foot taller at least, heavily mus- cled, their heads identically shaved. One had no eyebrows, which gave him a misleadingly babyish appearance. The other had an unusually narrow skull and slightly sloping eyes, more likely a legacy of foetal alcohol syndrome than any exotic ancestry.

"I asked yer a question, Paki."

Indignation rose in Sam like acid. "I'm not a Pakistani."

Dink's approach to racial profiling: anyone who wasn't pure white like him simply shouldn't exist. His eyes blazed. He jabbed Sam in the chest. "You're all Pakis to me, you Paki fuck."

"Okay, whatever."

Sam knew Dink's story—in fact, he had thought of him when he was preparing his last lecture, "The Gang as Family". A textbook example of what he'd termed "Son of McDad", the product of a "domestic void", the child whose father only shows up from time to time to take the kids to McDonald's, the mother on benefits, a stream of adult males through the home treating it like it was theirs, and Mom telling him to piss off out when she had company. The child, neglected and constantly out on the streets, falls prey to the gang, who brutalize him, then test him with tasks—at first relatively trivial, such as a mugging, then increasingly violent. As they absorb him, they put him to work, teach him how to steal, how to threaten, how to be feared. He gets respect, status. It's addictive, like the stuff they're dealing. The gang becomes his family, their values his.

Dink had done well. The teeth said it all. As the older members were picked off—killed or maimed or sent to jail—he had risen through the ranks until he was number one. Respected, feared and rich, everything he wanted out of life.

But right now, all of Sam's insight counted for shit.

Dink snatched his bag.

"Please—careful." Sam's voice sounded more officious than he meant it to, a habit Helen had reminded him to check. Dink pulled out his conference ID.

"Whooo! *Doctor* Arsehole!"

Sam was twelve again, hurrying back to do his homework, Dink and his posse blocking the sidewalk, his satchel grabbed, the precious textbooks emptied onto a waiting heap of dog shit. Only this time it was his brand-new MacBook Air.

"All my work's in that."

Dink smoothed his hand over the surface of the lid, then flipped it open. "We'll look after it, don't worry."

He passed it to one of the henchmen.

"Now fuck off where you came from, Paki. You're trespassing."

"Come on, this is my street."

Dink stepped back in mock horror. "'My street', is it now? Next it'll be 'my country'." He looked at his henchmen, who arranged their pudgy features into expressions of dismay. He waved a tattooed hand at the smashed shops. "Your lot started this. Who's gonna clear it all up?"

"My 'lot'?"

"All you Paki Muslim cunts gotta go back where you came from. It's over, mate. You've had your fun." He nodded at the henchmen who each grabbed one of his arms while Dink patted him down, then pulled out his wallet. It flapped open, revealing the picture of Helen.

Dink's eyes bulged with indignation. "You dirty Paki fucker." Dink flashed the picture at his mates, shaking his head with theatrical sweeps. "Big mistake, Arsehole. Big mistake."

Sam was terrified and confused. This time indignation and rage overcame his fear. *"Fuck you!"*

Dink's features seemed to crowd even further into the middle of his face. Then he grinned and put his mouth close to Sam's ear. "Anyone doing the fucking, it's gonna be me. Pakis fucking white women should know what they got coming from Dink." He pressed himself closer, the smell of the various intoxicants rising from him, thrust his hands into Sam's pockets and pulled out his mother's keys. He dangled them from his little finger. The flat was only a few meters away. "Is Mummy home?"

He shook his head. That much he was grateful for.

Dink reached into his pocket, pulled out a bunch of surgical gloves and gave a pair to each of his mates. "Then it'll just be us chickens."

32

He had no idea what time it was. Daylight streamed in through the kitchen window, which seemed to loom above him at an unfamiliar angle. His eyes widened as he realized where he was. There was a strong smell of piss and alcohol. He glanced at the floor. The lower half of his body felt cold. And wet. He looked at himself. He was naked from the waist down, his linen pants round his ankles. With a jolt, it came back. As he moved, pain flashed between his buttocks. He turned his head and vomited.

He dragged up his pants and pants, felt the pockets. His phone was gone. Then he remembered the laptop. Ignoring the pain now, he pushed himself up to a sitting position, pulled on his clothes. The fridge door yawned open. In the pool of water in front of it his bag and wallet lay open and face down. His cards were still there but the cash was gone. The bag was empty, the laptop gone. Using the table he had once sat at to do his homework, he hauled himself up, then slowly sat in a chair.

Then he remembered Nasima. She couldn't see him like this. He got to his feet and saw himself in the mirror, his face bruised and bloody. Then he noticed the clock on the oven. It was seven a.m. He must have missed her—or maybe she hadn't come, after all.

He threw himself into a frenzy of activity, clearing up the kitchen, mopping the floor. He stripped off his clothes and threw them into the trash or garbage. In Karza's room he found a pair of jeans, a T-shirt, and a hoodie. They would have to do. In the bathroom he did what he could to clean up his face, but tears of rage blurred his vision. When the doorbell rang he jumped.

"Who is it?"

It was Nasima. He opened the door and her mouth dropped open. "What happened?"

"What does it look like?"

He shut the door quickly and showed her upstairs, steering her towards the front room.

"Who did this?"

"Thugs."

"Whites?"

Waves of shame and embarrassment welled in him. He couldn't hide it. His humiliation was complete. She stood in the kitchen and surveyed the scene. Then she came towards him and embraced him. He resisted at first, then gave in, put his head on her shoulder and cried.

"Fucking bastards. Fucking white fascist bastards!"

She soothed him. "It's okay, you're safe now."

He pulled back. "Safe? That's about the last thing I feel."

That he had been singled out made a mockery of all his years of trying to blend in. But she held on to him. "For what it's worth, I know just how you feel, believe me."

Her words calmed him. He felt less alone. She sat him down and made him a cup of tea. Then she sat opposite and held his hand while he sipped. He tried not to catch her eye but when he did he saw how different she looked. She had lost the reserve she had shown when they first met.

"I'm sorry I couldn't come last night—I got held up."

"Maybe it's just as well. You might have got caught up in this—this . . ." He let out another anguished sob. "I hate you to see me like this."

She smiled. "I saw you on the TV." She leaned closer. "You were very good. Does that mean you'll be meeting members of the government?"

He snorted. "I had a breakfast meeting with the home secretary. Now look at me!"

"No one need know. Don't give them the satisfaction of seeing your pain. Don't give up on what you're doing."

He shivered at the thought of his words about restraint and the need for perspective. "Well, I don't expect you to agree with any of it."

"You put your points very convincingly. I believe you're sincere."

"I just want to make a difference."

"Maybe you haven't found the right kind of difference yet."

"What do you mean?"

She smiled and reached for his face. Her touch was soothing. "Let's not have this discussion now."

"What about Karza? Do you know any more?"

She put her hands into her lap. "Well, we've made contact with the group he's with. He is alive, that's been confirmed."

He felt a huge rush of relief. "So he's safe?"

"Well, no one is safe in Syria right now."

"Of course—stupid."

She laughed. "I can see you're new to all this."

"So you might be able to get him back?"

"It's not as simple as that. We've yet to make direct contact. MI6 monitor all emails and Twitter feeds now so the fighters have gone quiet. I should know more in a few days."

Sam felt a twinge of irritation. "So you asked me to come up here just to tell me you might know more?"

She focused on the cut on his cheek. "You're bleeding again. I'll sort that out."

In the bathroom she dabbed the wound with a piece of gauze. Her bag seemed to contain a substantial medical equipment.

"You came well prepared."

"Well, I am a doctor, and I do work for a medical charity."

She produced a small plaster, unwrapped it and applied it to his cheek. "I hope that's better." She bit her lip and dropped her eyes, but her fingers lingered on his face. "There's a favor I wanted to ask."

"Name it. After all you're doing for me it's the least I can do."

"It's a big favor."

"Well, go on."

"You saw we're closing down here. I have to come to London, but I don't really know anyone there and I was wondering if you had a spare room where you could put me up." She gave a small laugh.

"Well, I'm staying at a friend's myself."

She gazed at him. Her whole persona, so cool and reserved when he had first encountered her, had softened. Her eyes were

163

wider, her lips slightly parted. Then she looked away. "I'm sorry, it was inappropriate . . ."

"No!" He felt a surge of pleasure at her attention. Helen suddenly seemed like a world away. "I'd be happy to help."

33

Victoria, London

From the edge of St. James's Park, Tom had a clear view of Invicta's headquarters, and the Bentley parked outside. He hadn't got back to Rolt yet. He wanted more time and he needed some answers, some that the boss of Invicta couldn't give.

Once Rolt had left the office with Jackman, Tom approached the door. The police waved him away.

"Closed for the day, sorry."

"I left my glasses here yesterday—just wanted to pick them up."

"Okay, ask at the desk."

Inside, the receptionist made a call to Phoebe. "She'll be down in a minute."

Tom settled himself in one of the big leather armchairs and picked up the *Evening Standard*. Rolt had made the front page.

Invicta Founder: "Send Them Back."

Before he could read on Phoebe appeared at the top of the stairs, wearing a big smile.

"So how was your visit to the campus?" She took her time descending, her skirt swaying compellingly as she moved. Her hair looked as if she'd given it a quick brush before she left her post.

"Nice of you to ask. A learning experience. Your boss has quite a thing going on up there."

She reached the bottom of the stairs. Tom noticed his gaze was starting to make her feel self-conscious. She gave a small, very attractive laugh. "Is there something I can help with?"

Tom pretended to look blank. "Oh, yes—I thought I'd left some glasses here but then I remembered I don't wear any."

She gave him a mock-scolding look and laughed again, her eyes shining seductively. If he hadn't been so preoccupied he would have had to admit he was powerfully attracted.

"I'm staying at my father's club. I wondered if you'd like to join me for a drink."

She put on an apologetic face. "I've got something on."

"Vernon's offered me an assignment. To be honest, I'm in two minds. Thought you might give me the lowdown on working for him." The work angle should swing it, he calculated, and as she hesitated, he gave her one of his trademark looks, designed to melt the most obstinate woman at fifty paces.

She lifted a stray strand of hair and tucked it behind her ear. "I'll make a call."

Job done. He watched her go back up, taking in all her movements. A few seconds later she reappeared at the top of the stairs, tapping something into her phone. She dropped it into her bag as she came down.

"Who did you have to put off?"

"Oh, a girlfriend. It's not a problem."

"Not a boyfriend, then."

She frowned slightly. "As it happens, no."

"Sorry, just being nosy, forgive me."

166

"I'll let it go this time."

Formality was slipping away. He needed her nice and relaxed to maximize the element of surprise.

He turned into the street and gently took her elbow as he steered her through the traffic. "Your boss is a very persuasive man."

She nodded eagerly. "I'll say. He really motivates people."

"You enjoy the job?"

"Oh, yes, very much but it pretty much takes over my life."

"Judging by the headlines, you'll be having to work even harder now."

"It looks like it."

The doorman greeted them as they entered the club and climbed the stairs to the foyer. Tom hoped his father wasn't around: the last thing he needed was parental disapproval of his chatting up another woman behind Delphine's back. He guided her to what had been called the smoking room, then to a table in the darkest corner. "They do a particularly mean mojito here."

"I'll have a soda . . ." She sighed. "Oh, all right." She grinned guiltily. She was good, thought Tom, but not *too* good.

He summoned a waiter, who took their order, then leaned forward and gave her all his attention. "You must forgive me for seeming so forward but I've been away in the most god forsaken place, surrounded by hairy, perspiring males with varying standards of hygiene, on a military base totally devoid of any beauty."

She raised an eyebrow. "So you've got me here under false pretences. I thought this was strictly business."

"I've always had difficulty finding the line between where business ends and pleasure begins."

Tiny movements around her eyes suggested to Tom that she was torn between attraction and wariness. Fair enough, he thought. She has no idea what's coming.

"But I really do want to talk about the amazing Mr. Rolt. He's shown his hand with that interview. I expect your life's about to get a lot more complicated, as a result."

The waiter arrived with the drinks. Phoebe took a tiny sip and sat back in her chair. "It's been relentless today. He's going to get a lot of flak but he's very resilient."

"Are you a big fan of his views?"

She seemed taken aback by the question.

"It doesn't take much to see what he's saying adds up to a pretty extreme position."

"He's never said he has any personal political ambitions."

She hadn't answered the question but he let it go for now. He picked up his glass. "What shall we drink to?"

She grinned at him, waiting for him to choose.

"To Invicta? And all who sail in her!"

"To Invicta."

They each took a sip.

"That's better." He resumed his probing. "Rolt does seem to have taken control of the political agenda. The government must be reeling. He's just come out and said what half of them think but are too scared to admit in public for fear of being labelled racist. How long have you worked for him?"

The question tacked on to the end of his speech seemed to take her by surprise. "Oh, not long. Only a few months."

"And before that?"

She rolled her eyes. "A stint for the MoD press office, then an attempt to be a freelance journalist, God help me."

Her answer had slipped out too easily, Tom thought. He took another sip of his mojito while she made an attempt to deflect the conversation from her. "So what's he offered you?"

"Oh, a sort of envoy role."

"Gosh, wow."

Her excitement seemed out of proportion.

"I thought you would have known that."

She shrugged. "He keeps his cards very close to his chest."

"He's been very open with me."

"He makes up his mind about people very quickly. Everyone's either friend or foe. Nothing in between. I'm sure you made the right impression. Besides, he's been looking for someone like you for a while."

"What does 'someone like me' mean exactly?" Tom watched her closely; on the surface she appeared to be quite relaxed, in her stride.

"You might have noticed on the campus that the men, they're . . . well, a lot of them have had a bad time and they're mostly . . . how do I put this? From less advantaged backgrounds. He doesn't get many of your sort. That's why he was so keen to meet you. Or meet you again, I should say."

"Clever of you to track me down. Was it hard?"

"Part of my job is to be a talent scout for him. He needs what he calls a better class of ex-servicemen, not just victims but victors. People who can act for him on the ground. It's my job to know everything about his background and who he knows or has known. When I discovered you were on your way back from Afghanistan, I thought he'd like to know. He's always looking to recruit new blood."

A very well-crafted answer, thought Tom.

"And how did you do that?"

"Do what?"

"Track me down."

She held his gaze. Tom decided she must have been well trained. "An old contact at the MoD, who's also an Invicta supporter. He helps where he can with lists of returning soldiers."

"And you happened to recognize my name because you knew Rolt and I were contemporaries at school."

She smiled a bit too eagerly. "Yes, that's right."

"And you managed to get hold of my phone numbers."

She gave a coquettish smile and took a sip of her drink. "Well, I was a journalist."

"He must have been very pleased with you."

She looked temporarily lost. "He expects a hundred and ten percent."

"And total loyalty."

She smiled emphatically. "Mm."

"So he'd be pretty pissed off with you if he found out you were working for someone else."

She closed her eyes and gave an exaggerated shudder. "God, yes."

"But you'd tough it out, wouldn't you—if he accused you?"

She stared at him with an amused smile, as if she was pretending to enjoy not knowing where this banter was going.

"And you'd be very plausible. You'd challenge him on it— insist he backed up the claim."

She took a much bigger sip of her mojito.

"Well?"

His whole demeanor had changed. Not overtly threatening, just a cold, penetrating stare.

She put her glass down and positioned it on the coaster. "Yes, I would."

"And if I went to him and told him that you couldn't have seen my name on any list because the MoD never lists the movements of the SAS, and that my phone number is privileged, is never on anyone's file . . ."

Her calm and seductive serenity was starting to fray. Tom suspected that inside she felt as though she was clinging to a very slippery windowsill.

". . . and that therefore I've been set up . . ."

"I'm sorry, Tom, but I really don't understand what you're saying."

A last-ditch attempt. She was off the windowsill, falling to her doom. A bit of him felt sorry for her—she was only doing her job. But mostly he was angry. He'd been played in Afghanistan, humiliated in front of senior officers, made to carry the can for a brutal murder. And now someone else was manipulating him.

He leaned across the table and put his lips very close to her ear. "Take out your phone and call your case officer. Say you'd like him to join us for a drink."

34

"This is all rather awkward."

Tom said nothing.

Woolf's eyes had a slightly desperate look, like that of a man who had had a stroke and was thinking far more than his features would allow him to express. He and Tom had met before, on the Eurostar hijacking: Woolf had been MI5's man on the ground when the SAS had gone into the tunnel. Unlike the suits and mandarins, who had rushed in after it was over to claim their slice of the credit, he had taken a back seat. And for that Tom had reserved a molecule of respect for him—until now.

They were seated in a private room in his father's club that Tom had commandeered for the meeting.

Phoebe, looking fragile, stared hard at her nails as she waited for her boss to explain himself.

"Sorry to hear about the business in Bastion."

Tom glared at him, feeling nothing but cold anger. It came as no surprise to him that the spook knew about his exit from Afghanistan—but how much? "Let's just get this done, okay?"

Woolf sighed, with an air of defeat uncharacteristic for someone in his line of work. These people were used to calling the shots. "Okay." He took a deep breath. "From the top?"

"From the top."

"The shooting in Walthamstow. We think it connects to Invicta."

"How?"

Woolf looked at Phoebe but she was still studying her nails. "Our suspect is on their payroll."

"Who is he?"

Woolf hesitated. Tom laid his hands flat on the table. "Come on! You've fucked me around enough."

Woolf swallowed. "His name's Vestey."

Tom laughed. "No way."

Woolf's eyes widened. "You know him?"

"I saw him in action today. He's not your man. His sniper days are over."

Woolf reddened. "His brother's a commander in SCO19. He was on duty that night."

"Take it from me. Vestey could not have been your shooter. He's past it." Tom gazed at Woolf as he digested this news. "Is that it?"

Woolf blew out a long breath. "All right. We don't have much to go on, even less now you've . . . enlightened us about Vestey. And I'm grateful you did. There are plenty in the Service who would happily see me fall flat on my face on this one." He leaned back and gripped the edge of the table.

"This shooting of a blameless respected Muslim—set up to look like it was done by the police—has, in my opinion, all the hallmarks of a deliberate act of provocation. Remember what happened after Stockwell and Duggan? The outrage. Only this time the cops did *not* do it. So who was it? Our focus has been on Muslim extremists and returnees from Syria. But why would

173

they? They may have the motivation to do harm, but do they genuinely have the capability to carry out an attack with this kind of precision? You and I both know that's highly unlikely. My colleagues in the security services are looking in the wrong direction."

He blinked as he waited for Tom to respond.

Tom knew what he thought. A returnee might have the motivation and have done a bit of time in a training camp, but you didn't learn to be a sniper by messing around in a war zone shooting off an AK at anything that moved. However, he wasn't in any mood to give Woolf the benefit of his wisdom. "You're the spook: you tell me."

"Well, the key question is motivation. The killing has brought Muslims out onto the streets and, in turn, all those who hate them. Someone is deliberately trying to polarize the two sides. To push us beyond the limits—perhaps even to the edge of civil war."

Tom folded his arms. "And the hostel bomb? Genuine reprisal, or . . . ?"

"Or an attempt to raise the temperature further. Exactly. We've had 7/7. We've had Woolwich. Each time we've stepped closer to the edge of popular outrage. Now the government's tearing itself apart trying to be all things to all communities, but it's losing the battle. The whole—ecosystem we're living in has changed."

Tom glanced at Phoebe. "And you suspect Rolt because he's gone out of his way to articulate it?"

"A year ago Vernon Rolt would have been ostracized for talking about removing the extremist element," he began, "whereas today . . ."

174

Tom looked at Phoebe again.

She nodded slowly. "He's extremely secretive, and extremely well connected. He's worked long and hard to build and maintain his position as a pillar of society. An entrepreneur who's not only plowed millions into a good cause but befriended, and championed, a very particular kind of underdog."

Woolf took up the thread. "The underdog with a grievance, with the capacity to turn on his former masters. Potentially, Invicta isn't just a refuge. It's the perfect incubator for the disaffected ex-soldier with a grudge to nurture."

A waiter put his head round the door. "Anything I can get you?"

Woolf looked as though he badly needed a drink but Tom wasn't in the mood to show mercy. "We're fine, thanks." He waved the waiter away and turned back to Woolf. "Let me get this clear. You believe someone inside Invicta is training former service personnel—people like *me*—to be terrorists?"

Woolf took a breath. "Maybe. That's what we have yet to verify."

Tom turned to Phoebe. "Well? You're the one who's been cosying up to him all these months."

Phoebe glanced at Woolf, who signaled for her to go ahead. "They prefer to think of themselves more as crusaders or freedom-fighters than terrorists. But unfortunately we're not that cosy. Rolt plays everything close to his chest, as I said. He makes lots of his own arrangements, doesn't keep records, sometimes avoids using email even. I'm pretty sure he doesn't suspect me, but he knows that the Service is likely to be watching him, as it does all right-wing groups, so he never lets me see anything sensitive."

175

"So you've actually got nothing concrete on him?"

Woolf parried this before she could answer. "You know what keeps us spooks awake at night? The white terrorist, the one no one's looking out for. The one who looks and sounds just like us. The next big one won't be a bus bombing or a plane, it'll be a smart surgical strike on people in power and that will need operators who can pass for insiders—who are hiding in plain view."

"Except you've got fuck-all to implicate Invicta, especially now I've shot down your claim about Vestey."

"Maybe he *recruited* the shooter."

"*Maybe*. You're grasping at straws."

"Straws are sometimes all we have." Woolf leaned forward, propping his head on the tips of his fingers, as if fending off a headache. "Look, you've just spent some time with him. Isn't there anything about him, about Invicta, that gave you pause for thought?"

Tom stared at him for several moments. The claims were outrageous, bordering on the deranged. Rolt was unusual, eccentric, even. But he had shown Tom respect and confidence, which was more than he could say for his former paymasters. "My first impressions are that Invicta's doing a good job for soldiers who've been fucked over or abandoned by the system. Without his commitment and dedication most of them would have been lost, ending up a danger to themselves and a menace to society." He stood up. "I think we're done here."

Woolf held up his hands in surrender. "Please, Tom. We need someone on the inside, no disrespect to Phoebe, who can get closer—"

"One question. Why didn't you go through the normal channels to try and recruit me? Was that such a crazy idea?"

Woolf shook his head. "If we'd gone through the normal channels, at least ten people in the MoD would have had to know. There'd have been emails, forms, countersignatures. Just getting it signed off by your CO, you'd have been blown before we even got airborne. Apart from the DG and a couple of my counterparts, no one knows about this. It's completely off grid. I couldn't risk anyone inside the MoD apparatus knowing."

"In case they tipped Rolf off?"

"As Phoebe says, he's that well connected. He gets one whisper of this, I'm out—and my boss will probably have to fall on his sword too."

For all Woolf's pleading, it was still clear to Tom he had been played. Woolf had used him as the Service always used people, like avatars, in a game they thought they could control.

Tom took out his phone. Woolf opened his mouth, closed it again and sighed. "Look, I apologize. It was bad judgement. If you make the call to Rolt, I'm history. Invicta will become even more impenetrable and we'll never know. We won't even know if we were wrong."

Tom looked at Phoebe. Her eyes were glistening. "This what you signed up for—to fuck over members of the armed forces?"

She didn't speak but her eyes said it all. *Keep this to yourself, please, for my sake as well as yours.*

Tom looked at them both. "Okay, I've heard what you've got to say, now piss off."

Woolf got to his feet. "So—will you help us?"

"I haven't decided yet. Right now I need a holiday."

177

Woolf buttoned his jacket. He looked like a man who could have done with a week's sleep.

After they had left Tom stayed in the room alone, very still for several minutes. Then he took out his phone and dialed Delphine.

35

Westminster

"My God, I'm so sorry. The bastards." Pippa's face was a picture of concern.

Not even Nasima's expert attention could entirely disguise Sam's bruises. He had done a bit of improvisation with some foundation of Helen's he'd discovered in the bathroom but the finish was uneven. How did women get that stuff to go on properly? Fortunately, the worst of the damage was not on his face or hands. "I think they came off worse," he joked.

She laughed along but Sam doubted she believed his lie. "Well, I'm sure the police will get them."

"Ah, I didn't report it."

"Why ever not?"

He felt like saying, *You just don't get it, do you?* The assault had been a wake-up call, a reminder of who he really was and where he had come from, but that wasn't what he had come to talk about.

"It's not that simple. There could be reprisals. Look, there's something I was hoping you could help me with. I've been chucked out of my flat."

It was sort of true. It was only a matter of time before Helen would want the place back. He had decided Pippa was the best

179

person to broach this with. Derek Farmer was the decision-maker but Sam didn't think he could stand his particular brand of bonhomie just now. Uppermost in his mind was finding somewhere he could also accommodate Nasima. Her imminent arrival in London dominated his thoughts.

"Oh dear. That's not good, is it?" She shook her head in sympathy.

"Things aren't as easy as they were, put it that way." That much was true. Things weren't. Everything was different. The attack had knocked away the foundations of everything he held dear, as if he had been punished by some malign force for clinging to his values of tolerance and inclusion. But almost as powerful had been Nasima's response. First, her concern, the professional way she had taken charge of his injuries. How much his life had changed in just a matter of days. This new job and now this woman. Helen was history. What was the point of having some white trophy girlfriend when there were people like Nasima out there?

Not that she was his girlfriend. Not yet.

Pippa listened, her head tilted to one side as he spoke. She reminded him of a kindly headmistress, even though she was probably not much older than he was. "Well, no. Absolutely. We can't have our star spokesperson living on the streets. Stay here while I make a few enquiries. I might have just the thing." She gave him a broad smile and glided out of the room.

It had been Nasima's idea to ask the Party. It wouldn't have occurred to him, and when he had said he didn't like to ask, she had become quite frosty. "They're in government and they're your employer. What's wrong with asking?"

180

In less than a minute Pippa was back, triumphant.

"Courtesy of one of our recently disgraced members, it seems we have a rather nice little *pied-à-terre* in Victoria going begging."

"Disgraced?"

She rolled her eyes. "Shared a bed in Brussels one night with another man—not a problem *per se*, but his wife wasn't terribly happy. And his constituency party is—shall we say—very old guard."

Sam nodded noncommittally. "It sounds perfect. Does it have two bedrooms? My girlfriend is very modest."

There was a beat while she took this in. He could see her thinking, *They're a funny lot.*

"Oh, yes. Right. Of course. As it happens, it does, though the smaller one really is a bit *bijou*, as the agents like to say."

"I'm sure we'll manage. It's very kind of you."

"The furnishings aren't much to write home about, but as you'll be out and about most of the time, I don't imagine that'll be a problem. And it is very central. The neighbors may be a bit old-fashioned, but I'm sure you'll use your charm on them."

He assumed that by "old-fashioned" she meant likely not to want Muslims living among them. Whatever, it wasn't his problem. His life was evolving and he was taking charge of it, leading his destiny in a new direction.

From a drawer she produced a large gold-edged invitation card and held it out to him. "Welcome to the next level."

He gazed down at it.

The Prime Minister requests the pleasure . . .

"Beware, you're going to be bombarded with these. We want you at all the PM's VIP bashes. We're keen to widen the gene

181

pool around him—and you're, well, the best thing that's happened to us in a while."

Sam stared at the card.

"And I can make them plus one if you like."

He grinned. "Wow, thanks."

His life was on track. He was someone. He couldn't wait to tell Nasima.

36

An hour later, Sam was leaning against the wall in a fourth-floor mansion flat two blocks from Victoria station, getting his breath back.

Inside it smelt faintly of mildew and instant coffee, and bore all the signs of a hurried departure: curtains drawn, a large drift of post piled against the inside of the door, an iPhone charger hanging out of a socket and half a packet of chocolate digestives on the small kitchen table. He bit into one: still crisp.

He sat down in a black leather swivel chair, running his hands up and down the chrome frame and grinning to himself. He had gone to work for them; now he was making them work for *him*. He stood up and explored the bedrooms. Nasima wasn't actually his girlfriend yet—that was more at the planning stage. He hoped she'd be okay about being his date at the PM's events. Would that kind of thing impress her?

So far, she had shown the right signs. One room had a king-size bed, the other a narrow single. He gazed at the king size and wondered how she would look on it, naked.

He called her but the number was unrecognized. He tried it several more times and got the same message. A sense of doubt welled up in him. Had he let his imagination run away with him? His mother used to tell him he was a fantasist, dreaming of all the things he wanted to do. He began to wonder if she'd been right. Why would Nasima, who seemed so capable, need *his* help to find somewhere to stay? There was so much about her that both excited and mystified him. He knew almost nothing about her, or her family, or how she had come to be connected with the charity in Doncaster.

Just as he was starting to give up hope an unknown number came up on his phone.

It was her. "I lost my phone."

He could barely disguise his relief.

"Were you worried?"

"Well, yes."

"That's nice of you."

He delivered the good news about the flat. "Just temporary, but it has two bedrooms."

"See? I told you. They're very lucky to have you, right now."

"Yeah, I should remember that."

"They must really think they need you on their side. Not many people like us would be so willing to speak up for the government, especially at a time like this."

"There's something else." He told her about the Downing Street do: an invitation from the prime minister, no less. There was silence at the other end of the line.

"Are you still there?"

"That's—well, it should be very interesting."

Oh dear, had he gone too far? "You don't have to come. I mean, it was just I thought . . ."

"Sahim, that's wonderful. I'm sorry, I was lost for words. You really are amazing."

A warm glow of confidence flooded back. Even over the phone the force of her appreciation was unmistakable. All he had to do now was tackle his next challenge: to convert it into something tangible.

37

10 Downing Street

The reception room was a sea of people. Waitresses glided between them with trays. Over a marble fireplace at one end of the room hung a portrait of Elizabeth I, standing on a map of England. But Sam's attention was on Nasima as she gazed at the crowd.

"It's much bigger inside than it looks from the front, isn't it?" he said.

"What is?"

"Number Ten. A bit like the Tardis."

She seemed mystified, a reminder that they were worlds apart. But he could see she was captivated by the event. Her whole manner was so different from that of the distant, wary woman he had first encountered in Doncaster. Her dress had also surprised him. She had really gone to town: smart black suit with a skirt above the knee, white blouse and high-heeled boots. Her eyes were subtly enhanced with kohl and her lips were a glossy rose. In this gathering of powerful, famous people, he wasn't the only one whose attention she was attracting.

"If you don't mind me saying, you look terrific."

She gave him a wry smile. "Just trying to blend in."

The spell was broken by Derek Farmer bearing down on them. "Well, look at what we've got here." His lips were shiny with alcohol. He licked them as he spoke. "I hope I'm worthy of an introduction."

"This is Nasima. Nasima, this is Derek, my boss."

He added the last words as a warning signal. He was ready for Farmer to disgrace himself and wanted to alert her in case she decided to take against him. But she rose to the occasion, smiled and even gave him a flirtatious laugh. Sam's chest swelled with pride at her taking charge of the encounter with such confidence. Farmer leaned down and spoke in his ear in a stage whisper. The smell of drink was almost overpowering. "I'd keep her under a burka if I were you."

Nasima laughed dutifully as he trundled away.

"I'm sorry about that. You handled him brilliantly."

"Yes, he is quite disgusting," she said, without breaking her smile.

They sipped their elderflower cordial as a couple of reporters came up and complimented Sam on his TV appearances. He'd kept his studio makeup on, so what remained of Dink's inflictions were now fully concealed. He could feel Nasima's admiring gaze as he fielded their questions.

"What's your comment on the identity of the bomber?"

Sam frowned at the man, who was glancing at his iPhone as he spoke.

"Kevin Hagerty, *Daily Mail*."

"Which bomber?"

Hagerty looked askance. "The hostel bomber, just been ID'd. Returnee from Syria."

Sam's stomach lurched. Hagerty continued talking while simultaneously scanning the room for anyone else of interest.

"Nurul al-Something-or-other, got back three weeks ago after a nine-week tour. They found half his head in the rubble."

The reporter fixed his eyes on Nasima, whose expression remained studiedly neutral. Then he called across to Pippa, who was talking to one of the presenters of *Newsnight*. "You need to brief the new boy."

Pippa turned and said, without smiling, "Kevin, if this is about the hostel story, you know very well that's unconfirmed speculation."

Sam took a breath. He wasn't at all clear what the rules of engagement were here, but Nasima was right beside him, watching intently.

"Well . . ." he ventured ". . . whatever the outcome is, I can say this much. Some of the people returning from Syria are very damaged."

"Oh, so you don't condemn them, then?"

Sam reflected briefly on how much his life, and his thinking, had changed. Dink had committed that brutal assault on him for the same reason he was here now, so close to the seat of power: it was because of his *difference*. All this time he had been living his life believing he was no different from the mainstream. Now he was being sought out for his views *because* of his background. He didn't know whether to be amused or outraged. It was as if he had been both alienated and empowered at the same time. How weird was that? He cleared his throat.

"I do condemn the bombing, utterly. But it is important to understand the motivations of those who go to help in Syria, the desire to help their brothers, to do some good. Many of them come back utterly traumatized by the experience of war. Rather than just punish them, we should offer them support."

The reporter let out a long, garlicky sigh. "Blimey. I wonder what your new mate the PM's going to say about that."

Pippa was suddenly by their side. "Kevin, this is a *reception* not a bloody press conference." She turned to Sam. "He can't use a single word."

"What—really?"

Sam looked at the smiling reporter in bafflement.

"Yes. Really. Now run along." She held out a newly manicured hand to Nasima. "Philippa Kendrick, head of communications. Thank you so much for coming." She gazed at them approvingly. "Would you like to meet the prime minister?"

38

Across the room, Stephen Mandler, director general of MI5, was working his way through a much-needed glass of claret. He observed the entourage swirling around the PM with a mixture of pity and contempt. From his perspective the man was out of his depth, splashing away frantically, trying to keep his head above the waves.

On the other hand he felt a bit sorry for him, having constantly to come up with sound-bites that spoke to an increasingly fractured electorate, while his cabinet briefed and schemed behind his back. Yet there he was, making exactly the wrong call: tanned and buoyant, fresh from his trip to the President's retreat, aglow with the excitement of standing shoulder to shoulder with "POTUS". And he'd accepted one of those ridiculous Camp David jackets they made everyone wear as if they'd joined some fraternity, all the more to talk up the revived Special Relationship, while in his own country the streets burned and the people were in uproar. His assessment was that both of them, the President and the PM, had buried their heads in the sands of Afghanistan, while all about them the danger signs much closer to home were flashing red. He'd seen it all before, heads of state shoring up their crumbling reputations with lofty promises about international partnerships. And there was more to come. A full-blown Anglo-US summit right here in the middle of London, sprung on them out of the blue when there was still glass all over the streets, to show that it was "business as usual" in the capital. All Mandler could see was more overtime and canceled leave—and, as always, no extra budget to cover it.

As he took another gulp of wine he reflected that never in all his time in the Service had the country seemed so unstable; he felt a mounting discomfort that bad things were happening, and at a pace he could neither understand nor control. It was one thing to know what the problem was, quite another to know how to fix it.

To complete his misery, Alec Clements sidled up, rosy-cheeked with wine. "Ghastly news, isn't it?"

"The summit?"

"Good Lord, no. The bomber, of course. I thought you of all people would have that front of mind." The cabinet secretary eyed Mandler reproachfully. "Confirms everything I've been saying all along about the Syria problem, as no doubt you're aware. At least it's out in the open now. Time to face the facts."

This was neither the time nor the place for an argument. Mandler decided no response was the best policy as Clements went on. He wondered if he was going to tell him how to do his job, one of his trademark characteristics and why so many people couldn't stand him.

"And I do happen to know that the PM would be jolly glad to hear that you've got your A Team covering the returnee threat. Woolf seems a bright chap."

Was there nothing that escaped his attention? How he had any idea of what Woolf or any of his staff was doing was a complete mystery. Mandler gazed at him with barely suppressed contempt. A morsel of roast beef from a mini Yorkshire pudding had anchored itself to Clements's lapel. He decided not to point it out. Instead he responded with one of his deathly smiles. "Jolly good idea."

Mandler glared at the retreating back of the cabinet secretary as Sarah Garvey appeared at his elbow.

"What a cunt," she muttered.

He and the home secretary did not have a lot in common but they shared a loathing for Clements. "Quite."

She emptied the remains of her Chablis as if she was doing shots. "Never passes up an opportunity to do someone's job for them." She leaned towards Mandler. "You should know he's already told the PM you'll be stepping up your watch on returnees. And since he's mentioned Woolf, you'd probably better make sure you've got him aimed in the right direction."

They exchanged a glance. He could see she was in a corner. Had Clements got at her as well?

"Look, I know it's all part of your job to think out of the box et cetera, but this is *force majeure*."

He turned and bent his head closer to her ear. "Anything you say, Home Secretary, but *entre nous*, the pathologist's report on said returnee, whose body parts were sprinkled over the hostel site, rather tends to suggest that the unfortunate fellow was almost certainly dead *before* he supposedly blew himself up."

Her eyes widened as he nodded slowly. "I shit you not."

She let out a long, mournful sigh. "Are you going to tell me what you think about that?"

"Honestly?"

"I know it means breaking the habit of a lifetime."

He shrugged. "God's truth, I haven't got a bloody clue."

39

BA 195 London–Houston

It was the call to Delphine that settled it.

"Please, Tom. I need some time with my family. I've been too long away from France."

Tom decided not to argue. He knew only too well how stubborn she was. In fact, he respected her for it. They were kindred spirits in that way, though he realized now, with a stab of regret, that it worked against them as a couple. His mother's words echoed in his head: *Don't rush her*.

He raised his seat to upright and gazed down at the Texas landscape as the 747–400 started its descent towards George Bush Airport. When he'd called to accept his invitation, the founder of Invicta had let out a huge sigh of relief.

"I knew I could count on you. I hope it won't be too onerous. You'll have to press a lot of flesh, wow the crowd, spin a few yarns about your time in the field. They need to know we're for real. And they want to feel reassured that I've got the right people around me."

Rolt clearly felt Tom was doing him a favor. The man was hard not to like. And so far he had seemed to be completely straight with him, which was more than he could say for Woolf.

"We'll keep this to ourselves, shall we? With all the heightened tension around the hostel, we don't want any unnecessary attention, do we?"

"Fine by me," Tom told him.

On his iPad was the file Rolt had sent him. It was sketchy: a profile of Skip Lederer, boy genius and founder of Oryxis, a dramatically expanding software start-up, and a bit about the chairman, Aaron Stutz, a seasoned operator with a raft of business interests, including oil exploration, risk management and private security. He was more than twice Lederer's age. Quite what their interest in Invicta was he would have to find out. Even after he had digested the details, Tom was hardly any the wiser about that aspect of it. And Rolt had not revealed how much he was hoping they would invest.

"It's a very large figure," Rolt had told him, "but I don't want to tempt Fate by telling you. All you have to do is make them want to open their pockets just that bit more. Also," he added cryptically, "they may put you through a few hoops. But nothing you'll be unfamiliar with."

Tom had made a few notes for his speech, and chosen a mission from his past, which he thought would be just the sort of thing they'd want to hear. In 2006, as part of a four-man squad, he had sprung a CIA operator from a heavily defended house in Kandahar. Using the rescue drills they had perfected under live fire back in Hereford, they had fast-roped onto the roof from a Black Hawk, blasted the occupants with flash-bangs, and snatched the chained and blindfolded agent from right under the noses of his captors. It was a do-or-die operation in the best tradition of the Regiment, all done and dusted in under twenty minutes. He would leave out the

194

fact that the American was a total arsehole who had demanded to know what had taken them so long—and that they had been seriously tempted to boot him off the deck of the Black Hawk as soon as they were in the air.

At the arrivals gate there was a line of drivers holding up name cards. As he scanned them, a tall young woman with a 1000-watt smile came towards him, as if out of a dream. She was blonde, gorgeous and, even allowing for the heels, close on six feet, most of which was legs. Her silky hair was in a ponytail, her lips heavily glossed, as if with varnish. Her red skirt was tight but not so short as to attract the wrong kind of attention, and the crisp white shirt was open to show enough cleavage to stimulate interest without looking what his mother would doubtless have called "inappropriate".

"Hey there, Tom! Beth Adams. Welcome to the Lone Star State!"

How had she recognized him? Everyone in the Regiment closely guarded their image.

"Delighted to be here."

"We're very honored to have you visit us this day."

As they stepped out of the arrivals hall Tom was mugged by the summer heat and, for a moment, he tensed. But it wasn't the same as Afghanistan's debilitating, angry heat, and accompanied by the big Texas sky, it invited him to relax and pretend he really was on holiday. Beth lowered the sunglasses that had been perched on her head and clicked across the parking lot in her vertiginous heels. Oppressive, troubled London already felt a long way away.

She gave him a big grin as if they were about to embark on a ride at Disneyworld. "We're all *really* excited about your

195

visit. So here's what we're gonna do. I'm gonna run you up to Skip's compound right away. He's *dying* to meet you. You can freshen up there. Then we'll take you back downtown and get you checked into your room. The reception's in the same hotel. Oh, and Mr. Stutz will be there to greet you."

"And he's dying to meet me as well?"

There was a beat as the irony failed to penetrate, then she giggled to fill the vacuum. He had limited appetite for this level of enthusiasm, however long the legs that went with it. Maybe after a few bourbons she would mellow.

She marched him towards a gleaming metallic black Chevy pick-up, sporting a *Don't Mess With Texas* bumper sticker. She remotely popped the tailgate, which lowered in time for him to drop his bag on the deck.

"That all your stuff? I do hope you won't be leaving us too soon."

He shrugged. "I guess I've been trained to travel light. So, tell me, what's your role at Oryxis?"

"Oh, I just help out." She giggled childishly. "Look after Skip and stuff. He's a really fun guy. You're gonna love him." She laughed again.

It was impossible to know how much of it was genuine. Tom reminded himself to behave and resist the temptation to provoke her with any more cheeky Brit cynicism. Her laugh was full of sunshine and optimism, and he found himself smiling back as he opened the passenger door. "I'm sure I will."

He climbed in beside her. The seats were upholstered in something reptilian. "I assume a lot of snakes were harmed in the making of these seats?"

196

Again she laughed, but was clearly baffled.

The engine growled thunderously, and they were engulfed by a gale of aircon and country music.

"Everything you heard about Texas, it's all true." She turned to him with an even bigger smile as she threw the shift into drive. The truck leaped forward.

"So, tell me about the event. Who's coming?"

"Aw, it's just, y'know, guys networking."

"That's a bit vague."

"They're all friends of Oryxis. And they're just dying to hear what Invicta's doing for y'all."

"I just like to know who my audience is. In case they've heard it all before."

She laughed yet again, probably to cover up the fact that she didn't have a clue what he was on about.

On the way he quizzed her more but her answers were all frustratingly vague: "Aw you'll see," or "The guys'll fill you in," each accompanied by her sunny laugh. So he just let her talk, pointing out roadside features, like a drive-through liquor store called Beer Barn, which was, unsurprisingly, styled to resemble a barn, and Freakin' Pecan—"The best place in the universe, like *ever*, for pecan pie. Don't you go and leave without trying it now, y'hear?"

"Okay, promise," said Tom, his resistance wilting in the Texas sun.

Despite feeling carpet-bombed by her enthusiasm, he had fewer problems with Americans than some of his fellow Brits had. He admired the can-do mentality, the refusal to compromise and even the tendency towards overkill, which could make British methods seem tentative and half-arsed. As he considered this, he realized

197

how detached he had become from his roots. In the space of just the last few days he had already begun to change his thinking. But whereas before he had felt angry and disillusioned, he now felt energized and refreshed. The Texas sun, the country music, Beth's enthusiasm—and her long legs—were working their magic.

At an intersection they pulled up behind another pick-up with a gun rack carrying a Mossy 500A and a Winchester 94.

Beth grinned. "Betcha don't get to see a lot of *that* back home."

His thoughts drifted back to the Invicta campus, and to Woolf's claims about Vestey. What would his hosts make of the hostel bombing and Rolt's views about dealing with the current crisis back home? Just as he was deciding to put those thoughts aside, he felt his phone buzz in his pocket: a text—from Woolf.

He was tempted to delete it without reading it, then decided to leave it for later.

40

Lederer's place looked more like a country club than a home. A vast golf course occupied the grounds on one side of the drive for as far as Tom could see. On the other side was a lake with several brightly colored pedalo-type boats tethered to a landing.

"Pirates is one of Skip's favorite games. He is just so much fun." Behind a line of trees he could see a Ferris wheel: full size.

"Yep, that's our Skip. Basically he's just one big kid."

"With an oversized brain, though, right?"

Beth laughed yet again. How long could she keep this up? Was it really natural?

"You got it." She brought the truck to a halt outside the main door of the mansion and parked next to a silver and blue Bugatti Veyron, covered with road dust, a deep scrape down its left flank: a million dollars' worth of car and it looked as though it had been driven along a wall.

"Looks like it could do with a bit of TLC."

"He's got a new one on order. Let me show you to where you can freshen up. And when you're ready I'll find him for you."

She led him through a hallway made almost entirely of dark gray marble with a fountain in the middle, which produced a fan of blue-tinted water. It reminded him faintly of a crematorium, albeit a very expensively designed one.

"Why blue?"

199

She looked thrown for about a second, then said, "Skip's favorite color."

She opened a black polished door and waved him in. "You can freshen up in here—if you'd like."

"Jesus."

The bedroom looked about big enough for tennis. One wall was all glass, looking out onto the golf course; another was all TV, playing a film of dolphins frolicking in an expanse of turquoise sea. A gleaming, piano-black wardrobe, when he opened it, turned out to be a fridge with a temperature-controlled wine section and a cocktail cabinet. What a pity they'd put him in the hotel.

Another black door led to an equally vast wet room.

Beth hovered in the doorway. She seemed in no hurry to leave. "Want me to fix you anything?"

Tom grabbed a glass and helped himself to some iced water. "This is fine. I'll just be ten minutes." He found a remote and switched channels from the dolphins to CNN. The top story in the UK was still the hostel explosion. The bomber's ID had been confirmed: Nurul al-Awati, from Coventry, recently returned from Syria. A montage of reactions followed: a mixed group of women crying; crowds of chanting shaven-headed men; a train ablaze outside Birmingham; police behind shields being pounded with bottles and bricks.

Then he remembered Woolf's text. *Call—urgent*.

He texted back, *Can't—later*, then deleted both messages.

41

"Hey, Tom! How's it hanging?"

Skip was perched on a silver mesh swivel chair, hunched over a bank of screens, most of them filled with numbers. One was showing a war game, a Black Hawk banking and turning into a fireball. He didn't look round but waved a hand before returning it to his keyboard. From behind he could have been fourteen.

"He'll be right with you," said Beth.

When Skip finally did look round, Tom saw the face of an aged teenager, almost grotesquely disfigured by sleep deprivation. The dark pits under his eyes resembled wounds rather than shadows. His mop of curly yellow hair clearly needed a good wash, as did the Beavis and Butt-Head T-shirt that hung off his slight frame, above a pair of baggy checked shorts. Teenager was only slightly pushing it. Tom knew he was twenty-six, had grown up in New Mexico, had dropped out of Stanford University, had never travelled out of the US and had only in the last year moved out of his parents' house into this purpose-built compound.

He swivelled round and got to his feet. He was small, five six or so, and almost painfully skinny. The hand he offered was clammy, the fingers clawed from years of keyboard work. "Looks like it's all kicking off in jolly old England."

"You could say that."

"Man, I love your British understatement."

Skip's eyes slid across to Beth and her cleavage. Her face registered nothing, the blissed-out gaze aimed over his head.

"So, Tom: Del*phine*. Way to go, dude!"

"What?" Tom felt every muscle in his body tense.

"God, I love French chicks. *Zat accent*. And waaay hot. Too bad she bailed on your ass." He swung back to his keyboard, hit a couple of keys and her image appeared on a couple of the screens: a CCTV shot of her getting off a French train, then another of her in a street, in a café, coming out of a shop. Tom leaned forward to see the date: yesterday.

Skip wheeled round, grinning.

Tom glanced at Beth, the smile on her face fighting for its life.

"C'mon now, Skip. Be nice, remember."

"Superfast global facial recognition. Neat, huh? It's still in Beta but we're in the home stretch. All you need's a passport image or a photo off of Facebook, input that with a few coordinates, frequently visited locations, don't even need a name, hit send and *voilà*. When we get it running right, it should relay in about fifteen seconds from anywhere round the globe. Cool or what?"

Skip paused for him to respond, but Tom was too stunned to speak.

"Want me to set up an alert and patch it to your phone so you can keep check? Case you're worried about all them smooth French dudes hitting on her? I know I would be."

Tom swallowed, holding down the urge to deck the little prick. He couldn't remember a time he had taken such a dislike to someone so quickly.

Beth glanced anxiously at him, then went into over-drive, laying down a big apologetic laugh, like covering fire. "Really, Skip, you're just too much. What kind of a welcome is that to show our guest? I'm so sorry, Tom, he's just real keen for you to see his ideas. Ain't you, Skip?"

Skip giggled and raised his hands in surrender. "Hey, Tom, don't take it personally, okay? I'm just a geek with a hard-on for my new equipment." He pointed at Beth. "You should see what I got on *her*."

He hit another key and the screens filled with images of her in every stage of dress and undress, eating, swimming, shopping, driving, right up to meeting Tom at the airport and getting into the Chevy. Creepy didn't even begin to cover it.

He wagged a crooked finger at her. "See, babe? Nowhere to hide." He bowed as if responding to applause, his eyes hovering somewhere round her chest. Still she continued to smile, as if it was actually a clause in her contract. Maybe it was. But, almost to his relief, he thought he saw the mask slip for a millisecond.

Tom swallowed his disgust and reminded himself why he was there. *Press the flesh, secure the cash, then get the hell out.* "So, what's your interest in Invicta?"

Skip looked over Tom's shoulder, towards the door. "Ask him."

42

Aaron Stutz, chairman of Oryxis, came towards them: late fifties, balding, gray suit, dark blue tie, round wire-rimmed glasses, reminiscent of the US bureaucrats Tom used to see in the Green Zone, the ones who wore suit jackets over their body armor. He wondered if Skip's miraculous facial-recognition software would work on Stutz. His face was so uniform and featureless; surely it couldn't be picked out from a crowd. Nonetheless, he had to have something unique about him: everyone did. He cracked a brief, almost subliminal, smile and held out a chubby hand. He might have looked like a Central Casting average corporate animal but the small blue eyes blazed with intelligence. "Welcome to Texas, Tom. It's good to have you here."

Stutz glanced briefly at the screens and shook his head. He had evidently heard the last part of Skip's informal presentation. "Please forgive the boy's . . . enthusiasm. His work gets him so carried away he forgets his manners. So, you're gonna be Vernon's new recruit? Congratulations. Vernon is a very dear friend of mine, so you can believe me when I tell you he has no greater admirer than myself."

Recruit? That wasn't how Tom saw it. "Well, let's say I'm just here to do my bit, for the moment."

Stutz put a hand on Tom's shoulder and guided him away from Skip towards the door. "We just got the news about the bomber. How's that for timing?"

Tom frowned. "In what sense?"

Stutz smiled grimly. "The folks you'll be speaking to tonight, they know you guys are on the front line over there. They know what's wrong and what it's gonna take to put it right. You're among friends."

Tom was mystified. He nodded while he digested this and struggled to find some appropriate reply. "Well, that's good to know."

Stutz clasped Tom's arm. His grip was surprisingly firm. "Vernon's lucky to have people like you around him, men he can count on."

"Thanks for the compliment, but I'm pretty new to this."

The grip tightened. "I'm familiar with your story. So believe me when I say how deeply I feel your anger about what happened in Afghanistan with that ANA arsehole. Don't forget, we're grateful for your service alongside our people."

Stutz's cheeks had started to go an alarming purple color.

Skip's pictures of Delphine, and now this. Tom felt as if he was being sent a covert message. *We know a lot more about you than you've bargained for, so watch it.*

He held Stutz's gaze. The door he had tried to close on Afghanistan had just been wrenched open again. But what was Stutz's agenda? The best way to find out, he reminded himself, was to play along, for now. "Well, thank you for acknowledging that. I appreciate it."

Stutz's face began to ease back from purple to light plum. "Son, I'm getting the feeling we're gonna get along real fine."

205

43

Crown Plaza Hotel, Houston

Tom's room was on the forty-eighth floor. He gazed out at the Houston panorama, where streaks of pink cloud were ranged across the darkening sky. He had shaken Beth off in Reception, resisting her pleas to check his room was okay, and was making the most of a few hours alone. In any normal circumstances a tall blonde offering to make sure his pillows were plumped would have been ushered in, not shooed away. But these were not normal circumstances, and to him, her solicitousness smacked more of anxiety to please her bosses than the desire to get closer to those pillows.

Tom checked himself in the mirror. Hugo Boss tropical-weight wool suit, Sea Island cotton shirt and Regimental silk tie: his body armor for the evening, plus a crossed-flag pin in his lapel—Stars and Stripes with the Union flag. As well as a first-class ticket, Rolt had provided him with a generous float. "Anything you need, any gear, it's on me, okay?" He certainly wanted Tom to impress his Americans. But Tom wasn't ready to feel too beholden to him, not yet anyway.

His own phone was buzzing again. He decided to put Woolf out of his misery and took out one of the pay-as-you-go Samsungs he had taken the precaution of buying at the airport.

Woolf was as breathless as ever, diving in without a greeting. "You saw the hostel damage for yourself. Was there anything at all that struck you as strange?"

One detail had stuck in Tom's mind. "The damage was pretty extensive for explosives carried in a vest. Why?"

"There's a suspicion the bomber was dead before the device was detonated. CCTV from the street has two men, both white, making a delivery an hour before the blast from a van that was subsequently found burned out forty miles away."

"Has Rolt heard any of this?"

"No, and we're keeping it out of the press. But you know what this means?"

"That's two incidents now that have been deliberately made to look as if someone else was responsible for them."

"Glad you see it my way."

"Are you having trouble convincing them?"

"You could say that. Also I've been reassigned. They're trying to clamp down on returnees from Syria, Mandler's insisting. Phoebe stays in place for now. But I'm afraid you're rather on your own. That is, if you're still speaking to us."

Well, that's just great, thought Tom. *First they trick me into working for them, then they cut me loose.*

"So, if it's not an impertinent question, where are you now?"

"Houston."

"As in 'Houston we have a problem'?"

Tom could tell he was trying to stifle his disappointment.

"I'd hoped you'd come around, you know, to giving us a hand."

"It's not quite a vacation. I'm here for Rolt, standing in for him, sort of."

Woolf sounded genuinely alarmed. "Look, you do realize we've got no backup for you out there?"

"I'm perfectly capable of looking after myself. This isn't exactly Kandahar. The biggest danger is dying from a surfeit of enthusiasm."

Woolf sounded like he was on the move, running up some stairs. "Well, I'm late, as usual. But, if anything, this business about the bomber has made me even more suspicious of Rolt. Keep your eyes and ears open, will you? Something really isn't right about this."

"I will," Tom found himself saying.

There was a gust of relief from Woolf's end. "So you are with us. Thank fuck for that."

"Don't push your luck."

There was a cheery knock on his door: Beth.

"Gotta go."

44

Victoria, London

Sam wanted the first impressions to be the right ones. Earlier in the day, he had put new sheets on the beds, and bought a large bouquet, which he laid on the coffee table in the living room. He had drawn the curtains, which were heavy and plush. He had then spent some time fussing around, turning up the lights, then dimming them and moving them around to create the most welcoming atmosphere. Eventually he settled for just the single table lamp, which gave off the cosiest glow. The low light and the enclosed feeling, with the outside world and its distractions now excluded, made the place feel much more intimate. Even as he was denying it to himself, he was hoping this would create the right conditions for what he wanted, which was to shut out the rest of the world and be alone with her. The rest of the night lay ahead, full of possibility.

At last they were alone.

The big flat-screen TV faced them across the sofa. Nasima, remote in hand, was flicking between BBC News and CNN. He looked at her luggage, a small wheelie case collected on the way there from Victoria station.

"Is that all you have?"

"I don't need much."

He was starting to notice how deftly she rebuffed any questions she evidently construed as intrusive. Fair enough, he thought. Take your time. But where was the rest of her life?

"Would you like to see the . . . rooms?" He couldn't quite say "bedrooms".

"Sure," she said, as if she didn't much care either way.

"Obviously, you should have the double, the bigger one, I mean. If you prefer."

He showed her the small room as well—"for comparison". The more he said, the more he sounded like an estate agent. In his fantasy, which he had already replayed many times, she would be so intoxicated by the excitement of the evening, of having mingled with so many powerful, famous people, that she'd be desperate to leap into bed with him. But he knew that was what it was, no more than a fantasy. All the same, he ached to see her naked skin, and to touch her.

"You choose. I don't mind," he said needlessly. His heart thumped against his chest.

She put her bag down on the double bed and smiled. Should he make his move? As he hesitated, she moved towards the door to get her case, and he realized she was waiting for him to leave.

He went into the living room and sat on the sofa. Was she coming back? He put on the TV to drown out the sound of his blood pumping round his body.

He was still in a state of excitement from the evening at Downing Street. He had had a whole two minutes with the prime minister, with Nasima looking on.

"You're very good on camera—you've got the knack," the PM had told him. "So I rather fear we're going to be ruthlessly exploiting you over the coming weeks. Are you getting everything you need?"

"Oh, yes, thanks." He had started to describe the flat, then quickly stopped when he saw the PM wasn't paying any attention: his eyes had flicked to Nasima.

"And what do you do?"

"Oh, I've put everything on hold to support Sahim."

Her well-chosen answer pleased the PM, and Sam even more.

"Well, then, he's very lucky—and so are we that he's got you. You know what they say, behind every great man and all that . . ."

But by then someone was at his ear and he was gone.

Sam turned to her and grinned, delighted by the PM's reaction, but her face had gone blank, just as it had when he'd first set eyes on her.She shrugged. "Well, I guessed it was what he wanted to hear."

In the car back to the flat she had hardly said a word. To fill the silence he thanked her for being there, twice, to which she had merely nodded acknowledgement. Perhaps she was tired. He was exhausted too, but the adrenalin rush from the evening— rubbing shoulders with the mighty, her by his side—was almost over-powering. He had never felt like this before.

"I hope you don't mind that everyone thought we were—you know."

"No, it was fine."

Again, the slightly unnerving lack of response. At least if she'd been bothered by it that would have been something. He got the impression she didn't want to discuss it, but wasn't hugely moved one way or the other, as if the idea of being with him, like that, didn't engender any emotion at all. That was the ultimate failure, to provoke indifference in a woman. Maybe she was conscious of the driver's presence. It was one of the Party's regulars, a Polish guy with whom Sam had already had one touchy discussion about the current situation.

The bedroom door opened. He turned, he hoped not too quickly. She had removed her makeup and was wearing a long dressing-gown, buttoned up to the neck, and slippers.

Never mind, he told himself. There will be other opportunities.

And now here they were in front of the TV, still not talking. Every now and then his eyes flicked away from the screen to her, in the passion-killer garment. His desire hadn't been quelled at all. She could have been wearing a black sack for all he cared.

Eventually she switched off the TV and turned to him. His whole body glowed under her gaze. "I have some news about your brother."

He felt the atmosphere in the room change. It was as if they were back in Doncaster, in that kitchen, the first time they'd met.

"It's not good."

The coverage of the hostel bomber had already reminded him about Karza and, to his alarm, Sam realized he hadn't lately been giving his brother much thought. Her words brought him back to earth with a bump.

"Is he still alive?"

"Yes. He was wounded and is being treated. But it's compli-cated."

"You know for sure he's all right?"

"All I know is what I'm telling you."

"How did you find out?"

"They have representatives here."

"Returnees?"

"Since the bombing of the hostel they have to be very careful. Surveillance is being stepped up on them so communication is hard. They are also very angry with Britain."

"Because of the targeting of returnees?"

She shook her head. "Not just that. The rebel army council, which was funnelling help through Turkey, has been disbanded. The supplies promised by the West haven't materialized so they've lost all credibility with their fighters on the ground, who were desperate for ammunition. Those groups like the one your brother was with had no option but to side with the more militant ones. It was that or die. They feel very bitter, very let down. They feel the West has betrayed them."

"But they are looking after him? Karza."

Her look was quite cold. Was it selfish to be so concerned about one man when the whole struggle was at stake?

"They are, now they know who his brother is. They've been told to keep him alive."

What did she mean? He opened his mouth to speak but so many thoughts were crowding in that he couldn't think what to say.

"They want something back."

The conversation seemed to be veering into alien territory. Less than an hour ago they had been mistaken for a couple; now she was becoming more business-like, more distant. He battled to manage the torrent of confused emotions swirling inside him.

"What exactly?"

"Their people here want to meet you."

This was a world he had never had any contact or rapport with. He felt as though he was being pulled along on a conveyor-belt, outside his control. "Why?"

213

"As I said, they know who you are, what you do."

"What difference does that make?"

"They want to deal with you direct. There is only so much I can do, Sahim."

He sensed her exasperation. He felt his face heating with embarrassment. "Of course—how stupid of me. I'm so grateful to you for doing this. How can I ever repay you?"

She allowed him a small smile. "Well, you are giving me a roof over my head."

He felt the warmth come back a little, as if she had just flipped a switch.

"So we are in each other's debt."

He seized the moment to take her hand. She didn't resist, just let it lie there. Should he go further? He didn't get to find out.

"They want to see you tonight."

"But it's—" He looked at his watch: 01:12. "Now? Really?"

"Yes."

She released his hand and got up.

"They will text me when they are near. And you mustn't be alarmed: they will have to take some precautions, for security. I suggest you get some sleep until I need to wake you."

45

Crown Plaza Hotel, Houston

There was a long line outside the reception room. To get in, the guests had to pass through a full security check and give up their phones to meaty, dark-suited guards in shades straight out of *Men in Black*.

Beth steered Tom past the line and straight through, where she broke away and went into full meeting-greeting-laughing mode as she guided people to their seats. Tom scanned the crowd: mostly male, almost uniformly middle-aged and white. A lot of the men had the square-jawed, whitewall haircut look of former military personnel. Others were clones of Stutz—gray men in gray suits. But there was another contingent somewhat less formally dressed, with beards and ponytails, who looked as if they had just ridden in on their bikes from the desert. What kind of big idea would unite these disparate factions?

Stutz clambered onto the stage. "For those of you who don't know me, I'm Aaron Stutz."

There was a ripple of laughter—as if to acknowledge how ridiculous it would be not to know who he was.

"And I want to thank you most sincerely for joining us tonight. You're about to experience an evening to remember. But you don't want to listen to me. Without further ado, let me introduce you to the brains behind this project, the reason you all have come here tonight—Skip Lederer!"

To wild applause and whooping, Skip ambled in, sucking a popsicle. Beth had evidently not persuaded him to change: he was still in the Beavis and Butt-Head T-shirt, his only concession to the occasion a small radio mic. Instead of standing at the autocue, he chose to sit on the edge of the podium, his legs swinging like a toddler's. He didn't bother with an introduction. Instead, he took out the popsicle and examined it, then reached into his jeans pocket and held up a smart phone and an American Express card. "Most folks think these are what freedom is all about." He waved them in the air so everyone could see them.

"Uh-uh. Not so. In fact they're quite the opposite. These babies are the spy in your pocket, channels through which we can discover everything we need to know about an individual: what he buys, where he goes, who he meets, who he screws, what he reads, who his friends are, his enemies—and what they're saying about him. We can find out more about a guy than he knows about himself. Great, huh? So, what's the problem?"

He waited, ostensibly for someone to answer, but really for dramatic effect. They were hanging on his every word.

"The problem, girls and boys, is not the collection of the intelligence, it's what happens to that information. That's the NSA's problem number one. Their other problem, of course, is that they think they're hot shit."

He shook his head. "Know what? In actuality they are *full* of shit."

216

A few of the audience whooped.

"I mean literally. Their server capacity is maxed out. They got so much data on us they don't know what to do with it all. Like, they've built the world's biggest vacuum-cleaner to suck up all the intel, and it's gummin' up the works. They can't process it. It's too freakin' much for them."

He paused briefly to finish the popsicle, then gestured with the stick.

"All that precious intel is mountains of information they don't have the resources to begin to mine. Thar's gold in tham thar hills, but where's the manpower to go panhandling for it? Sure it's fine if you know who you're looking for, which bad guys you're on to. But what happens when you don't know who the hell they are?"

He paused and surveyed the sea of rapt faces. Then he turned to the giant screen behind him and aimed a remote. "I'll tell you what happens. The Boston Marathon happens ... Fort Hood happens ... Times Square happens. No warning. No intelligence."

The faces of the perpetrators of each attack flashed up, followed by the burning Twin Towers.

"Another problem. 9/11. Some of those guys were in the system. They had a few names, but no one joined up the dots."

The screen changed to an image of a huge soccer crowd: faces of all types, all ages, all colors.

"Where's Waldo? Where's the next guy on *no one*'s radar who comes out of *nowhere* and goes bang? Does the NSA know about *him*? The hell it does. Even though he's in their system somewhere."

217

Skip was rewarded with a volley of evangelical *Right ons* and *You said its*. Evidently his appearance and mode of delivery had done nothing to dampen the audience's enthusiasm for his pitch. He shook his head mournfully and jumped up into a standing position.

"Here's the thing. The NSA's retrieval technology is supposed to be state-of-the-art. Their programs have cool names like 'Prism' but they suck. Why? Because their systems can only tell you the *past*, what the bad guys have *done*. And if they haven't done anything bad *yet*? Who's watching out for them? The freaks who blew up the Boston Marathon. Who knew? How long are we in America gonna have to go around looking at the guy next to us on the street, at the bus station, on the subway, wondering what's in his backpack, what's under his vest? Well, let me tell you, the wait is almost over."

The audience were now on their feet, clapping and cheering. What they were hearing made George Orwell look like an optimist, but they were loving it.

"For those of you who are tired of wondering when the next bomb is coming, when the next lone bomber is gonna strike, Oryxis has the solution."

He turned to the screen again and waved the remote. Over the Times Square throng appeared the words *Threat Elimination*.

"Our software is designed not only to mine the information, but to process it *in real time*. Soon, what NSA desk jockeys take a *week* to do, we'll be doing in thirty *seconds*. And we can do a thousand times the *volume*."

He paused while the room erupted with more whoops and applause. They didn't need convincing.

"But here's what else we can do."

The screen flashed with another headline: *Predictive Tracking*.

"What Oryxis can do, with intelligent use of all this data, is model what an individual is going to do *before* he does it. Our algorithms penetrate the data, looking for patterns in behavior that conform to our profiles. We then isolate our POIs, our Persons of Interest. And then we go deep. We go in and get it all. We can know so much about a guy that we know what he's going to do *before he's even thought of doing it*. Welcome to the future. Suck on that, NSA! We are gonna build the digital fortress to keep this country safe."

To thunderous applause he came and sat down beside Tom, who leaned towards him. "Interesting. And what happens to the POI after you've identified and predictively tracked him?"

Skip shrugged. "Hey, I just write the code." He nodded at Stutz. "I leave the outcomes to the grown-ups."

Stutz was on his feet, clapping along, his face turning purple again, but with elation this time. "People, let's hear it for Skip Lederer, the cleverest man in America—hell, the world!"

He smiled indulgently, like a headmaster waiting for his pupils to stop chattering. "Now, I'd like for you to meet our next speaker, a very special guest, who's come all the way from war-torn London to talk about the work of our friends at Invicta. Tom Buckingham has, for the last fourteen years, served his country in their most elite military group, the British Army's Special Air Service, better known as the SAS."

All eyes were now on Tom.

"Please join me in giving him a real down-home Texas welcome. Tom Buckingham!"

As Tom approached the podium to loud cheers, Stutz came forward and gave him a firm photo-opportunity handshake and a big grin. Only there were no cameras tonight, that was for sure. Stutz whispered in his ear, "Give 'em hell, son. Tell it like it is."

Public speaking was a necessary evil, something to be trained for, like suiting up for a gas attack. He knew several in the Regiment who would rather die in a fire-fight than get up in front of an audience but he was ready. He shut his mind to everything but the job he had agreed to do and what he was about to say.

He needn't have worried. They were attentive, leaning forward to listen and laughing in all the right places, as he took them through a few highlights of his life in the SAS. And when he moved on to describing the men he had met on the Invicta campus, whose lives had been turned around by Rolt and his program, there was a reverent hush. From there, he pulled no punches in his description of the hostel bombing. If this was what it took for Rolt to get his money, then why not go for it? If there was one thing that would surely clinch it, it was this.It almost alarmed him how easily it came to him, finding the words that could mesmerize the audience. Was this how the politicians did it? The hate preachers? And all the time in another part of his brain he was asking himself what any of this had to do with Invicta. The questions were piling up. And as his eyes drifted from face to face he caught sight of a figure at the back of the room, leaning against a pillar: just the man who might have some of the answers.

46

"Hey, partner." Kyle Pope eased himself away from the pillar and stepped forward. "Of all the gin joints in all the towns . . ."

"Who does that make me, Ingrid Bergman? And, by the way, you're no Bogart."

"Didn't think you'd recognize me."

Tom punched his shoulder and was enveloped in a big man-hug. "I'd smell you a mile off."

Even with the mirror Aviators and the chin-muffler beard, there was no disguising Kyle Pope. Six foot four in his bare feet, he had towered over his adversaries in Iraq. Yet his black eyes and olive complexion, from Tartar stock somewhere on his mother's side, gave him a look of the universal citizen, and an almost legendary capacity to blend in. When you were in a minivan stuck in the middle of a traffic jam in Baghdad, he was the one you wanted to keep close to. The man led a charmed life, a major reason Tom was still alive.

"Nine years—Jeez, where did they go?"

The joint SAS-Delta Force assault had been on a compound in Ramadi, about a hundred klicks west of Baghdad. Local resistance was anticipated, so Delta operators in tracked and tur-reted Bradleys had mounted over-watch. The intelligence had told them the house was occupied by a large extended family so casualties had to be minimized. House clearing was second nature in the Regiment. Tom had practiced this sort of drill *ad nauseam* with live-fire exercises in the Killing House back at Stirling Lines. The trick was to be confident enough to fire without hesitation, yet spare the innocent. Flimsy, rusted metal gates protected the entrance. But before they were through they were met with a hail of fire from the upstairs windows and he was hit in the thigh.

The wound itself wasn't life-threatening, but he was pinned under one of the gates and part of the wall that had exploded with an RPG fired from the house. Trapped, without help, he could have bled out. They couldn't call in the Bradleys as he knew that others firing from neighboring buildings couldn't see him. In a brief lull, Kyle had run forward, but as he bore down on Tom another volley of AK opened up. Kyle wheeled round and sprayed the windows, while hauling Tom out of their arcs to safety. It had been the first day of the rest of his life.

"Good to see a friendly face out there tonight."

They moved a couple of steps away from the crowd.

"Yeah, these dudes ain't exactly top of my list of drinking buddies. They lapped up your spiel, though. You sure hit the high notes."

A couple of well-wishers headed towards Tom but backed off when they saw Kyle.

Tom noted the Glock holstered on his friend's hip. "Who are you expecting?"

"Comes with the territory. I help Mr. Stutz with his security."

"That a full-time job?"

"Twenty-four seven." Kyle nodded at the men in black, chests straining at their suit jackets. "Yep, that's my team."

"How're the kids?"

Tom remembered he had twin boys and a baby girl.

"Good, I guess." Something in his tone indicated that that was as far as he wanted to go on that subject.

"How about we get some beers? Take a break from all this flag-waving."

Tom looked round and saw Stutz deep in conversation, Skip fiddling with his phone and Beth smiling relentlessly. Maybe he should have been working the crowd, flying the flag for Invicta, but getting an inside track on Stutz's operation from an old buddy was too good an opportunity to pass up. Kyle gripped his arm.

"C'mon. Those guys seem to have it covered."

Tom saw him catch Stutz's eye. Stutz looked up from the group he was talking to and nodded. Tom grinned. "Okay, partner, let's ride!"

47

Tom did a swift change into jeans, T-shirt and bomber jacket. On his way out he waved at Beth and, for the first time since he had set eyes on her, thought he saw the smile fade. Was that wistfulness he detected? Maybe she had been hoping babysitting him would be a respite from Skip. Maybe she had been thinking more than that. Yeah, and maybe he was kidding himself.

The hot night air was full of the sound of cicadas and the aroma of barbecuing meat laced with traffic fumes.

"Ah, the sweet smell of Texas."

Parked on the hotel forecourt was Kyle's Harley, a classic early sixties Panhead but straight, no ridiculous *Easy Rider* forks or crazy chrome. A workmanlike machine.

"Still tearing up the Badlands?"

"You wanna take it? I gotta bring the van anyhows. No helmet needed here. You get to feel the wind in your hair."

Tom zipped his jacket and climbed aboard. He kicked it over and the pushrod twin exploded into life. He hauled it off the stand and eased out behind Kyle's Chevy van. The height of the gas tank raised the center of gravity, which was only somewhat counteracted by the low seat. The riding position, feet forward, made for a distinctly laid-back driving style, which was fine since the machine was in no hurry to climb up the revs. After the BMW he was used to, it was monstrously heavy. But there were upsides to the design, which had barely changed in more than a century. This was a bike on which you could cruise all day across America.

After ten minutes the city fell away and they were in open country. Kyle veered off the freeway onto increasingly smaller and rougher back roads where the Harley came into its own, soaking up the rough surface and floating through ruts, like the dirt roads it had originally been built to conquer. It was a mean, slug of a machine, which would only grow old grudgingly, like its owner.

At the end of a long wooded track stood a weathered-looking ranch-style house. There were several other vehicles pulled up in front: a pick-up with a gun rack, a dusty Chrysler 300C with a bullet-hole in the wind-screen, and a van with tinted windows that said *Bob's Pool Maintenance* on the side. Tom didn't know if there was a Bob. But he was pretty sure that pool-maintenance vans didn't need tinted windows.

Kyle was waiting, a six-pack of Southern Star dangling from each hand as Tom pulled the Harley to a halt beside him. "As time passes, the more I find love in inanimate objects. Less complicated." Tom killed the engine. "They also find me more reliable."

Tom heaved the bike onto its stand and stared into the darkness. In the yard he could see the ghostly shapes of a swing, a slide and a large wooden climbing-frame; the weeds around them suggested they hadn't seen too much action lately.

From inside the house came the sound of an American soccer game, a crowd roaring and a hysterical commentator.

"Some of the boys are home. Come and say hi." Kyle waved him in.

Three large men were lounging round a huge TV, surrounded by cans and Chinese take-out cartons. There was a strong smell of cannabis.

225

"Y'all meet Tom Buckingham, recently liberated from Her Majesty's very own SAS."

The men favored the same fashions as Kyle: big beards and shades, fatigues and sleeveless denim over wife-beaters. They each raised a hand at Tom through the fug and returned to the game.

"Come on back out into the fresh air." At one end of a wrap-around porch were a dog's basket and two old Adirondack wooden chairs with wide armrests. Kyle indicated the chairs and tossed Tom a can as they sat down. He followed Tom's gaze beyond the cars to the play area. "Gabrielle and the kids been gone a few years now. Some of the boys' situations were similar to mine, so I invited them to move in. And we get along just fine."

He popped his can and drank deeply. There was a big empty silence but as soon as Tom drew breath to ask a question Kyle continued. "I got this place because it was safe and out of the way, thinking it was my job in life to protect them. I didn't know back then that what they needed protectin' from was *me*. Ain't that ironic."

It was not a question.

"Do you see them at all?"

"I don't get to go near. I hear stuff about how they're doing and that's about it. Gabrielle doesn't want me around them and the sheriff knows that too."

Tom decided not to ask why.

"Eleven tours, six in Iraq, five in Afghanistan, and I didn't have a scratch, not one. I thought I was fuckin' immortal. Guys dug operations with me because they figured I'd bring them good luck. But I knew my number was gonna be up sooner or later. So did

Gabrielle. She persuaded me to quit. She said, 'You've served your country. Now come home and look after your family.'"

He gazed dispassionately at Tom. "Guess you've got the same problem coming at you. Only you're lucky you don't have a family to fuck up. Some shit-for-brains shrink asked me how I fill the void. I told him them being gone wasn't the void."

His eyes looked tired from staring into the sun too long.

"The fuckin' void I got to fill is not having a war."

He took a long pull on his can.

Tom shifted in his seat. He'd known too many evenings like this descend into booze-fuelled self-loathing and recriminations. He needed to move the conversation away from domestic matters; he wanted Kyle's perspective on Oryxis before he got too drunk to be useful. "Tell me about Lederer and Stutz."

"You seen *The Truman Show*, right? Lederer's Truman."

"And Beth's in the Laura Linney part?"

He laughed uproariously. "Ain't she somethin'? What she puts up with from that kid, watching his damned videos of her with his hand in his shorts . . ." He leaned across and lowered his voice.

"Know what? She's actually Stutz's girl. Took me a while to figure that one out."

"Doesn't he mind?"

Kyle shook his head. "He's a busy guy. Ain't got no time for stuff like that. If Beth's what it takes to keep Skip amused and on the job all day, then all well and good. How *she* stands it . . ."

"And what keeps Stutz busy?"

Kyle looked at him. "Who's asking?"

For a second Tom thought he had zoned out. Far from it. He fixed him with an unexpectedly cold stare, as if reassessing him.

"What I'm saying is—is that Tom Buckingham, ex-SAS sergeant, or Tom Buckingham, associate of Invicta?"

"What's the difference?"

Kyle just gave him a look.

"Well, is Stutz a good guy?"

"He threw me a lifeline."

"How come?"

"After Gabrielle left it was a bad time. I didn't do too well on my own, and I craved excitement. I got into some arms trading, working cartels across the border: AR-15s, AKs, FN semiautomatics, M4s, M203 grenade launchers. I made a lot of money. But I knew that sooner or later the ATF were gonna catch up with me—it was just a matter of time. Stutz got me out of it."

"How did he do that?"

"He has his connections."

"And in return?"

Kyle laughed to himself. "He says I was his inspiration."

"Meaning?"

"Me and my kind. Our kind. Who did what we did but don't like the outcome. Who trained and fought to protect this country, to secure our borders, to remove the threat. No one's facing up to the fact that we failed. They sent us off to fight unwinnable wars. All the guys who were in Fallujah, the ones who got out. Now they see Al Qaeda back in town like it's '04 all over again. All that blood spilled—and for what? They're mad as hell and they want something back for their sacrifice. Stutz wants to channel that anger, put it behind some proper action to protect the country. And know what? It goes all the way up the food chain. You saw the crowd tonight. Pentagon people, private operators, all players who want a better outcome."

He reached across and gripped Tom's shoulder, just as Stutz had done. "See? You're far from alone, man. Help is at hand."

Tom didn't feel that he was in need of any help, but he went along with it. Kyle was on a roll: no point in distracting him.

"In 2005, more people from Islamic countries became US residents than in any previous year: ninety-six thousand. 2009, the figure's up to a hundred fifteen. We got a time bomb ticking." He crushed the can and helped himself to another.

Tom made sure he was drinking only half as fast. "How does Stutz plan to achieve his 'outcome'?"

"You saw Skip's presentation. Stutz wants to deploy it to weed out the bad apples. That's where he's focused. Forget Afghanistan, forget Iraq, Syria. Protecting the *homeland* from what's coming down the pipe. That's what he's all about."

"How's that going to work?"

"First you gotta convince people it's worth believing in. Maybe scare them some. Show 'em why it's gotta happen. And let me tell you another thing. Stutz has the network, the manpower. You want in?"

Tom tried to look thoughtful while he came up with an appropriate answer. Rolt had won some of his sympathy. But nothing he had seen of Stutz and Lederer made him want to get any closer to them.

Kyle was staring at him as if waiting for an answer. "You been fucked over. You wanna chance to fuck them back?"

"You're still not telling me what it involves."

"It ain't that simple. To get to that level, we need an indication."

229

Was this what Rolt had meant by "jumping through a few hoops"? He hadn't counted on this.

"What sort of 'indication'?"

"You made a good impression on Stutz, I'll tell ya. He likes guys like us. Gets off on the whole Special Forces thing. And you can talk the talk, all right. But if Invicta wants his dollars it's gonna take more than a few fancy words and a coupla handshakes." His eyes were sparkling with intrigue.

"He needs to know how far he can trust you, how far you're prepared to go."

"How's that going to happen?"

Kyle grinned and poked himself in the chest. "I give him the word. But I gotta know where you stand first."

Was this all bullshit—the self-important ramblings of a former elite soldier gone down in the world?

Kyle's phone buzzed in his pocket. "I gotta take this." He got to his feet and moved a few yards away, glancing back as he spoke.

Tom processed what he had heard with a mixture of curiosity and distaste. Kyle was smart, he had trusted him, and he was utterly fearless: Kyle had risked his life to save him. What had changed? He was bitter and angry with the world and he had good reason to be. Was this what Tom could look forward to—now he was out of the Regiment? Was Kyle just further round the curve? Perhaps this encounter was going to prove a valuable wake-up call. But right now there was a choice to be made. He was sounding as if he was about to set Tom some kind of challenge.

Suppose Woolf was right, that there was a more sinister element to Invicta and Rolt. Could that element be Stutz? For better or worse, Tom had got himself this far under the wire. He was being given a chance to go deeper. In the interests of getting to that next level, of penetrating Stutz's operation, of finding out more about their plans, it had to be worth it.

Kyle finished his call.

Tom stood up and grinned. "Okay." He held out his hands. "I'm in."

48

Victoria, London

How could he sleep? The adrenalin that had been coursing round him seemed to intensify until he thought he might have a stroke. Then she was shaking him awake.

"They are ready for you. Turn left out of the front door and go to the corner. You will see a black people-carrier."

"Is there a name?"

"They'll make themselves known to you. Go."

He pulled on his jacket and shoes. He hadn't undressed.

She followed him to the door and closed it behind him.

Close to the junction the people-carrier, an old Toyota Previa, was parked with no lights on. As he came towards it the side door slid open. "Sahim?"

"Yes."

He couldn't see who was speaking. The voice came from deep inside the vehicle.

"Come to the door." A small sharp beam of light was pointed at his face. "Get in."

He hesitated.

"Now, please."

The engine started. He climbed in. It was very warm inside. There were four of them. He saw a phone, its screen glowing with an image. They thrust it in front of him.

"Watch."

It was a video of a man lying on a mattress. Whoever was recording him moved closer and pulled back the sheet covering him. The figure on the bed shrank away as if he was about to be hit.

Something was shouted that Sam didn't understand. A hand grabbed the man's head and turned it to face the camera.

"Is that him?"

For a second he wasn't sure. The eyes were completely blood-shot. The face had several weeks' growth of beard and was shrunken and emaciated, but when the camera was pointed at him the eyes lit up. He whispered, "Help me, brother."

A wave of shock and relief came over him. "That's him."

He felt something sting his arm, then everything went black.

Sometime later, he had no idea how many hours had passed, he came to. His head was resting against the glass. He could see road rushing by. Three lanes. A highway. He tried to lift his head to see who else was in the vehicle but he couldn't move. Then he felt a pain in his upper arm and was out again.

When he woke the next time his hands were tied and some fabric covered his face. A voice he hadn't heard before addressed him. "Sahim?"

This was a new voice, older, with a strong accent he couldn't place.

"What's happening?"

"Sahim Kovacevic, confirm your name."

"Yes, that's me. But I need the bathroom."

He was led through a couple of doors, his jeans were undone and pulled down and he was manoeuvred onto a lavatory seat. There was a strong smell of oil and he heard an engine being revved. Maybe they were in a garage. He was led back and put on a hard chair.

"Can I have a drink?"

There was some mumbling, then steps, then a door being closed. The hood was lifted just enough to uncover his mouth. Sam could see part of a face: a man in his early twenties, Asian, with a small scrub of beard round the outline of his chin, holding a can of Coke to Sam's mouth. He smelt of tobacco and garlic. Sam drank, the Coke running down his chin. The hood came back down.

The older voice spoke again. "You are the brother of Karza, that is right?"

"What's happened to him?"

"He is injured. You will pay for his release or he will be killed."

"Who has him?"

"One million dollars."

"*What?*"

This couldn't be happening.

"I don't have anything like that. I'm just an ordinary person."

"You are in the government."

"I'm just a spokesman."

"Then he won't survive."

"But this is madness! He had no idea, he went to help. He was just an innocent—"

The older man cut him off. "What are you?"

"What do you mean?"

"What are you?"

"I'm a British citizen."

"That's what your passport says. When you walk down your street at night, is that what you think? That you are one of them?"

"I've never thought of myself as particularly different."

"You've never *thought* at all. Have you?"

"This country hasn't done anything bad to me."

This was not the right thing to say.

"This country and its allies, its coalition of infidels, is killing your brothers. When you turn on the television and you see the dead and dying Muslims, mutilated by bombs and bullets, do you not see your brothers?"

Sam was starting to sweat under the hood. He could hear the older man's anger rising.

"Do you understand anything about what is happening in Syria?"

Sam shook his head. This wasn't a time to bluff. "Only minimally."

"Since you are a servant of this government, you should inform yourself so you better understand what your masters are capable of."

He was tired, frightened and now angry. Two days ago he'd been assaulted by Dink for his race; now this. What had he ever done to deserve it?

"Okay. Inform me, then."

"You know who encouraged us to go to Syria at the beginning?"

Sam shook his head. He could feel a lecture coming his way.

"The British government. They sponsored us to go and help the resistance. Go and be heroes, liberate Syria from the dictatorship. So we went to help our brothers. Young Muslims from Britain, many without jobs, without respect, feeling isolated by the licentiousness and decadence that surrounds them, spat on, shunned because they were obedient to God, because they prayed and didn't drink. A chance to do something worthwhile, to attain some worth in the service of Allah, praise be upon him.

"So we jumped at the chance. We trained, we prepared, and we saw for ourselves the suffering. But where were the arms we were promised, where were the bullets? They didn't come. So we rationed the bullets, we shared the weapons. We had to steal to eat, to get fuel. We, who had come to be liberators, were stealing from the people we had come to liberate. Imagine, if you can, the shame, the betrayal.

"The men your brother was with, they are surviving on almost nothing. The West has deceived them, and they are trapped. Every day there is a choice. Do we buy bullets or food? They can't even come back now. Because the government that encouraged them to go now looks on them as criminals. So they have no choice but to side with the Islamists who have bullets *and* food."

Where was this going? Sam's neck and back ached. The man leaned forward suddenly and he felt his breath through the hood.

"Find the money. You have a week."

He was pulled onto his feet, frogmarched back to the van and sedated again.

236

When he came to he was lying on a bench, with traffic whizzing past a few feet away. He looked round. Cockfosters tube station was just up the road. He got to his feet and stumbled towards the entrance.

49

Sam sat on the tube, watching the commuters nodding to the music in their earbuds, eyes glued to iPads, Kindles and tabloids: "My Serial Sex Cheat Shame" and below it "TIME TO STOP THE TERROR". The whole front page of the *Sun* was devoted to a statement by someone—perhaps the paper itself. "The government must bring itself to think the unthinkable . . . The time has come to stop the talk and take action . . . The enemy within . . . Time to face the facts. Where all the terror is coming from and what we need to do to stop it. Stop it now."

The words swam in front of his eyes. All he could see was the film they had shown him of Karza. *Help me, brother.* Before, he had been quick to dismiss him and his absurd delusions of being a warrior. Now, for the first time he could remember, he began to think of him differently. In the past, he had never had any reason to admire him. Now he saw that each of them in their own very different ways had gone searching for meaning, for validation, to do something that made a difference. And here he was and there Karza was.

He thought about throwing himself on the mercy of Pippa. She had been very understanding. They would want to avoid a scandal. And they had rich donors. Or just go to the Foreign Office. No! How could he be so naïve? He thought of his mother seeing the footage he had been shown, the last sight of her son alive, pleading for her other son to help him. He would have to do something . . . but what?

He became aware of the other passengers looking at him. A girl reading a Kindle seemed to be frowning. An elderly red-faced man was also looking askance at him, as if Sam himself was the enemy. Was this tolerant country, which had welcomed him with open arms, now turning against him?

50

When he got back to the flat the door of the big bedroom was shut. He went into the bathroom and cleaned himself up, then made himself a coffee. In an hour he had to be at Party Headquarters for a briefing with Vernon Rolt, the man from the organization called Invicta which had been bombed. But he couldn't think about anything other than Karza and the dreadful situation they both now found themselves in. His head throbbed painfully. He had only wanted to help. Now catastrophe was just around the corner and there was nothing he could do to prevent it.

He was sitting on a stool at the breakfast bar in the kitchen, staring into his mug, when the bedroom door opened and Nasima appeared in a pant suit and hijab. He turned away. Tears were rolling down his cheeks and converging under his chin. His nose was running. He didn't want her to see that, to see his helplessness. But she came up close, put a hand on his shoulder and pulled him towards her. His tearstained face pressed against her chest for several comforting seconds until she gently moved him away.

She listened in silence while he told her what had happened. He didn't know who they were or where they had taken him but there was no question about the video. After this she was quiet for some time. He felt himself sinking back to the frame of mind he had been in during his visit to his mother. He should never have agreed to try and help Karza. And judging by the blankness of Nasima's gaze, he could not expect any sympathy from her.

"Maybe I should go to the Foreign Office."

Her face was like thunder. "Are you crazy? This group is classed as a terrorist organization—both here and in America. And your position with the Party would be compromised."

She looked away, as if what she was about to say pained her deeply. Then she nodded thoughtfully. "It's a lot. And it's non-negotiable. Now they know someone's looking for him, they will at least keep him alive. But because they don't have any support from the West, they have to ration their medical supplies. Don't imagine they will look after him indefinitely. So we have to do something fast."

Sam pushed the cup away. He felt sick. The thought of his brother, and then his mother, shook him to the core.

"Plus the cost of transport. Depending on his condition we might have to airlift him back, which could add another half-million."

She waited while Sam digested this, her eyes trained on his face. He felt stupid. It hadn't occurred to him that any kind of payment would be demanded, let alone a ransom. He hadn't given it any thought.

"What do you think you want to do, Sam?"

This time her whole attitude was different. None of the flirting that he was sure he had detected last time. She was direct, business-like.

"I don't know where I could get that kind of money."

The thought came back into his head that he could ask his new employers, after all—or maybe one of their funders. No, no, that was too naïve, and what would they think of him if they knew about Karza? He wasn't about to jeopardize his new status with the revelation that his brother was a jihadi. He felt desperation pressing down on him.

"I have to find a way. I don't have any choice."

It had just the right effect. Her face softened. She took his hands. "I know how hard it is when there's only one option, believe me. A brother is a brother."

It was the nice Nasima again, the sympathetic friend who might one day be something more.

"You should go. You mustn't miss your meeting." She wrapped him in her arms, then held his face apart from her and kissed his forehead. "There may be something, some other way of doing this. I have some contacts, sympathetic people who may give us advice. Go on, go. Whatever happens, you mustn't let this get in the way of your job."

51

Texas

Tom drove because he had had less to drink. After eighteen hours awake he was relying on the adrenalin to deal with any fatigue.

"They're real bad, that's for sure."

"How bad?"

"Remember Timothy McVeigh, the Oklahoma bomber? That bad. One part Nazi, one part Survivalist, three parts fuck-brain. Their target's a building downtown."

"What is it?"

"It belongs to some associate of Stutz's."

"Who?"

Kyle shrugged. "That's not for us to know. We just do the job. We don't get the whole scoop. But we have all their moves from Skip's surveillance. They're all ex-National Guard and crazy gun freaks. Jefferson's the leader, supposedly, but he ain't too bright. We'll be paying him a visit at his trailer. He's OTH—other than honorable discharge from the Marines. He didn't make the grade. He's a loner, no personal life, spends a lot of time honing his shooting skills. And he's the designated asset of a local chapter of neo-Nazis. He's got no idea we're coming."

From the back of the van, he produced a Glock 9mm with a titanium suppressor and an extended twenty-round magazine.

At a set of traffic lights, Tom racked back the top slide to check the chamber and make sure it was empty. He wouldn't ask if the rounds in the mag were subsonic. If they weren't, the suppressor was useless—but of course they would be. He had just got the weapon from Kyle.

"Keep it, at least while you're with us. It'll help you sleep nice and peaceful too."

He directed them on to the Loop going east, then north on the 45 towards Conroe. Tom needed to find out how prepared he was, without appearing to question his judgement. He kept his eyes on the road.

"You reconned the place?"

"Yep. It's pretty secluded, next to the lake. There's a few other trailers, trees and scrub, plenty of cover. Easy."

Tom could see Kyle was nervy, pumped. Had he thought this through? "You want to be a little more specific?"

"I'm saying relax, the set-up's fine. Jefferson's routine's pretty standard. This time of day he'll have had a few beers and some weed so he'll be nice and mellow. He doesn't have any reason to believe he's under threat so shouldn't be thinking he's expecting anyone."

"How often does this sort of job come up?"

"When it does."

Kyle's answers were getting more cryptic. This had better be worth it.

Twenty minutes later they were bouncing down a pot-holed road. Lights from a few single story homes set back in the trees provided the only illumination. While Tom drove, Kyle was bent over an iPad, studying the latest feeds from Lederer's surveillance.

"Nothing to suggest he's with anyone. He's busy with his phone and laptop. No other signals coming out of that location."

"Any dogs?"

Kyle shook his head. "Don't need none. He's handy with his weapons and this is Texas."

As soon as the trailers came into view Tom slowed to walking pace. They were spaced quite far apart, some with chain-link fences around them, cars and vans parked nearby. Music and TV sounds spilled out of them and merged together.

"Which one?"

Kyle pointed. It was painted yellow, an awning on one side under which was parked an ancient pick-up. The fence around it was higher than the others and the gate was shut but not, they hoped, locked. The blinds were down and the door was closed.

"We'll go on foot from here."

Tom turned the van so it was facing the way out. They agreed that since they couldn't get eyes on Jefferson inside the trailer they would have to lure him out: Kyle up front, Tom covering from the other side of the fence.

Tom rammed the mag into the pistol grip until he heard it clip home, and racked the top slide, letting it return under its own power: it would pick up the top round from the mag and ram it into the chamber. To make sure, he pulled back gently on the top slide until he could see the brass case in the ejection opening. The last thing anyone wanted to hear was the dead man's click when firing. "I'll take a shot at the wing mirror on the pick-up: that should generate enough of the right kind of sound to bring him out. You hang in that shadow to the left of the door. It's the hinge side so you should see him before he sees you."

245

Kyle nodded. "We don't have to worry about being interrupted. Neighborhood like this, they hear a gunshot, last thing they're gonna do is call the cops. They keep their heads down."

They moved together up to the gate. Tom lifted it silently and moved it enough for Kyle to get through. Tom skirted the fence so he had a clear shot at the pickup and the trailer door from a shadow under one of the trees. When Kyle was in position, he signaled.

Tom aimed at the mirror and fired. A dull *phut* from the suppressor was followed by a tinkle of splintering glass.

A light came on inside the trailer, then went off. Thirty seconds passed.

Tom felt his pulse move up a gear. He had the Glock in his hand, with a nasty feeling that that was just where he was going to need it. Then Kyle took a step towards the door just as it burst open, slamming back against the trailer's side. But the doorway was a black void. Jefferson must have been hovering a few feet inside, in shadow. Kyle stepped away from the trailer so he had a better angle but, in doing so, showed himself to Jefferson. Any element of surprise was gone.

The shot came from inside the trailer. Kyle's legs buckled under him, but he still had his Glock raised and fired wide. Now Jefferson appeared in the doorway. Tom aimed center mass of the dark doorway and rapid-fired until the door slammed. It was pointless putting subsonic rounds into the trailer hoping to hit the target; it'd just waste ammo. Tom sprinted over to Kyle, who waved him away.

"Deal with him first. Get over there and get it done."

Tom ignored him and started tearing at his T-shirt to get a look at the wound but Kyle pushed him away. "Finish it."

The choice was made for him. The trailer door opened again: a shotgun muzzle pointed straight at Tom. He fired again and the weapon fell limp before hitting the metal steps up to the doorway. He ran forward and wrenched the door open, then lunged at Jefferson, who was struggling to pull himself up.

"Back in there—*now!*"

Tom thrust the muzzle of the suppressor into Jefferson's neck, grabbed him by the belt and dragged him deeper into the trailer. Jefferson lashed out with a foot. Tom managed to keep his balance and smashed down on his face with his boot.

Jefferson started to roar. Tom bore down on him, ramming the Glock's fat suppressor into his mouth. He kept his voice low. He didn't want Kyle hearing this. "Any noise and you're gone, okay? You will die."

Jefferson got the message and calmed down, his breathing heavy and noisy as he tried to exhale through his nose now that his mouth was blocked.

Tom reached up and hit a lamp switch that dangled from the unit above them. He quickly took in the features and general state of the place: a small hob with a filthy pan on it, a screened-off bathroom and shower and an unmade sofa-bed, with a half-smoked joint in a saucer on the pillow. Hanging on one wall was a Confederate flag—nothing unusual about that in this part of the world but, above it, a poster of a swastika left no doubt as to his political affiliations.

The man below him was mid-thirties, shaved head, steroidal frame.

Tom stared down into his eyes. "You want to live?"

Jefferson nodded and the weapon slowly moved with his head.

"Right. The other guy was here to kill you. I'm not. You get that? I'm going to deal with that wound, and you're gonna tell me *why* he was here to kill you. Answering will save your life. Understand?"

He took the Glock out of his mouth and pressed it against his head.

"I got no fuckin' idea, man."

"Don't fucking waste my time. Who's your enemy? Who's your target?"

Jefferson still looked blank, but he wasn't about to give it up.

"Give me a name."

He stared back into Tom's eyes, cold and clear. Okay, thought Tom, have it your way. He took a step back so as not to get blood spattered over him, raised his weapon and took aim.

"Zuabi."

"Zuabi? What's that?"

"*Mullah* Zuabi."

"Where?"

"The fucking mosque. You—"

"What mosque? Where?"

"You fucking white traitors . . . brainwashed . . . destroying our— "

Jefferson lashed out with his good hand, only this time there was a knife in it. In the semi-darkness of the unlit interior, Tom had missed it. He sprang back but there was nowhere to go, and he smashed into a closet, breaking off the door—just as the blade sliced through the arm of his jacket. Every instinct said, *Fire,* but he resisted. He had come this far, he had to get more out of him. He wasn't done.

He smashed the knife hand with the Glock repeatedly until the weapon fell to the floor.

But in a mammoth display of brute strength Jefferson reared up and lunged. Tom slipped in the pool of blood growing on the floor and lost his balance, his head slamming back onto the wall cabinets in the cramped kitchen area. He felt himself sinking, the Glock slipping from his grip as Jefferson prised it away and turned it on him.

But he didn't fire. The muzzle shook wildly and Jefferson started to convulse, his tongue thrust out in a bloody mass as his teeth chewed into it, his eyes wide, swivelling uncontrollably as if loose in their sockets. The Glock dropped to the floor and Jefferson's whole body flexed in a mad, manic dance until he crumpled in a heap.

Tom struggled up and started to get his breath back. As he reached for the Glock he saw he wasn't alone.

"Easy now."

Kyle was at the door, his weapon pointed straight at him.

52

Kyle had overheard Tom's exchange with Jefferson. "Like I told you, we just do the job. We don't ask why. That's not part of the brief."

There was an empty look in his eyes.

Tom struggled to move. "For fuck's sake, Kyle. What is this shit?"

"Too many questions."

"Just listen a moment. Let's calm down, shall we, and talk this through?"

But Tom could tell that wasn't going to happen. He dived out of Kyle's line of sight just as he fired.

The shot slammed into the cabinet door he had just been leaning against, narrowly missing his shoulder. A cloud of wood chippings erupted and scattered over Jefferson's body. No more negotiation. Tom's reflexes took over and his shot burst a hole in Kyle's forehead as he collapsed in a heap in the doorway.

Tom didn't move for several seconds, struggling to absorb what had just happened. He had killed a man who had once saved his life. But he had been left with no choice. Whatever Kyle had signed up for, it didn't take account of friendship. The only other sound apart from his heaving chest was the chorus of cicadas outside. He reached forward, and pulled Kyle's corpse further into the trailer.

Mullah Zuabi—who the fuck was he? How did he fit into Oryxis's agenda? Too many questions were mounting up.

Tom knew he needed to get the hell out of there before anyone came looking, but the opportunity to search the place for more information about what Jefferson was up to was too good to pass up. He reached over Kyle and closed the door. Then he pulled him over to the seating area and folded him as best he could under the table. He wouldn't be entirely hidden but was at least less obvious if someone were to peer in. Then he pulled up the blinds to let a little more light in. He ducked while a pick-up rolled past, blaring Johnny Cash, a couple of dogs perched on the deck, then began his search.

He didn't have much time. Eventually someone would notice that Kyle hadn't shown up, and as for Jefferson, even neo-Nazis looked out for their own. Luckily, since he was definitely a minimalist in the furnishings department, there were very few places to look. On the table was a yellow legal notebook. He flipped it open and read the large, childlike handwriting.

Today, according to the latest U.S. Census—only 23% of the American population under the age of 18 is WHITE. Already, four U.S. states are MAJORITY NON-WHITE, and 10% of all counties in America are MAJORITY NON-WHITE. World-wide, white women of child-bearing age comprise only 3% of the earth's population. Do these FACTS disturb you . . .?

It was disturbing all right. But he put it down when he spotted a rectangular shape under the thin bedcovers: a laptop. He carefully lifted the lid and stroked the trackpad: it came to life. Nolene's

Escorts. *Proudly serving Houston surroundings, available 24/7. A girl for every taste. What's yours? Call now to meet one of our fifty luscious babes.* So far, so normal. There was an AOL email account, one of the last in existence, but it needed a password. He clicked on the Search History. The last twenty or so pages were more of Nolene and her luscious babes, then some local news pages: *UH tops Florida on Senior Night.* Evidently his racial obsessions didn't get in the way of his interest in basketball. Then *Teen leads cops on high speed chase . . . Arms seized in South Houston drug bust . . . Grand Mosque nears completion.* He opened it: a front page from the *Houston Chronicle—Houston's largest mosque nears completion.* The photo: a group of men in suits and hard hats, posing in front of a tower of scaffolding, with a much shorter, smiling bearded man, olive complexion, in a white *topi* and white robes. The caption: *City councilors get sneak peek at Houston's newest Islamic Center Masjid As-Sabur, hosted by Mullah Asim Zuabi.*

Asim Zuabi—this guy was Stutz's "associate", whose would-be assassin he had sent them to kill?

From down the road not far away came the sound of sirens. Blue and red lights flickered in the distance. Tom closed the laptop and turned his attention to Jefferson. He took a photograph of the corpse, then patted down the pockets. Then he relieved him of his phone, pulled the blinds down, closed the door behind him and stepped out into the night.

53

Whitehall, London

Cabinet secretary Alec Clements was in the chair. "Thank you all for making the time to be here. The PM sends his sincerest apologies but, as I'm sure you can imagine, he is rather busy just now. I will relay to him whatever comes out of our discussion. In any case this is a good opportunity for those of us who don't know him to get to know Vernon Rolt."

He indicated Rolt, who smiled and raised a hand. Clements went on, "There is no formal agenda, hence the mix of attendees. May I remind all those here that this is a background briefing? Chatham House rules: nothing said here leaves these four walls."

Sarah Garvey scrolled through the emails on her BlackBerry. They were the same messages she'd read twenty minutes ago, but she felt the need to concentrate on something else while Clements was speaking. She was by far the most senior politician present— the others were all comparatively low level—yet she had been added to the list at the last minute. Was this some kind of slight, to get back at her for her robust chairing of the COBRA meetings? Whatever was behind it, she smelt a rat.

Clements referred once again to his star guest and this time put on his grave face. "I'm sure I speak for everyone present when I say how profoundly shocked we all were by the atrocity at the hostel. And may I add my personal compliments to you, Vernon, for the restraint and moderation with which you have chosen to respond. An example to us all," he added, with a glance at Garvey, whose short temper and fondness for rapid-fire expletives were notorious in Whitehall.

She focused on Rolt. She found it disturbing that opinions which would have been considered toxic a matter of months ago were rapidly gaining credibility. Before, just being in a room with someone holding his views would have been political suicide, yet now his presence was regarded as a lifeline, politicians virtually queuing up for a photo-opportunity.

He was very seductive, no question. Partly it was his looks. He was timelessly handsome. With his thick, short dark hair and clear blue eyes, he could have been a film star: Sean Connery in his Bond days. Also his composure, the apparent lack of outrage combined with the quiet passion, were all great attributes, all the more so when he was seated beside Clements, whose oily manner and imperiousness were so repellent to her. She suspected *his* sexual proclivities did not even involve other humans.

Clements was still talking, ranging over the events of the past few weeks, firing out statistics of casualties, damage. He was in his element, presiding over his favorite kind of situation, semi-covert, with the promise of confidentiality for all, so he could soak up whatever thoughts people were having and pass them back to the PM. She was alarmed at the extent to which he'd had the top man's ear since he'd returned from Washington. And she was not a little piqued at how her own role seemed to have been subtly down-graded.

Privately the PM had been full of praise for her handling of the unrest, but publicly he talked as if he had been in complete charge—even while he was poncing about at Camp David. But what could she expect? With an election coming, if he didn't look strong and decisive he could take them all down with him.

Early that morning she had called Mandler, MI5's director general, to tell him about the Rolt meeting.

"We're still watching him, but I'd be lying if I said we had anything concrete."

She was grateful for his honesty, something that seemed to be in increasingly short supply. "I thought you were putting someone inside his camp."

He sighed. "Well, that's proved more difficult than we expected. Our man didn't exactly take the bait. And now I've just heard he's buggered off to America. Woolf made a total dog's breakfast of trying to recruit him. It seems they all underestimated him. On the other hand, his attitude makes him perfect for the job, since there's no way Rolt would suspect him. I think we just have to play a slightly longer game."

"There isn't time for a longer game. Rolt's becoming a power to be reckoned with. It's time you started joining up some dots, Stephen."

She could hear the strain in his voice. She knew that sceptics in the Service were arguing—with some justification—that they were on a fishing expedition where Rolt was concerned. She had some sympathy for Mandler, being pulled as he was in different directions, but she could see the fight going out of him and it wasn't an edifying sight.

"This wretched hysteria about returnees isn't helping. Pulling people off the streets with virtually nothing to go on, other than that they spent a bit of time in Syria, is just inflaming an already combustible situation. There aren't the resources for much else."

"Well, give it another week," she had told him, "but don't let Rolt go off your radar. I don't have a good feeling about him."

Watching Clements's body language, it was clear that, as far as he was concerned, Rolt was the most important person in the room—after himself, of course. The cabinet secretary was positively fawning over him. She looked round at the young Muslim, Derek Farmer's new find. He had a Bosnian name, but scrubbed up well as a Party man, the acceptable face of young Islam. What was he making of all this? She watched him as Rolt spoke.

"All I've really said is that there are limits to tolerance if we are under siege from people who have different beliefs, many of which are entirely obnoxious to the vast majority of us. And may I add I've had numerous messages of support from a wide range of faiths and communities."

"Would you like to come in here, Sahim?" Clements pronounced his name *Saaheeem*. "Ladies and gentlemen, for those who haven't yet met him, Mr. Kovacevic is doing sterling work waving the flag for the moderate Muslim. Our secret weapon, if you like."

Sam scrabbled to separate the warring thoughts over-lapping in his brain. He felt he had lost control of his life, that he was being pushed and pulled in different directions. He had been hired as the voice of moderation, the young Muslim who could speak up for tolerance. Now he was torn. Before, part of him had agreed with Rolt; now what the man was talking about sounded like nothing short of ethnic cleansing, in which he, Sam, would be tarred with the same brush as Karza, and Bala, with his leg injury and electronic tag. To have escaped deportation in Bosnia then find it here, being openly discussed by supposedly civilized people? It was unthinkable. What could he say? His mind had become a complete blur. He opened his mouth, hoping fervently that what came out would not be too incoherent.

"Thank you. Well, I think it's a time for care, for restraint, for keeping open lines of communication with all sections of society. We should extend a helping hand to the returnees, rather than punishing them. We need to help them find a way back into society. And those who have been traumatized by their experiences, I think we should be helping them, just as Invicta helps ex-servicemen and women, who've fought for their country."

That seemed to make sense. So why was there an uncomfortable silence when he finished? He noticed that almost everyone was staring into their own laps. No one was looking at him. Had he crossed some kind of line?

Clements struggled to find the right response. "Well, that certainly sounded like it came from the heart. Thank you, Sahim."

Sam's heartbeat was hammering in his ears.

Rolt engaged him with a cold stare that sent a shiver through him. "It's a laudable position, and I don't doubt your good intentions," he began, "but I'm afraid we've passed that point. Where do you think you're going to find the popular support, now we have seen what they—some extremists—are capable of ? The people we are talking about are not the well-meaning Muslim running their halal business or corner shop. We're talking about another thing altogether: the menace in our midst, who've taken all our hard-fought-for values of tolerance and free expression and crushed them underfoot. They want Sharia law. They want a caliphate. They want women segregated, shrouded, deprived of education. And they are prepared to blow up my men to scare us into making concessions. No, we need to be rid of them, whatever it takes."

Sam's mouth went dry. Those words would be Karza's death sentence. Before, he had relished this sort of meeting, enjoyed the cut and thrust of the debate. Now he was lost for words, and terrified of what the future might bring.

54

Party Headquarters, Westminster

"What the fuck have you been saying?" Derek Farmer grabbed Sam's arm, swung him round and pulled him into an alcove. Sam tried to edge out of his grasp. He didn't like being manhandled by anyone, let alone a large, sweaty, shouting man—and, above all, not this one.

"Sorry? What d'you mean?"

"'Give returnees support'? What? Welcome them at Gatwick with tea and bloody sympathy, and sorry it didn't work out? You've gone way off base, matey."

"It was a closed meeting. Chatham House rules. They said so."

"Chatham House—what century are you in? You'll be all over the papers tomorrow, I guarantee it. The *Mail Online*'s already got it: *Government's Muslim Poster Boy Goes Rogue*. You are going to be in so much shit you'll need a fucking snorkel."

Where was all the "Thanks for helping us out here, Sahim" and "Marvelous to have you on board"? What had happened to change their attitude?

"Then I resign."

Farmer wagged a chubby finger under his nose. It smelt of old cigarettes. "No way, José. Not an option. We'll end up looking like the total muppets we were for ever taking you on. Here's what's going to happen, sunshine. You're going to do an interview with the *Sun*, and I'm going to give you the script, which you are going to stick to, word for bloody word."

Sam attempted to breathe slowly. He thought he had spoken sensibly and moderately, and now he was being vilified by yet another faction. Or, to be more precise, the people he was meant to be working for. It had all started so well. And now everything—everything to do with his life in Britain—was turning to shit.

"What if I refuse?"

"We'll comb through your history, your family, your uncles, your aunties, your girlfriends or boyfriends and pets until we find some dirt. And don't tell me there isn't any because there always is. We'll go to town on you. We'll make you so unemployable you won't even be able to get work as a fucking cabbage picker with all the other immigrants."

He held onto Sam's arm with one hand while he gesticulated with the other. "Think about it. You think about the one thing you wouldn't want the world to know about—and imagine it as a headline. A nice big one. Then imagine your mother reading it. We'll ruin you."

Sam didn't have to think about it. He was trapped.

"And not only will you be out of a job, you'll have nowhere to live. And I don't fancy you and your bird's chances of finding any room at the inn with a name like yours right now." Farmer sighed and let go of his arm.

"Look, Sam, we're on a war footing, and we can't have any deserters. Rolt knows this is his moment. Right now. And if we don't bring him into the tent, he'll go to the opposition's and piss into ours. As it is they're already sniffing each other's butts.

We have to nip *that* romance in the bud before they get into each other's Y-fronts and right up the fucking aisle. *Capisce?* We'll craft you some well-chosen words about the merits of what Mr. Rolt's been saying and we'll forget all about your little— diversion this morning. All right?"

And he was gone, with a rush of air like a train roaring out of a tunnel.

55

Victoria

Sam watched her as she read it, his heart sinking to new depths.

"They made you say all this?"

"I didn't have any choice." He told her what Farmer had said. "They would have found out about Karza. And that would have been his death sentence. I did it for him."

He searched her face for some expression, something to show she understood. One by one he was disappointing everyone who mattered to him and he couldn't bear it if she was next. "I hope you don't think any the worse of me."

"You need to be careful. You shouldn't have got their backs up in the first place."

"What do you mean?"

"Your position, right inside the Party, the contact with the prime minister and his officials. From now on, do nothing to upset them. Stay on message: remind them what an asset you are. That's the way you're going to save Karza *and* make a big difference."

Sam didn't know what she meant.

She came and sat close, put a hand on his face. The effect was electric. "You are very alone, aren't you?"

He felt the tears welling again. This so wasn't the image he wanted to project right now. He nodded. Yes, he did feel desperately alone.

She smiled. "That's how we all feel. This is how it is. Before, you were getting on with your life without a thought about your brothers. This has brought you closer to them."

"I have just one brother."

"No, you don't. You have thousands of brothers—millions— and they feel like you. But they are with you. You've got them— and they have you. Do you understand that?"

"Maybe."

"And you have me."

She looked at him with a gaze that melted his anguish. But then he was jolted with another realization. He slapped the newspaper. "The people who—the men I met, they'll see this and they'll . . ." He felt ineffectual and weak.

"I know what you're thinking, but that won't happen."

He wanted to believe her, but couldn't begin to imagine how this could end other than badly. Very badly.

56

Texas

Tom got to the van just as the cops came past in their cruisers, three of them, in a big hurry, bouncing across the ruts. Tom put himself in plain view: appearing to skulk furtively wouldn't help him. He raised a friendly hand and smiled as they went by.

As soon as they were past he jumped into the van, fired up the engine, yanked the shift into drive and floored it. If the police were definitely there for Jefferson he needed to put as much distance as he could between them and himself. He kept going south until he hit the Loop, went east to the next exit, then dropped into a side road and pulled up at the curb.

He turned on the interior light and checked himself over. There was a fair bit of Jefferson's blood on him. He looked into the back of the van, evidently Kyle's cell headquarters. There was a stack of listening equipment, a bunk, some cabinets and a fridge. He helped himself to a Coke, which felt wonderfully cool to his parched throat. Then he checked the closet and found a pair of camo cargo shorts and a khaki T-shirt. He changed into them, then took out the pay-as-you-go phone and dialed Woolf. It went to voicemail. He didn't fancy risking that so he tried Phoebe.

"Tom!"

"Can you talk?"

"I'm just on my way to Invicta."

"I need a name checked out. Asim Zuabi. He's an imam based in Houston, Texas. Whatever you have on him."

"Okay, hold while I text that in."

"How long does it take?"

"Only a few minutes. Tom?"

"Yes?"

"Thanks for not blowing us. I do want to say how sorry—"

"Never mind, it's fine. Just get me the info. How's Rolt?"

"I've hardly seen him. He's been caught up in a whirl-wind of meetings in Whitehall. The hostel bombing has changed everything. They're taking him very seriously. There are some in the cabinet wanting him to join some kind of crisis task force. Hang on while I see what we've got on your man."

While Tom waited, he took out Jefferson's phone and looked at the call log. All the names in his contacts were abbreviated to one or two letters. One number he had dialed twice, and received four calls from, in the previous twelve hours belonged to a *CF*.

Phoebe was back on.

"Okay, Zuabi's showing no POI status: not a Person of Interest. Appears to have no form at all. He arrived in the US as a refugee from Syria in 2006, and seems to have carved out a presence for himself in something called the Southern States Caucus for Interfaith Learning. Otherwise, no profile. He's not even showing up on the FBI's Watch List."

"Okay, thanks. Look, if you've got the time to go deeper, he seems to be heading up a very generously endowed new mosque, part of the regeneration of a rundown part of Houston. It's massive. Be good to know where the money's come from. And something else: I need a caller ID."

He read off *CF*'s number. There was a pause.

"It's a gun shop. Confederate Firearms, proprietor one Lester Colburn. There's a red flag against him. He also runs a website called Refugee Resettlement Watch. I don't much like the sound of that. Look, Tom, you can obviously handle yourself, but these are very murky waters."

"Yeah, I know. Hey—thanks."

"Can I ask how this connects with Invicta?"

"I'll have to get back to you about that. Thanks again."

He killed the call and searched Confederate Firearms on his phone. *For your weapon of choice, look no further. We have the most extensive range in the county . . . friendly attentive service.* He looked at his watch: 4 a.m. A bit too early to go and buy a gun, even in Texas.

57

Confederate Firearms was in the Northside district of Houston: a windowless, metal, single-story structure in a street of anonymous warehouses. He parked Kyle's van and went inside.

Even to someone with his experience of weaponry, the sheer scale of the place was breathtaking. Rack after rack of rifles, pistols and assault weapons and even a "ladies" section in one corner with small, pink-finished handguns for girls. Welcome to Texas.

Colburn was behind the counter: late fifties or thereabouts, thin, with a florid John Wayne kind of face and small, squinting eyes that stared at Tom suspiciously. He was flanked by two larger men, one of whom looked younger, their checked shirts bulging over their belts.

"Good morning!" Tom figured a friendly demeanor, plus the accent, might help break the ice, along with a few knowledgeable but generic questions about the merchandise. He glanced up at a wooden plaque with the motto "*sic semper tyrannis*". "Thus always to tyrants".

Colburn nodded. "That there's the state motto of Virginia, my home state."

"And the words shouted by John Wilkes Booth after he shot Lincoln, I believe."

Colburn nodded again, slowly. "God rest his soul."

"Lincoln's or Booth's?"

Colburn's mouth came close to what might have been described as a smile. "Ain't it obvious?"

"Yes, of course."

"You figuring on making any purchase today?"

"Absolutely." Tom took a step closer and lowered his voice. "Actually, I was also hoping to find out about Refugee Resettlement Watch."

Colburn changed his tone. And the two assistants moved closer. Their earnest expressions struck Tom as faintly comical. Their name tags said "Don" and "Phil", one late forties, the other maybe sixty: weightlifters, but sluggish with it. "What's your interest in that?"

"Well, you've seen the news about Britain?"

"We sure have. You guys having a lot of trouble with your Muslims?"

"Not just them."

He reeled off a random list of gypsies, Africans, Indians and other "undesirables", with a bit about the "Jew-controlled media" for good measure.

Phil and Don started nodding. Tom kept his gaze guileless and open.

"I believe you've got the same problem we have."

Colburn kept still, his eyes on Tom.

"And what problem exactly might that be?"

Whatever brand of fascist Colburn was, he was no fool. Tom guessed he'd been under the spotlight of the security services at some point, so wouldn't be about to share his deepest-held views with just anybody who walked in. He would have to make the running.

268

"But Muslims are the worst problem. They're the ones who bombed our capital on 7/7. They're the ones trying to destroy Christian values and bring down Western society. And it's reached the point that back home some of us want to do something about it."

"Like what?"

"Well, you know what it's like there." Tom gestured at the merchandise. "We don't have the . . . resources you guys do."

"You said it, boy." Don grinned widely, revealing intermittent brown teeth. "Judgin' by what I seen on the news, it's gettin' a little outta hand over there, wouldn't you say?"

"We do say. And that's why I'm here."

Colburn seemed to be buying it. Tom breathed out a little. "This is it. And I gather you've got a particularly big Muslim problem right here in Houston."

"Sure have. And it ain't going away."

"What do the authorities say? Are they concerned?"

The ice broke. Colburn thought this was hilarious. He looked at Don and Phil. Don joined in the laughter. Phil was examining something on his phone.

"Concerned? Rollin' out the red fuckin' carpet's more like it."

Tom put on a slightly puzzled face: keen to learn.

"See, they're real good at making the right friends. Money talks loudest here, and some of these guys got serious megabucks. One of 'em, he's got billions coming in from somewhere."

"Who's that?"

"You seen the mosque going up? The imam there, Zuabi, he's loaded, enough to wage global jihad right from his pulpit. But he's wised up. He's got PR men and lawyers and all, got the mayor and Chamber of Commerce kissin' his dirty fuckin' brown ass."

Don chipped in: "He's a fuckin' Syrian, for Pete's sake. Very pious and God-fearin'. Only it ain't God he'll be fearing, right about—"

Tom saw Colburn throw a warning glance at Don, who stopped in mid-sentence.

"That right?" said Tom, casting an admiring eye over the racks of guns surrounding them.

"Hey, Lester, over here a second."

Phil had wandered towards the front of the shop and was looking out of the door at Kyle's van.

"I'm shootin' the breeze with our English friend here."

But Phil clearly wanted his boss's attention urgently. It had to be the van. As if they were telepathically connected, all three now had their weapons in their hands, each of them close enough to get a clean shot but not so close that Tom could do anything about it. Welcome to Texas.

58

"Is there a problem?"

Tom maintained the dismayed-visitor pose but he knew it was timed out.

Colburn was keeping his weapon in his hand below the waist but his eyes fixed on Tom. "In the back, motherfucker."

Tom raised his hands.

They reached the doorway of the back office, where a desk was piled with paper and a monitor showed the CCTV. Phil was already through the door so there was going to be a second pair of eyes and another weapon on him when he passed through.

This was Texas; their buddy was dead and they were looking at the reason. Tom knew there was no thinking about what he had to do, he just had to get on and do it—and maybe come out of it the other end. He kept his eyes down, focused on Colburn's gut with the weapon in the right hand, down by the thigh. He slammed his shoulder hard into Colburn, who toppled over, taking Don with him. This gave Tom just enough space to get past and through the doorway. He started towards Phil.

Everything was now in ultra-slow motion. Phil and Tom had eye-to-eye. Phil should have known what Tom was going to do; he could have stopped, he could have put his hands up.

Tom heard shouts behind him. He caught the reaction in Phil's eyes as he jinked to the left and out of sight of the other two just

271

outside the office, his left hand reaching down. Tom kept looking at the target. With his left hand he grabbed a fistful of his own shirt front and yanked it up, his elbow held high to make sure he could clear the material from his stomach and expose the pistol grip of the suppressed Glock. He'd only get one chance.

They still had eye contact. Phil started to shout but Tom didn't hear. He pushed the web of his right hand down onto the pistol grip. If he got this wrong he wouldn't be able to aim correctly: he would miss and die. As he felt his hand make contact with the pistol grip, his lower three fingers clasped tight around it. His index finger was outside the trigger guard, parallel with the barrel. He didn't want to pull the trigger early and kill himself. Phil was still looking, still shouting.

Phil's hand was nearly at his pocket.

Nothing else mattered for Tom, apart from bringing his weapon into the right position all in a fraction of a second.

Their eyes were still locked. Tom knew he was faster, and he saw that Phil knew he had lost. There was just a curling of the lips. Phil knew he was going to die.

As Tom's pistol came out he flicked it parallel with the ground. No time to extend his arms and get into a stable firing position.

His left hand was still pulling his shirt out of the way and the pistol was now just level with his belt buckle. There was no need to look at it: he knew where it was and what it was pointing at. He kept his eyes on the target and Phil's never left Tom's.

Now the muzzle was clear from his waistband, Tom simply brought the weapon up, twisting his wrist to raise the weapon's barrel until it was parallel with the ground and against his hip, making sure he cleared his body away from the muzzle as much as possible.

Bend that hip back and he knew he'd have a firm position for the pistol.

He pulled the trigger.

The weapon report seemed to bring everything back into real time. The first round hit Phil. Tom didn't know where; he didn't need to. His eyes told him all he wanted to know.

He kept on firing low into Phil. There was no such thing as overkill. If Phil could move, he could fire. If it took a whole magazine to be sure, then that was what he'd fire. He took three rounds until he was down onto the ground, writhing in pain and shock as blood spurted out. Tom could no longer see Phil's hands. He was curled up in a ball, holding his stomach. Tom moved forward and fired two aimed shots at the head, then spun round.

The other two were now in the room. Tom kept firing low until they, too, were down, in a lake of their own blood. As their legs flailed, they smeared it, like angel wings in the snow. The men's screams sounded muffled for a moment; it wasn't until Tom started to move that the volume bounced back up.

Colburn collapsed into the doorway, blocking it, but for now that didn't matter. All that did was getting the weapons away from reach.

Colburn tried futilely to grab hold of him. Tom turned, brought the pistol down against his thigh and zapped off another round.

That one definitely hit the bone. He heard the thud and crunch. Colburn's screams drowned out the others'.

Tom grabbed him by the feet and pulled him into the room. The expanse of blood on the floor made it easy. He closed the door.

Don was closest to him. Tom bent down into his face and screamed at him: "Why are we all fucked up because of the van?"

All Tom got was a mouthful of blood spat out at him. There was no time for this. Don got another round, this time into his gut, before Tom turned and went back to Colburn.

Colburn had got the message. "It's been seen."

"By who? By Jefferson?"

He got a shaky nod.

"Zuabi? You know who I'm talking about, don't you? What about Zuabi?"

He didn't give any indication whatsoever. Tom leaned down again. "What the fuck has it got to do with Jefferson? What was his problem with Zuabi?"

Colburn hesitated.

"Yes, Jefferson's dead. Want to join him?"

Tom could see it clearly in his face, even if it was screwed up in pain as he breathed in short, sharp pants: message received.

"Mogadishu—Black Hawk down, man. He lost his brother. Those fuckers cut him into little pieces. Motherfuckers cut him up. And now they're over here, taking over the country. *That's* the fucking problem."

Tom went over to the CCTV and ripped out the hard drive. Some wires were screwed in, some clipped. Leads dangled out of the back, like long, slim dread-locks.

Then he grabbed hold of the cordless phone as the monitor started to pixellate and threw it through the door to join the weapons in the shop.

Colburn gave a sob and his breath came shorter and weaker.

274

Tom stuck his head back through the door. "If you fuckers tell anyone about what's happened here, you know I'll be back looking for you."

He closed the door, then wiped the handle with his sleeve and headed for the van.

59

Back in his hotel room, Tom showered off the dust and blood, then had a much-needed shave. He put on his lightweight Hugo Boss suit with a fresh shirt and studied himself in the mirror, checking for the moment he turned back into the polite, reasonable envoy from Invicta. There were two missed calls from Rolt, neither of which he had acknowledged. Instead he texted a non-committal *All good so far. Stutz meeting next.* He knew what he needed to do and didn't want to have to talk to him right now. He went downstairs.

Beth was waiting for him. "Howdy! How was your night?"

"Good. Yours?"

She giggled. "Aw, just fine. You have a good time with Kyle? You two go way back, right?"

"Yeah, that's right."

A slight dilating of the pupils suggested she wanted to know more, but that was all she was getting.

Stutz was in the boardroom, alone, hunched over some documents. "Just waiting on Skip. He needs to be here for the formalities. How was your evening with Kyle?"

Tom closed the doors behind him. "I've got some good news and some bad news."

Stutz looked up.

"We paid a visit to Jefferson. Kyle didn't make it." Stutz's eyes narrowed. "But neither did Jefferson."

Relief spread over Stutz's face. Tom described the ambush much as it had happened, with a few cosmetic changes. When he was done, Stutz's expression softened into a grin. He stood up, came round the table and pumped Tom's hand. "I knew I could count on you."

That confirmed he had arranged it. How far had he expected Tom to go?

"Kyle was loyal, but he was losing his edge. Good job you stepped up."

"You'll look after his family?"

"Oh, yeah. You can count on it."

There was a pause while Stutz returned to the document in front of him. Evidently it was no trouble for him to digest the news about the loss of one of his closest lieutenants. But Tom couldn't leave it there, couldn't walk away from two corpses without knowing more about them.

"So Jefferson was a problem for you—what had he done?"

"Not what he'd done, what he was going to do. That's what Skip's software is all about, catching them before it's too late."

"Who was his target?"

Stutz smiled. "Let's just say he was a threat. Better you don't know. It's less complicated that way."

There was an air of finality to his reply, and in the interest of keeping in with him, Tom changed the subject. "The presentation last night, the whole digital fortress concept, Skip really blew me away."

Stutz grinned. "Drives me nuts, but the kid's a goddam genius."

"Other than taking them out, like we did Jefferson, what happens with all the others? When you've run your checks on the individuals you've decided are a potential problem."

Stutz got up and indicated the huge picture window. Forty-five floors down, office workers criss-crossed the plaza, oblivious to the ambitions of the man looking down at them.

"See those folk down there? We've not done right by them. We've spent their taxes on two expensive wars supposedly to protect them. We've failed to win either, and we haven't made those people any safer. We owe them, big-time."

Tom waited for him to go on.

"What's happening in Britain right now, the same could happen here, maybe even worse. But our government's hands are tied. After Nine/Eleven we should have pulled up the drawbridge, built the fortress. Instead, we send our best people, men like you, like Kyle, God rest his soul, to risk their lives in yet more costly and futile conflicts we're still kidding ourselves we're gonna win—you get what I mean?"

He looked at Tom, to gauge his reaction.

"Yeah, I follow."

"And down there, they're all still looking around, watching their backs, wondering if they're standing next to a jihadi. There are people right here in our midst who want holy war, want terror, want a caliphate, want revenge for Iraq and Afghanistan, want to take us back to the Dark Ages. So we're gonna find someplace else for them to live."

There was an alarming messianic zeal in Stutz's expression.

"How will you do that?"

He grinned. "Simple. We have money, we'll do deals with those countries, pay them to take them back. One payment. Job done. Imagine freedom from fear, at a fraction of the cost of Desert Storm, Iraqi Freedom, even Enduring Freedom."

Tom kept his composure. The sincerity behind Stutz's vision would have been laughable if the implications weren't so shocking—and naïve.

"So, no more 'Give me your tired, your poor, your huddled masses . . .', then?"

Stutz nodded. Evidently the prospect of sweeping away the fundamental principle on which his nation was founded was not keeping him awake at night.

"What about the moderates? The guy running a café or driving a cab? Or his cousin, who wants to come here and open a shop? Won't they get caught in the net?"

Stutz tilted his head and pressed his lips together in a way that implied both regret and finality: a man of integrity just telling it like it was. "We got a full house. America is closed."

And yet you had Jefferson killed because he was threatening an imam. This still didn't add up, not by a long way.

"Now, you tell me, son. Do you think Invicta's up to the job?"

It was clear there was only one answer he wanted to hear. Tom had come this far, he might as well keep playing the game.

"Absolutely. You bet."

"God bless you. Britain and America should stand together. We're done with being the world's policemen, sending our best people to be blown apart. It's way too costly in money and lives—and it doesn't work. Let them put their own houses in order. We need to protect our borders, conserve our resources. *This* is what this century needs. The world's changing. We got our own gas and oil now. We can cut 'em all loose—the Saudis, the Iraqis, Syrians, Afghans. All of 'em."

Tom looked at him steadily, letting none of his revulsion show. "Your backing will make all the difference."

Stutz put an arm round his shoulders. "You know, Tom, I had a good feeling the minute I set eyes on you. I don't warm easy to people, but we put you in the line of fire and you came through. And you've been straight with me. I'm proud of you, and it makes me sick what you went through at Bastion."

He bent forward so his mouth was close to Tom's ear. "That fuck Qazi, you say the word, he's gone." He nodded gravely. "I mean it. One word, and it'll be done."

From anyone else it would have been ridiculous bravado, but Stutz gave a convincing impression that in his world nothing was beyond his reach. Perhaps Stutz had another Kyle right there in Bastion, on standby, ready to do the job and not ask any questions. "Thank you. I'll bear it in mind."

But behind all the talk, what was he actually planning? Never mind Qazi. What insane horrors were these people planning to unleash? Tom put on a calm smile. "So, what are the next steps?"

"People on the front line, in command—at Langley, in the Pentagon, all over DC and in Whitehall too, for sure. Vernon's got a lot of people quietly moving in the right direction. Quietly and determinedly. You can be sure of it. But we need to speed up the process, one more outcome that'll be the tipping point."

Woolf's claims, which had seemed so outlandish a day ago, were starting to look less and less far-fetched.

Tom was about to probe for more on the "outcome" when the door opened and there stood Skip, the rings round his eyes even grayer. "Hey, guys, we ready to close the deal?"

60

Tom declined the offer of a driver and walked back to the hotel, a lone figure on the sun-blasted sidewalk. The hot Houston air felt unexpectedly cleansing after the oppressive atmosphere in the Oryxis boardroom. Stutz had made the call to Rolt but Tom didn't get to hear what was said. Now Rolt was calling him.

"This is it! We're on our way. I owe you, Tom."

"All I did was trot out a few old war stories and shake their hands."

"Stutz told me you did a lot more than that. I'm proud of you, Tom."

There was a beat while Tom absorbed this. But Rolt was still talking.

"He says you passed with flying colors. He says you're a great asset."

So that was what it took. It might as well have been an initiation into a Hell's Angels chapter. Kill to order to get to the next level.

"Well?"

"It's very flattering. I don't know what to say."

He was in. Right under the wire. Woolf had put him there and he had come good. But where was Woolf now?

"Look, give it some thought on the way home. You coming back tonight? We certainly need you. The bombing has raised everybody's game."

Right now all he could think of was sleep. "I'll keep you posted. It's been a long twenty-four hours."

Tom dropped his phone back into his pocket. He was on the forecourt of his hotel, just a few feet from the revolving doors, when he was halted by an unfamiliar voice.

"Tom!"

He turned to see a stunning young Black woman, dressed impeccably, if a little warmly for the weather.

"Alicia. UNHCR, Baghdad. Remember?"

She had a British accent and a beautiful smile: not the sort of combination a man would easily forget. He smiled back. "I'm sorry—who?"

She laughed. "You really don't remember me?"

She was moving towards a side-street. As he rifled through all the faces he might have remembered from Baghdad, and that was a lot of faces, he followed her. She turned and came up very close as if she was about to kiss him, and as she did so her expression changed. Something made contact with Tom's thigh and he heard the sigh of compressed nitrogen. He couldn't do anything except take the pain as the Taser barbs embedded in his flesh and the force of the electric shock slammed him into the ground. Apart from fifty thousand volts, the only thing that went through his mind was the idea that he should try to curl up and protect his head as he tumbled off the curb.

As he tried to retake control of his legs, a blacked-out MPV screeched to a halt at the curb and two men jumped out.

They bundled him into the vehicle as easily as if he were a child and accelerated away.

Tom had no energy left for any of this—whatever it was. "Look, it's been a long day and I'm fresh out of moves. Could we just cut the foreplay and I'll call you in the morning?"

Tom turned to find himself in the center well of the MPV. The memorable Alicia sat up front with the driver, and with their backs to them, facing the rear, sat two compactly built young bloods in shades, with blandly inoffensive faces, like shop dummies but with less personality. They looked alert and fresh from a good night's sleep; just gazing at them made him feel weary.

"Buckingham, listen up. Look at me."

Opposite them was the talker, a tall, patrician man with neat silver hair, the sort who might have been a prefect at his old school.

"You are Tom Buckingham?"

Tom struggled. "Who wants to know?"

The patrician bent down and thrust his face close to Tom's. "Don't be tiresome, Buckingham. We've had the FBI on our backs, wanting to know why you're here. They seem to know things we don't and that's not how we like it."

"Sorry, I can't help you."

"They know all about Bastion."

"Yeah? Apparently so does everyone. Have you honestly got nothing better to do than swoop out of nowhere with—Beavis and Butt-Head here and bother a private citizen on his holidays?"

The shop dummies looked at each other; clearly they'd been called worse things.

"The FBI are concerned you may be seeking some kind of revenge."

"In Texas? That's a bit paranoid even for them."

It was Alicia's turn to chip in: "For fuck's sake, Tom. Everyone's on edge back home and there aren't any easy strategies. We can't put tanks on the streets. We're not the Russians. We need all the support we can get from the US and stuff like this makes them feel we're not playing the game."

Tom sighed. "Look, you can drive me around all day, if you like, but spare a thought for the poor old British taxpayer footing the gas bill for this barge, not to mention keeping these two fat and happy."

The boss sighed heavily and rubbed his eyes. It was clear they were on a fishing expedition. They had no real idea why he was there.

"Look. Just be out of here by tomorrow. All right?"

This was madness, one arm of the secret service trying to employ him, the other trying to expel him. But in fact Tom was hoping to get out of there sooner than that.

"Fine, whatever. Just let me out."

The car lurched to a halt. He turned to them. "There is one thing. Masjid As-Sabur?"

The patrician frowned. "What's that?"

"'As-Sabur' is one of Allah's ninety-nine names. Depending on your interpretation of the translation it means either the 'Timeless One' or the 'Patient One'. 'Masjid', I'm sure you know, means 'mosque'."

"So?"

"Asim Zuabi, imam and Syrian refugee."

They all looked at him blankly. "Check him out. He's building a big new mosque here. Some of the locals aren't happy but he's loaded so he's bought off the authorities, apparently."

"What's the significance?"

"Honestly? I have absolutely no idea."

61

Tom was in the bathroom doing some maintenance on the previous night's damage when there was a knock at the door.

"Room service."

He looked through the peep-hole: Beth, carrying a bottle of champagne and two glasses. He had been looking forward to some time alone and catching up on some much-needed sleep. Besides, he didn't feel like celebrating; Kyle's demise and the carnage at the gun shop had left him feeling deeply troubled. But maybe this was a chance to get another angle on Stutz. He reached for a robe. The accumulated damage had left him with a number of welts and angry-looking bruises.

He opened the door and she strode in on those end-less legs.

"Courtesy of Mr. Stutz. I believe congratulations are in order!"

She looked different today, less of the efficient PA, more Jack Wills at the Beach. She had on a vest that clung nicely, shorts and trainers, evidently her off-duty equipment. He took the bottle from her: Krug, Clos du Mesnil 2000.

"Mr. Stutz says you Brits know your champagne."

"Very thoughtful, thanks." He glanced down to see that one of the cuts inflicted by Colburn and Co was oozing onto the carpet. He pulled the robe closer round him. "Just give me a minute."

She brandished the bottle. "Would you like me to open it?"

"Go ahead."

He went back into the bathroom and put on a long-sleeved fleece and pants to cover the evidence.

"Where did y'all get to last night?"

He laughed. "I'm afraid I don't remember. We rather overdid it, I'm ashamed to say. I think I might have come off his bike at some point."

He heard her turn the inside lock on the door. That wasn't right.

He was only halfway through the doorway when a jolt stung him on the thigh and he went down for the second time in less than an hour.

What was this, Groundhog Day?

He lifted himself up a little and, without even turning, she jabbed her left elbow into his chest, forcing all the air out of it. Then her face followed, like thunder, as if she'd just ripped off her happy mask to reveal the scary android beneath. She smashed the back of her hand across his face. This helped him focus just enough to grab her wrist and pull her down. He didn't see the foot heading for his left temple until it was too late.

He was on the carpet. His limbs felt like sludge, but he grabbed the foot and twisted it hard. She rotated with it, trying to avoid the crack, and crashed into the side of the minibar. He grabbed her ponytail and pulled her head down. She fought hard with her fists, hammering his face, chest, shoulder—wherever she could land them—twisting all the time like a hooked marlin. With a huge effort of will he forced her off him, but as he did so, she used his momentum to send him smashing into the wall.

He tried to open his eyes. The room was on its side, a blur. He twisted to try to see the right way up, but it was painful. When he recovered a little, he found he was on the floor and she was standing over him, the Glock in one hand, a small black wallet open in the other. He focused on the wallet, in particular the three white letters: FBI.

62

"What happened to the nice, smiley Beth? The one who doesn't Taser guys in hotel rooms."

No sudden moves, he told himself—at least, not until you know if everything's working.

She glared at him with contempt. "What are you—some kind of one-man crime wave?"

He lifted himself an inch. She pushed him back down with her heel. "Okay! Okay!"

The muzzle of the suppressor was less than two feet from his face. "Believe me, I am more than capable of using this."

"I believe you. Can you just move it out of my face?"

"I'm calling this in, Tom Buckingham—if that's even your name. You just booked yourself a long-stay cell in Huntsville."

Tom had never heard of the place but he was pretty sure it didn't have sun loungers and a pool. He adjusted his sore leg. She raised the weapon again.

The thought flashed through his mind that this was another test, commissioned by Stutz, but the badge and the wallet looked like the real thing, as did the way she handled the weapon.

"Can I at least straighten up a bit?"

His head was wedged half under the table and his zapped leg was smarting unpleasantly.

"What do you know about Zuabi?" She took a half-step back.

"What's that?" Tom tried to straighten his legs.

"You don't know? How long did you say you'd been under cover?"

He gave her the heads-up on the mystery mullah.

She listened, saying nothing, which suggested that it was all new to her. Since he had her attention, he went on: "What's in this for Stutz? Seemed to me his thing is sending people like Zuabi back where they came from."

She sighed, her patience running on empty. "Okay, you're still fucking with me, Tom. You need to get yourself a better scriptwriter."

"Syrian refugee builds mega-mosque in downtown Houston. Nazi nutter plans to kill him. Stutz sent me with Kyle. What else could I do? You know the score. Under cover, you get to do all kinds of surprising stuff—like being filmed by Skip, yeah? How does that feel?" He thought he had crossed a line but she didn't rise to it. "He was testing you. That's what he does."

"Then I guess I passed." She sat down on the edge of the bed, keeping the Glock trained on him, not letting down her guard, but at least she was responding. Tom pressed on.

"MI5 think Invicta is deliberately provoking the unrest in the UK. They put me in to see if I can join up some of the dots. The dots led to here."

"And a lot of collateral."

He shrugged. There was no point debating that. "Okay, I showed you mine. How about you show me yours?"

She shook her head in mock-disbelief. "Jeez, you Brits are something else."

"Well, go on. Why have the FBI got you running around for these creeps?"

"That's none of your fucking business."

"But maybe what I have is *your* business."

She shook her head again. It was getting to be a habit. "I just don't get it, what are you trying to do here?"

"We can help each other."

Her eyes narrowed.

"Look, we both know Stutz's ambition is for Skip to deliver the software equivalent of ethnic cleansing. Rolt's been talking up something similar in the UK—and he's getting an audience. There's evidence he's been helping the process along—stirring up ethnic hatred. Stutz talked to me about the Invicta hostel bombing like it was preordained. What if it was planned—by them? The FBI could be missing a trick here."

"Meaning?"

"That you and I may have a chance to stop the biggest orchestrated terror initiative since 9/11."

She looked at him for several seconds. Tom could almost see the debate going on in her head. *Is this guy for real or some fuckwit?*

He noticed the Glock wasn't pointed at him now. Beneath what was left of the shiny gloss of her cover, he detected the frustrations of her assignment coming to the surface. She looked at him for a long time. When she spoke again, it was through gritted teeth.

"Stutz is impenetrable. He's very meticulous, and very secretive. He's got all the detail in his head. Maybe working with Skip has convinced him that, no matter how many firewalls you put in, nothing is safe. He hardly uses the phone, he doesn't do email. Everything's word of mouth. He has people from his security outfit couriering messages all over. And they're all totally loyal to him, just like Kyle was."

Tom looked at her afresh. She was in deep, risking her life, putting up with everything Stutz and Lederer threw at her for the Bureau. He bet her paymasters had never imagined, when they had instigated the War on Terror, that they would be tracking the likes of Stutz.

She put up a hand as if to wipe out the previous thought. "Wait, roll back. You talked about Rolt, the Invicta guy?"

Tom nodded.

"Rolt was here a month back. He met with Stutz at his penthouse. That's not usual—he takes work there sometimes but doesn't do meetings there. He had me bring up a package, and when I went in he had this purple folder open, stuff spread all over the table. They looked like résumés, mug shots on them. The men with beards, women with headscarves. Never saw Stutz with anything like that before or since. Anyhow I'd come in without knocking and he went apeshit. I didn't get near enough to see names or anything but I saw letters on the corners of some of them: SAR."

"Syrian Arab Republic."

"And we know he's not hiring them—doesn't even want them here. So why's he looking at their details?"

"What was the Bureau's interest in him, originally?"

She gave him a withering look.

"Okay, hand me over to the authorities, if you want, but I guarantee you, no one wants a fuss right now. They'll most probably ship me back to the UK and pretend it never happened."

She took a deep breath and let it out slowly. "Before 9/11, Stutz was in the oil business, supplying infrastructure and personnel to the high-risk fields: Iraq, Libya, Azerbaijan, Nigeria.

293

With the Iraq invasion in 2003, he teamed up with the CIA to supply contractors. As the war dragged on, the demand for all kinds of off-book operatives increased. Congress got interested in how much public money was flowing to these private contractors, but they were protected with all kinds of National Security provisions that meant there was a whole bunch of stuff they didn't need to declare. Langley and the Pentagon closed ranks to protect Stutz, which pissed off the Bureau."

"Have you managed to get anything?"

"Some numbers. Bank details. Raw data from transactions. Something to feed Carter, my contact agent in DC, so he can follow up the financial leads while I keep working on getting closer to Stutz."

"And Skip?"

"Don't even go there, okay? The guy's a class A pervert."

"Sounds like you got the assignment from hell."

She stiffened again. "Why should I even trust you?"

"Remember 'Mutually Assured Destruction'? We both know what he'd do if he found out about either of us. And we both have enough on each other to give him cause to want to do that. So we have an incentive not to blow each other's cover. Where is Stutz now?"

"In DC. He doesn't get back before midnight. He drives himself from the airport and at that time there's no traffic. The building has a parking garage in the basement. He has his own elevator, which bypasses the offices and so forth. Just goes straight up. I sometimes go in there to pick up stuff so it's not unusual for the guards to see my pick-up. So far I've never been in alone but my company pass gets me into the garage. And I've memorized the elevator and door codes."

"Any other way up or down?"

"The emergency stairs, but it's forty-five floors. Access is through the bedroom. The door doesn't open from the outside, though, so it's exit only."

"Can you get me in?"

63

She left the radio off in the pick-up and they drove in silence.

"You okay?"

"Sure."

Her silence felt unnatural.

"So why take the assignment?"

"I didn't. I mean, I didn't choose it. I was on probation."

"How come?"

"My previous assignment was a drug bust. I had to get close to some dealers in Miami, be their girlfriend and whatever. And I ended up getting too close to the product. When the case came up, their defense argued my evidence was inadmissible on the grounds I was addicted, and they walked. The FBI doesn't hold back. It was either this or get out."

The penthouse was invisible from the street.

"It's set back. There's a deck all around it with trees and stuff. Kinda wasted on a guy who never goes outside."

She looked wistful for a moment, then turned into a side street. "You need to get under the dash, there's cameras on the gate. Stay down till we've stopped. I've learned where the blind spots are. When we leave the truck, you follow my route exactly to the elevator."

Tom crouched in the footwell. She swiped her card and the barrier to the parking lot flipped up. They dropped down into the underground garage. It was only partially lit.

"Okay, now come out my side."

There were a dozen other cars, BMWs and Audis, a black Lincoln SUV, a yellow Lamborghini Huracán and a classic Jaguar E-Type.

"Any of these his?"

"Just the Jag. His favorite toy, supposedly, but he never uses it. He also has a blue S Class—he's out in that now. The Lambo's one of Skip's. Think he forgot it's here."

They parked next to some Dumpsters and walked to the elevator door. She punched in the number: 5121861.

"Looks familiar."

"May twelve, 1861. Wouldn't mean anything to a Brit."

"Start of the Civil War, when the Confederates fired on Fort Sumter."

"You know your history."

"I know the battles."

The elevator opened and they stepped in. The inside was leather, studded with matching buttons.

"Like a padded cell."

"That's where I'll be when this ends."

"You and me both."

"Well, maybe they'll let us share."

The elevator stopped. The lobby was deep-pile cream carpet.

"Let me go in first: I need to put in the code."

She opened the door. Inside it was pitch dark except for one tiny red light that might have been the TV. She disappeared into the murk. He waited for his eyes to adjust. A dull orange glow from the streets far below filtered through the gaps in the heavy curtains.

They moved down the hall. She had sketched the layout for him: master bedroom to the right, living room and kitchen next door on

297

the left. The doors to the living room and bedroom were opposite each other. The kitchen had two, one onto the hall, the other to the living room. Tom followed her in there. She switched on the light, revealing a wood-floored room with leather sofas arranged round a vast glass and granite coffee-table, a roll-top desk and two walls covered with bookshelves. Above a fake fireplace hung a pair of Civil War Harpers Ferry rifle muskets.

Tom couldn't help admiring them.

"The Confederates captured the Harpers Ferry Armory and took the whole shebang, weapons, tools, back to Richmond where these were made." She pointed at the letters carved in the stocks. "See those initials, AS? These were made for one of his ancestors."

Tom scanned the room. He tried the drawers in the desk and the lid: all locked. He could have forced them but that would alert Stutz to intruders and quite possibly blow his cover, hers too.

"Tom."

She picked up a framed photograph and handed it to him.

It had been taken at the Invicta campus. A group shot: fifteen men. He recognized Philips, Vestey and Jackman. Rolt was at the center with Stutz, looking faintly awkward in a US Marines APECS parka. He flipped over the clear plastic frame. The date showed it had been taken four months ago.

"Keep looking. I'll check the bedroom."

It was a faint hope that the purple folder of résumés would still be there. Stutz was the last man to leave anything significant lying around but perhaps there might be something tangential that shed a light on his connection with Zuabi, some clue as to how their interests could have converged. He was pondering all this when he heard the elevator approaching. It came to a stop.

He switched off the light and stepped back into shadow just as the door opened.

It was Stutz.

64

"What the fuck you doing here?" His voice was quiet but full of rage: a disconcerting combination.

Beth sprang back into cheerleader mode. "It's a surprise, honey—I thought that maybe tonight, you know, it's been a while."

From the shadow in which he hid, Tom could see it all. Beth stepped towards Stutz and placed a hand gently on his chest. He grabbed her wrist and pulled it away.

"You know I don't do *surprises*." He still had his hand round her wrist.

"I'm so sorry," she cooed.

Ignoring the grip she leaned towards him, giving him the full force of her magnetism. He pushed her hand away. "Get in the bedroom."

He didn't look the sort who would take his time or spend too long on foreplay, more the "wham bam, thank you, ma'am" type, and that probably without the last bit. So time was short.

There was only the glow from the night sky of the city and a greasy yellow moon. Tom took out his phone and used the light on that. He embarked on a shelf-by-shelf search of the books, a comprehensive library of American history and political biography. In one space there were a couple of photographs, a young Stutz in his Marine dress blues and in a combat desert jacket from the first Gulf War. He moved on to more books, all neatly stacked. He returned to the coffee table. There were sounds coming from the bedroom, all Beth, working hard for her country.

The coffee table had three large books on it: a glossy catalogue of weapons of the Civil War, an album of Residences of the United States Foreign Service and a thick, embossed tome of photographs of London. The last had something sticking out of it—the corner of a piece of paper. It was a compliments slip with the British coat of arms printed across the top: "From the Office of the Cabinet Secretary". On it was a handwritten message.

A memento of your visit. With all good wishes, Alec.

Alec? Cabinet secretary? Stutz's London connections ran deep. He lowered the book to put it back, then noticed a file that had been lying underneath.

It was similar to the one Beth had described: purple with a small castle-like logo in the top left-hand corner and beneath it the word FORTRESS. He flipped it open and came face to face with his own photograph.

It was a copy of his military record.

The bedroom door opened. He put the file back under the book and darted for the kitchen, which was nearer the elevator.

But that couldn't be his exit. He couldn't risk the noise. And she had told him the only way to the emergency stairs was through the bedroom. Stutz crossed the landing to the lounge where Tom had just been. There was the small "snap" of a box being shut, a lighter flicking on and off, and the smell of a cigar, then two feet coming towards the kitchen.

Tom stepped behind the door. Stutz was in a dressing-gown, the fat Cuban clenched in his teeth and an ashtray in his hand. He put down the ashtray, took a glass out of a cabinet and filled it with iced water from the refrigerator. Then he took a small tube for pills from his pocket—it was empty. He cursed, put down the water, placed the cigar in the ashtray and left the room. He would be back any second. Tom was trapped.

He had already clocked a hinged panel in the wall, about a meter square: the garbage chute. Madness, obviously. But leaning beside it was some cardboard packaging, a large piece, about two meters by one. He bent it into a large U, opened the chute, stuffed in the cardboard and got in after it as if it was the finger of a giant glove. It was a desperate measure, but staying in the kitchen wasn't an option. The lid sprang closed behind him and he was in total darkness, sliding earthwards in near freefall, buffeted and hammered by the sides of the chute. The card protected his legs, head and face from the worst of the friction, but the clothing round his shoulders and hips was soon shredded. He prayed that the Dumpster below was full, that there would be something to cushion his fall.

Everything went black.

The Dumpster was not full. But there was just enough rotting refuse to prevent him breaking a leg. The smell of it all around him brought him back to consciousness. His whole body ached, but nothing was sprained. He still had to extricate himself from under the mouth of the chute and climb out of the enormous, fetid container. He heaved himself out and caught his breath, taking lungfuls of the comparatively fresh air in the underground parking lot, before dropping behind the Dumpster to evade the cameras.

He hadn't bargained on leaving the penthouse alone. From his limited vantage-point he spent some time scouting the cameras and the layout of the space. There was no pedestrian exit. The gate—operated by the card he didn't have—was shut, but it didn't look particularly strong. It could almost certainly be rammed. Beth's pickup was right in front of him. It wasn't locked but, of course, she had the key. He opened the driver's door and, still in a crouching position, tore off the plastic cowling round the steering column and examined the ignition assembly. No chance. That was the problem with modern cars: too thief-proof. He looked round at the others.

Then his eye fell on the E-Type Jaguar. His father had had one, in British racing green, fast but serially un-reliable—though easy to hot-wire if the battery wasn't flat.

He rooted around in the garbage till he found what he was looking for: a mesh vegetable bag. Perfect. He put it over his head. Then he hunted some more until he found a coat-hanger, which he bent into a hook. This would have to be done fast. He dashed round to the driver's door, inserted it between the window and the canvas hood and fished for the lock, which clicked open satisfyingly.

He was in. Now there was just the small matter of getting it started. He yanked the wires out from under the dash, and several came away in his hand. He worked his way through them one by one. Testing each against another. The starter whirred, slowly at first. Nothing. He found the choke, pulled it out, pumped the throttle a couple of times. Then the wires again. There was a splutter and a cough and the old Big Six barked into life: a shattering sound in the cramped confines of the parking lot. He moved the choke in but not too far: he couldn't risk it stalling. Now there was just the matter of getting through the gate. With enough of a run at it, he could hit it at about thirty. It ought to do it. He put on the waist-only seatbelt. He revved the engine, found first, let the clutch bite and shot forward, then reversed to get as far from the gate as he could. Then he shoved it back into first and floored it, his arms now extended and locked to push him back against the seat.

There was an explosion of grinding metal and glass. Despite his locked arms, his head hit the windshield, which exploded over him, and for a few seconds he was gone. When he looked up, he was still on the wrong side of the gate, but had forced it open a few inches. He extricated himself from the driver's seat, stepped over the crumpled bonnet and tried to squeeze himself through the narrow space the Jag had prised open. To whoever was watching through the cameras, it would look like a not at all grand theft auto.

The gates weren't giving but Tom pushed and squeezed, eventually twisting himself through the narrow gap.

"Freeze, you fuck. Don't move!"

Two guards were standing at the top of the ramp, their big old Colts trained on him. He raised his hands. He still had the mask on. They mustn't hear his voice.

Cautiously they approached, one a chubster, the other skinny with bow legs. "Okay, we're calling this in. You stay right there."

Tom gestured at his chest and mouth.

"Hey, Sal, maybe he ain't breathin'."

Sal wasn't so sympathetic. "Fuck him. Wait till the cops get here."

The skinny one had his doubts.

"He stops breathin', we'll get it in the neck. He can see we're carrying. He ain't goin' nowhere."

"Okay, okay."

Sal swiped a card on the reader and the gates lurched open.

Tom collapsed onto his knees, clutching his chest.

"Jeez, will you look at what he done to the Jag-war?"

The skinny one stood over him and reached down with his left hand to pull off the vegetable bag.

Tom grabbed the weapon barrel and simply twisted. The shock the guy got when this happened so quickly made it easy to yank it out of his hands. The hard bit was then making use of the weapon fast and in such a way that the other one knew he had a problem. Shooting them was the ideal option, but that wasn't going to happen and Tom jammed hard between his skinny legs. That always grabbed people's attention.

Tom put on his best and worst American accent. "Tell him to throw me his weapon—now!"

The command was quickly shouted out and ended with a "Jesus, Sal, just do it."

Tom took off on foot, not looking back, just making distance as he wiped the weapon and dumped it as soon as he could. It was maybe half a mile of hard-sweat running before he spotted a cab and flagged it down. The driver began to pull away.

"No way—you're fucking rank, man!"

"There's an extra hundred in it if you take me."

"Okay, get in."

65

The phone woke Tom from a brief but incredibly deep sleep.

"You find anything?" Beth was on the move, walking quickly. He heard the sound of a car unlocking.

"Yeah, maybe. We should talk."

"I've got a crash meeting with Carter, my contact agent. He's flying in from DC."

"How come?"

"I called him about Zuabi, asked him to run a check. I guess he has something big, so we should meet after that. I'll give you the address."

It was a motel out on an exit from the Loop to the southwest.

"Why there?"

"His choice. We should be done by noon. Text me when you're near."

He picked up the keys to his hire car at the desk and headed out into the hot, smoggy morning. A silver Toyota Camry was about as anonymous as you could get, the automotive equivalent of a Styrofoam cup. He took out his iPad and tapped in his destination, the Tijuana Motel, then searched for the location of Zuabi's mosque and put that in as well. He had some time to kill before meeting Beth; a good opportunity to check it out.

Before he set off he called Phoebe again on his throw-away phone. She sounded stressed: phones were ringing and beeping in the background. "Tom, have you talked to Rolt?"

"Why?"

"He's over the moon about something, but hasn't said what. He's keeping his composure in public but when he's in the office it's as though Christmas has come early. And everyone wants to talk to him, government, media—even more than before. It's gone mental."

"Well, he's got some new investment. Another name for you: Aaron Stutz. That one ever come up there?"

"Can you give me more of a steer on it?"

"Big shot. Chairs a software company called Oryxis. He's the guy Invicta's getting new funding from. Rolt and Stutz are close. Also anything that cross-references the name 'Fortress' with either of them."

"Doesn't mean anything but, as you know, there are whole channels of his activity we don't have eyes on."

"Well, you need to get eyes on them. Woolf needs to raise his game. You need to go a lot deeper."

"Why the change of heart?"

"Because I don't like what I'm finding out."

66

Tom slowed the Camry and pulled into the parking lot of a dry-cleaner's where he stopped, facing the building site of the mosque. Maybe Stutz's interest in Zuabi had nothing to do with the construction. None of it made sense.

It was the scale of the place that struck him first: not just one hall of worship but a whole complex of buildings rising out of the ground in an otherwise forgotten neighborhood. A high wall of pale pink stone had already been built. The minaret was complete, and where the main dome would be there was a huge edifice of scaffolding. He was weighing the pros and cons of trying to do a decent recon when a coach pulled to a halt in front of the entrance. Out poured a group of about twenty people, most of them in suits, who gathered round the luggage hatch at the back where white hard hats and hi-viz safety vests were being handed out.

He left the car and crossed the road, then came round the side of the coach and joined the queue for equipment. When he got to the front the guy doing the handing out gave him a strange look. His name tag said "International Confederation of Structural Engineers". "You on the list?"

"Roger Symes, Royal Institute of British Architects. I only just landed—got a bit delayed. They probably didn't have time to add me. I'm most awfully sorry."

The guy handed him a hat and a vest. "Whatever."

Tom inserted himself into the group as they headed through the entrance, following an enthusiastic guide in a yellow hat, who was in full flow.

". . . and to produce the activation heat for this system, we're using roof-mounted parabolic solar collectors, working on a higher than usual temperature . . ."

Tom soon tuned out. He was in the building, which was what mattered. He smiled at a woman studying her BlackBerry, who rolled her eyes. "There's only so much of this stuff I can take." She leaned towards him. "How many mosques d'you think there are now, operating in the US?" He smiled again and shrugged. "Twelve hundred."

"Wow."

"And eighty percent of them built since 9/11. How does that work?"

"Are they all this big?"

She shook her head. "Oh, no, this fella's in a whole different league."

"Know anything about the guy behind it?"

Another member of the party who appeared equally bored chipped in, "Got his hand deep in Saudi pockets. Which ain't right."

At this point a third man, the only one of the party who looked like he might have actually built anything, waded in. "Hey, give the guy a break. He's spending his dough here, not on guns for A-rabs." He drawled the "a" so it came out as "*Ayrab*". He waved in the direction of a cluster of men erecting a crane. "They're all American workers too."

"Guy's a refugee, came here with nothing."

"Yeah, so did my granddaddy, but then they start sending for their families an" all."

"I heard it's gonna be dedicated to his daughter."

"What happened to her?" Tom asked.

The third man shrugged. "Guess she didn't make it. They got all kinds of trouble in Syria now, ain't they?"

They moved towards the scaffolding where the dome would be. Another man with a well-scuffed hat came forward and was introduced as the site manager.

Tom tried to listen but his attention was caught by the purple folder under the man's arm and the logo in the corner. It was the same castle design and the same color as the one in Stutz's apartment. He turned to the BlackBerry woman. "D'you know that logo at all?"

"New to me. Some construction outfit, I guess."

67

The Tijuana Motel had seen better days. A low, L-shaped structure, it had been painted a lurid orange, evidently some years past,
perhaps in an attempt to attract the attention of passing trade.
But time and the seasons had not been kind to it: so much of the
orange had flaked away that the mottled surface now looked more
like some misconceived kind of camouflage than the outside of
anywhere people would choose to stay.

There was no reply to his text so he waited another ten minutes.
He chose not to call Beth's cell in case Carter was still with her.
But after half an hour he began to get impatient. Her pick-up was
still there, and the only other car in the lot, a beaten-up Ford, didn't
look like it was going anywhere. He decided to take a closer look
at room forty-five.

There was a do-not-disturb sign on the door. The curtains were
closed and there was no light on, except from the blaring TV. He
knocked once, then again. He tried the door. It was open.

Beth lay sprawled on the bed. She was cold. He probed desperately for a pulse, hoping, yet knowing there was no hope.
There was foam on her lips, and blood from where she had
evidently bitten them. A needle hung from her arm below the
latex glove that had been used as a tourniquet. On the nightstand
there was a lighter, a spoon coated with residue, a syringe pack,
bottles of hydrocodone syrup and promethazine, and an empty

foil of oxycodone pills. Some of the powder clung to a small knife, which had been used to chop up the pills. On its side on the bed was a bottle of Streak vodka.

Whoever had done this knew their stuff.

He lifted the pillow beside her. The underside was speckled with blood. They had smothered her to finish the job. Tom thought of closing her eyes but thought again. Then he turned back to the door, pausing only to wipe the handle on the way out.

68

Washington DC

"Dean Carter?"

"Who wants to know?"

Before following him up from the parking lot, Tom had been in and rung the bell to make sure that no one else was home. According to Phoebe, the FBI listed Carter as single, but he had to be sure they'd be alone for their talk. He had also reconned the building for security cameras.

Carter stood at the door, his key in the lock, as Tom came towards him. He was in his early forties, balding, but his hair was an unnatural jet black; his fierce little eyes had flabby bags under them. His thin beige raincoat hung off him and his shoulders had the droop of a man who spent a lot of time at a desk, carrying too much around in his head.

Tom pressed the Glock into his right kidney.

"Hey, what is this?"

"It's a gun. Let's go inside, Dean." He gave him a shove so that he stumbled into the room, then quietly closed the door; no need to disturb the neighbors. It was stifling inside. There would be an AC unit but they tended to be noisy.

He indicated the balcony doors.

"Open them, just a little. Then sit down on the sofa. If you try to make any kind of noise I'll kill you."

His flat, quiet tone seemed to get the message across. Carter slid the glass door open, then sat.

"Okay, if it's cash, you're wasting your time, and there's nothing of value here."

"Dean, listen to me. Do I look or sound like I'm interested in your crap? Why don't you use some of that special-agent intuition and try to work out why I *am* here?"

Carter turned his palms skywards; he couldn't work it out.

"Okay. Just answer a few questions honestly—that means without lying to me—and we'll get this over with."

Carter flicked his head from side to side as if more mystery men might have come in behind them. "Who the fuck are you?"

"I've just got in from Houston. I stopped by the Tijuana Motel on my way out of there."

Carter blinked but that was all.

"And do you know what I saw there?"

He wagged a finger at Tom. "Now let's get something clear here. I'm a special agent of—"

"Yeah, yeah. And Beth Adams's CA."

His forehead creased into a frown. "Wait—are you Buckingham, the SAS guy?"

Tom didn't answer, which Carter took as a "yes". Relief spread over his face. "Ah, okay, so, yeah, it's a kinda complex situation we have here. Beth's not been in a good way for a while. It started with the coke—as you probably know. And, basically, she went rogue on us."

He shook his head in mock-regret. Tom sat on the coffee-table opposite him, keeping close, while Carter improvised a few more

314

details. "We kinda had to rein her in and she couldn't take it. If you knew about her habit, she was on notice . . ."

Tom remained impassive.

". . . and it all got too much for her. It's really very sad." He looked up at Tom, seeking some sort of acknowledgement.

"What? Oh, I get it. You actually think I believe this bollocks? This pack of fucking lies? My God, where do they find you people?"

At this conclusive evidence that his performance had not won an Oscar and sent the gullible Brit obligingly on his way, Carter's indignation got the better of him. "Now, I don't know who you've been talking to, fella, but you're a foreign national and this is US-government business. You need to understand—"

"What I *understand* is that she died between ten and twelve this morning in room forty-five at the Tijuana Motel."

At the revelation that Tom knew something—anything—a look of panic crossed Carter's face. "Well, I don't have any of that exact detail."

"Supposedly of an overdose."

Though his ordeal was far from over, Carter clung to this apparent concession on Tom's part. "Yeah, that's what I'm saying."

"Except she couldn't have. Ask me how I know that." He shoved the weapon closer.

Carter looked profoundly uncomfortable. Clearly he hadn't been briefed on this eventuality.

"How do you know that?"

"There was blood on the pillow from where she was smothered when the 'overdose' didn't work. Where I come from we have a word for that."

Carter glanced up at him, and this time Tom detected a flicker of guilt pass across his features.

"We call it *careless*." Tom whacked him across the head, not enough to knock him out but enough to quench, at least temporarily, his desire to rip the man's head off and shoot several rounds down his neck.

There was momentary silence while Carter took this in. He was cornered but he wasn't throwing in the towel yet. Amazingly he came back for another go. "Ah, no, listen—she was a real car crash. She really was getting into all kinds of shit—"

"Look, *Dean*. Let me stop you there before you make me want to hurt you even more badly than I already do. I'm giving you a chance to make a clean breast of things, but badmouthing Beth is only going to make me want to snap every bone in your pathetic, cowardly little body. She trusted you to look after her. And instead you had her killed."

"Look, I'm not gonna sit here and listen to any more of this shit." Tom loomed over him and put the muzzle of the suppressor next to his left eye.

"'The Contact Agent can provide physical and psychological support, can be available in times of danger . . . at any sign of danger the Under Cover Agent is extracted.' That's straight from the FBI Career Guide, Dean. That means it's your job. Maybe you need to go on a refresher course."

At the words "refresher course", Carter looked truly frightened.

"The FBI *Career Guide* also says that only one undercover agent has ever been killed on duty in the Bureau's entire history, which I find hard to believe, and now you've doubled that. So, Dean, let's discuss what leads an agent with an unremarkable record like yours to resort to having his own colleagues murdered. Let's start with some names, shall we? Zuabi, Fortress, Stutz."

"I'm not—I can't—"

"You are and you can. This—" he indicated the weapon "—says you don't have a choice. Zuabi, Fortress, Stutz. Come on, join up the dots."

At the mention of the names again, Carter's expression changed. His face was starting to glisten, as were his eyes, which were opened very wide, as if something was pushing his eyeballs out from behind. When he spoke again, his voice had gone up an octave and came out as a childish whine. "You think I can walk out of here if I tell you what I know? You have no idea what you're dealing with, fella. No idea!"

"Enlighten me."

Carter breathed deeply, as if he was trying to compose himself, as if whatever he was about to do there was no going back.

"Zuabi doesn't know zip about Stutz or Fortress, okay? Not a thing. He thinks his finance comes from the Saudis. He's just the conduit to his people."

"What people?"

"Sleepers."

Carter was panting hard, hyper-ventilating. "I gotta get some air."

Tom nodded. Carter struggled to his feet, a hand against the wall for support. His face was as red as a traffic-light. Tom kept his weapon trained on him as he felt his way to the balcony window.

"So Stutz is running Zuabi without his knowledge?"

Carter turned back to him, the desperation on his face that of a man who had given up his most precious secret and was trying to absorb the consequences of having crossed that line. He shook his head. "You can't stop him. He's too well connected."

317

Then, as if jolted by a freak burst of electricity, he darted forward through the open window to the wall of the balcony and leaped over. Tom lunged after him and wrapped his arms round his left leg. Carter shook his head frantically. "No, no! Let me go!"

Tom fought to get a better grip but he was thrashing, gravity sucking his body out of Tom's clutches. Tom grabbed the end of his coat but it was no good. The coat detached itself and he was absorbed into the darkness below.

69

Pall Mall, London

There was something deeply comforting about walking back into his father's club. After all that had happened in Texas, Tom felt calmed by the wooden panelling, the quiet, understated tone of the place. Even the frayed edges of the rug on the landing outside the members' dining room was strangely reassuring.

"There you are!" Hugh rose to his feet. "I was starting to think we'd lost you."

Tom glanced at his watch: thirty minutes late. It was odd that, after all his years in the Regiment, his father should fret about his being half an hour late for dinner; ridiculous, and rather endearing. He felt surprisingly happy to see the old man.

"Sorry, I was in the bath."

"You?"

"I needed a serious soak to get some of that oily American grime off me." He didn't say that he had stood under the shower in his hotel room before he flew home, watching the last flecks of blood floating off him: his own, Jefferson's, Kyle's, Colburn's and, most distressingly, Beth's. A lot of people's blood, not to mention the memory of Carter going over the balcony. It wasn't the sight of blood *per se*, or death, that was shocking to him, but the world he seemed to have stepped into. The rules were different. And he didn't like the people who made them. Worse, he didn't trust them.

His father peered at him. "You look exhausted. But never mind. Sit down and have a drink. This Cabernet Sauvignon's really quite good. A Le Bonheur 2006. Or would you prefer to open with a G and T?"

"No, pour me some of that. Thanks."

"Did you have a good trip?"

Tom couldn't think of when he had ever been more glad to be back in London. He sniffed the wine—it smelt like an old cigar box—then drank. It was rich, dark and oaky.

"Hey, take your time, we've got all evening."

"Don't tell me to slow down, Dad."

"Sorry."

Tom could see his father's concern etched on his face. He knew he must seem tired and distracted, as his eyes roved around the room.

"Tom, is everything all right?"

Tom looked at his father, his worried, careworn face. "I can't begin to tell you how good it is to be back."

"Was it successful—your mission?"

He had told him it was for Rolt but hadn't gone into any more detail than that. "You know I can't talk about it."

"Oh, come on, it was only a PR job for Invicta—wasn't it?"

"PR job?"

"Oh, come on! You're not in the SAS now."

"Look, it was and it wasn't. It's complicated, okay?"

All his working life he had made a point of never lying to his parents. There were many things he could never tell them about his work but he refused to lie about it.

Hugh looked uncomfortable as he took another gulp of wine. "Dad—what is it?"

"It's just that . . . . I rather feel I owe you an apology."

"Why?"

"Getting you involved with him."

Tom put his glass on the table. Yes, he probably did need to slow down. Right now he felt like getting well and truly shit-faced, but that wouldn't do at all, not here, and definitely not in this company. "How d'you mean?"

"I think I may have been a bit—premature."

"Well, you weren't the only one pushing me in his direction as it turned out, but why the change of heart? You were so gung-ho before."

Hugh Buckingham paused while the wine waiter topped up their glasses. "I think we'll need another of those when you have a moment."

The waiter nodded and glided away. Hugh leaned forward and lowered his voice. "The last few days, seeing him all over the media and so forth, I mean it was terrible what happened to his hostel, awful—those poor men—but it's put him even more in the spotlight."

"And?"

Hugh blew out a long breath. "Well, he's very presentable, very calm, very reasoned. But when you actually add up what he's saying—well, stop me if you think I'm wrong—it's pretty inflammatory."

Tom found himself on the spot. He played for time while he worked out how to respond. "Go on, then. Get it off your chest."

"Well, in the past people like him were always banging around. They'd make a bit of a noise, get a few headlines, then

321

disappear back into the swamp they came from. But Rolt, with his reasoned tone and presentable looks, he's gone mainstream, if you like. And instead of putting a *cordon sanitaire* round him and giving him a wide berth, everyone seems to be climbing on his bandwagon. Half of Westminster is queuing up for a photo-opportunity with him, as if he's some kind of magic bullet for their fading popularity. I have a bad feeling in my water that something quite fundamental is happening and I don't like it one bit."

"Is that so?" Tom knew he was coming over as defensive when he had no need to be. Was it that he didn't want to go down in his father's estimation—even if it had been his idea in the first place?

"Well, you must have noticed."

"I've just been in America, remember, but go on. I'm interested in your point of view." Tom sat back, prepared for a lecture.

"Well, if you follow his argument to its logical conclusion, it's damn near forcible repatriation. Even Enoch Powell didn't advocate that. And in some cases, because we're also talking about people who were born here—there's no other way of putting it—it's deportation. And I'll tell you something else."

He gestured discreetly at the other diners and lowered his voice. "It's putting the jump leads on some of these old farts who've been minding their Ps and Qs, toeing the politically correct line and so forth. There's all kinds of nasty stuff coming out of the woodwork. In fact," he jabbed a forefinger at the table, "it almost smacks of what went on in Germany in the thirties. And I don't say that lightly."

What could Tom say? There'd been many times he and his father hadn't seen eye to eye, but this wasn't one of them. In fact, he agreed with every word.

And he now saw very clearly where he stood. He had gone to Texas with an open mind, pissed off with the Army, with MI5, in fact the whole British Establishment, and had plunged head first into an entirely alien world, like nothing he had experienced before. Having seen what he had seen—and survived—he had emerged with a burning desire to get to the bottom of what Stutz and Rolt were up to and stop it in its tracks. He had successfully inserted himself into Invicta so was better placed than anyone to chase down what was going on. It would be madness to bail out now.

But he couldn't let on to his father, not yet.

"Look, Dad, it's difficult."

Hugh looked indignant. "I don't see what's difficult about it at all. You don't owe the man anything. I apologize for ever having got you involved with him, but I'm not happy with the idea of my son going around with a man who's talking up what amounts to ethnic cleansing. One more atrocity like that hostel and he's going to have public opinion right alongside."

Hugh's voice had risen a couple of decibels as it was apt to do when he was on a hobbyhorse. A couple at the next table were staring at them.

Tom raised his hands to his father in a placatory gesture. "Please, Dad, can we not discuss this now? I've had a pretty gruelling few days and I just need to chill. Okay?"

But Hugh wasn't looking at his son or listening to him: his eyes were fixed on something behind him. "Well, talk of the devil."

323

Tom looked round. Rolt had just entered the dining room. He seemed to be lingering in the doorway, as if to make the most of his entrance. Conversations petered out and there was a hush as everyone gradually became aware of his presence.

All eyes were on him, the man of the moment. The whole atmosphere of the room had changed. Someone started to clap and soon a ripple of applause spread throughout the room. Tom glanced at his father, whose hands remained firmly clenched in front of him, a knowing eyebrow raised. Less than a week ago such a display of impromptu adulation would have been unimaginable. But Hugh was right: Rolt had picked a scab and uncovered a festering sore underneath. And it alarmed Tom to see just how vulnerable people were to his charm and charisma.

He looked away, but it was too late. Rolt had spotted him from his vantage point in the doorway and was striding towards their table, with another man in tow. There was nothing else to do: Tom got to his feet as Rolt bore down on them.

"Tom, you dark horse! You slipped back to London without passing by. I'm crestfallen." Rolt pumped his hand.

"You remember my father, Hugh Buckingham."

Hugh, ever the gentleman, stood up and they shook hands.

"I really am in your debt for sending Tom my way. I don't mind telling you he's the best thing that's happened to Invicta in a long while."

"Well, it's very nice to hear that. Always good for a father to see his son getting rave reviews."

Rolt turned to the man he was with. "Alec, meet Tom Buckingham, my latest recruit, who's been doing sterling work for me across the pond. Tom, Alec Clements, cabinet secretary."

From the Office of the Cabinet Secretary. The "Alec" on the compliments slip in the book on Stutz's coffee-table.

"Delighted." Clements nodded to both of them, his lack of interest transparent.

"Tom, can I have a quick word?" Rolt put an arm round him and moved him aside, leaving Hugh with Clements.

Rolt put his mouth close to Tom's ear. "Well done. You really stepped up. As I said on the phone, Stutz filled me in. I seriously owe you. Come by first thing tomorrow, promise?"

Tom had already agreed to meet Woolf for a debrief. "Can we make it the afternoon? I seriously need to catch up on some sleep."

Rolt sighed, then smiled. "Of course. But the pressure's on now. Lots to do."

They made their farewells and Clements steered him away. Tom and Hugh sat back down again.

"Well, that was extraordinary. I've never seen adulation like it in this room, apart from when Andy Murray came in. Proves my point. Something big is happening."

But Tom wasn't listening: he was thinking about Rolt's companion. "Tell me about Clements."

Hugh's contempt was only too evident. "An operator *par excellence*. A ferociously bright Civil Service official who's clawed his way to the top post in the Cabinet Office by stabbing his rivals in the back. The cabinet secretary is basically the most powerful unelected official in government, the main source of policy advice for the PM. That means he's at the very heart of where the most important decisions are made."

"So being seen with him is a vote of confidence for Rolt."

"You bet. Clements is the type whose every action is a calculation. Bringing Rolt to dinner is *de facto* his endorsement of the man, and that will reverberate round Whitehall. Shocking, really."

"Why?"

"People in Clements's position don't change when there's an election. They're in for the long haul. Chances are he's laying down a marker for whoever is in power now or *after* the election."

"Aren't you crediting him with too much power?"

"Not outright power. Let's call it influence."

"So Clements wouldn't associate himself with anyone he didn't regard as useful to him in some way."

"Absolutely."

"So giving a present to or having himself photographed with the wrong kind of person . . ."

"Just wouldn't happen. He's much too smart. But why the sudden interest in Clements? I thought this sort of political minutiae bored the pants off you."

"Maybe I've changed."

Hugh put down his glass and put his hand over Tom's. They didn't go in for physical contact: Tom had made that clear years ago. "All I can say is, I hope you've not got yourself into something you can't get out of."

But he was already in, and in deep. It was time to move the conversation on. "I'll do what I have to do, okay? Trust me on that."

Without knowing it, his father had just confirmed Tom's suspicions. Stutz's connections didn't just stretch up through the

Washington bureaucracy. They ran deep into Whitehall. But for now he had to keep this part of the jigsaw to himself. With some careful handling he managed to move his father to other matters while they ate their steak, but the relaxed evening he had been hoping for had turned into just the opposite.

All through the meal, he noticed Hugh had been glancing at his phone a lot. As the plates were being cleared, it buzzed and he announced that Tom should head out to the front desk. "Someone's waiting for you."

70

She was sitting in a leather armchair with her back to him. When the porter announced him and she got up, his heart turned over.

"Delphine!"

She smiled, lighting up the lobby. Under her trench coat she was wearing a low-cut black dress and black boots. Her hair was glossy and her skin glowed.

"You look amazing."

"Well, I've had some time at home, time to relax."

He was lost for words, still absorbing the surprise of seeing her.

"And your mother's been so kind. She's offered me to stay for a few nights. I know you're—busy."

Tom felt a flicker of irritation: he had had enough parental interference for one day.

The possibility—myriad possibilities—hung in the air. She went on, "I've had a think."

Tom was aware of the porter shifting uncomfortably behind his desk. He gently touched her arm—sending an electric charge through him—and steered her down the stone steps into the street. "Let's get out of here."

It was still light, though the street-lights had just come on. The air was cool on their faces.

"I've been doing some thinking and I—I was wrong. Right to go home for a break, perhaps, but wrong to run away as I did."

"I don't blame you."

She looked down uneasily at the ground. "I do! I do blame me." She smiled again: that intoxicating beam of light. "I think we should try again. I know it's very forward of me but you know what we French are like when we want something . . ." She giggled flirtatiously, but there was an underlying nervousness.

Part of him would have liked nothing more than to leap into a taxi with her there and then and head off into the night, into the future.

"I've missed you." That much he could say. "Life has been . . . rather complicated lately."

"I've missed you too—very much. Can we—go somewhere? Alone?"

Tom gestured back at the large old doors. "I've left Dad in there."

"No, I mean away. Somewhere hot and relaxing and . . ." He could see the disappointment starting to cloud her gorgeous face. "Please believe there's nothing I'd like more . . ."

"But?"

She was clearly heartbroken. He fought with himself. Looking at her, standing on the damp sidewalk, her face so full of hope, he realized this was something he wanted now, had wanted all along, without knowing it, and it had come at the worst possible time.

"But I can't go anywhere right at this moment. It's very complicated."

"Is it the man you're working for? The fascist, Vernon Rolt? Your father told me."

"He did? It's not how it looks. I'll be able to explain, but not yet."

He knew, even as he said it, that the last thing he could do was explain, probably ever.

"So it's true, then. In France in the papers they say he's like Le Pen—even worse. What's happening to you, Tom? Is this some kind of revenge for what happened with the Regiment?"

What else could he say? There was no explanation that would work right now. He was in too far and too deep. He reached out to her. If he could just get closer, maybe he could communicate how he felt, transmit the truth of his emotions without using words. But she pulled away.

"I'm sorry, Tom. I'm sorry for this country, which I did love. And I'm sorry for you."

She turned and walked briskly towards Piccadilly. He knew it was useless to follow.

71

Westford Airfield, Oxfordshire

"And that's everything?" Mandler peered at Tom over his half-glasses, his arms tightly folded over his chest.

"Chapter and verse." Well, sort of: he'd glossed over some of the more extreme moments and left out any mention of the Clements connection. He wasn't going to share that with the group. It had to be for Mandler's ears only.

"Quite a frantic little city break you seem to have had."

As Tom sat down he scanned the listeners. There were seven of them round the table: Woolf on his immediate left, looking like he had neither slept nor changed his clothes while Tom had been away; Rafiq and Cindy, his sidekicks, whom he had contrived to keep from being reassigned; and Deakin and Brandeis, a pair of geeky analysts on loan from MI6 for their expertise in US affairs. The draughty hangar groaned and creaked in the wind.

"Was it really necessary to dispatch Carter?" asked Mandler.

"He dispatched himself."

"And if he hadn't?"

Tom gave Mandler a cold look. They both knew the answer to that one.

"Either way, you risked blowing your cover."

"My judgement at the time was that it was worth the risk. Beth was killed because she'd asked him about Zuabi. Kyle Pope decided I had to die because I'd heard the same name. For God's sake, Zuabi's connection to Stutz is one that people are prepared to kill to hide."

Brandeis raised a finger. "If I could come in here, our reading of the reaction in Washington suggests the Bureau haven't exactly put the flags at half-mast for Carter. He wasn't top of anyone's Christmas-card list. They seem content with the conclusion that it was suicide. More than content, I'd say."

Mandler gave a grudging nod.

Woolf was wagging a finger to get attention. He looked like he badly needed some sleep. "But it still means we have to be extremely careful with the Americans. We don't know how far Stutz's influence spreads into Washington. We go to them for help, we risk blowing it all. Could we please turn to what we've got on your imam?"

Brandeis got to his feet and plugged his laptop into the screen. A long-lens shot of an elderly man appeared, partly obscured by the crowd around him. He was swathed in white, with a stiff embroidered hat, and had a bushy gray beard. His heavy-lidded eyes were lowered as if in prayer. The same man Tom had seen on Jefferson's computer in the trailer.

"Okay, we *think* this is the most recent shot of Asim Zuabi, taken four months ago. And here's his mug shot when he first came on the grid."

An emaciated figure, his head shaved, eyes sunken. He looked nothing like the later shot.

"It's early days so what we have is sketchy. In 2004, he walks into the US Consulate in Beirut. Why they didn't spit him straight back out is still a mystery. It suggests he had names or some information that gave them cause to hang on to him. We don't yet know where he was born or raised. He told them he was based at a mosque in a village north of Aleppo, which has since been shelled to fuck. But another source tells us that, prior to becoming a cleric, he spent some years working oil wells round the Gulf. Maybe that's where he hooked up with Stutz. Whatever and wherever that connection occurred, the speed with which he was processed suggests that someone had a hand in fast-tracking his exit. He had an American passport and a green card in two weeks."

"What about family?" asked Tom. "The mosque is supposed to be dedicated to one of his daughters."

"There are five known children by three different wives, none of whom accompanied him to America. We don't know where they are now. If they're still in Syria it's going to be hard to get any reliable data but we're working on it. He's believed to live in a house close to the mosque. He has a couple of servants and a secretary, all men, who live there as well."

Brandeis flicked through several more shots of the mosque under construction, the *Houston Chronicle* photo-op Tom had seen, the house and neighborhood: it all looked very suburban-American, all incredibly normal.

"There's nothing ostentatious about his lifestyle. This is his car, a 'ninety-eight Chevy Impala. He lives a very low-tech life. Just a landline into the home, no Internet on site. And no email ID that we've found so far. We think this is significant."

Mandler peered at Brandeis doubtfully. "There's a lot of 'maybes' to this story."

Woolf came straight back. "Doesn't that strike you as odd? That he's in charge of the biggest new mosque in the area, the focal point for the Muslim community across Houston and for miles around, yet the guy has no email account? Terror networks are bypassing electronic communication altogether to the extent that they're using messengers and couriers. His lack of visibility makes him all the more suspicious."

Brandeis was clearly relieved to have his point endorsed. "And as Tom told us, before Carter in-conveniently jumped to his death he said Zuabi was a *conduit*, didn't he? That he had some kind of network."

Mandler's impatience, which Tom had been aware of all through the briefing, was starting to make itself felt. "Well, thank you for that rather inconsequential appraisal."

Brandeis, cowed, sat down again as Mandler took the floor. "So, if I might sum up, we have Rolt and Invicta handsomely financed by an American benefactor, with deep links to the military industrial complex, whose company is also pioneering— what was it?"

"Predictive tracking," said Tom.

"Which, frankly, strikes me as voodoo but there you are, call me old-fashioned. And Lederer and Stutz seem to be singing from the same hymn sheet as Rolt—that some kind of mass deportation is the answer to all our ills. We have Stutz's dark hints of something around the corner but we've no idea what, and tenuous links to an obscure cleric with no form who seems to be a virtual recluse yet has apparently nothing particular to hide. What's more, there's nothing whatever to connect Zuabi to the UK or Rolt and Invicta. I'm sorry to have to bring you all back to earth, people, but if it's

334

not domestic, it's not MI5's responsibility to chase it up. Can we please move on to more pressing matters closer to home?"

"Suppose Rolt is just an appendage of Stutz's operation? Stutz is where the finance is coming from."

Mandler eyed Tom wearily, then unfolded his arms and raised his hands heavenwards. "Which strengthens the case for briefing the Americans about what we have."

Woolf was almost out of his chair. "If we do that, we lose all control of what we've got! There's every chance it will get straight back to Stutz and all our leads will go cold. Tom—who's risked his neck to get on-side with these people—would be blown. We'd be back to square one. Can I ask that we, please, park talking to the Americans at least until we're further on with Invicta?"

Mandler sighed heavily, his exasperation with Woolf plain for all to see. "I don't have to remind you that this is an extremely sensitive time for our relationship with the Americans. The PM has staked the election on this summit with the President. We're all going to have to be on our best behavior for this wretched event. If it comes out that my Service is intimately connected to the deaths of not one but two FBI agents, a lot of toys will be thrown out of the pram, even more if they find we've withheld information because we don't trust them. I hope you follow my line of thinking—I'm only stating the bloody obvious."

Mandler paused. To Tom, it looked as if MI5's DG had let too much of his own exasperation with his political masters show. Mandler turned back to Woolf. "So how *do* you propose to get further on with Invicta?"

Woolf had been caught off guard. He hadn't bargained for Mandler's dampener. It was time for him to come to the rescue.

"Go back to Vestey and the shooting in Walthamstow. We know about his connection via his brother to SCO19. I know I said that in my judgement he's not a good enough shot to have been the perp, but maybe he's the connection to whoever did the job. You either need to eliminate him or find a stronger link."

They all looked at him.

"You have his entire history. He's at the shooting range most days, isn't he?"

"Or doing security for one of his VIP clients."

"Right. So why don't you get him out of the way? And we'll go and have a look round his place. And the supposed hostel bomber. Are you still sitting on the evidence that he was DOA at the scene?"

Woolf glanced at Mandler and nodded. Mandler shook his head.

"You do realize the consequences for our relationship with Scotland Yard when they find out? So, the sooner you have something concrete the better. What else do you know about him, other than that he's one of the returnees?"

Rafiq, who had been studying something on his phone, looked up. "We've only just tracked down his family. They went to ground after his name was published."

"Well, if he did die before the blast, how come he was there at all? And what about survivors? Do any of them remember anything?"

No one spoke. It was becoming horribly clear to Tom why these questions had gone unanswered. It wasn't for any lack of commitment to the investigation but a consequence of Woolf's lack of resources. What had changed, Tom realized, was his own position. Having been furious with Woolf at the start for his clumsy attempt to recruit him behind his back, he now had a grudging respect for his staying power. He could also see how Mandler was between a rock and a hard place, knowing he would have to carry the can for a wayward investigation that stepped all over the toes of the other services and pissed off the Americans.

Mandler folded his glasses and slipped them into his top pocket. "I'll have to go to the home secretary if we're going to be turning over Vestey's place without the Plod."

"Well? Can you?"

Tom felt his frustration with all this procedure getting the better of him.

"All right. But if you draw a blank there, I'm shutting you down."

He turned to Tom. "Sorry to be a killjoy, but these are hard times. Thanks, all."

The meeting was over. Mandler was on his feet and heading for the door. Tom followed him out.

Halfway to his car, Tom caught up with him and put a hand on his shoulder to turn him round. Mandler stepped back abruptly as if he thought he was about to get a fist in his face.

"Barely a week ago I was made to carry the can in Bastion. You fold on this, I'm going to be right back where I was, in the shit for sticking my neck out, but this time I'll have the wrath of Rolt and Stutz to deal with, and after what I've seen of them, I don't fancy my chances. You've got to come off the fence and get behind this. Woolf's operating with one hand tied behind his back."

Mandler sighed, as though the fight had gone out of him.

"And there's something else you need to know." Tom told him about the gift from the Cabinet Office in Stutz's penthouse, and the photo of Clements.

Mandler listened without comment, which Tom could only hope was a sign that it had sunk in, then shook his head mournfully. "Do you have any idea what pressure I'm under? The country's in uproar, the PM's polls are flat-lining, and he's only a few months away from an election. Plus the cabinet are all scheming against each other, and most of the Whitehall departments are at each other's throats. The home secretary and the Met are barely on speaking terms. Now we've got this bloody summit, which the PM's staked his survival on, so London's going to be on lockdown. I've got a lot bigger worries on my plate than what happens to you."

"I'm not just thinking of myself. Don't you understand that? The stability of the whole country's at stake."

Mandler nodded at the hangar. "Get me some red meat and you'll get the resources to fight your battle."

"*Our* battle," said Tom, but Mandler was already in the car.

72

10 Downing Street, London

Everything about the prime minister should have suggested a man at the top of his game, thought his home secretary. Sprawled over his sofa he was tanned, with not a single gray hair and no unattractive bags under the eyes, the signature facial feature of anyone in the top job. The neck was developing a bit of a wattle, Sarah Garvey noted, a hangover from a crash diet he had embarked on a year ago. And he was doing his best to look relaxed in a polo shirt, lightweight chinos and loafers. The trouble was, he was in the shit and he knew it.

"Okay, Derek, hit me with it."

Farmer glanced at her. "Sure you wouldn't like to clear the room first?"

The PM smiled grimly. "I think Sarah will have heard worse things about me than anything you can deliver, and said them too, most probably."

She gave him a grim smile back, relieved that she was still a confidante, that she hadn't been eclipsed—yet.

Farmer sighed and launched in. "Okay, so this sample's taken from the party faithful, which is what makes it particularly worrying as they were giving you a pretty easy ride before all this chaos. Sixty-five percent of those polled said they thought the PM had not handled the crisis well, seventy percent say you should have broken off your meeting at Camp David and come home to take charge."

The PM showed no reaction.

"And seventy-three percent say they don't believe the enhanced Anglo-American relationship will deliver either prosperity or security."

Garvey noted a pink tinge spreading over the PM's cheeks. He lurched forward and jabbed the air. "Yeah? Well, bollocks to that. And POTUS and I won't be announcing any detail before our summit anyhow. How the fuck do they think they know? Honestly, Derek, where do you find these people?"

His neck quivered, causing her to wince inwardly. She also disliked his un-ironic use of the presidential acronym, one of his other less attractive features being his fondness for diminutives and nicknames to denote new best friends.

Farmer plowed on. At least he didn't mince his words. "Understood, Prime Minister. But the fact remains that, with an election five months away, the other figures are troubling."

"But, as you say, the sample is just the party faithful. They're always at their worst when there's a bit of bother on the streets."

This was too much for Garvey. "Geoff, really, you can't go around downplaying what's uppermost in people's minds right now."

"I know, I know. It's just a turn of phrase. You know me, never knowingly overstated."

And this with half the country going up in flames. He really was the limit.

Farmer looked up from the pages of figures perched on his knee. He had evidently detected an unexpected ally in his midst.

"Well, to the home secretary's point, there's a further question in the same sample it's worth drawing your attention to."

"Go on. Hit me while I'm down."

"Eighty-five percent of those polled said they believed that Vernon Rolt's call for a crackdown on suspected terrorists should be heeded by the government."

"Oh, for God's sake—"

"And if I could just finish? Sixty-five percent of them said they would vote for the opposition if they were to adopt the same measures."

"Well, bollocks to that as well. Five months is a very long time in politics."

Farmer wasn't backing down. "We can't overlook it. The party chairman has been onto us about it."

"Well, he can sod off."

The PM got up and started moving round the room, fiddling with his many knick-knacks—evidence of his supposed popularity in various parts of the world the voters weren't interested in—but Farmer wasn't to be deflected. Garvey braced herself for what was coming.

"Look, just as a holding measure, how about a meeting—you and Rolt? Nothing formal, just so we can get a photo of you together. You don't have to show your hand, just listen to him for ten minutes."

The PM didn't seem to be paying attention. Farmer added: "All right, five. It might help check the rumor that you're not receptive to fresh ideas."

The PM's face was very shiny now. "It's his ideas I'm not bloody receptive to. I've nailed my colors to the multicultural

341

mast and I'm not taking them down, especially for that—I know it's terrible what happened to his hostel and after all he's done for our boys and so on, but I refuse to be associated with a proponent of deportation. Derek, I'm disappointed in you. Sarah, where do you stand on Mr. Rolt?"

"I'm with you, Prime Minister—sorry, Derek. We're a nation of moderates, and whatever the polls say, when the chips are down, we don't like extremists. I say, stand your ground. Besides, everyone knows that the right message at a time like this is one of unity—the very opposite of what he's trying to promote."

Farmer gave an almost inaudible grunt of reproach.

Garvey glanced at her watch. "We need to cover security arrangements for Friday."

The prime minister was clearly glad of a reason to get shot of Farmer. "Sorry, Derek, let's pick this up later."

Farmer gathered up his papers and got to his feet. "So you'll give it some thought? Only we're inundated by press enquiries about where you stand . . ."

Garvey knew this was a bridge too far. When the PM flipped he turned an alarming heart-attack red, reminding her of an angry tomato.

"I'm not going to be pushed around by some Oswald Mosley wannabe with delusions of grandeur. Make it go away, Derek. Do your job."

Farmer collected up his papers and shuffled out of the room. The PM shook his head as the door closed. "He may be right. A handshake would probably suffice. He can be invited to some low-level do or other and they can get their picture—but I'm buggered if I'm going to give him a personal audience. You know, they've got the same problem in the US, the rising tide of bigotry. The President and I compared notes."

There was a wistful look in the PM's eye, as if he was remembering a romantic weekend, before he'd had to come home to his wife.

"Yes, and on that note, I really must give you a run down on the security for the summit."

The PM groaned. "Must you, Sarah? I'm sure you've got it marvelously under control."

What was wrong with the man? He was hopeless on detail. Besides, she was going to tell him whether he wanted to hear it or not. Then if anything went wrong, God forbid, he couldn't say she'd kept him out of the loop.

"Basically there'll be a total exclusion zone around Number Ten and Whitehall for the whole day. All the roads will be closed around the ambassador's residence in Regent's Park for his motorcade, or if he's delayed he can helicopter in from Stansted, once they've parked Air Force One, and land in St. James's Park. Any hiccup at all, we have the place secure. Every pedestrian within a mile will be stopped and, if necessary, searched. The police have authorization to turn away anyone they don't like the look of. We will also be closing Westminster, Charing Cross, and Victoria tube stations and rerouting the buses. The only press invited will be ours and theirs, staff only, no freelances."

The PM's eyes had already glazed over. "As I said, I'm sure you've got it all under control."

A senior PA put her head round the door. "The cabinet secretary's here, Prime Minister."

The PM sprang to attention. "Jolly good."

Garvey got swiftly to her feet. The last thing she needed right now was to be cross-examined by Clements in front of the PM.

"And, ma'am, Stephen Mandler's waiting for you in your office. He said it's urgent."

73

Mandler was perched on the edge of the sofa, half folded over as if he had a stitch.

"You look like a man who's painted himself into a corner."

He shrugged dejectedly. The comment had hit home, as Garvey's comments usually did.

"So, let me see if I've got this right. You've got Rolt being funded by people in the US who do surveillance software and private security. And you've got an Invicta man whose house you want to turn over without tipping off the Met."

"All I'm doing, Sarah, is keeping you in the loop."

And possibly looking for somewhere else to lay the blame, once it came to it, which it usually did. "Thank you, Stephen, that's most considerate. What is it you actually want?"

"Leave to keep going, but without involving the police. We may need to lift a few people and question them without sending any shockwaves that might alert Rolt's friends."

"Are you saying Rolt is somehow complicit in the bombing of his own hostel?"

"Not in so many words—but you're aware of what we know about the supposed 'bomber' and that's still under wraps for now. But if we take the two incidents together, the shooting in

345

Walthamstow and the bombing, what do they have in common? It would now seem that both were planned specifically to deceive us about who was responsible. The first outraged the Muslim community because it appeared that the police had shot an innocent man, and the second got the rest of the population very worked up—not just over Syrian returnees, but just about everybody with a Koran in the house. If anyone wanted to split the public and turn the two communities against each other this has done it, and Rolt has stepped into that divide. It's extremely bad news."

"But apart from your belief that trouble always comes in threes, and a nasty feeling about Rolt, this doesn't amount to much."

"Look, can I just say, re the location for the summit—"

"Stephen, there's no way that's going to change. The PM has staked his reputation and, indeed, his political future on pulling off a deal with the US that should put the economy back on the rails. What's more, moving it away from Downing Street will, he thinks, make him look weak. I don't like you going behind the backs of the police. As it is, there's too much friction between you lot."

She held his gaze. They both knew what she was talking about. 9/11 might have been averted had there been better communication between the US security services. 7/7 had caught them unawares here, yet the perpetrators were found afterwards to have been on the watch lists. And with Al Qaeda urging returnees from Syria to make lone-wolf attacks on any significant targets this was no time to be fomenting disunity between MI5 and the Met.

"How's your man inside Invicta? Has he made any headway?"

"It's a little early to say, but he's certainly got stuck in. He's the reason I'm here basically."

"His name wouldn't be Tom Buckingham, would it, by any chance?"

The blood drained from Mandler's face. "Wherever did you get that idea?"

She gave him a wry look. "You're aware that our mutually esteemed cabinet secretary has a soft spot for Rolt. Turns out they dined at Clements's club and Rolt was waxing lyrical about an ex-SAS man of that name. If he's your man, and Clements is aware of him, I fear his number may be up pretty soon."

74

Tom walked past the SO6 cops outside Invicta's headquarters and through the front door, held open for him by another cop with an MP5. Inside, the security guard gave him a friendly nod. No questions, no search. And the receptionist greeted him as if he'd worked there for years.

"I'll sign you in, Mr. Buckingham. Just go straight up," she said, with a sunny smile.

"Thanks. It's Hattie, isn't it?"

She beamed.

Phoebe was waiting for him at the top of the stairs. "Hello, Mr. Buckingham. How nice to see you again."

She was so convincing, he wondered for a moment if she had just had a serious attack of amnesia. "Good to see you too—er?"

"Phoebe."

"Of course, how could I forget?"

He took her hand and gave it a discreet squeeze.

"Good trip, I hope?"

"Yes, thanks."

A couple of Invicta staff came past and smiled at him.

Phoebe was staying in character. "We've lost Vernon, I'm afraid. He went off to see a group of MPs and he's not back."

"No problem, I'll wait."

Phoebe's eyes shifted pointedly towards the doorway of the room next to where they were standing. Inside, a woman was sitting on a chair, facing the desk: fortyish, attractive, with dark shoulder-length hair, in a dark coat and low-heeled shoes; professional, he guessed, educated. Phoebe leaned towards him. "Mrs. al-Awati, the mother of the hostel bomber. Vernon invited her."

If she heard them talking about her, she gave no indication of it. Instead, she stared into the middle distance, as if to avoid focusing on anything.

"How come?"

Phoebe leaned closer. "He wants to show some magnanimity. He thinks it's a good message to send out that he's capable of forgiveness—and, of course, it's a great photo-opportunity." She gestured at a photographer sitting on a bench further down the corridor, surrounded by his equipment, reading the *Sun*. "Give me a sec, will you?"

Tom went into the room. "Mrs. al-Awati, good afternoon. I'm Tom Buckingham. I work with Mr. Rolt."

She started to get up.

"No, please."

Her face was etched with grief, her eyes marbled with red, as if she had been crying for days. A handkerchief was balled up in her fist. Tom took her other hand as he sat down beside her. It was stone cold. He was tempted to keep hold of it just to add some warmth. "I'm sorry for your loss."

Over the years he had had to comfort the parents of fallen comrades, but nothing like this. Her face crumpled. She lifted the handkerchief and pressed it to her eyes. "Thank you. Do you know you're the first person to say that to me? I still can't entirely believe it. Maybe I never will."

"That's an understandable reaction."

She began to cry again.

"It's very courageous of you to come here today."

She said nothing to this, just stared into her lap.

"Why don't you tell me a bit about him? He was in Syria. For how long?"

"Why he went—I'll never understand. He had a good job with the Co-op, a pharmacist. Not medicine, as we'd hoped, but still—respectable, you know. Then last September I got a text. He said he'd flown to Turkey. I thought he'd gone on a last-minute holiday. He was there five months. They wanted him for his shooting skills."

"How do you mean?"

"Clay-pigeon shooting was his sport. He won a lot of cups for it—he was so skilled. They're all still in his room."

"Did he come back to you when he returned to the UK?"

"Yes."

"And what was he like, when he came back?"

"He wouldn't talk, wouldn't see his old friends. He was on his phone all the time, I don't know who to."

"And what happened—with the authorities?"

"They came down on him very hard. Detention, took his passport away. Nothing excuses what he did, but I think that was the worst part, the treatment he got when he came back. He thought he had gone to do a good, courageous thing . . . and then that." She gazed up at Tom, with a look of desperation. "Do you know what fighting is like?"

He nodded. "And when he was back home, how was it?"

"He went away for a couple of weeks, suddenly. Said he couldn't stay there. I hoped his girlfriend would help."

"Did he avoid her as well?"

"Oh, no, she was new. They only got together after he was back is my impression. I saw her just the once. He didn't introduce me. She was very devout. I don't know if he feared I would disapprove of that in some way, because we weren't. But I thought it was a good sign, you know, that he had some kind of emotional stability in his life."

"Have you definitely not seen her since?"

"After what's happened? Poor thing, she can't have realized what she was getting into."

"Do you know her name, where she was from? Perhaps you could track her down, support each other." She seemed not to hear this. "He always wanted to be in the Army. From when he was a little boy. It was his dream."

"Mine too," said Tom.

She looked up. "And did you fulfill your dream?"

"I've been very lucky."

"Nurul's father wouldn't allow it. He told him that after 9/11, they wouldn't take Muslims. I knew that wasn't true but you couldn't argue with my husband. He died a few years back." She bowed her head and shook silently as more tears came.

"Do you know where he was living? Nurul."

She sniffed. "The last time I saw him, he had overalls on. He said then he'd been working at a garage in Hatfield." She shook her head as if that, too, was mystifying.

"Was that with the girlfriend or any others, do you know?"

351

She was looking past Tom. He turned. Rolt was standing in the doorway. For a fraction of a second Tom felt a stab of pure hatred towards him, but he checked himself and made a mental note to be ready to show unswerving loyalty at least for now.

"Thank you, Tom. Mrs. al-Awati, I'm so sorry I'm late. It's unforgivable."

"It is most considerate of you to invite me."

"It's very courageous of you to accept the invitation."

"I'll leave you to it." Tom put out his hand. "I'm glad to have met you. Again, I'm very sorry for the loss of your son."

She took his hand and gave him a thin smile. He watched her and Rolt go down the corridor together. Rolt held out an arm as if to guide her along, then retracted it.

Phoebe came out of another door. "He'll only be five minutes or so. He just wants the picture."

"Did you get any of that?"

"Mm. I texted Woolf about the garage."

It didn't take Rolt long to dispense with the mother of the man who had allegedly bombed the Invicta hostel. A four-minute chat, a flurry of camera flashes and it was all over. By the time Tom entered Rolt's office she was gone and he was shouting down the phone. As soon as he saw Tom he finished the call. "That fuckwit. He's so going to regret this."

"What's happened?"

The prime minister had refused to meet him. This was the first time Tom had seen him angry.

"With the state of his popularity you'd think he'd have more sense."

"Perhaps he'll listen to his cabinet secretary. You two seemed to be getting on pretty well the other night."

352

Rolt frowned, as if his memory of their recent encounter at Hugh's club had been obscured by whatever else had happened to him since. Then he brightened. "Ah, yes, at least he's got some clarity about him. And the way things are going, probably a more useful ally in the long term."

"Can't he get you in with the PM?"

Rolt shook his head. The PM's stonewalling had evidently stung him deeply. "You know what? Fuck him. I'm part of the future, he's not."

There was something messianic about his gaze, deluded and disturbing.

"That was a bold move, inviting Mrs. al-Awati."

Rolt sighed. "Well, we don't want to completely alienate the Muslim community. And I had her thoroughly checked out first. She's a GP—almost one of us, really."

"It's strange, isn't it?" said Tom. "You'd assume that suicide bombers are poor and unemployed, with no hope and so forth, yet a lot of them come from decent backgrounds, which makes understanding it all the harder."

"Well, if things work out as planned we won't need to be worrying about suicide bombers soon." He grinned. "So you were impressed with Skip and his vision for the future? I was worried you might be alarmed by it."

Don't overdo it, Tom told himself. "Well, it's a bit *1984* when you first hear it, but it's hard to argue against. The challenge is how you follow through, once you've isolated the people you want to move."

Rolt moved to a sideboard and a tray of drinks. "What'll you have?"

"Not for me, thanks."

Rolt raised his glass. "To order out of chaos. Who was it said that people don't want to be free but safe?"

Tom didn't know, but he tried to look as though he endorsed the sentiment.

"You made a hell of an impression on Stutz. He certainly put you through your paces, I gather. And now we know what you're capable of . . ."

Stutz had clearly briefed him about Jefferson. And since they both knew what he was talking about, Tom couldn't resist the direct question that might take him closer to what he needed to find out.

"You going to ask me to do more of the same?"

"God, no, I've got far more expendable people who can take care of things like that for us, should the need arise. It's the loyalty that matters and you more than passed that test."

There was a manic gleam in his eyes. They had crossed a line. But who were the expendable people? Were the hostel victims expendable? Tom tried another tack. "After what happened at the hostel, I imagine a good few of those lads on the Invicta campus wouldn't half like a chance to get stuck into some serious revenge."

"They're all right as foot soldiers but no more than that. And a lot of them are too winged, or too dim, to be of much use. Something I learned from Stutz, you need professionals all the way. Emotion's useful but it's hard to direct."

Suddenly he veered off the subject—or appeared to. "Remember that fight at school? You gave me a damn good hiding."

"When I should have been doing my prep. I probably spent more hours in the ring than in the classroom!"

"And why not? You were damn good. And it was a valuable lesson for me. Afterwards, I promised myself I'd start winning. Had to go to America to learn how to do that, of course. But who would have thought the day would come when you'd be working for me, eh?"

He was basking, gloating almost. Had that really been his motivation? The psychology was interesting—belittling and flattering at the same time.

"Well, forgive my impatience but I'm used to action. I'm not wired for a lot of waiting around."

Tom decided he should sound sceptical enough not to alert Rolt's suspicions that he was being recruited too easily, and keen enough for him to feel that his new team member was going to be a hundred percent loyal. "Look, I have to know exactly what you want from me. If I'm going to be on the team, I need to be clear about what the structure is here and what you're planning. Basically, I just want to know what I'm letting myself in for." He hoped to God he'd judged it about right.

Rolt put an arm round his shoulders and steered him towards one of the huge windows that overlooked the park. "It won't be long before everything gets a lot clearer. It has to get worse before it gets better. The country's had a couple of shocks, but it's not enough. We've had some outbreaks of violence, a few folks are probably thinking about jumping ship for Spain and wherever, but most people are getting on with their lives, back to business as usual. We need another event, something that will really change the climate—politically speaking."

We need another event. We. Tom was struck by a terrible realization, so terrible that he had to push it temporarily out of his mind

355

in order to stay in the room. He tried to finish the conversation with his voice level. "Well, if there's a seat, I want in."

"Tom, I really applaud your sentiment. But we've done our bit on that front for the moment. Stutz's crew will handle the rest. He has the men and the means. His network—it's fantastic. He's got his people in over forty countries, for God's sake. He's been prepping them for years."

Tom blinked with what he hoped resembled admiration while he digested this. Mandler need be in no doubt now about Rolt's connection to Stutz.

"I understand your impatience. I know what happened to you in Afghanistan made you thirsty for revenge. Come back in twenty-four hours and I'll see about giving you a heads-up."

Phoebe put her head round the door. "Sorry, Vernon, your four-thirty's here."

75

Vestey's house was a new-build on an anonymous estate outside Basingstoke, one of four that sat at the end of a cul-de-sac behind neat, square lawns with no flowers.

The van said *"Lawlor Landscaping"*, with a green tree logo on the side. They left it on the main road, and walked up: one from MI5's digital intelligence team and the other a forensics specialist, trained to work under severe time pressure. Woolf had asked Tom along on the grounds that, with his background, he might notice something they would overlook, though he didn't need much persuading.

The two techies were kitted out in anonymous, greenish-hued overalls that suggested gardeners, and each carried a dusty rucksack that contained, inside sealed pouches, all they needed for the job: gloves, card readers, a pair of hard drives in case one failed during the uploading, and a lightweight forensics equipment with all the essentials for the recovery of fibres, fingerprints and any kind of sample likely to yield DNA. Woolf had gone to town and had a folder tucked under his arm also marked *"Lawlor Landscaping"*, with the same tree logo as on the van. For a team so short on resources, they'd risen to the challenge quite impressively.

The house was like countless soldiers' homes Tom had seen in the past, soldiers with OCD to be exact: the downstairs open plan and dominated by a huge flat-screen TV, the sofa and other furniture arranged exactly to line up with it, as if on a grid. Most squaddies were untidy, just like Tom. It was the NCOs' griping that kept them in order. Otherwise most blocks would have looked like a gorilla had gone crazy during the night.

Even the magazine on the coffee-table, *Autocar*, was placed in one corner, the edges flush with those of the table. On the mantelpiece above the fireplace, a collection of memorabilia from Vestey's army days gave the only indication of his previous calling: a nickel-plated SA80 bayonet with "Farewell and good luck" engraved along the blade; a brass Arab coffee pot with the obligatory matching little goblets; a picture of his old rifle company. Three rows of men in their number-two service dress, medals glinting in the sun. The first row sitting crosslegged, left over right and closed fists resting on thighs, the center row standing at ease, and the rear the same but with their legs cut off by bodies as they stood on chairs to give them height. Tom smiled to himself as he looked down at the company commander's feet to see the obligatory yellow Labrador lying in front of him. Vestey was, no doubt, one of the young bloods standing proud, but the photo was years old, from his glory days.

He touched the edge of the frame with a gloved finger: not a speck of dust. Even the trash or garbage in the kitchen, for which Woolf made a beeline, was spotlessly clean.

"Nothing," he announced, when he had taken out the garbage bag, shaken it carefully and replaced it, taking care not to rearrange the single fish-finger packet and used teabag he had found within. Tom watched him with interest; his kind were easier to admire when they were quietly deploying their core skills, i.e. doing the actual physical snooping, than when sitting round boardroom tables blowing hot air at each other.

"I must say it's been a while since I've done this," he said. "I've rather missed it." He winced as Tom moved the kettle to look behind it. "Just make sure—"

"—it's in exactly the same place. I know."

Woolf opened the oven and the microwave while Tom took the fridge.

"Careful when you open the freezer. That's when you get bits of ice on the floor that thaw out into puddles and give you away."

Tom knelt down and opened both of the two freezer drawers: nothing other than a box of Iceland burgers and a four-pack of Cornettos. No ice to drop. "He defrosts regularly. My mother would be impressed."

The venture was beginning to look futile to Tom.

"Hard to look for something when you don't know what the fuck you're looking for."

The digital techie had already done Vestey's computer, a laptop he found under some socks in the nightstand. He plugged in his gear and sucked up the contents of the hard drive in less than a minute. Tom didn't have a lot of faith that it would reveal anything, apart from porn. His gut feeling was that if Vestey was their man he would have covered his tracks very carefully.

While Woolf worked through the bookshelves, drawers and cupboards, moving items and carefully replacing them, Tom

359

stood in the middle of the room for a few moments and tried to imagine Vestey at home, here, the sort of life he lived, his routine. Did he have any girlfriends, or any friends for that matter? A lot of men didn't and, once out of the beehive that was the services, became loners, adrift from the normal social networks. He looked in the bathroom cabinet for any evidence of female visitors: nothing. The only other room was a spare bedroom that looked as if it was never used. Nonetheless he went in and studied the single bed, the small nightstand and lamp, and the narrow wardrobe, empty except for five hangers and two spare blankets.

The only other item in the room was a mat beside the bed, the default souvenir brought home from Iraq or Afghanistan by countless service personnel. Tom had given his mother at least three over the years. In the pattern of this one were images of a comb and a jug, reminders to the faithful to perform *wudu*: to wash their hands and comb their hair before coming to pray.

Woolf appeared in the room beside him. "*Nada*, I'm afraid. He doesn't even have any dirty socks." He bent down to lift the mat.

For a moment Tom was lost in thought, staring at it. "Wait!"

Woolf looked up. "What?"

"It's not straight."

"So?"

"Everything in this place is lined up exactly or at a right-angle to everything else."

"Ye-es . . . And?"

"This is out by at least a hundred mill."

Woolf's face showed his confusion.

Tom took out his phone, touched the compass icon, and held it out for Woolf to see. "This mat's facing Mecca. Someone's prayed here."

76

"What's going on with you?"

That was Sam's mother's way of starting a conversation. Not a hello or a how-are-you. Since she'd discovered Skype it was even worse.

"Hello, Mother. How are you?"

"How do you imagine I am? All these days I've texted and you don't reply back."

She was dressed in a beach robe and her hair was wet, as if she had just come in from a swim. So she was managing to enjoy herself a bit, then.

"I'm sorry, it's been frantic."

"Frantic? I'm the one who's frantic. Worrying myself to a frenzy about your brother while you're doing God knows what. What you dressed up for?"

Sam had on a suit and tie from another of the Party's endless policy reviews. They always placed him somewhere prominent for the cameras but seldom asked for a contribution.

"It's just a suit for work."

The truth was, he felt guilty for not keeping her informed, but explaining Karza's situation was out of the question. She would just blame him, then hassle him even more for news.

"I'm sorry I haven't any concrete news. I'm making enquiries but as you can imagine it's very tricky, very delicate, okay?"

"And with your fancy new job you don't have time for your brother, while here am I crying not sleeping. That's right, isn't it, Jimmy?"

Sam heard a non-committal grunt from Jimmy somewhere in the room. "Of course I do. I've had a meeting with the people who sent him to Syria."

"Oh, a meeting, very good. And do they know, your government employers, that you have a brother in Syria? I bet you've hidden that from them. Pretending he doesn't exist, like you always did."

There was another off-screen mumble from Jimmy.

"Jimmy says I'm too hard on you. He's probably right. It's my grief, my grief for my Karza. No one else."

She broke down into floods of tears. Jimmy appeared from behind and put an arm round her, nodding at the camera and giving a half-hearted little wave. At least Sam didn't have to put up with this every day, like he did. The man's patience was something to behold.

"Look, Mom, the good news is he's alive."

At this she shrieked and pushed the long-suffering Jimmy away. "Who said he wasn't? I never doubted he was alive. That's why you must help him. Tell your bosses you have to go and help your brother or I will ring them up and tell them and tell the papers. They have people right here in Spain, the tabloids do."

"For God's sake, have you any idea what that would do? It would hurt *him*, not me. Just think!"

Sam canceled the call and his mother's face disappeared from the screen. But there were no tears of desperation this time or any self-pity. Instead he felt a cold, dark, vengeful rage. "Fuck them all."

Only then did he become aware that Nasima had slipped into the room and was watching him. During the past twenty-four hours she had been cool and distant. He had tried to phone her from work but the line seemed to be dead. When she finally called back it was from another phone.

He looked at her. "My whole life has been a mistake, a lie. I've spent all this time pretending I was something I wasn't. I tried to belong, played the game, learned the moves. The Party—I thought they hired me to tell them what to think. Now *they're* telling me what to think, or not to think anything at all, just be there, like a bit of set dressing so they can say, 'Look, we've got a nice little Muslim boy on our podium.'"

He stared out of the window at the darkening sky. "You know who I feel I have most in common with in all the world? Karza." He gave a mirthless, sardonic laugh that he barely recognized. Then he turned back to Nasima. "So, I'm sorry. Sorry if you thought I was something else, if I misled you. If you had the impression I amounted to something, or ever would. You're wrong and I apologize for being so fucking pathetic. I'm finished with this. I'm done. I don't know what hopes you had for me but I've got nothing to offer you. If you want to go I'll understand . . ."

While he was speaking she hadn't moved, but remained on the other side of the room, watching and listening without expression. Now she came forward and gently put her arms round his shoulders. Then she pressed herself against him. "Make love to me."

77

Afterwards they lay still for some time. Nasima seemed calm and complete, with her beautiful face so close to his. He was intoxicated by her smell, the sound of her breathing. Once he might have wanted to jump up and down on the bed and celebrate, let his joy burst out round the room—the world. Now it was different. He knew that beyond the bed, outside the door, the world hadn't changed; the same forbidding problems lay out there. He had only to listen to the endless drone of police and emergency-services sirens outside. How familiar they were now, as trouble rumbled on. But with her he felt closer to peace than at any time he could remember. He had spoken from the heart, confessed his darkest thoughts, and now she was reaching out to him.

"You've been very patient with me. You've respected my privacy. Yet there are so many things you must have wondered about me."

She pulled him back towards her. "When you were speaking just now, I got it absolutely. You said so much about how I have felt so often, never more than now."

He reached forward and kissed her. "Tell me something then. About yourself."

She turned away, her face clouded with regret. "Do I have to? There's so much that is sad and ugly." Then she turned back to him. "Does it matter? Does what we have here right now have anything to do with what has gone before? Can we just be us together and not think about all that stuff before?"

He smiled and touched her cheek with his lips. "Sure, but I want to know you. Properly. And one day I would like to feel that you can tell me."

"Thank you for not prying, for being so patient. You will be rewarded." She rolled on to her side, still facing him, pulling the sheets up to cover herself. He sensed the mood changing.

"There is a way to save Karza. Without money. And there is a reward. A big one."

78

Tom's phone buzzed.

Woolf was on a speakerphone. "Bingo. We have a match. The hair we lifted from Vestey's prayer mat is one of Nurul's." He was practically hyperventilating with excitement.

"For sure?"

"A hundred percent. Good call, Tom. Bloody well done."

Mandler was in the room as well.

"So you got your red meat," said Tom.

Woolf didn't wait for his boss to reply. He charged on: "This changes everything. Nurul stayed with Vestey, which connects Vestey with the hostel. And here's another thing: MI6 has put together a record of Nurul's time in Syria. The rebel group he was with wanted him as a sniper, as you learned from your conversation with his mother, and he was bloody good at it. They only let him go home because he couldn't cope with all the carnage he saw. He was on his way to full-blown PTSD and would have been no use. With his connection to Vestey and his marksmanship, this puts him bang in the frame for the Walthamstow shooting."

"We have to bring Vestey in."

It was Mandler's turn. "Steady, Tom. Let's think this through. We do that, it could put Rolt on alert and might blow your cover."

"I don't remember that being a problem before."

"Not to mention letting the trail go cold. Which *would* be a problem."

Tom felt that the value of potentially getting something out of Vestey outweighed the risk of tipping off Rolt. "The man's complicit in blowing up his own on top of the shooting of a civilian, for fuck's sake. If you don't talk to him, I will."

"Now, Tom, careful. I suggest you calm down a bit, and think before you speak."

"Why? I don't work for you, remember."

He heard Mandler's trademark weary sigh down the phone.

"You do, you know you do. Tom, whether you like it or not, and I don't care which, you're in our gang. Let's not fall out now. This is important and we need you. But don't imagine you're indispensable. No one is."

"So what? Look, the fact is you don't have a choice. Rolt made it pretty clear there's something big in the pipeline. He said that, whatever it was, Stutz's people would be in the frame. Maybe they're complicit in the hostel and sourcing Nurul. You've got half the fucking White House landing in twenty-four hours so you have to take the risk. We pick up Vestey and find out what the fuck is happening."

There was silence.

Eventually Mandler spoke. "And we can't just put him back on the streets after we've talked to him. You'd better think about *that*."

79

Vestey's voice was croaky, full of sleep. "Who is this?"

"Tom Buckingham. Rolt told me to call you. We need to talk."

"You seen the time?"

It was just gone two.

"Yeah, but this can't wait. It's about the hostel."

There was a long silence at the other end.

"Is there a problem?"

"Yes. I'm outside. The Prius."

"You'd better come in, then."

"No. The car's safer."

It was a risk, but one worth taking. Would he go for it? They could have gone in and lifted him from his bed, but that would have meant noise and vans, and some civic-minded neighbor might have called the police. Getting him to leave the house voluntarily was Tom's idea, but as a precaution Woolf had placed three of his team round the house just in case Vestey was a lot more switched on than they thought and took flight.

Three minutes passed and Vestey had still not shown himself. But that wasn't a problem just yet. GCHQ were monitoring his landline, email and cell to see if he was checking up on Tom's story. But there was nothing to listen to or read from the house: he was just getting dressed. Then the front door opened. Tom flashed his interior light on and off and Vestey moved towards the car.

369

"Sorry about this, mate," said Tom. "Get in."

As soon as the door shut, he moved off.

"Put your belt on—we don't want to get stopped."

One good thing about a Prius, and there was only one: no starter, no revving—it just glided away soundlessly.

"What's happened?"

"We have a problem with the bomber. The police know he didn't blow himself up."

"Who's saying?"

Tom took a left at the bottom of the road, then sped up to a roundabout, took the third exit onto the bypass and pulled into a layby, the designated meeting point. He came to a sharp halt behind a white Transit.

"What the fuck's this?"

As the Transit's rear doors opened, and Woolf's team of heavies spilled out, Tom cleared the Prius.

Vestey, wide awake now, had taken the precaution of pocketing a weapon and was struggling to reach it as he tried to undo the seatbelt. But it was all too late.

Woolf's guys pulled the door open, grabbed the small .22 revolver from Vestey's front jeans pocket as the belt was cut and, in a swift and smooth motion, bundled him into the back of the van.

The whole action took less than ten seconds and they were on their way.

80

The safe house was in the grounds of an old hospital, a modest pebbledash structure from the 1930s that had once been the home of the caretaker. Although it was superficially furnished like a normal house, the lack of detail among the uniform Ikea fittings—no postcards on the mantelpiece, no messages on the fridge, plus a lingering smell of disinfectant only just covering something organic and ominous—gave the place an institutional feel. A flat-screen monitor mounted above the kitchen counter showed a grainy image of Vestey seated at a table, his hands manacled to a bar. He had been there for four hours.

Tom was on his third coffee, wondering why he was there, when Woolf emerged, looking drained.

"It's hopeless. He's saying nothing and I'm running out of ideas, not to mention time. Plus I'm getting to the point of wanting to resort to the sort of career-ending tactics we aren't supposed to use on detainees any more."

"Let me have a go. You don't get him. He's still a soldier and that will never leave him. You spooks know nothing about people like him."

"Go for it, then. See what you can get out of him."

Tom let himself into the room, and told the guard to unlock Vestey's cuffs. The man hesitated. "Go on—there'll be no drama."

He did so, and lingered by the door.

Tom took the seat opposite. "You want a drink?"

Vestey made no response; his eyes were fixed on some invisible point in the middle distance. Tom filled the plastic mug that was on the table and pushed it towards him.

Vestey stayed in the same position.

"Mick, you have to remember what they taught you. Your conduct-under-capture training? You take food and drink whenever you can because you don't know when you'll get more. Here." Tom placed the water closer.

It took a couple of seconds but Vestey broke his focus and drank the water as fast as he could—just as he'd been taught, in case it was taken away from him.

"Look, mate, you've done your job not talking to the people who are avoiding the pain route. But we're both switched on and we know how this works. You know what's going to happen now, don't you? We both know I have a job to do. We both know that I'm going to crack on with mine and there will be pain."

Tom took a breath, checking that what he had been saying had sunk in. It had. "But I'm thinking I don't have to do that. I'm thinking that there is another way."

Tom leaned closer, his hands flat on the table. "Mate, we're both from the same tribe. We're soldiers—we have standards. And values, that bind people like you and me together, makes us special, better than all those pencil necks the other side of that door. You remember those values, Mick, you remember what we're about? Courage, discipline, respect for others?"

Vestey kept his focus on the floor as Tom continued with the fundamentals, which every soldier knows and which have saved lives during a fight.

"You remember integrity, loyalty, selfless commitment? I know you remember them. I know you once believed in them."

Tom let Vestey stew a little. "I met Nurul's mother yesterday. Did you ever meet her? She's a nice lady, a GP. Spent her life serving the community. She's wondering where she went wrong with her poor little boy."

Vestey didn't move. Neither did he tell Tom to shut the fuck up. So Tom kept talking. "Did you know Nurul was her only child? And now she's got to live with the knowledge that her son is a notorious suicide bomber, the first returnee from Syria to blow himself up in the UK, and the one who's pretty much split the country in half. Only we both know he didn't do it, don't we, Mick? Was it you who shot him? They're still sifting through the wreckage. And eventually they'll find the piece of him where the round entered."

Tom refilled the mug. Vestey brought it up to his lips, then paused. "He wanted to die: it was his choice."

Something—which was always better than nothing.

"And you understood that, probably better than anyone. He must have trusted you, recognized a kindred spirit who, like him, loved guns but had seen too much war. Most people would have just written him off as a crazy jihadi. Probably Rolt would have, but you saw beyond that because you'd been there too—your mind full of those pictures you couldn't stop. The dismembered kids in bomb craters, the families dead in their beds. I know those

373

pictures. I've got them too: Kandahar, Kajaki, Basra, all those shit holes."

Tom was improvising wildly yet something was working. Vestey was nodding slowly, as he rolled out the names, no doubt flash-banging images in his head. A hand came up to his face to wipe away a tear.

"You understood that, and his need to make a difference, to make something happen, and you fixed it for him. Was it at your place he said his last prayers, on the mat in your spare room?"

Vestey registered a flicker of interest but said nothing.

"And his girlfriend's out there somewhere. She's seen his name all over the media, but who can she go and grieve with? Who will hold her hand and say—"

"She's not grieving."

"How come?"

"She sent him."

"What d'you mean?"

"He did it for her. That's how strong their tribe is. Mine, I just fucked them up." Tears were now falling down his face, into his lap. He suddenly looked fragile, like a sad schoolboy.

"Mate, have some more water. You want a brew, two sugars?"

Vestey kept his head low. "I don't need anything."

Then he jumped up and charged at the guard, who was still by the door.

Tom sprang after him. He knew what was happening.

"Mick, don't!"

But it was too late. Vestey had got both hands on the guard and was using both hands to try to get his pistol from him. Two more guards came in, weapons drawn.

374

Tom was now on the other side of the table. "No!"

But he knew it was too late and that the guards would do the right thing. As soon as they saw Vestey had physical contact, just a touch of the weapon, two loud, dull thuds filled the room.

81

The garage had once been a KwikFit, but had changed hands several times and was now owned by a company called Expo. The main windows had been bricked up with breeze blocks and there was no sign of any business being done. It was on a back-street of lock-ups and small industrial units, none of which seemed to be much in use.

Rafiq touched the wipers and the Transit's screen cleared of the gray, greasy rain that was bucketing down. Of all the short straws, this one beat the lot. It was moments like these when he had to have a quiet laugh about signing up for MI5. Recruitment had warned him to forget James Bond, that much of the work was mundane, but that didn't begin to cover it. And he had turned down Goldman Sachs. His best mate, who had graduated from LSE with him, was now in Manhattan pulling in a hundred K a year. And here he was sitting in a surveillance Transit on a back-street in Hatfield. Hatfield! And now it was raining. Was twenty-three too early for a mid-life crisis?

The only people he could find were a couple of guys with industrial face masks re-spraying some car wheels in a lock-up down the street, one stripped to the waist with a Union Jack tattoo on his back. At first they had paid no attention to his polite enquiry about the former KwikFit, but he persisted.

"Do you know any of them—the guys who've got that place?"

The man shook his head and turned away.

"Only I'm trying to find my brother. I think he may be working round here."

That got them going. The tattooed man took off his mask. "Too many of your fuckin' brothers over here, mate. You know what you lot should do? Fuck off home, back where you came from."

Rafiq nodded, as if he would indeed give it some thought. "So they looked like me, the guys who worked there?"

"Yeah, like you couldn't tell them apart."

Rafiq gave them a big smile and thanked them.

He had found forty-five garages in or near Hatfield. First he eliminated the franchised dealers and service stations, which brought the figure down to twenty-two. Then he visited each one, armed with enough innocent enquiries to get him into the back offices and have a cursory look round. Of the last three, one was a burnedout shell, the second was occupied by very pale squatters and an alarming canine menagerie—and the third was this one.

On the face of it, it appeared that no one had been there in months. There was an overflowing wheelie-trash or garbage outside and the letterbox had junk mail oozing out of it. But to Rafiq's trained eye, it was evident that the locks had recently been turned, and there was some tell-tale condensation on a small, high window. He slipped the probe of a Borescope inspection camera under the roller door, which revealed a black people-carrier with a current tax disc.

He retreated to the Transit, reciting the registration to him-self to keep the letters and numbers in sequence, and called up Cindy in the hangar for a plate check. It was with a company based in Sheffield. Fifteen minutes later she was back on the phone. "Interesting. The address for Expo's in Sheffield, but the company's been dissolved and the property in Sheffield has been re-let. I got on to the agent for the landlord, who said it was some kind of medical-aid charity. He told me it was wound up very suddenly a few weeks ago. The woman he'd been dealing with, a Leanne Grove, vanished, owing them three months' rent. He was about to get an officer onto it when out of the blue all the money was wired to him from an overseas account. I persuaded him to go through his records and he found it had come from a bank in St. Croix."

"Where the fuck's that?"

"Virgin Islands."

"Not famous for their terror cells."

"Not famous for anything much, apart from beaches and tax avoidance. Interesting, though."

"Okay, keep digging."

He called Woolf, who told him to stay put and keep watch for anyone coming or going. The rain began to come down harder. He was about ready to pack up and leave, when the roller door started to move and the black van pulled out. Three men—two his age, one older—who could all have been his "brothers" were on board.

He gave them a minute to clear the street, then returned to the garage with a parcel he had prepared and labelled with the address. He hammered on the door good and hard, shouting that he had a package needing a signature. Then he held open the letterbox and listened. The only sound was a low, intermittent murmur, which could have been a radio. He tried the camera probe again, and saw some large white tubs and cardboard packaging.

His phone buzzed.

Cindy was almost hyperventilating. "Are you ready for this?"

"Go on."

"The account the money came from for the rent, the one in the Virgin Islands, is held by a company called Excelsior, described as an international courier company, a subsidiary of another firm that's an agency for offshore contractors—they supply infrastructure and personnel to the oil and gas industry. I got a contact at Vauxhall Cross to see if they could dig any further into their dealings. They couldn't come up with any names of the board or employees or anything, but elsewhere in the account details there was a big fat debit: one million two hundred and seventy-five thousand dollars. It's from a numbered account but it has a forwarding address in Houston."

Rafiq was excited now too. "Oryxis?"

"No! Better than that. Remember Brandeis's slide of Zuabi's house? All innocent-looking and suburban?"

"No shit!"

"Yes shit. That's the forwarding address!"

"Mother of fuck."

82

Bob Heron, the chief constable of Hertfordshire Police was not in the habit of getting personal calls from the home secretary, and certainly not at two a.m.

At first he assumed it was someone's idea of a hoax, a bloody unfunny one. But something about Sarah Garvey's free use of expletives—to the effect that he'd better sit the fuck up and pay fucking attention NOW—suggested this was the real thing.

"Yes, ma'am. I completely understand, ma'am. Consider it done."

In any other circumstances he would have been inclined to have a quiet word with the Met commissioner about this, but the home secretary had made it very clear that his promotion prospects—and Herts, let's face it, was a bit of a backwater—were directly connected to his ability to keep this one to himself and just get it done.

So he did what any sensible chief constable would do in those circumstances and called his deputy with the details of who to liaise with at MI5. "We've got next to nothing to go on, so belt and braces. Firearms team fully bombed up. Maximum care—we don't know who's in there, what they've got and if they know how to use it. But keep the guys under control—I want no dead bodies we have to go to court over. Just get it done quickly and do not advertise. Use some tact and surprise for once."

But the occupants of the garage had prepared for just such an eventuality. The blast blew the front roller door clean off and littered the street with shrapnel from the disintegrating breeze blocks. And by the time Tom and Woolf rolled up, forensics had found the remains of three men and, on the face of it, not much else but a charred mess.

"Basically they had the place wired and ready," the Herts DI, who had taken charge of the site, explained mournfully.

A team in white coveralls were picking over the place with scrupulous attention. Even in this blackened, ruined state it was a potential treasure trove of information. There were several round plastic tubs about a foot deep, containing wholesale quantities of chapati flour and black pepper, along with plastic jerry-cans of hydrogen peroxide, every bomber's hairdressing product of choice. Littered about the floor were a lot of triple-A batteries and the remains of several digital clocks and cheap cell phones—all the components for homemade timers and detonators. And every one of these items, one of the team noted drily, was freely available on the high street.

But the premises wasn't just used for bomb making: there was evidence of makeshift sleeping quarters, with three camp beds and inflatable mattresses, a washing machine and a clothes rack hung with T-shirts.

Tom found Rafiq in less than triumphant mood. "Hey, you tracked it down. This is a direct connection to Zuabi. It changes everything. We'll find out who these guys were and we've got their vehicle, so we can do retrospective license plate recognition. You should be very proud."

Rafiq looked pained. "After everything you went through in Texas, the least we could have done was not fuck this up."

"Bullshit. These guys had planned and prepared for this shit. If you'd gone in there you'd have been history. No amount of planning would have guaranteed against this going tits up. So don't worry about it. You're still alive, they aren't—simple as that."

One of the men in white chipped in: "And at least it's over. The clock's not ticking on this little bundle of fun. So we can take our time and make the most of what we've got here."

Tom didn't feel that it was over, but he had no concrete reason for thinking that. Just as he was reflecting on it, another of the forensics team yelled for quiet. Everything stopped.

The forensics guy was a small man in a disposable suit and shoe covers. He'd stepped back from a now pitted and scorched green-painted door. It was clearly reinforced, having taken the concussion wave of the blast and all the secondary missiles that the explosion would have ripped apart and hurled about the garage at supersonic speed.

The forensics guy put out a hand to open the door.

Tom grabbed Rafiq and pulled him with him as he instinctively stepped back. "Stop! Stop!"

It was too late. The door was open, but only to reveal darkness. The guy's flashlight penetrated the gloom. "We've got a body," he said. "I think it's alive."

Tom let go of Rafiq and headed for the door. "Leave it! Don't go in!"

He took the flashlight from him. "Get a couple of firearms guys."

The forensics techie ran off and Tom scanned the darkness with the flashlight. First impressions had been right. There was a body, face-down, feet towards the door, about three meters in.

And there was movement.

Shallow breathing.

Tom shone the flashlight on the soles of the feet, which were grimed with layers of filth as if their owner had walked through tar. He tilted the flashlight to try to get eyes-on, see if the guy was reacting to the light. He couldn't even tell if his eyes were open—it was the wrong angle. "You! You on the mattress! Sit up and show your hands!"

Tom got no reply. He quickly checked the doorframe, then around the narrow, damp concrete cell.

Two firearms officers turned up in full black gear, slightly out of breath with all the body armor on. They peered into the darkness.

"I think he's breathing but I'm getting no reaction to commands. I'll go in, but here's what I want you two to do."

Tom rested his hand on the taller one's shoulder. Physical contact was always good in these situations. It made things more personal: it meant they might go the extra mile if Tom landed up in the shit.

A small crowd had gathered in the doorway to look at the body. Tom kept his hand on the policeman's shoulder, but directed himself at the crowd first. "If it's booby-trapped, we're all going to be history. You need to move out now, go on—go."

His hand was still on the taller officer's shoulder. "Switch on your weapon flashlight and keep aiming at him all the time. Center mass of his head. Don't aim at the body. If he's got a device and the explosives are homemade, a round will detonate it. And don't come in. Get an angle into his head from the doorway."

Tom turned to the other policeman. "Okay, what I need you to do is get down on the ground right on the threshold, and use your flashlight to check under the body when I move it. You okay with that?"

There was a nod.

So far, so good.

"I'm going to lie down on his right, right against him—almost spooning him. I'm going to grab him and lift him up, almost over me, so you can check there's nothing underneath. All right?"

He faced the taller one. "That's when you're going to come into play. If anything is under that body, your mate will shout, 'Device!' I'll drop him and roll out the way, and you just get rounds into his head. You need to drop him like liquid so he can't detonate. Easy . . ."

Tom gave a little smile. These guys were doing thirty-seven-and-a-half-hour weeks; they went home; they had mortgages; they had loans on their cars—and they'd be going on holiday with their wives and kids. If they didn't get blown up.

"Just one thing. If I shout, 'Fire!' that's what you do. All right? Let's go."

Tom let the two officers take position as he waited to the right of the doorframe. As soon as the body was illuminated once more, he started in.

"If you're injured, show me. Move your leg, move your foot, move your toe. Just use your feet to show me that you understand. Move nothing but your feet. Can you hear me? Do you understand?"

There was no response as Tom moved to the right side of the body. The two police flashlights shone on it, illuminating the left wall of damp and pitted concrete.

He moved to the right of the ripped and soiled mattress to be out of the taller one's arc of fire. His flashlight picked out the mass of hair on the head and the beard. He checked the floor for any tell-tales, any wires, any tape, anything that could indicate there was a device, even under the body. As he got closer, the smell became more rank. The guy hadn't washed for weeks, maybe months.

Tom could finally see parts of his face in more detail. The beard was matted, wet with saliva that dribbled out of his mouth. Tom lay down to his right, hard up against him so the body would partly shield him from any blast that came from under him. He didn't bother trying for eye-to-eye.

"Ready!"

He pulled back so the stinking body was almost halfway over him and what he got in reply was what he wanted to hear.

"Clear!"

Tom let go and the man rolled back onto his face, Tom rolling the other way and back onto his feet. He grabbed hold of the heap and, as he turned it over, twisted a fistful of face hair to get a reaction.

The lips moved, but that was it.

83

Sam had never been completely smitten before. It was as if he had been drugged. He couldn't stop thinking about her. Nothing else mattered now—except Karza. After all, it was he who had brought them together. And together they would free him. That was her promise.

He slept deeply and by the time he woke, she had disappeared into the other bedroom. He had to get to Party HQ, so he showered and dressed. As he was about to leave he tapped gently on the door. She answered and he went in. She was preoccupied, as if Sam wasn't even there, and barely acknowledged him.

Then she looked up. "You understand?"

He nodded.

He hoped this wasn't how it would be from now, that she would still show him the attention she had earlier. But he had a new bond with her. He had seen these mood changes before and decided not to sweat it. The least he could do was cut her some slack after she had been so good with him. He told her he would be back in a few hours. She didn't seem to hear him so he shut the door and left.

All the things that had besieged him before, Karza's fate, his mother's hassling, the ignominy of the assault by Dink, the threats from Derek Farmer, were diminished now, so much so that he hardly noticed them. He felt a heady kind of freedom.

Pippa was delighted to see him. "I'm so glad you're still with us. It seems the line you took at that meeting with Vernon Rolt definitely resonated elsewhere." She gave him a conspiratorial look.

He waited for her to go on.

"Number Ten, no less. I know this must seem a bit arse about face, but the messages coming down from the PM's office now are to keep the faith, not to throw multiculturalism under the bus just yet. We've had some terrible setbacks but we mustn't be deflected by them and so forth. We need to keep a bit of outreach going. Okay?"

And that after the humiliation of having his words written for him by Derek Farmer. Sam was almost amused at how much party policy got made on the hoof when there was a panic on, not that he cared any more. All the same he grinned enthusiastically. "Right. Got it."

She thrust a folder into his hands. "We've prepared a little road trip for you. We want you to make some strategic visits to key constituencies. Sit with the MPs at their surgeries, let them be seen with you. Take your girlfriend along. It's good they see you as part of a modern couple. People warm to that sort of thing." She gave him a sympathetic smile. "I'm sorry you've had a bit of a baptism of fire with us, and the different messaging that's been going to and fro. But the PM's hoping that the fruits of his summit with the President will send the right message to the country about the economy—which, after all, is what people really care about, isn't it?"

Sam tried to think of something to say that made him sound as if he was paying attention. "No question that job insecurity and unemployment are an accelerant to civic strife."

She clapped. "That's the spirit. You really do have a talent for these one-liners. You're going to go far, you know."

He smiled at this. "Thanks, I intend to."

He looked at the folder. Various letters of invitation and tickets to party events were paper-clipped together: Brighton, Bristol, Birmingham, Crewe, Sheffield, York—an itinerary covering half the country.

"And, as promised, tickets for the summit events over the next few days. Don't miss any of them. The PM thinks you're just his sort of guy." She studied him, almost with a frown. "May I say, Sahim, you look much happier?"

He smiled serenely. "You're right. I am. Much happier."

84

Victoria

When he got back to the flat, Nasima was in the bathroom.

He went into the large bedroom, where they had spent such a wonderful night. Her small case was open on the floor as before. And on the nightstand was the locket she always wore round her neck.

He sat down and glanced into the case. There were a few clothes, a spare pair of shoes, a small bag of makeup. He didn't want to intrude, let alone snoop, but there was so much he didn't know.

Last night he had tried quizzing her again. And again she had told him that her family story was not a particularly happy one, and that she didn't want to spoil the mood by going over it. "I try to keep facing forward, living in the moment."

That, he had agreed, was well worth doing, especially when the moment was as good as this.

He glanced again at the locket on the table. Surely looking at that wouldn't be wrong. He picked it up, his pulse racing. He opened the clasp. Inside was a tiny oval photograph: a picture of a man in his sixties with a full beard.

Then he looked up. She was standing in the doorway, a towel round her, holding out a smartphone, a different one from the one she had had yesterday. "Are you all right?"

"Fine," she said, her face a blank mask. She looked as she had that first time they had met on the doorstep in Sheffield, as if last night hadn't happened.

"There's a video from your brother." She passed him the phone.

He touched play. Karza seemed less distressed but his beard was more unkempt, and he looked really quite sick. This time the appeal was addressed directly to Sam.

"Brother, thank you. Thank you for saving me. I'll never forget you. I will be in your debt for ever. I love you, man."

Tears filled Sam's eyes. He couldn't remember a time when either of them had ever said anything to each other about love. And now he felt overwhelmed, remorseful, too, for having been such an inattentive brother. He played it again, studying the image more closely. The ripped and soiled mattress lay on a damp, pitted concrete floor. The walls were the same. The room was tiny. Was he in a cell? It looked like it.

Nasima held out her hand for the phone and took it back.

"So he knows?"

"He knows that you are going to free him."

Her eyes flicked to where she had left her locket. He had dropped it on the bed when she appeared.

He held it up. "I'm sorry. It's unforgivable."

He was covered with embarrassment. She looked blank. It was impossible to know if she was annoyed.

"Can I ask who it is?"

"It's my father."

"Where is he?"

She didn't answer.

"Is he dead? I'm sorry for asking."

390

She reached out for it. "He's building a mosque. And he's going to dedicate it to me."

She looked at the picture for a few seconds with no reaction, then snapped it shut. Her eyes had that far-away look again. He turned to her, flushed with relief after his invasion of her privacy. "Nasima, we're going to be together for the rest of our lives."

"Until we die?" she asked, in a clear voice.

"Yes."

"I can't think of anything that would make me happier in all the world. You've made my life complete."

The light came back into her eyes.

"We will make our lives worthwhile. And Karza will be safe."

She let the towel drop to the floor. She was naked, standing in front of him like a perfect statue. He was mesmerized.

Her eyes shone. "Do you know my favorite Western song, by David Bowie, 'We can be heroes' . . . ?"

He smiled.

"'. . . Just for one day . . .'"

She climbed on the bed and pulled him towards her.

"'For ever and ever.'"

"'For ever and ever . . .'"

85

Westford Airfield, Oxfordshire

They had regrouped at Woolf's hangar. The numbers on the team had swollen significantly. Fifteen more staff were seated at laptops and a big screen had been erected, showing detailed images of the garage. Finally Woolf was getting the support he had been arguing for. But Mandler was in there as well, arguing with him about the merits of alerting the Americans to the connection with the Virgin Islands company and Zuabi.

Woolf was emphatic. "How can you trust them after what happened with Carter? Stutz's influence stretches right up the food chain in Washington. We know he's a regular contractor for all their security agencies."

Mandler was sticking to his guns. "But you still don't have a direct, verifiable link between Stutz and Zuabi, and it's not MI5's job to make it."

"I'd say Jefferson was a pretty firm connection."

"Whatever you think, it's off our remit. I don't need to remind you that our focus is domestic. As it is, I've got Vauxhall Cross jumping up and down about what our man was doing in Texas. Plus the pressure's off us here. We've found the bomb factory. The three Rafiq saw in the people-carrier, they're likely to be the three who blew themselves up."

"But we still don't know who they were, and the fourth man, the one in the inspection pit, we don't know who he is either—or why he was there. It appeared that he was being held against his will. What's that all about?"

Tom couldn't resist pitching in: "Don't forget that Vestey and Nurul's mother both mentioned a girlfriend. It was the only thing that Vestey gave us before he topped himself—that she was the one who'd brought him."

His phone buzzed; it was Phoebe in PA mode. "Mr. Rolt would like to see you."

"When?"

"ASAP. He has some kind of live-link presentation for you. The tech guys are rigging it in his office right now."

"Okay, I'll be there, but answer me this: has he any awareness of Vestey's absence?"

"No, I don't believe so. So you can come along in an hour?"

"That's a no?"

"Absolutely. See you then. Bye." And she was gone.

86

Westminster, London

When Tom arrived at Invicta there was still a strong security presence outside, including a couple of police BMWs in the street, which had been cordoned off to all traffic.

He bounded into the building and up the stairs.

Since his return, Rolt had been full of praise for his efforts in Texas but so far had failed to be specific about any further duties, which Tom took to be a sign that he was still on probation in some way.

When he came into his office one of the tech guys was fiddling with a computer screen that had been set up on the boardroom table. Rolt was animated. "Ah, just in time."

Phoebe followed him in with a pair of envelopes. "The reception tonight. You'll need these." She handed one to each of them.

Tom opened his.

The United States Ambassador to the Court of St. James, Denham Smart III, requests the pleasure . . .

"Fuck that," said Rolt.

Phoebe looked taken aback. "But it's come from Number Ten. They said it's in recognition—" She stopped when she saw Rolt's face reddening.

"Yeah, yeah, in recognition of the fact that the PM hasn't got the guts to meet me in person. Well, fuck him. I'm not some groupie who's going to wait in line for a handshake."

Tom glanced warily at Rolt. It was a side of him that he hadn't seen before, a fragile ego, enraged at being spurned.

"I'll send your apologies, then."

"If you must." He shooed her out.

The techie was finishing up. "Should be okay for you now, sir. You want me to stay and check the signal doesn't cut out?"

"No, off you go."

Rolt waited until the man had gone. Then his whole demeanor changed. The outburst forgotten, he was now shining with almost child-like glee. "You're going to appreciate this."

"What is it?"

"What shall we call it? A bonus? A consideration for your good work in Texas."

"It was nothing much."

"Nothing much? You were on test—and you passed with flying colors."

"Okay."

"It wasn't just you who was being tested—it was Invicta. Stutz doesn't put his money out there until he knows what he's investing in. You delivered, big-time. We got the investment, and this is a gift from him. Sitting comfortably?"

Tom smiled and nodded.

Rolt reached for the remote. "Okay, we're live from Kabul. And . . ."

The screen came to life. A bare room, a man hunched over, manacled to a chair, stripped to the waist.

Someone out of vision prodded him with some kind of stick or baton, then placed it under his chin to lift his head. The face came into view.

Tom felt every muscle in his body tense.

It was Qazi, the Afghan National Army lieutenant from Bastion.

Rolt was grinning. "Stutz felt he owed you this, after what you did for him in Texas." He leaned towards the microphone on the computer. "Okay, gentlemen, we're ready this end."

An American voice, presumably the person off-screen with the stick, addressed Qazi.

"Okeydokes, friend. Ready and waiting. Do your stuff, like we agreed."

Rolt leaned towards Tom as if this were an everyday occurrence. "See? Stutz has his people embedded all over. He had them track Qazi down. They lifted him in Kabul yesterday. He's in one of their secure compounds."

The American prodded Qazi. "Let's get this show on the road."

The image was monochrome but it was clear that blood was all over Qazi's chin, his eyes were bloodshot, his face was battered and swollen, and when he opened his mouth his front teeth were gone.

"I—" He erupted into a series of choking coughs. The American stepped forward and slapped him hard on the side of his head. He started to fall sideways out of the chair. Another man appeared and pushed him upright.

". . . Second Lieutenant Amhamid Qazi, committed the . . ."

"C'mon, spit it out."

". . . murder of Sergeant David Whitehead of the . . ."

He doubled over and vomited.

Tom glanced at Rolt, whose face wore an expression of triumph. "No court, no drawn-out inquiry, no compromise, no plea bargaining. This is how to get things done."

Tom said nothing. Inside he was revolted. He could see Qazi had had the shit beaten out of him so the confession was worthless. Those men would never put him back on the streets. He knew he was looking at a dead man. This was no kind of justice that he subscribed to, but the intensity of Rolt's gaze told him that what happened in the next seconds would decide his own future with Invicta. And he figured that another five thousand miles away, in Houston, Stutz was watching—most probably with Lederer sucking a popsicle. Another day, another test. Tom drew some grim satisfaction out of stringing them along.

"This is your opportunity. You say the word. What happened in Bastion was wrong. These guys'll see that justice is done for your friend."

The American with the stick now had a pistol in his hand. He turned and looked down the lens. Tom turned towards Rolt. He was holding open a door. All he had to do was step through. Tom leaned forward so his command would be loud and clear.

"Do it."

Qazi's head snapped back as half his skull blew away with the blast. The force sent the man and the chair slamming onto the floor. It was all over.

The shooter turned to the lens and gave a small salute. Job done. The screen went black.

Rolt reached over to Tom and shook his hand. "Welcome to the next level."

"Thank you. I'm honored." Tom swallowed. "What does it entail, the next level?"

Rolt got to his feet and strode over to the fireplace, then stood in front of it, as if he was about to recite a prepared speech. "Invicta is becoming a force to be reckoned with in the country. Politicians are beating a path to my door. The public are listening. We've warmed up the climate of fear. Yes, we've had to make our own sacrifices to get there. The hostel was one of those. But gestures like that speak louder than words."

Tom noted the admission—or as close to one as Rolt had got—of his complicity in the carnage Vestey had arranged. He carried on listening as if he was hanging on his every word.

"There may have to be others but this is a fact of war, and we are waging a war we are going to win. Not in some far-off desert but right here in British towns and cities. Invicta needs to be ready—it has support, in the Army, the police, from friends all the way up the Establishment—ready to rid the country of the cancer that's eating us from within. We've started a fire and we need to let it burn just a little longer before we put it out for good."

"More 'gestures', you mean."

"To bring things to a boil."

"And where do I fit into this?"

"We need to be more visible. We need to look the part."

"And what's in it for me, exactly?"

"You're the model, Tom. You have the skills, the experience, you've proved your worth, and you're as comfortable in the gentlemen's clubs of Pall Mall as on the battlefield. But your story will also resonate with the servicemen and women who've risked their lives for their country in unwinnable wars overseas, only to be dumped back on the high street with barely a thank you. I need your help to mobilize them."

Tom said nothing. Rolt was in his stride: he didn't need encouraging.

"We don't need to deploy the rhetoric of racism, we don't need to scare off law-abiding people of other faiths and backgrounds, if they accept the rule of law. We don't need paramilitary paraphernalia. We want to look—aspirational. And promote ourselves as the only sane alternative to chaos."

Rolt came back towards him and sat down, his face close to Tom's. "So, to cut to the chase, Tom, I want you to be my number two, by my side, speaking for us and planning our future with me, handling operations, setting an example."

Rolt outlined the "package": triple what he'd been getting in the Regiment, plus allowances, car and accommodation. "Well?"

"I'm very flattered. I need to think about it."

Rolt looked put out. He'd clearly been expecting an instant yes. Tom stood up.

"Tomorrow, okay?"

87

Winfield House, Regent's Park
Residence of the US Ambassador to the Court of St. James

As he approached, Tom scanned the building and smiled at the thought of the pained expression it would provoke on his mother's face. This neo-Georgian—not real Georgian—edifice had been the 1930s creation of the hugely wealthy Woolworth's heiress and socialite Barbara Hutton. With its huge central door flanked by Ancient Greek-style columns and a parapet featuring a relief of the seal of the USA, it was a classic example of an American's idea of a British stately home. Perhaps she had been seduced by the fact that Henry VIII had hunted wild boar in the forest that had become Regent's Park. When the Second World War broke out, it was commandeered by the RAF, and after it had fallen into disrepair Hutton had sold it to the US government for a token dollar. It had been the residence of the American ambassador ever since.

A covered walkway had been erected on the drive that reminded Tom of the hasty arrangements after the security panic following 9/11. The Americans weren't taking any chances. Teams of men and women in black overalls were at the ready to pat, prod, probe and inspect the guests. He joined the queue and, as he waited to be cleared, listened to the two Americans in front of him as they complained about the heightened security. They agreed, however, that with all these measures in place because of the current troubles, this was probably the safest place in Britain right now, especially with American security being run by US personnel. A Brit said defensively that they had been dealing with terrorist threats for forty years, since the bad old days of the Northern Irish Troubles and the IRA. The two Americans seemed somewhat baffled. *Come on, they were funded by you lot,* Tom felt like reminding them. Sure the Brits were old hands at this, but even at the height of the IRA's bombing campaign here, a typical security check mostly amounted to no more than a cursory glance into bags and briefcases. Now, the War on Terror had provoked a massive boom in private security, with entirely new industries generated. Would that be his future too, Tom wondered, as the line edged slowly forward.

His eye was caught by a striking young woman in a deep blue dress further up the line, leaning close to her partner. Immediately he thought of Delphine, and how she would have appreciated an event like this, something impressive and glamorous to make up for all they had been through. There was no point in dwelling on how their last encounter had ended: he must put it out of his mind and focus on tonight. To pass the time he did a mental audit of recent events.

With the bomb factory now history, he felt some comfort that his efforts with Invicta had been worth the grief, but ringing in his ears was Rolt's talk of further "gestures", to stoke the fires of public anxiety. All through his last meeting he had been conscious of Stutz's shadow looming over Rolt, with his global connections, his people positioned in all the corridors of power. It gave credence to Woolf's fear of more and bigger things to

401

come. Mandler needed to understand that the bomb-factory discovery wasn't the end of something but an opening chapter, if Rolt was to be believed. It was Woolf's suspicions about Rolt that had kicked all this off. Tom had moved from irritation to respect for Woolf and his cussed determination to follow his instincts.

So much was unresolved. Rolt had admitted his collusion in the hostel bombing but no more than that. Stutz's connection to Zuabi, and indeed Zuabi's significance, was also still a mystery. Mandler had even cast doubt on his existence. And what was Clements's connection with Stutz all about? Or was there nothing more to it than the photograph and the Cabinet Office compliments slip?

Tom imagined Clements presiding over all of it, a visit with Stutz here, a dinner with Rolt there, but keeping a safe distance when anything unseemly occurred, then slipping back into his lair in Whitehall, uncontaminated by whatever fallout followed. Perhaps that was where the real power lay, with people like Clements, who controlled much of the fate of the country: unelected, unaccountable and ultimately unassailable.

The sight of an Oryxis logo on the security staff's epaulettes confirmed his sense of how far Stutz's tentacles reached: a measure of his influence that was plain for all to see. No better place to hide than in plain view. What bugged Tom most was knowing that the dots they had joined up fell short of Stutz himself. And echoing in his head were Stutz's words about change coming, Rolt's coy hints about what lay ahead, and Woolf's fears about a "spectacular". Whatever Mandler said, all of this led Tom to suspect—to know—that the job was far from done.

Eventually he reached the front of the line.

As the man patted him down Tom nodded at the epaulettes. "This a good gig, with Oryxis?"

He said nothing. Tom noted he also sported an 82nd Airborne tie pin. "You still in Fayetteville? When I was there I spent all my money at the Mash House and Hooters."

The eyes lit up, an instant connection between the two ex-servicemen. Fayetteville was the hometown of Fort Bragg and the 82nd Airborne. Bragg was a city in itself and not only housed the 82nd but also Delta Force. Tom had spent many months with them over the years.

"Yeah, still there."

"I came over and did your jump course. Happy days."

"Good as it gets, sure."

A voice piped up behind them: "Hey, can you hurry it up along there? We want to get in before midnight."

The guard waved him on. "Thank you, sir. Enjoy your evening."

Tom moved up the stone steps and, once inside, instinctively scrutinized the layout. The hall was dominated by a grand, sweeping staircase, with a balustrade of wrought iron. The vast reception room ran the depth of the house to the french windows that opened onto another terrace and garden at the rear. The drawing room was to the right, the state dining room to the left, the kitchen and staff offices evidently beyond.

The strains of some Bach wound their way through the crowd from a chamber orchestra. A greeter swooped down on him. "Hi, my name's Charlie. Can I help you with anything tonight, sir?"

"You could tell me the order of ceremony."

403

"Sure. So, in about a half-hour the President will be joining us for a few minutes' walkabout. Then, with your prime minister, he'll do a short welcome speech and there'll be a line-up for a few handshakes with selected guests."

"How do I get on the list for that?" Tom wasn't too fussed about meeting the prime minister, but it wasn't every day you got to shake hands with the President of the USA.

"Aw, I'm real sorry. That won't be possible this time." Charlie looked genuinely disappointed on his behalf. "The President and prime minister's staff do the list. It's prepared well in advance."

"Of course. As long as I get to see them, I'll be happy."

A waiter with a tray of drinks swept towards him. "We have a Californian champagne from Sonoma County."

Tom knew that wines from outside that region of France weren't called champagne, but let it pass.

"And a very fine 2007 rosé from Gloria Ferrer."

Tom declined. He needed to keep his head clear. "I'll take a Coke, please."

But he could sample the food: orange morsels of Alaskan salmon—so said the woman in the Stars-and-Stripes vest serving it—with pickled ginger on "wild rice blinis", seemingly some kind of tiny pancake. Another was carrying a tray of dates stuffed with almonds, wrapped in bacon. Pass on that one. He swallowed two of the salmon things, then took a mini steak sandwich with a little American flag on a cocktail stick in it. Not bad.

"They're steak and Stilton," explained the waitress, "to represent the Special Relationship between Britain and the United States."

And sure enough, after the delicious steak, an un-welcome lump of cheese dissolved on his tongue. Special Relationship—perhaps, in an unsubtle, blundering way.

He sipped the Coke as his gaze swept the crowd. A couple of retired generals he recognized were deep in discussion with a former British ambassador to Kabul, now an academic. And the home secretary who had a crowd of suits round her, was looking as if she wished she was somewhere else. He caught sight of Mandler, who raised an eyebrow a millimeter.

Tom decided to let his guard down and came up along side him. "Rolt's not coming. He was pissed off about not getting a one-on-one with the PM." He nodded in the direction of the home secretary. "You briefed her yet?"

A gale of laughter exploded around Sarah Garvey. She managed a wan smile.

"Somewhat," Mandler replied, with a guarded look. "We got an A-plus for the garage, but I chose not to spell out all the loose ends. She's got enough on her plate as it is."

"Did you mention Clements?"

"Mm. She didn't react. They're not exactly each other's greatest admirers. If we were to start poking around in *his* dark corners, it might look as though she'd put us up to it. Westminster's a very small village."

He deposited his empty glass on the tray of a passing waiter. "Anyway, I can't hang around. It doesn't do for Madam to think I'm bunking off at this hour of need."

"She's not exactly looking overworked herself."

The suits had moved off and Garvey was now talking to the old generals. Mandler shrugged and, with another raised eyebrow at Tom, melted into the crowd.

He would hang around for the President, then make his escape. He could call up his dad, see if he was still free for dinner. He had been a bit sharp with the old boy about his scheming with

Delphine, and owed him an apology. He was musing on whether he could ever come clean with him about his true role at Invicta when he felt his phone vibrate. He moved through the french windows onto the terrace.

It was Woolf.

"Tom. The man in the hole: he's been stabilized and is able to talk. His name's Karza Kovacevic, a Bosnian by birth, now a British national and a returnee from Syria. He's not making a whole lot of sense yet. He claims he wasn't a member of the group in the garage—says they abducted him."

"Okay . . ."

"But here's a thing, we're checking out his family and—get this—his brother's working for the government. 'Speaks on multiculturalism', according to the Party's blurb."

"If they lifted him, they wanted something."

"Anyhow, we haven't got to him yet."

"What's his name?"

"Sahim Kovacevic."

Tom stood, the cell to his ear, thinking. The only reason to lift someone and keep them is leverage.

"Tom? You still there? Tom?"

"Forward me a mug shot. I'll find out if he's here."

88

Tom went back inside to find Garvey. An admiral was now bending her ear.

"Excuse me. Good evening, ma'am. I'm Tom Buckingham."

She peered at him. "Do I know you?"

"Not exactly. I work for Stephen Mandler."

The admiral looked particularly perturbed at the interruption. Tom ignored him, keeping his focus on Garvey.

"Do you know a Sahim Kovacevic? Do you know if he's here? I need to talk to him."

Garvey's frown deepened. "Oh you do, do you."

"You know if he's here?" Tom repeated the name. "This is important."

The admiral stepped between them. "Look here, I don't know who you are but the home secretary does not want to be interrupted."

Something about the directness of Tom's look and tone must have made her realize that he wasn't wasting her time. "He's with a pretty girl in a blue dress. Should I be concerned?"

"Not for the moment. Thanks."

He snaked back into the crowd and wove his way through the guests, searching for a blue dress. The throng was getting thicker as the minutes ticked down to the President's appearance.

The woman in the blue dress—the one he had seen in the queue—was about fifteen feet away, with a young man, black hair, who could have been from Bosnia or Blackpool or a hundred other places. They weren't with anyone else. Tom's phone buzzed: a photo from Woolf of Sahim in a TV studio. Definitely the same guy. When Tom looked up again, the woman was alone.

Tom stepped left, then right, and got eyes on him moving off to the left and away from the main crowd. Tom followed. Sahim went out into a wide carpeted hallway with fancy Regency-type lampshades on the walls. He seemed to be heading for the Gents. Ahead of him was a security guy, easily identified by his shoulder epaulettes, carrying a white cardboard box gift-wrapped with red ribbon. He went through the door to the cloakroom and Sahim followed.

Tom waited outside. He wasn't going to let Sahim see his face. There might come a stage when he had to get up close to him. But for now there was no need: he knew where he was; he wasn't going anywhere. Tom carried on to the other side of the door, where there was a row of chairs. Before he got there, the security guy came out again, but he was no longer carrying the box.

Tom was committed to passing him. The security guy was walking with purpose, and as soon as he'd disappeared, Tom went straight to the door and stepped inside. He was confronted by a bank of four cubicles, all with beautifully varnished, full-height wooden doors.

The door at the far end was engaged, so he stood at a sink, ready to wash his hands if someone came in.

He stood stock still, listening, but couldn't hear any sound at all. He walked very slowly and quietly into the cubicle next to the one that was occupied and closed the door. He put his ear to the partition, eyes closed to help him focus. Clearly the one next door was not being used for its intended purpose. There was far too much body movement, and too many rustling sounds. And then the unmistakable sound of Velcro.

That stopped the instant the door from the corridor opened and the hustle and bustle of the outside world filled the room.

Tom heard a guest go into the cubicle at the end, the seat being lifted, and a stream of urine fired into the pan. The flush was activated, and there was a quick wash of hands before a burst of hustle and bustle from outside as the door opened again, then silence.

Tom waited with his hand on the door as a bit more Velcro was ripped and there was more movement. The cubicle door opened, and footsteps went past. The door to the corridor opened and closed, Tom came out of the cubicle. In the waste-trash or garbage below the basins was the white box, collapsed and neatly folded, along with the red ribbon.

Tom followed Sahim Kovacevic as he joined the crowd heading for the ballroom. The cell in Tom's pocket vibrated but he put his hand in and cut it. Woolf was surplus to requirements just now. He had got his target. All Tom's efforts now, both mental and physical, were focused on the man who was gently and politely edging his way through the throng. He didn't appear to be hurrying; he wasn't even sweating; he was perfectly calm. He was even smiling his thanks to people as he split up their little cliques to move through.

Sahim Kovacevic being calm meant nothing. It didn't mean that nothing was going on. He could be on a high, in a good place in his head because he thought he was doing the right thing. He could be almost floating on air at the moment—either because he'd been promised a place in Paradise or because this was what had to be done to get his brother released. This must be what the leverage was about, Tom thought. It had to be.

Sahim was still easing his way through the crowd. Tom focused not on his head—he didn't want to risk eye-to-eye with him—but on his nicely polished black shoes under the dark blue suit, on his way to his place in history. Stutz's "outcome"; Rolt's "gesture". This was what was playing out right in front of him, right now.

Sahim's jacket wasn't bulging at all. Whatever device he had attached to himself didn't have to be that big. He was there to kill one man—maybe two, if he did it well. All he had to do was make contact with his targets and they would be history. A couple of thin slabs of PE, no more than a kilogram each, rolled out over him like pastry, a battery and a detonator: that was all it took to do the trick. All he had to do was bide his time, then run, barge, push, whatever it took, to get within a couple of meters, make a grab for his target and detonate.

As Tom followed the polished black shoes through the crowd, nothing else mattered. He barely noticed when, from above him somewhere, a band struck up the rousing chords of "Hail to the Chief". The President had arrived.

The shoes stopped next to a woman's. Tom looked up at the blue dress just in time to see Sahim hand her something half the size of a cell phone. She didn't look down, just palmed it. The initiation device. He almost smiled: it was such a simple plan. Sahim would do the running and grabbing; she would do the detonation. He might get only halfway to his target before he was shot; he might grab hold of the President but be unable to detonate because he was restrained at the last second. It was a simple plan and a perfect one. She was detached from the action, had a clear line of sight . . . She was using him as her own personal human drone.

Tom shifted his attention. All his focus now was on the woman and the small device she'd been given, which she held in her left hand. All he could hear was his pulse pounding in his temples.

The President and the prime minister were stepping up onto the podium at the far end of the room, doing a stilted double-act as they each encouraged the other to speak first.

There was an eruption of polite laughter as the music stopped and the prime minister said something amusing to the people in the front row, which they heard before all the mics went on.

Sahim looked at the woman and they stared into each other's eyes. She finally broke the spell and kissed him on the lips, just as the prime minister began to welcome everybody to the event.

Sahim eased his way forward again and Tom let him go. The monkey didn't matter, only the organ grinder. She was the one with the fate of the world in her hands.

The nearer he got to her the more tightly packed was the crowd. Some people were almost on tiptoe as they jostled to get a look at the most powerful man on the planet. It wasn't so easy any more to pass them. Nobody likes queue-jumpers. Tom had to be careful: he didn't want to alert her.

Yet he had to be very fast. She had to be dropped—instantaneously—to have no chance whatsoever of detonating. It was no good fighting her, no good trying to grab the device. If it was just a button that had to be pressed, she had to go down immediately.

He didn't worry where Sahim was: he just had to keep pushing forward without her being aware. If he was too slow, he would find out very soon, when bits of president and prime minister sprayed the room.

The glimpses of blue were now three deep away from him and the cell was vibrating once more in his pocket. The blonde woman to his right, standing immediately behind the woman in blue, gave him a smile and took a sip of champagne.

Tom knew that the woman in blue would be doing exactly the same as he was, only she would be focusing on Sahim, all her attention on that drone of hers delivering his payload to the front of the crowd, waiting for the moment when he would jump onto the podium and she would complete the mission.

A scream sliced through the crowd as it surged back. Members of the presidential protection team were leaping from the podium. Sahim must have broken free and was making his bid.

Tom grabbed the blonde woman's champagne flute and snapped off the base as he zoned in on the right of the exposed neck of the woman in the blue dress. With his left hand he grabbed a handful of her hair to keep her head in position and rammed the shaft of glass deep into her neck.

The screams around him were joined by gunshots. Sahim was being taken down. But it wasn't over yet. Tom kept all his focus on the deep gash in her neck as he plunged the glass down again and again into the mess of tendons and flesh. Blood spurted like a geyser from her disintegrated jugular and arced into the air. She buckled straight away but he kept ramming and twisting the glass stem as she went down. If she could move, she could detonate the device. If he had to sever her entire head to be sure he'd stopped the threat, then so be it. He fell with her, leaving the stem in her neck, both hands scrabbling for her left arm. He ended up on top of her and saw the detonation device by her hand on the carpet. As he went to grab it and get control, three weapons carried by dark suits bore down on him.

"Freeze!"

Epilogue

The first reports to emerge from the US ambassador's residence were confused and contradictory: a shooting, a frenzied stabbing, a bloodbath. All three were true.

Throughout the night, Downing Street and White House press officers vainly attempted to impose news blackouts, which simply fanned the flames of rumor online as well as on TV. By the end of the night people at home on either side of the Atlantic could choose from at least twenty interpretations of what had just happened.

By seven a.m. London time, some of the rumors had solidified into confirmed reports. The frenzied attack of a lone female guest had been eclipsed by a much stranger and even more compelling claim. The *Mail Online* dubbed it a "Romeo and Juliet attack", the suicide pact by a pair of doomed lovers who had given their lives to jihad.

At ten a.m. a joint press conference was convened, but only after several hours of wrangling had taken place between the two governments over what could be said, should be said and definitely could never be said. The agreed line was that the US Secret Service had magnificently thwarted an audacious attempted suicide bombing. But nothing could be done to cover up the fact that the young male bomber had actually been in the pay of the UK's governing party. As for his lover, the woman known only as Nasima, her identity remained a mystery.

Five thousand miles away, Aaron Stutz stood alone in his penthouse, watching multiple screens featuring TV and online attempts to get to grips with the story. Either way, for him it was a win: whether the two premiers died or survived, both outcomes guaranteed that anti-Islamist tensions would escalate to new heights. Public demand for stiffer measures against Islamist extremism was inevitable. Getting the incumbent President and prime minister off the stage would have ushered in successors who would be obliged to consider the case for the digital fortress—and almost certainly act on it. But even if they survived, and in any case both of them were up for election within the year, they would have to be seen to act. The digital fortress would become a reality now.

Stutz helped himself to a tumbler of Jim Beam Black and turned away from the screens to the picture window that ran along the whole side of the room. He looked in the direction of the mosque rising in the southeast of the city and raised his glass to the memory of the young woman who had given herself so bravely and so audaciously for the cause.

In Thames House, inside Mandler's glass refuge, Jonathan Rhodes, his opposite number from Vauxhall Cross, was just finishing his briefing. It had been an awkward encounter.

"Our conclusion so far, Zuabi doesn't exist. He's a clever construct. Someone's been fucking with the systems, some digital *über*-geek has created a persona for financial purposes. But we'll keep digging."

There were also a lot of difficult questions about Buckingham and his antics in Texas. "Your man pissed in our tent big-time."

Mandler didn't attempt to protest.

"And now he's untouchable, I suppose."

Mandler gave him a curt nod, not wishing to rub it in. "I think that's the right attitude."

"What will you do with him?"

"That's probably up to him, I suspect."

It had been a long night for Tom. After the Secret Service heavies had fallen on him he was cuffed and carted off to a secure room where they'd tried to question him. He had told them to piss off and call Mandler. In the end Sarah Garvey had come to his rescue. She had witnessed the whole incident, and after one of her trademark bollockings, during which the men of the US Secret Service heard words they had never known a female politician to utter, she had sent them off to find him somewhere to shower and a change of clothes and Tom was released into British custody. Even then there were a lot of questions about what had made him focus on Nasima. The device in her hand was the answer. But what had also come back to him, from among the many mysteries about his time in Texas, was what he had heard on the building site. And as he had zeroed in on her, the thought had flashed through his mind: was she the woman to whom the mosque would be dedicated?

Woolf caught up with Tom later that night. He had been at Karza's bedside, piecing together his story and wondering how long he could hold off telling him about the fate of his brother. They had contacted his mother, who sounded like a handful, and she was coming in by plane that morning.

Woolf didn't go in for jubilation. "I think a drink is in order," was about the sum total of it. Very British, for two men who together had just saved the lives of the leaders of the Western world.

"Your round, I think," said Tom.

"So, what now?"

"I'll let you know when I know," he replied.

Low cloud hung over the city. Central London was still on lock-down. The tubes and buses weren't running, checkpoints had been set up all round Westminster, and what looked like every serving member of the Metropolitan Police had been called out onto the streets. As Tom walked across St. James's Park, he marveled at how only the ducks were calm, happy in their oblivion. The question on everyone's lips: was this a one-off, or was there more to come?

The few pedestrians he encountered eyed him, and each other, uneasily. Not a good day to be carrying a backpack—or sporting a dark beard. A row of police vans with armored mesh over the windows parked nose-to-tail formed a cordon around the Invicta head-quarters.

Inside, Phoebe was still at her post. The look in her eyes as Tom approached suggested Woolf had kept her up to speed. She came out from behind the desk and put her arms round him. "So, I guess this is it?"

He smiled at her.

But before he could answer Rolt was at the door. The gleam in his eye said it all. "A good night for Invicta, you might say."

No pretence now, no frown of concern.

Tom nodded. "Yes, you might say that."

Rolt let him into his office and closed the door. The sun was blasting in through the huge windows. The Turner over the mantelpiece looked fabulous. "Well, what's your decision?"

Tom clasped his hands. There was a tiny fleck of Nasima's blood under a fingernail. He scooped it out, then looked up at Rolt. "Count me in."

Turn the page for a preview
of Tom Buckingham's next mission
in

1

02.45 GMT
River Thames, London

The inflatable bucked and kicked as it skimmed the surface of the Thames. A stiff breeze flustered the water, sculpting it into small waves that smacked the bow as the craft progressed upriver. The low cloud pressing down on the capital glowed a dull orange, reflecting the city lights on to the deserted waterway. A lone night-bus made its way across Battersea Bridge, empty of passengers, like a ghostly *Mary Celeste* on wheels.

The only interruption to the boatman's progress had been a River Police launch heading downstream to its base at Wapping. He had throttled back to tick-over and steered into the shadow of one of the few remaining Thames barges moored on the sea-ward side of Tower Bridge. As the launch came past he flattened himself against the hull, clenching his teeth against the cold. The launch slowed and veered so close that for a few seconds he could hear the radio coming from it—the sound of cheering. The election results were coming through. He stayed like that until the sound of the launch had faded into the night. The snow was starting again; welcome additional cover to obscure the small craft, fine flecks that swirled uncertainly in the biting wind.

All but his face was covered by the marine dry-suit. The chill sliced at his features, freezing the moisture in his nose and round his lips, a warning that whatever snow made it to the ground would quickly freeze. Already, ice was crusting along the water's edge. He decided to ignore it. Years ago he had taught himself not to worry about things that were out of his hands and focus on what he could control—and what was ahead.

Although he had never been there, he knew the layout of the hotel inside out. He had started with YouTube, and the news reports of the opening, then read all the entries on TripAdvisor— it was amazing how much time people wasted recording their visits in mind-numbing detail. From there he had graduated to a presentational CGI animation prepared by the architects, and finally the plans themselves, until he could conjure up the whole layout in his mind's eye, like a hologram. He had two entry-point options: one through the kitchens, the other the laundry. But the kitchens even at three thirty a.m. were unlikely to be empty. A skeleton crew would still be on duty, handling room-service requests and keeping the last of the revellers fed and watered. The laundry should be deserted. He had to find somewhere to slip out of the dry-suit and ditch the backpack after he'd pulled out the less conspicuous overnight bag that held the equipment he needed: the weapon, a Glock 9mm with a titanium suppressor and an extended twenty-round magazine—much more than he required for what he expected to be a surgical strike—a Bowie knife, smoke canisters, a mask. From his research, he knew that there was a locker room and a bathroom to the back of the laundry: he needed a mirror to check himself over before he moved into the public area.

In the first plan there were to have been three of them: two for cover. He hadn't liked it. Too conspicuous. "But who's going to watch your back?" they'd asked. He'd said he'd watch his own. He was used to it: why break the habit of a lifetime? Alone, he had complete control, no one else to consider if he had to make a change of plan. The truth was he didn't much care about his back, didn't want to be encumbered. This was his idea, his plan. "We won't forget this, Fez," they'd told him.

Whatever.

The hotel came into view: the "Ice Palace". These days, all new buildings in London seemed to acquire nicknames—the Gherkin, the Cheese Grater and so on. And Ice Palace sounded better than "Battersea Regina"—some smartarse had already called its giant three-story atrium the Battersea Vagina. True to its name, though, this one looked the part, all tiered glass, like something that had time-travelled out of the future. And, like all good palaces, it was surrounded by a vast fortified wall to keep out any trouble. But not the river front. Didn't the architects have any sense of history?

As the craft made its way towards the target, he reviewed his route once more. He was right to avoid going through the kitchens. Unless he could slip past the staff he would have to take down whoever was there, which would be messy and risky. He didn't want collateral: there was only one target. The better option was through the laundry. He smiled grimly as he thought of the heavy security out front, ever vigilant, never imagining the threat that was coming by river on a frozen February night.

He slowed as the hotel came into view. A giant slab of glass and concrete bordering the southern bank of the river, so new there were still traces of the last construction work. He unclipped the oars and dropped their paddles into the water. Short, shallow scoops brought the craft noiselessly up to the jetty.

Over his shoulder he spotted a lone silhouetted figure on the broad apron that separated the hotel from the river, leaning against the balustrade, the orange dot of a cigarette glowing minutely as the smoker drew on it. The figure straightened, the cigarette suspended in front of him. As he watched, he unzipped the suit, felt for the Glock. One well-aimed shot and it would be that smoker's last gasp. But before he drew down his weapon the man flicked the butt into the water, turned and ambled back out of the cold.

The craft nudged the jetty and he reached for one of the polystyrene bumpers that dangled from it, tugged it and drew the craft towards a metal gangway. The whole structure was encased in a thick glaze of ice. He struggled for grip through the waterproof gloves. The boat slid from under him and, for a few seconds, he feared he would drop into the icy river. He was out of shape: he hadn't done shit like this in a long while. After several tries he managed to haul himself high enough to get one foot on the structure. Then he kicked the inflatable away. He wouldn't be needing it. Maybe someone down-stream, Gravesend perhaps, would be the lucky owner of a new boat by the end of the night. There was no exit from this, no going back now.

Half crouching, he moved swiftly along the gangway, which bucked and creaked under him. The snow was thickening: bigger, heavier flakes falling with more purpose now, already laying the beginnings of a carpet of dull white across the hotel river front. He fixed on a point some four meters beyond the west wing of the façade. From his memory of the plans he had studied, there was a ramp from which vehicles could reach the lower-level service area, bordered by a metal fence. He was just about to set off towards it when he saw the camera tower. That wasn't in the plans or the photos. It was new. Builders' plastic barriers were grouped around the base. Were the cameras live? He would stand out a mile against a white background. But then he remembered the havoc snow played with night-sights, filling the image with miniature starbursts of reflected light. He decided to risk it, moving nonchalantly with a civilian gait.

He vaulted the fence and dropped on to the ramp, paused, scanned the area for any more new cameras, any more smokers. Nothing. He moved down towards the laundry service door, unzipped the suit and took out the precious key card charged with that day's code. In his mind it was the one weak link in the plan, the only thing for which he'd had to depend on someone else. But it had given the others something to do so they felt part of it. He approached the door beside the shuttered vehicle entrance. The key reader was at eye level, just to the left. He went up to it, swiped the card. Nothing. He tried it again, pushed the door again. Then he saw the hinges. It opened outwards. One more swipe and a tug. He was in.

He moved between the vast stainless-steel machines that by day could handle the four-hundred-plus bed sheets but were now silent. It was almost completely dark, just a pinprick of blue light: the master switch for the machines at the end of the row. He took out the mini-Maglite so it was ready in his hand. The smell of trichloroethylene went straight to the back of his throat. How did the poor fuckers who worked here put up with it? Probably they were illegals who'd got in hanging on to a cross-Channel truck. After a trip like that it didn't matter what the world smelt like. He reached the end of the row and paused, considering whether it was time to step out of the dry-suit.

A flurry of rustling said panic and flight. His first thought was rats. Then, in the pencil beam of the Maglite, he saw them: what little of the woman that was still dressed suggested she was either a waitress or a cleaner, the man harder to tell in just the wife-beater that clung to his heaving chest. There was no choice. The woman was about to scream, but the sound never made it. All that came out of her throat was a gush of blood. The guy got his in the forehead. The suppressed coughs of the pistol seemed to hang in the air as they dropped, still entwined, on to the heap of clothes beneath them.

He sighed, holstered the weapon, dropped the back-pack, unzipped and stepped out of the dry-suit.

2

The hotel had a network of service passages so cleaners and maintenance staff could move throughout the building unnoticed: perfect. The suit, white shirt, and black tie had the right anonymous security-operative look about it. He had a fake ID if anyone queried him. And if that didn't work there was always the Glock in its polymer belt holster. The bag was more of a giveaway.

Six months ago, he would have been on the guest list, a valued comrade, a loyal brother. But he had burned those boats. Two waiters came past bearing silver trays of glasses. They didn't give him a second look. Good. He moved on closer to the room where the reception was.

"All right, Fez?"

He wheeled round. How he hated that name. He'd been stuck with it since Helmand. Something to do with the shape of his hair. Protesting had only made it stick.

He nodded at Ballard, reached for the Glock. "You lost?"

Ballard swayed a little on his feet. His blazer was flapping open, his tie loose. "Story of my life." He raised his hand, too late to stifle the belch that erupted from him. "G'night?"

He had nothing against Ballard. They'd both done two tours in Afghanistan, both seen the same shit, had been discharged the same year and joined Invicta a year later, among the first to sign up. Both of them had been through the rehab program, only Ballard had clearly lapsed. Perhaps Fez could talk his way past.

"Yeah." He nodded, a hand reaching round the grip of his weapon. "Good night."

He tried not to infuse the words with deep irony. It was good that Ballard was too shitfaced to register any surprise at seeing him, as if it was quite natural that he would be there to join in the celebrations. Maybe Ballard had forgotten Fez's sudden exit from the organization. Maybe he could be spared.

Ballard leaned closer. "So where'sa Gents?"

"You've taken a wrong turn. Back into the main hall and left."

Ballard looked relieved. *Go on then, fuck off.* But he didn't. He leaned against the passage wall, frowning at Fez's suit. "So— whya you here? Thought you'd packed it in?"

He shrugged. Maybe in Ballard's alcoholic haze he would accept that as some kind of answer.

Ballard frowned, trying to focus as he stepped away from the wall, his face just centimetres from Fez's. "Here—you're banned. Shouldn" be here."

Nothing for it. Fez slammed a flat left hand into Ballard's chest so he fell back towards the wall, leaving enough space between them for him to draw down the weapon in his right. Keeping his left high and out of the way of the shot, he pivoted the weapon as soon as it was free of the holster and fired.

Immediately he stepped back to ensure there was no blood on him as Ballard slid down the passage wall. Shit, what now? He looked up and down the corridor, got his bearings and, gripping Ballard by the armpits, pulled the lifeless body towards the door to a store room.

He had to move quickly now. A loud pumping beat of the sort of music he loathed thumped above the hubbub of partying revellers behind the swing doors. He put his head in and spoke to the nearest couple. "The guv'nor still in there?"

"He was 'bout half an hour ago."

"Thanks." He moved on through the crowd. He saw a pair of bouncers standing sentry in identical suits, little coils running from their ears into their collars, their ISA ID armbands ungainly over their jackets. They looked ridiculous, bloated by steroids and too much muscle to be useful. More like a pair of bouncy castles. They were preoccupied with a group of pissed hoorays, who were arguing loudly. He steered away from them, deeper into the throng, a heaving mass of mostly young bodies, the same age as the ones he had just dropped downstairs. He felt his pulse step up a level. Two banners had been hung across the room. One said, "Victory!" and the other "Tomorrow Belongs to Us". On the stage a youth with a ludicrously exaggerated blond quiff was crooning into a mic but his voice was inaudible. He saw one of the party officials and elbowed his way towards her. She was well pissed, gyrating drunkenly against her partner.

He nodded towards the stage. "Where is he?"

She frowned. "Who are you?"

And who the fuck are you? he felt like saying.

"Oh, yeah, right. Probably gone to get his head down, I should think." She gestured upwards. "Been on his feet the last two nights, poor man."

Her partner pulled her back towards him. He thanked her with a curt nod, extricated himself from the crowd and headed in the direction of the elevators.

3

Ed lay on the bed, grinning up at the chandelier. He spread his arms and legs as if making a snow angel, feeling the luxurious sheets slide under his limbs. He'd never been in a five-star hotel before, never mind the presidential suite. It smelt of new carpets and fancy soap. He glanced at the wall of window to his left, the curtains undrawn. Across the Thames, somewhere on the north side, a column of fiery smoke funnelled up from a blazing building. The river was invisible, except for a row of lights on the opposite bank, the rest obscured by snowflakes floating down, tinged orange by the hotel lights.

He smirked. Christmas had come right in the middle of February. Jennifer was in the bathroom getting ready for what was left of the night. Although he'd had the bare minimum of sleep for the last three crazy days' campaigning, the election-day adrenalin, plus a cocktail of Pro Plus and Red Bull, kept him buzzing. He glanced at the massive muted TV, churning out election coverage, the umpteenth replay of Vernon Rolt's moment of glory, the new MP punching the air, then the all-too-familiar sound bite about making the streets of Britain safe again, cutting out the "tumor of terror".

Jennifer appeared from the bathroom gift-wrapped in a voluptuous hotel bathrobe, her blonde hair draped about her shoulders in damp snakes.

"How d'you like me in this?" She did a twirl so the robe fanned out around her.

He grinned. "I'd like you better out of it."

She rolled her eyes, her attention caught by the TV. The image had cut to a heaving throng of protesters in Birmingham, pushing through a cordon of police riot shields, gas bombs arcing above, a news reporter ducking as one of the flaming missiles came his way.

Britain might be on fire, but right now Ed didn't give a shit. He snapped his fingers to get her attention. "Hey, it's a compliment." He pushed himself up on to one elbow. "Jen, babe, I've been meaning to say . . ."

"What?"

"Could you put my shoes outside?"

She groaned, picked them up, opened the door and was about to chuck them out on to the landing when they heard the first muffled thud.

She dropped the shoes, shut the door abruptly and looked at him, alarmed.

He sank back on to the bed. "Fireworks, probably. They're still celebrating downstairs."

"*Inside* the hotel? Like, I don't think so."

Jennifer wasn't giggling. That was a slight problem with her—a bit too serious. They'd met only three weeks ago in the queue of volunteers for Rolt's campaign. Having just lost another bar job and with fuck-all else to do, he'd thought it might be a laugh. That, plus doing his bit for the country, of course, making a stand against Muslim extremist nutters, putting them in their place—preferably back where they came from. He'd seen her in the line and couldn't take his eyes off her—she didn't seem to mind. When they'd got talking it turned out she was heading towards her university finals in politics and was on a mission to help right some wrongs. Her father, a cop just retired from the Met, had egged her on to support Rolt. "Dad says he's our only hope," she'd told him earnestly. He'd nodded vigorously. Next thing he knew they were paired up on the campaign trail. Bingo.

She'd agreed they would spend election night together, and he'd pulled off something of a coup by securing the suite that had been booked for Rolt, who hadn't even shown up at the victory party downstairs. Everything had come good, except now she was spoiling it by going all serious.

Jennifer stood close to the door, listening.

He beckoned her. "C'mon, get over here."

There were two more thuds, louder this time. She shuddered, gripped the lapels of the robe and bit her bottom lip as her eyes welled. He sighed as she wiped away tears. They had had their share of scares during the campaign and he had put on a show of chivalry, which he reckoned had only half convinced her.

"Maybe they're chucking furniture down into the atrium. Lock the door, come to bed and let the rumpus begin." He raised his arms in her direction and put on a sinister James-Bond-baddie voice, which seemed to go with the surroundings. "Come, my child."

The lights snapped off and the TV screen faded to black.

Shit, he thought. This really isn't how it's supposed to go. He levered himself up from the bed and marched towards the door. He was about eight feet from it when the lock exploded, taking a chunk of the door with it, spraying them with splinters. Jennifer leaped towards him, gripping so hard her fingernails dug into his shoulder. There was something in the air, not a smell as such but as it hit his lungs he felt as if he'd inhaled nettles. His eyes burned and filled with tears. He whirled her round and pushed her towards the bathroom, falling on top of her as he lost his footing on the wet tiles. He kicked out wildly at the door and it slammed shut. He thought of getting up to lock it, then realized it would be ridiculous after what had just happened to the other door. They huddled in a corner of the shower, behind a partition no more than three feet high, clutching each other in the total darkness. Something sticky ran down the back of his hand, too thick and cold to be blood—they must have collided with a soap dispenser.

Fuck, fuck, fuck. This was for real. Rolt's people had always said, "Be ready. Never drop your guard." Any jihadi just back from Syria might be out there waiting for them. But the hotel was ringed with security: they should have been safe here. Rolt had many fans, but he wasn't short of enemies sending death threats. For all his claims that he wanted to protect the patriotic Muslims, he'd pretty much alienated the entire lot of them. Ed and the rest of Rolt's team had even been given some basic self-defence tips by one of the tough guys from the MP's organization, Invicta: a jab in the eye, a boot in the balls but neither applied here. Jennifer's grip tightened on him.

"Hey, loosen up," he whispered. And then, uselessly, "It's gonna be all right, okay?"

"No, it's not. We're going to die, Ed. They want to kill Rolt and they think we're him," she said, through huge convulsive sobs.

He pressed a hand over her mouth and hugged her to him.

As he held her, he raised himself half an inch to peer over the partition. Through the crack between the bottom of the door and the floor tiles, he saw a light sweep past, then back across it.

"You want to get yourself beaten up? *Killed?*" That had been his mother's response to his signing up for Rolt's campaign. She always overreacted, always went for the negative. Now he wished he had listened, given the whole thing a wide berth. "They'll come after you. You'll be a target. Is that what you want, to spend the rest of your life looking over your shoulder?"

The light under the door reappeared, static this time. He thought he could hear breathing. Then the door burst open with such force it smashed into a glass splashguard, which exploded into pieces over them.

The light was coming from a flashlight attached to something. He couldn't see what or who was holding it. Someone stepped into the room and Ed ducked, but his pathetic attempt to hide was rendered useless by Jennifer's whimpering.

He could see the shape of the gunman now, his profile contorted by something—a face mask, sound coming from it like Darth Vader. He prised Jennifer off him and stood up. What drove him he didn't know: he was beyond scared, his pulse hammering in his temples, the taste of vomit in his mouth as he opened it to speak. "You want Rolt? He's not here. Just us. We're nothing, just—we don't even officially work for him."

His voice was hoarse. The saliva had vanished and his tongue felt like rubber.

The flashlight beam was now trained directly on him. The figure didn't move. Above Jennifer's whimpering he could hear hissing breaths coming from the mask. He could see more of the silhouette now, completely still, legs slightly apart. The flashlight was attached to something—a gun: a very big one. Ed thought of all the things he would promise to do in return for his life. All the clients he had ripped off whom he'd reimburse, all the teachers he'd apologize to . . . His life flashed before him—the fuck-all he'd achieved so far. If he could do one thing in the time left, like save Jennifer from this . . .

Behind the gunman, back in the bedroom, Ed thought he detected another movement. How many were there?

A tiny red dot danced above the gunman's left ear. Then there were two *thunk* sounds, plus the short, sharp, metallic grinding sound of a top slide moving, and the gunman dropped to the ground in a lifeless heap, the weapon clattering on to the tiles beside him. Jennifer screamed, a high-pitched distress signal shockingly amplified by the tiles, then dissolved into convulsive coughs. Ed squeezed her to him as his bowels trembled. Were they safe? Were they next?

A second figure stepped into the room, holding a dripping towel up to his face. Ed raised his hands, but the man didn't even look at him. All his attention was on the body twisted on the floor. He reached down, picked up the weapon and lifted the mask off the dead man's face. Despite the fear raging through him, Ed heard his own voice pipe up: "Who is he?"

The man didn't answer, but shone a phone flashlight on the unmasked face. A pair of empty blue eyes stared straight up out of a pale pink freeze-framed face. Ed looked away. It was his first dead body, a massive crater where the man's left ear had been. He looked back to the shooter. "So who are you?"

Tom Buckingham reached down and replaced the mask over the lifeless face. "Nobody."

Andy McNab is one of only two people since WWII to receive
the Military Medal and the Distinguished Conduct Medal.

He served for nine years and
survived capture in Iraq during the Gulf War.

For ten years he's worked with
Delta and SEAL teams,
as well as the FBI,
on covert surveillance,
capture, and hostage rescue.

Don't miss his explosive true story in

Seven Troop

coming in September 2021

Glossary

ACU	Army Combat Uniform
ANA	Afghan National Army
Bergen	Full size British Army combat rucksack
Bradley	US-made armored fighting vehicle
DSF	Director of Special Forces in the UK
Hesco barrier	A collapsible wire-mesh container and heavy-duty fabric liner, which can be filled with sand or rubble and used as a barrier against explosions or small-arms.
ISAF	International Security Assistance Force, a NATO-led security mission in Afghanistan established in 2001 by the UN Security Council. Its main purpose is to train Afghan National Security forces and assist in rebuilding key government institutions. It is also engaged in the war with insurgent groups.
ISO container	A shipping and storage container. ISO stands for International Standards Organization.
MPV	Multi-purpose vehicle
MTP	Multi-Terrain Pattern; a camouflage pattern printed on equipment issued to British forces.
NVs	Night-vision goggles
OBL	Osama Bin Laden

One-star	Brigadier general in the US Army
PE	Plastic explosive
POTUS	President of the United States of America
PSNI	Police Service of Northern Ireland
RPG	Rocket-propelled grenade
RTU	Returned to unit
SCO19	Metropolitan Police Service Specialist Firearms Command
Shura	Arabic word for "consultation"; used to describe a tribal gathering.
SO6	Metropolitan Police Service Diplomatic Protection Group
UNHCR	United Nations refugee agency
WO2	Warrant Officer class 2

WELBECK

PUBLISHING GROUP

Love books? Join the club.

Sign-up and choose your preferred genres to receive tailored news, deals, extracts, author interviews and more about your next favourite read.

From heart-racing thrillers to award-winning historical fiction, through to must-read music tomes, beautiful picture books and delightful gift ideas, Welbeck is proud to publish titles that suit every taste.

bit.ly/welbeckpublishing

WELBECK

ANDRE DEUTSCH

MORTIMER

MORTIMER

WELBECK